Selling Pencils, and Charlie

a novel

Penny Perry

Lymer & Hart
Rainbow, California

Lymer & Hart
Garden Oak Press
1953 Huffstatler St., Suite A
Rainbow, CA 92028
760 728-2088
lymerhart@gmail.com
gardenoakpress@gmail.com
gardenoakpress.com

First published by Lymer & Hart / Garden Oak Press on July 24, 2020.

ISBN-13: 978-1975889647
ISBN-10: 1975889649

Library of Congress Control Number: 2020941631

Printed in the United States of America

For

    my All-star: Jonathan

    my Janeites: Daniel and Rae Rose

    my Italian astronaut: Bill

Selling Pencils, and Charlie

a novel

Penny Perry

. . .and it was not very wonderful that Catherine, who had by nature nothing heroic about her, should prefer cricket, base-ball, riding on horseback, and running about the country at the age of fourteen, to books. . .But from fifteen to seventeen she was in training for a heroine.

JANE AUSTEN

Northanger Abbey
1797-8 (written)
1818 (published posthumously)

PROLOGUE

I close my eyes and see me in a puffy, white slip with pink bows. Now I put on my cotton skirt and it billows out like a lovely parasol. I know better than to ask for a crinoline slip. We can't afford it. Just last month, my father, Mickey, paid for my first bra, though he doesn't believe I have anything to fill it.

Still, I want one of those slips. Girls at my junior high wear them to make their skirts puff out like open umbrellas. Though I set my hair in bobby pins every night, and comb it into a perfect flip every morning, and though I wear just the right amount of pale pink lipstick, and I'm only an inch shorter than the perkiest cheerleader, I still don't look like the other girls. My skirts hang on me like soggy sheets on a line.

My mother Alice doesn't care that she doesn't belong. She nods to other mothers on Hibiscus Street, but never asks them in for coffee. She reads her English novels and weeds her garden and says she's happy not to have to listen to the hum of little minds. She's a better person than I am. She doesn't stand in front of the mirror, tilting her head back and practicing the right smile.

I sigh.

"You've been moping for days," Mickey tells me. His eyes look tired in his sun-burned face. He hauls junk for a living. He stares across the dining room table. His voice is mellow from four beers. Four is the perfect number. After five beers he'll start an argument about a song lyric or a ballplayer's batting average. With a six pack, he'll forget his promises. But four beers gives him confidence.

"I want a crinoline slip," I say.

He squints, confused.

Alice says, "To make her skirt full, like Deborah Kerr's in *The King And I*."

Mickey splashes gravy on his mashed potatoes. "Just because we live in ritzy Santa Monica and you go to school with the daughters of movie stars doesn't mean you have to dress like them."

Now I have made trouble between them. I should have kept my wishes to myself.

Alice stares into her tea. She has a dreamy heart-shaped face. She is pretty enough to be a movie star. When Mickey rails against Santa Monica and the demands of a middle class life, her face turns blissful. She travels back where she prefers to be, in Kelso, the small town where she had won essay contests and spelling bees. A place where she had all the answers. I hate her for leaving me here.

"This new boxer I'm working with has the hands of a champion." My father makes fists with his freckled hands and boxes the air. "When Gentlemen Bill wins his first bout, we'll get you that slip."

Mickey leans back and listens to the Minor League baseball game on the radio.

Alice plinks her fork on her plate. "Could we finish one meal without that racket? Imagine people caring so much about overgrown boys hitting a ball with a stick."

Seventy miles away at Ventura, California the baseball crowd starts to yell. Mickey pounds the table with his fist. "What happened?"

To thank my father for not giving up on my slip, I turn the volume up.

"After three years," the radio announcer says, "Crazy Sotto finally got that grand slam home run."

"See," Mickey tells me. "You should never give up on your dreams."

My father sips his fifth beer.

•

Mickey's pickup truck rattles out of view. Finishing the breakfast dishes, Alice whispers as if he could still hear, "How much do those slips cost?"

"I don't know. The girls on the dance committee bought their slips at Phillip Fine's, but Susie found one at Penney's." I sigh. Most months, even J.C. Penney's is out of our budget. I was proud to buy my new bra in the lingerie department at

Penney's instead of the *Distressed Merchandise* barrel at the Bargain Discount store.

On her knees, Alice searches for a Mason jar she had hidden behind detergent under the sink. She unscrews the lid and pours quarters, nickels, dimes and pennies on the kitchen table. "I was saving for Jenny Lee, a hybrid rose with butter yellow petals."

"I don't want you to give up your rose bush."

She shrugs. "I can plant yellow roses later. But you'll only be in junior high once." She starts counting the coins.

•

In Penney's dressing room, she hugs a purse heavy with change. "Maybe you don't need me at home so much anymore. I could get a job." She blows cigarette smoke at the mirror. "There must be something I would be good at."

"You could be a saleslady." I nod at the henna-haired woman, her thick bra straps showing like adhesive bandages under a thin white blouse.

"I like plants," Alice says. "I could work at Merrihew's Nursery and tell people they should dump coffee grounds on their roses and brew seaweed tea for their orange trees."

She might scare the customers at the nursery. They would worry she was a witch.

I study price tags with neatly typed numbers. All that money just for a slip. We could get a skirt or even a dress at Bargain Discount for the price of the cheapest slip. The more expensive slips, made of cotton and nylon and edged in lace, have three tiers. Each tier is fuller than the one above. Who would know that the lace, hidden under a skirt, was even there? The snottiest girl in school, Jamie Day, the daughter of the famous actor, James Day, would know for sure.

The cheapest slip is made of netting. It feels like horse hair and scratches my legs. It is shaped like a pumpkin, not an umbrella. "This one is fine," I say, hoping Alice can still get her rose bush.

As if she hadn't heard, Alice holds the more expensive cotton slip next to my waist. "This one is better."

Before I can ask her if she's sure, she smiles and says, "A girl as pretty as you should wear nice clothes. Soon, you'll be going out with boys."

"Impossible," I whisper.

"You have so much to look forward to." When she presses her full lips together, they become as thin as two strands of thread. "There are places to go here. The theater. Concerts. Not like Kelso."

Alice and I never go to the theater or concerts. Tickets are expensive. What makes her so sure any boy I would meet would have the money to take me to those places? What makes her so sure a boy would want to? Still. . .I run my hands over the cotton and lace and picture myself dancing with Tebb Moransky, the president of our ninth-grade class.

Her face dark with dreams, Alice leads me out of the dressing room. "You will fall in love and find out what life is about." She lines up the slip and her quarters, dimes, nickels, and pennies on a counter by the register.

A familiar silhouette appears on the other side of the glass door to the street. Jamie Day. Jamie Day in flats and a pink skirt that looks like spun cotton candy is standing in front of J.C. Penney's. She should have been on her way to Phillip Fine's. Just as her fingers reach the door handle, she sees me. Caught slumming at Penney's. And by me – a nobody. I tilt my head and send her my practiced smile. Then, I check to see how Alice and I look. I am wearing exactly the right clothes – a scarf tied around my neck, a blouse, straight skirt and flats. Although Alice admires the women who feel free enough to wear sports clothes – Capri slacks or trousers – she had settled for her favorite spring suit and heels. There is nothing Jamie Day can find wrong with us.

Jamie pushes the door open and steps into Penney's. Almost in. Cotton rustles. Hinges hiss. Skirt and crinoline crush together in the door. Jamie Day is caught.

Alice blows cigarette smoke at the door. "Girls pay to be beautiful."

The daughter of the actor famous for tap dancing up the side of the wall straightens her shoulders and tries to pull her skirt free of the door.

I step toward her to help, but the expression on her face makes me freeze. A sales clerk calls the manager.

Alice's face turns darker. She inhales smoke and watches Jamie struggle. "We'll be stuck for the rest of our lives in Penney's."

"She'll hear you," I say.

"A giant step back. That's what women are taking."

"Shhh. That's Jamie Day."

The store manager hurries over and tries to push the door. No luck. He opens a tool box, stands on tiptoes and loosens the first hinge

"Those damn slips are a plot," Alice says. "Men want to make us helpless again. Can a girl in a crinoline climb a mountain?"

Wide-eyed, Jamie stares at my mother and covers her mouth to hide a laugh. It comes out in a way that seems to say: "Why oh why would a girl want to climb a mountain?"

The last hinge loosens. The store manager gathers the door in his arms. Without thanking him, Jamie turns and steps back out onto the sidewalk. Her spun cotton candy skirt catches the afternoon light.

Alice's words chase her. "Fashion is a way of making women prisoners."

Jamie glares at Alice and me. Shoulders raised, she marches toward Phillip Fine's.

I'm ruined. It will be all over school Monday that my mother is a crazy lady who said mean things about Jamie Day. We only have one more week of school. I will be talked about all summer. Still, in a weird way, I admire Alice's nerve.

Alice squashes her cigarette in an ashtray. Her eyes plead with mine. Her fingers punch the same kind of mark in my skin that the net slip had made. "Don't fill your head with clothes and make-up and boys. Don't try to be like everyone else." Under lashes thick with mascara, her eyes are wet. "Don't waste your life."

Does she think she's wasting her life? Back in Kelso, teachers had told Alice she could do anything she wanted – teach or even write. But maybe back then she was too busy being a girl who practiced her smile in the mirror to listen.

"Jamie did look like a peacock with its tail caught in the door." I pick up the slip. "Let's put this back."

But Alice shakes her head and grabs the slip out of my hands. Her eyes brighten. "We're in Santa Monica. Not Kelso. You have more choices. You don't have to make the mistakes I made." With strong fingers, she pushes her coins toward the cashier. "I want you to have it all."

1

*T*all *and tan and young and lovely. . .*I hum along with the song on the radio, hit the brakes of my Plymouth at the crosswalk, and wait for girls in their bikinis and boys with their surfboards to cross the highway. For a moment, I see myself four inches taller, three shades darker: I'm that girl from Ipanema on her way to the beach. The light turns green, I put my foot on the gas: I'm Pamela again. I'm pretty in my new blue dress. My hair looks gold in the sun. I could maybe even be a model advertising Back to School clothes, but no one would mistake me for the girl from Ipanema.

I turn the Plymouth past a hand-printed sign – *Waitress Wanted* – in the window of the coffee shop and park in the side lot. Out of habit, I pick up my textbooks. Just having them with me makes me feel secure. I step out of the car. Roses bloom by a corner of the building. Yellow roses. "Don't read the tag," I tell myself. I want to run back to the safety of my car, but something makes me march forward. I bend to the tag. The rose name is a *Jenny Lee*.

My crinoline slip lasted through one summer, then fell apart in the wash. My mother died before she had a chance to plant her yellow rose bush.

I make myself look beyond the roses, down the highway, where Santa Monica, a city on a cliff, glints in the fog. After a moment, I turn back to the coffee shop. It was California modern 10 years ago: a trapezoid. A horror to look at, but the windows are clean. Letters are missing from the sign on the roof: *_IMMER'S COF_EE _HOP.* Pimmer, Bimmer, Wimmer's? This coffee shop is still an improvement over the Majestic Theater where I am paid to serve popcorn with butter and cockroaches.

The door is heavy. The place is empty. I take the sign from the window. Help is here. Now where is Mr. Pimmer?

I step behind the counter to the opening to the kitchen, where waitresses, if there were any here, would pick up their orders. A boy and a man, both in chef's hats, cook hamburger patties on a sizzling grill. A fan whirs, blowing greasy smoke toward a small window. On a radio, Vin Scully calls a Dodger game. "Excuse me," I say. "I want the job."

Neither cook turns. The smoke is seeping out under the cafe doors that lead to the kitchen. I push through one of the doors. It hits something hard. The boy's back. Dark blue eyes glare at me. I recognize the face. Those eyes belong to Charlie Fain, the shortstop for our college team who makes the game of baseball look like a Russian ballet. Charlie is even more gorgeous up close. The young Nureyev catches a beef patty before it hits the floor. He grins. "Good thing I'm an athlete."

For a second I forget why I'm here, then a voice says, "No strangers in the kitchen." The boss has a red nose and bloodshot eyes. Another healthy Californian. He waves an oily spatula at me.

"Take it easy, Howie." Charlie is still grinning at me. He's wearing a uniform under his apron. Number 9. "I'm the one she hurt. I might have a fractured rib here."

Charlie is looking at me as if I were someone else, someone spectacularly beautiful like the girl from Ipanema. Words come out of my mouth before I can stop them. "At least I didn't break your heart."

Charlie's eyes widen. Now that I have his attention I don't know what to do with it. I turn to the boss. The boss has a Z embroidered on his apron. Zimmer? I step closer. "Mr. Zimmer? I want the job."

"What? Shut that door before we asphyxiate the customers."

I peer through the open door – the dining room is still empty – and let the heavy door swing closed. "Who are you cooking for? "

Mr. Zimmer yanks a basket of fries from bubbling oil. "Any experience waiting tables?"

I stretch to my full 5 feet 2 and one-half inches. "No."

"I can train her, Howie." Charlie winks at me.

Mr. Zimmer flips fries from a wire basket onto a plate and nudges his assistant. "Stick them in the oven before they get cold."

Charlie's smile gives me courage. "This job pays a dollar and a quarter an hour?" I say. "Plus meals?"

Mr. Zimmer waves me away. "Busy."

"Howie, you put the ad in the newspaper. The least you can do is talk to the girl."

"Looks like you're doing all the talking for me," Mr. Zimmer says.

Charlie shuts the oven door and looks at me. "I know you, right?"

"No."

"I'm Charlie Fain." He looks so puffed up. "You sure you don't know me?"

"I've seen you play. You. . .pitch?"

"Shortstop." He blinks. My little joke has made him feel terrible.

"You're not bad with a bat," I say.

"You got that right." He's smiling again. "Wait. Don't you go out with the third baseman?"

Charlie's blue eyes made me forget Warren. I have the loyalty of a flea.

"Ashburn?" Mr. Zimmer looks stricken. "No hit, no field."

"He considers baseball a sideline," I say.

"It shows." Mr. Zimmer flips a hamburger on the grill. "That guy's so bad, he's illegal."

Warren doesn't deserve this treatment from Mr. Zimmer. Or from me. I've turned into a flirt. I head for the door. Charlie takes my elbow and turns me around. Those eyes stare at me. "I've seen you someplace else – besides with Ashburn."

He's wrong. I would remember. "Someday Warren will be a famous poet," I tell him.

"First he's got to learn how to walk across the street without getting killed," Mr. Zimmer says.

"I wouldn't mind having Ashburn's brains," Charlie smiles at me. For me. His smile says he wouldn't mind having Ashburn's girl either.

He backs through a door out to a pantry lined with shelves. The room seems empty without him. Maybe I'm misreading his smile. Maybe he's this friendly with everyone. Charlie returns with more patties. He should be wearing tights and leaping across a stage with some lucky ballerina in his arms. I finger the *Waitress Wanted* sign, study bits of tomato bobbing in chili that simmers on the stove. It would be wonderful to work in this place where something is always cooking. "Mr. Zimmer, I know I can wait tables."

Grease splatters on Mr. Zimmer's leathery arm. "I put that ad in before all this damn fog chased my customers away."

"We go through this every year," Charlie says. "The marine layer will burn off, the place will be packed, you'll complain you have no help."

The boss says, "I need someone strong to carry out platters."

"I do a lot of physical work." I flex my right arm and show him my muscle.

Mr. Zimmer frowns. "How old are you?"

"I'm 18. A freshman at SMCC."

"Me, too." Charlie snaps his fingers. "Do you go to Saint Monica's?"

"The church?" I shake my head. "I don't believe in organized religions." I sound like my mother. "I don't believe in institutions. Churches. Girl scouts. Marriage. In order to belong, you have to give up thinking." Just repeating Alice's words makes me miss her.

"Hire her," Charlie says. "She has a mind of her own."

"We don't need a mind," Mr. Zimmer says. "Do you cook?"

"My father is a gourmet chef. Sometimes I help him."

Charlie puts his arm on the boss's shoulder. "Howie, she's strong. She can cook. She's pretty. What more do you want?"

I catch my reflection in the oven door. Does Charlie think I could be the girl from Ipanema?

"You're hired, I guess." Mr. Zimmer says. "Get rid of those damn books. This isn't a library."

"You want me to start now?'

Mr. Zimmer makes a sour face. "Isn't that what we've been talking about?"

The dining room is empty. "But this is my new dress."

Charlie winks at me. "I'll get you an apron."

I've just agreed to work in a mad house. The boss puts *Help Wanted* ads in the paper and then gets angry when someone asks for work. Now, he wants me to wait on imaginary customers.

Something big and heavy roars to a stop in the parking lot. A school bus, loaded with Cub Scouts. Screaming, hungry little Cub Scouts. A pale man with glasses peers from the driver's seat over the dash.

Doors bang. Heavy little shoes slap asphalt, then thud on carpet. The Scout leader cowers by the restaurant door. I set my books on the counter. Charlie hands me an apron. Eager Scouts knock over chairs, bang forks on tables, empty sugar into salt containers. Airplanes fashioned from napkins sail across the room. "Don't worry," Charlie says. "These kids are so hungry they won't notice if you get their order wrong."

•

I dry the last plate, put it on a shelf above the sink. Mr. Zimmer almost smiles at me. "I was surprised when a little thing like you got that big, fat kid down from the table."

"She's a spitfire," Charlie hangs his apron on a hook and grabs a pair of cleats from under the table.

"Today's your last game, isn't it?" I ask. "You must be so excited that you guys are in the top 10 of the J.C. league."

He looks out the window at the highway and the gray ocean. "We could get our clocks cleaned today."

Could he really be worried? "You look so fearless when you're out on the field," I say.

He winks. "You mean when I pitch?"

Did he know all along that I knew who he was?

"I got the feeling today's your day," Mr. Zimmer tells Charlie. "He's going to be there."

Charlie slumps. "I just hope I'm ready." He glances at me and smiles. "I've been ready since I was a junior in high school."

What is he ready for? Maybe I shouldn't be listening to a private conversation. I sprinkle cleansing powder on the sink then turn on the water full blast.

"Just don't get cute out there." The yellow light in Mr. Zimmer's faded brown eyes brightens. "Play heads up. No heroics, a solid performance like Tommy Heinrich, Old Reliable."

His eyes shine with hope. He looks young. He looks the way he must have as a boy. Little Howie Zimmer would have had a thick head of hair and a heart full of hope. He must have been the reliable one, the one the team could count on to make the routine plays and the unspectacular but necessary bunts that move a runner up a base.

"Maybe I should just close the restaurant down so I could see you today," He tells Charlie, losing his grin instantly. "All those hungry Brownies are coming back from Paradise Cove. They'd smash the plants out front and leave their dirty fingerprints on my windows, if I'm not here. Charlie, you should give her some chili."

He turns to me. "I can't just keep calling you *her*. Name?"

"Pamela Carey."

"Okay, Pamela. Come in at 6:30. That's a.m." He grabs a broom and dustpan and heads for the dining room.

Just hearing the word *chili* makes my stomach growl. The girl from Ipanema wouldn't have a loud stomach. I tell Charlie, "I should study."

"All you do is study. Last week, when Warren made that great catch in foul territory and everyone else was on their feet clapping, you were sitting with your nose in a book."

A week before I ever came into this restaurant Charlie Fain had been watching me. He could have any girl he wanted. Why would he notice me? A vain little smile creeps across my face.

"Pamela is a nice name," he says.

"My mother named me after the servant girl in Samuel Richardson's novel." I stop myself from launching into the argument of whether Pamela was innocent and religious, or sly.

"I didn't know girls got crew cuts," Charlie says.

He noticed me because I'm practically bald. I pat my fuzzy hair. "It's growing into a pixie cut."

"What was it?"

"A mistake. I wanted to be a champagne-blond. But it turned purple. Lilac. I had my stepmother cut it off."

"You could be a movie star: the girl with the lilac hair."

He takes a ladle from a drawer and a bowl from a cupboard. "People who work in restaurants shouldn't look underfed. Bad for business. Don't they feed you at home?"

He thinks I'm skinny. Why should I care? I have a boyfriend who believes I'm perfect. I taste the chili. It's spicy and thick. Just what have I been doing all afternoon? I've been flirting with Charlie as if I were available. He may be gorgeous, but he's arrogant and a show off.

"Good, you're getting more color already," he says. "Was that your stomach growling or do we have a starved cat hiding somewhere?"

He's not only arrogant. He is also crude and nosy. "I skipped lunches to buy this new dress."

"It's too nice to wear in a place like this. How many lunches did you skip?"

"I'm not poor," I tell him.

"Me either. I only work here to be in touch with the common man."

Suddenly I'm sick of this snoopy shortstop. "Aren't ballplayers supposed to concentrate on their game?"

He looks surprised. "Mental discipline is a key element to baseball."

"So why do you spend so much time noticing what's going on in the bleachers? Is it because I'm skinny and practically bald?"

He spits water back into his glass. "You're nice to look at, but it's not you I'm watching. It's the guy next to you."

"But I sit next to different people all the time."

"You're just part of my fantasy. I picked you because you're easy to notice. You're the only one who's not paying attention to the game."

Is Charlie Fain some kind of weirdo?

He mashes saltine crackers inside their plastic wrappers. His stare is fixed on the coffee pot. "See, I look up and there he is. He's sitting there next to the girl who has her nose in a book. He's kind of tired from his 90-mile drive, but he's happy to be there to see me. I leap in the air and make this spectacular catch. He gets to his feet. Then, he leans down and taps you on the shoulder. 'Did you see that catch the shortstop made?' he asks. You look up from your book and shake your head. 'I didn't think anyone could do that.' he tells you. 'That shortstop – he's my son.'"

His eyes are shining. He cracks his knuckles, rubs his hand over his green and gold Saint Monica's High School ring. I'm not the only person who misses a parent. All season he's been looking in the bleachers for a father who would drive 90 miles to see his son play ball.

"Did Mr. Zimmer mean your father when he said someone would be there today?"

"Howie knows my father isn't coming. Howie isn't the one who believes in fantasies." Charlie sounds angry with himself for having hope. But isn't it good to wish for things? He gets up from the table, takes off his chef's hat and puts on his baseball cap, then steps back to me. "I don't know why I even told you those things. I never talk about my dad. Maybe you cast some kind of spell on me."

He picks up an equipment bag and walks out the door. Good. I have other things to think about. I have to finish my essay for my English class. But I'm grabbing my books and following Charlie to the parking lot.

•

Fog blows cool against my face. Charlie stops. "Looks like we have something besides baseball in common," he says. "We both collect antiques."

He's staring at my Plymouth as he walks me around the corner of the lot. Someone, I hope not Charlie, painted the dented '49 Ford, a monkey-vomit green. "Pamela Carey, meet Old Chartreuse."

Maybe he will ask me to drive out to the game with him. He opens the door to the driver's side then tosses the equipment bag into the passenger's seat. My seat? I swallow hard. He stares at me for a long moment, then grins, "Hope you get a lot of studying done out there today."

The motor sputters and dies. He looks at me as if he's going to say something more – maybe invite me along after all – but then the motor catches. Fog swallows Charlie Fain and Old Chartreuse.

2

I write: *All Portia wants is a home.* My eyes squeeze. I begged my English teacher to let me write this essay and now the opening lines hurt me too much. The girl in the Elizabeth Bowen novel reminds me of me. The notebook wobbles on my knees. My essay on *The Death of the Heart* slides to the ground. I lean down and pick up the notebook. Maybe I can write the essay from another angle. I hunt for the book in my stack. It isn't here. Then, I remember. I was so busy thinking about Charlie, I didn't check to see if I had gathered all my books. Perfect. *The Death of the Heart* is sitting on one of the pantry shelves at Zimmer's.

Out in the field, Charlie catches a ball.

I picture Charlie swinging me in the air and saying, "That catch was just for you."

But Charlie isn't looking at me. He's staring at third base. "Hey, Ashy," Charlie says. "Guard the line."

Warren starts, looks at Charlie, and then faces the plate. Just seeing Warren makes me ashamed. How can I treat him so shabbily? I'm to here to watch him play, and I'm either writing or daydreaming about the shortstop. Warren is a wonderful person. His red cap catches sunlight breaking through the fog. He looks handsome in his Number 7 uniform. His intelligent eyes stare out at. . .at what? Not at the batter. He loves baseball, but he loves poetry even more. Something about being on the field inspires him. Maybe he's writing a poem right now.

It's cold. I hug myself, stamp my feet on the bleachers that seem to invite the afternoon wind and fog from the sea. I should have brought a sweater. June is always such a wet, cold month. An afghan covers the legs of a plump lady next to me. She sips coffee from a thermos. She looks warm. She looks like somebody's mother. Mothers are everywhere. Outside the dressing room at the Bargain Shop, somebody's mother waits to see her daughter's new outfit. Mothers and daughters sit together at the lunch counter where I sometimes treat myself to a sandwich. I would give anything to have my mother again.

With the next pitch, Charlie starts running toward third. The ball cracks off the bat. Warren holds his glove up high. The ball bounces off Warren's glove, but Charlie's backing up the play, grabs the ball bare-handed and throws to first in time for the out.

Fans in the bleachers applaud as the shortstop leads his team off the field. He grins toward the stands. "You like that?"

"Wonderful," I shout back.

Charlie looks surprised, then nods and runs off the field. He probably wasn't even talking to me. I've made a fool of myself. Warren glances at me. I give him an encouraging wave. He trots to the dugout.

I look down at my essay. Without the book, I can't write about *The Death of the Heart* and this girl Portia, who no one loves enough. I look over my list of other possible essay questions, the questions my teacher wanted me to consider for the June Wells scholarship. Even though all state high school and junior college female students are eligible, my teacher thinks I have a chance. I might have had a chance if I hadn't been chasing after Charlie and forgotten the book. Warren never makes me forget anything. He's like a steady diet of wheat toast and tuna. He keeps me on track. Warren's the one who encouraged me to try for the scholarship.

The June Wells Foundation would pay my tuition at a four-year college. I study the words shimmering on the page. Why does Catherine Linton in *Wuthering Heights* go mad? She was torn between two loves: even-tempered Edgar and passionate Heathcliff. Love made her go crazy. Love does that to people. I glance at the bench, where Warren is sitting next to Charlie. My little attraction to Charlie Fain has turned me into a monster who flirts with another boy right in front of her boyfriend. Is arrogant Charlie Fain my Heathcliff?

"Twelve assists. He's all over the field." A stocky man next to me studies notes fastened to his clipboard. The scribbles are in a strange kind of shorthand, lines and arrows, partially filled in diamonds, numbers like 6-3 and 4-6-3. C. *Fain* is the only name at the top of the page. Why is this man writing about Charlie?

The stocky man has dark hair and a broad face. His eyes twinkle like Ozzie Nelson's. He looks like a TV daddy. Maybe he is someone's father. But he couldn't be Charlie's. He must be a scout. That's nice for Charlie, but has nothing to do with me. I grab my copy of *Wuthering Heights.*

A book slides onto the man's lap.

He rearranges my stack. "You're either studying to be a librarian or a weight lifter."

"Teacher."

The scout smiles. I smile back. The small bits of friendship I pick up here and there keep me humming along.

At home plate, Charlie lays the bat on his shoulder. He looks relaxed, confident, but his blue eyes say he can't wait to clobber the ball.

"He's going to hit another home run. Just like Old Reliable, Tom Heinrich."

The man looks surprised. "The way Fain's playing, I don't think he can make up his mind whether he's Joe DiMaggio or Jackie Robinson. I hope you're right about the homer. I'd like to see the game tied up. Your team could win in extra innings."

My team. It sounds nice. The scoreboard reads visitor's 5, my team 4.

I read Brontë's description of rain on the moor. I don't want to write about poor Catherine. I'll get depressed. I pick up my own old reliable, *Pride and Prejudice*. The title of my essay will be *Love Conquers Prejudice*. And how many zillion other college girls will be writing that same essay?

"My guess is Fain will go for a single," the man says. "He's trying to hit for the circuit." Stubby fingers point to the diamonds on the clipboard. "Double, triple, home run. A single's all he needs."

"He can do that easily." I'm like Pamela, who puffs herself up because she has a rich and famous master. I open Austen's *Persuasion* and read how much Lady Russell, a widow, is looking forward to spending time in Bath. She is an older woman, not obsessed with love. She has the time and money to enjoy life.

Charlie's swing misses. I cup my hands around my mouth. "A single's all you need." Charlie cocks his head, stares. Can Warren see me from the bench? I sit down. "Is hitting for the circuit good?"

"In the majors, sure. Happens all the time in college ball, though. A kid like that" – he points at Charlie – "can do just about anything he wants against this competition."

"What are all those diamonds and numbers for?"

He smiles one of those male, affectionate, but slightly superior smiles. "I'm keeping score."

"It looks fun. But I have homework." I open *Emma*. Miss Bates, also unmarried, is effusively thanking Mr. Woodhouse for some small favor. Why is Miss Bates almost always in a good mood when she has so little to make her happy? The unmarried women at the boarding house where I live also seem unnaturally chipper. Love doesn't make them crazy.

Charlie swings hard at the second pitch. He misses again. "He's aiming for another home run," I say.

"It's a decoy. To move the third baseman back." The scout poises his pen over his clipboard. He nods as the third baseman takes small steps away from home plate. "Five-to-one he lays the next one down."

The pitcher fires a fastball and Charlie lowers his bat and bunts toward third base. The scout was right. Charlie was going for the circuit all along, and now he races down the first base line. The pitcher and catcher scurry toward the ball that the third baseman can't reach. I am standing and yelling. Charlie's foot thumps against first base.

"Tell me, was it a close play?" The scout hands me *Persuasion* and *Wuthering Heights*, picks up his clipboard. His pants now look as wrinkled as if he had slid into a base.

"Sorry," I say. "Charlie's so speedy they didn't even try to throw him out."

"It must have been very exciting."

"I'm not usually such a fan. I'm not sure I even approve of competitive sports."

He inches away from me. "I can tell."

I nibble my pencil and lean back. I open *Persuasion*. Anne Elliot enjoyed at least some of her life before she thought she had a chance to win Captain Wentworth back. Jane Fairfax in *Emma* also hummed along without the difficult Frank Churchill. On a new notebook page, I write, *The Argument Against Marriage: The Paradox in Jane Austen's Novels.*

Charlie takes a lead off first base. While the pitcher glances over his shoulder, Charlie takes an even bigger lead. I carefully lay my book on the seat before jumping to my feet. The pitcher throws toward home plate and Charlie races toward second. "Run," I shout.

"Would you say he stole second easily?" The man isn't smiling anymore. His bifocals are crooked.

I don't remember hitting anything. "He stole second very easily," I tell him.

The scout adjusts his glasses, scribbles something on the clipboard. "Please let me know what happens next."

The pitcher throws a curveball. Charlie breaks toward third. The batter hits a long fly out to right field. Charlie dashes safely back to second.

"Too bad he didn't tag up." The man smiles at me. "He'd be on third, in position to score on a ground ball. Or wild pitch."

If the scout has a daughter, she could put a dent in the family station wagon and he'd still think she was cute. I open my purse and offer him a lifesaver.

"I like the green ones best," he says.

Charlie takes another lead. A new batter is up and after him it will be Warren's turn. I can't watch Warren's at bats. Warren has a deep, Dylan Thomas voice, and a lovely shock of Dylan Thomas hair that flaps across his forehead. He enchants me with his poetry. But when he steps into the batter's box, he starts to shake.

If only the batter before Warren could get Charlie home to tie up the game. Warren does better without pressure. The batter pops the ball to the shortstop. Warren is up.

The scout, with the lifesaver between his teeth, says, "Down to their last out."

"It would be wonderful if Charlie could steal third and home." I don't sound boastful, just stupid.

"Great way to lose a ball game, but the kid might get by." The scout nods toward Warren. "This guy will never get him in."

"Be very choosy," I shout.

Pleased, Warren looks up at me. A high and outside ball whizzes past Warren's ear.

"Way to spot them," I yell.

Charlie slides into third ahead of the catcher's throw. Maybe the pitcher will throw a wild pitch and Charlie can score.

"Ashburn, just get it out of the infield," Charlie shouts.

The pitcher starts to throw the ball toward home. Charlie breaks down the line – trying to steal.

Warren watches the ball.

"Don't swing," I yell.

He swings.

His bat slaps the ball. The ball bounces to the pitcher. The pitcher grins, holds the ball out to Charlie like a prize then lobs it to first. Warren is still puffing up the base line.

The game is over.

Charlie trots across the plate and kicks Warren's bat. "Damn it, Ash-head."

Warren bows his head. He turns and walks slowly to the dugout. Charlie runs ahead.

"Not a bad game." The scout smiles and hands me my textbooks. "Glad I was able to see some of it." He pockets his bifocal, and tucks the clipboard under his arm.

He steps down the bleachers, then stops. His eyes look wistful. "You remind me of a girl I once knew. She was a big fan, too." He walks onto the field.

The plump lady folds her afghan. "Ashburn's a clod. What a lousy way to lose a ball game." She has probably never hit a baseball in her life.

Juggling my textbooks, a few against each hip, I step down the bleachers. I promised myself I would have written two pages of my essay during the game. I should never have let myself get so distracted. Something gold glistens in the grass. I pick up the scout's pen. It's still warm from his hand.

•

Charlie, with Warren right behind him, charges out of the dugout and runs toward me. I don't want to hurt Warren by telling Charlie how wonderful he was. I press my lips together, but the words come anyway. "You were amazing out there. You were. . .?" What had the scout said? "You were all over the field."

Charlie stops just long enough to look at me. His fuzzy stare seems to ask, "Who are you?" He smiles. "Hi there, sports fan." He winks and runs on.

Cold mist welling up from the ground clings to my legs. I'm as special to him as one of Zimmer's burned burgers.

Warren jogs to me. His cheeks are red from exercise or from something else. "Why were you talking to that show off?"

"I sat next to a scout. He made notes, little diamonds and arrows. I never knew baseball was so precise."

Warren studies home plate. "It's a wonderful game. I wish I could really play it. I heard you yelling out there. I told you the game would grow on you."

"It was the last game of the season," I say. "Very exciting."

"So that's why you were cheering for Fain?"

"He talked his boss into giving me a job. I was grateful."

"Sometimes Fain can be a halfway decent human being, but don't get too grateful, OK?"

I brush the Dylan Thomas hair from Warren's forehead. Charlie Fain may have cast a spell on me for an afternoon, but that is no reason to hurt the boy I love. "That was a wonderful catch you made last week in foul territory," I say.

"You saw that?"

"It was spectacular." I sigh and wish now I really had seen the catch.

Warren rubs my arm. "Maybe we can go to a Dodger game this summer." He takes a last look at the field. "The *La Forgue* I ordered is in at the bookstore. We can read the poems and watch the sunset at the park."

Maybe a sunset over the ocean will help me get my mind off shortstops. But my mind isn't the problem. It's my body. Hormones. Charlie is a perfectly nice, ordinary boy. But he has golden hair and mysterious blue eyes that make my hormones go berserk. I tell Warren, "Just a minute. I have to give the scout back his pen."

Warren nudges my back. "Be quick, OK?"

I walk across the field toward Charlie. Moisture soaks the top of my shoes. The scout has his arm around Charlie's shoulder. I wave the pen. The wide-faced man sees me and nods.

Charlie doesn't look up from the dirt he kicks. "Mr. Reisner, we would have tied it if that jerk hadn't swung."

I look back at Warren watching me. At least he can't hear Charlie's words.

"They were pitching out to get you. They had you cold, kid. And you don't win games showboating. You're not Jackie Robinson."

"I just wanted to show you what I could do, Mr. Reisner," Charlie says.

"Next time show me what you should do," Mr. Reisner says.

Charlie's big shoulders slump.

"Pam, the bookstore is going to close in half an hour." Warren's breath tickles my neck.

I turn to Warren and put my fingers to my lips.

Warren glances at Charlie and the scout. "It would be amazing to play in a major league game even for five minutes."

I pop my last lifesaver in my mouth. "Charlie could do it."

"He has a lot of natural talent," Warren says.

"But Mr. Reisner says Charlie is a showboater." A sigh leaks out of me. Why should I feel sad? So what if the world has one less ballplayer? It's not the same as having one less Brontë. Then I remember. The world will have one less teacher and I will have one less scholarship if I don't stop mooning over Charlie.

"Let's go," I tell Warren.

"Wait," he says. "This may be our only chance to see a Major League scout."

Mr. Reisner drapes a fatherly arm around Charlie. "The truth is, you look decent out there. Nice play you made in the hole. You've got good range. Ever play second base?"

"I'm a shortstop, sir." Charlie sounds disappointed.

"Fain is an idiot," Warren says in a whisper.

"Our Cotton Valley club may need of a second baseman," Mr. Reisner says.

"I can play anywhere," Charlie says. "Second, third, the outfield, you name it."

"I just did. Second base."

Charlie stiffens. "You mean, you're going to sign me?"

"You have potential, Fain. You might be Major League timber. I can't tell yet. When I get back from up north in a couple of weeks, I'll see you play again. There's a semi pro league you can hook up with in Inglewood." He hands Charlie a slip of paper. "We'll talk then."

"The scout's leaving?" Warren says. "We can follow him to the parking lot."

Charlie is grabbing the scout's arm. "Why can't we talk now?"

"Because I have to drive to Salinas to see another shortstop who might also be able to play second base."

The scout walks toward the parking lot. Charlie follows him. Warren follows Charlie. I follow them all. We make an odd little parade. At the parking lot, Warren tugs my arm. "My car's over there."

I pause. I want to keep following Charlie, but luckily Mr. Reisner stops in front of a dusty sedan. He doesn't have a family station wagon. And he probably doesn't have a daughter. At least not one who would want to ride in this car with him to Salinas. Dirt and dead insects streak the windshield. He tosses his clipboard onto the worn front seat. "Stay healthy, kid."

I hold the pen out to the sedan. "Sir, you forgot this."

"Thanks." His television eyes twinkle. "A big fan of yours, Fain." He studies me in my new dress then eyes Charlie. "Stay in training, too."

"What did he mean – a big fan?" Warren says.

I don't answer. I'm too busy watching the car turn out of the parking lot and merging with all the other cars on the boulevard.

Charlie throws his cap on the asphalt. He looks so disappointed. I want to take that hurt look away from his eyes.

"You were great today," I tell him. "You, you. . ." What exactly did he do out there? "Mental discipline is as important as the physical aspect of the game."

Charlie's dark blue eyes squint at me.

Warren is staring at me, too. "You sit next to a scout for a single game and suddenly you think you're some expert like Jim Murray?"

I glance at Warren. "Who is Jim Murray?" I turn to Charlie. "You hit for the circuit."

Charlie's eyes widen. He picks up his cap and slaps the dust out of it.

Those dark blue eyes are like a magnet. I step closer. "Mr. Reisner said you can do anything you want against this competition."

"Tell me something I don't know," Charlie says.

"He said you can't make up your mind whether you're Di Maggio or Jackie Robinson."

Charlie frowns.

"You're one of the lucky ones," I say. "You have talent. Mr. Reisner says you could be a Major League log."

"Well, this has been riveting," Warren says. "But if we're not going to the bookstore, I'm going to take a shower."

"You should have spent the whole game in the shower," Charlie says.

"Warren shouldn't have swung," I say. "But you shouldn't take your frustrations about Mr. Reisner out on him."

They glare at me.

Charlie starts to smile. "You are a firecracker. Instead of going to a bookstore with him, maybe you'd like to come have coffee with me."

Is Charlie Fain asking me for a date? Not possible. I remember the way he looked at me as if I were a burned burger.

"Which is it, Pam?" Warren's gentle voice has an edge to it.

I can't hurt Warren. Spending time with Charlie would only get me in trouble. I'd stop running my own life and start running his. I'd turn into his manager, worry about his diet, his attitude. I'd take care of him, the way my father takes care of his boxers. "Warren and I already had plans. But you were wonderful."

Charlie slaps his cap against his knee. "Wonderful. And I have to have coffee alone?"

"You shouldn't drink coffee," I say. "Stick to the juices."

Charlie's frown is back. He starts toward the gym, then stops. "Hey, Ashy, you're really coming along."

"Sure," Warren says. "I made the last out and only two errors."

"You're too hard on yourself," Charlie tells him. "You made contact and you made that one big play in the first." Charlie takes a deep breath. His eyes lose that hurt look. He says, "Major League log." He whistles through a smile and trots up the path.

Past the row of trees, the locker room door bangs shut. Warren tugs my arm. "Well, Mr. Murray, are we finally ready to go?"

I want to run up the path and tell Charlie that I want to be with him. I take Warren's hand and look out at the grass and the boulevard that have both suddenly lost their glow.

3

He asked me out for coffee, I tell my blouse with the puffed sleeves and Peter Pan collar. I smooth the towel on my dresser. With the money I get from tutoring, I'm saving up for a real ironing board. I lick my finger and test the iron. My finger tingles from the heat. "He's going to be famous."

Just thinking about how Charlie winked at me makes my feet start tapping, makes my little room with my bed, dresser, and hot plate, shine like a palace.

I tell myself, "You have an essay to write." I frown at pink buttons. "Charlie's father neglects him." Will Charlie even like my favorite blouse? With the edge of the iron I try to smooth a crease on the collar. Something smokes. A brown and permanent triangle-shaped scorch mark brands the collar. The scorch mark is a sign, a punishment for my careless, daydreaming ways. I already have a wonderful boyfriend. This Charlie-itis has ruined my favorite blouse, the one that was supposed to last my entire college career.

I unplug the iron. At least the scorch is at the back of the collar. When my hair grows back no one will be able to see the mark.

Maybe Charlie asked me out for coffee so he could pump me for information about Mr. Reisner.

"Enough," I tell the fuzzy purple wildflowers I picked in the vacant lot yesterday. The flowers have moon white centers. I pull out my notebook and pen and sit on my bed:

> *Although Miss Elizabeth Bennett would benefit financially and perhaps emotionally by being married, she still has a sense of herself. She knows her likes and dislikes. She is content and doesn't need another person to complete her.*

Lucky Elizabeth.

Outside my window, old cars rattle across steel gratings on Ocean Park Boulevard. Night shift workers from Douglas Aircraft button frayed coats that only partially protect them from the biting fog. The plant and the working class neighborhood that surrounds it are part of the Santa Monica that no one prints postcards of – the other Santa Monica.

Someone knocks at my door. "Pamela." Mrs. Soame's deep voice is insistent. "Telephone."

I rush past my landlady and hurry to the lobby. Could Charlie be calling me? My feet almost skid on the polished floor. I pick up the phone. "Hello?"

"I'm having a heart attack." The soft voice sounds familiar. "Daddy?"

"I hurt so bad."

"Did you call an ambulance?"

"It's too late."

He should have called them before he called me. "I'll get one."

"Just come to say goodbye."

The line clicks dead. It's too horrible. I'm going to lose my father the same way I lost my mother. Dr. Hoffman warned me that Mickey had an enlarged heart. I call the emergency operator and grab my car keys.

•

I picture him in bed in his striped pajamas. His face is white with pain. He looks the way Alice looked right before she died. My hand shakes so badly I have trouble putting the key in the lock. The door opens anyway. I run through the living room. I shoot down the short hall to the bedroom. "Daddy, I'm here."

The rumpled bed is empty. Did the ambulance attendants already take him away? My knees buckle.

"Pam," a voice whispers.

He's sitting in an easy chair. His face is yellow. Is yellow better than white? He tries to speak.

"Don't say anything. Remember that's what they told Alice? You're going to be all right." I hear the false hope in my voice.

He crooks his finger at me.

"You have to stay still." Alice didn't listen to me either. She got up and went to the bathroom. If I had stopped her, would she still be here today?

He crooks his finger again. I whisper, "Stay still."

He has tears in his eyes. "Promise me you'll take good care of Duke. And don't give him dried dog food. He only likes canned."

"Of course I'll take care of Skippy. But you're going to be all right."

"You have all my estate." My father waves his hand. "This house. I'm a little behind on the mortgage. You can have my trophies. And my boxers' mouthpieces."

"Daddy, stop talking." I can feel tears building behind my lids. "I don't think I can make it on my own." It's wrong to worry about myself when Mickey looks so small and frightened.

He sucks in his breath.

"I'm so sorry you hurt."

"Poor Alice," he whimpers. "Now I know what she went through. The pains shoot right through your chest."

I kiss his forehead. "The ambulance will be here."

"The ambulance is no good. Call Dr. Cade."

I open the nightstand drawer. "I'll have Dr. Hoffman on the line in just one moment."

His face contorts.

"Another pain?"

"Call Dr. Cade."

He's disoriented. "You mean Hoffman," I tell him.

"Cade, God damn it."

I dial the number. Why do doctors take so long to answer? Finally, I hear a man's warm, reassuring voice. "This Is Pam Carey. My father Mickey has chest pains. The ambulance is on its way. Is there something I can do for him?"

Mickey sits up. "Cade."

"Daddy, please." It's taking all my self-control to sound calm. "I can't hear Dr. Hoffman."

"Cade, damn it," Mickey shouts.

"Dr. Hoffman is an internist. Dr. Cade was Alice's gynecologist."

"And I'm having a baby." Mickey jumps out of his chair and grabs the phone. "My daughter always overreacts," he tells Dr. Hoffman and slams down the phone.

I open my mouth, but no words come out.

My father takes a cigarette from his shirt pocket. Is he crazy enough to smoke while he's having a heart attack? His cheeks are rosy. His healthy farmer face could sell boxes of cereal. "Do you still have chest pains?"

"Waldo's damn onions on his cheeseburgers give me gas."

"So you're not having a heart attack."

He sighs through his grin. "Good news, right?"

I still have a father. I watch him puffing his Chesterfield. He's going to be all right. I want to kiss him and kick him at the same time. "You scared me."

"Me, too," he says. "I thought I was going to go, just like your mother. Pains shooting down my left arm. I didn't want to die alone. I was worried that if I died there would be no one to look after you."

He does love me. "So, when did you know it was Waldo's onions?"

"When I was bequeathing you my house – *poof* – the pains went away.

"Why did you want me to call Dr. Cade?"

"Heart attack, onions, I knew I had something that required medical attention."

He puffs cigarette smoke at my face. His breath reeks. Not a heart attack, a liquor attack. How could I have been so stupid? I've been summoned to kill imaginary snakes dangling from the shower rod and chase CIA agents out of the closet. "This was a Jim Beam attack," I say.

"I thought you loved your father. But no, you're angry that I'm. . ." He blows a smoke ring. "Breathing."

I should be relieved that he's all right, but I want to pick him up and throw him out the window. I'm as loony as he is and I don't even have the excuse of alcohol. "You re-enacted Alice's whole death."

"I thought I was having a heart attack. Is that a crime?" His face softens. "I didn't know you would get so upset."

I turn away from him and stare at a plastic wastebasket with decals of roses. "Where's Kathleen?"

"We had a disagreement." He runs his hand through the thick red hair he is so proud of. "She's overly jealous."

Kathleen may have terrible taste in wastebaskets, but she does know Mickey. "Did your disagreement have a name? How much younger than Kathleen is she? Did you bring her home to show her your trophies, your mouth pieces, your estate?"

He winces. Good. I want to hurt him as much as he hurt me. He scrunches in his chair. He looks smaller, older. If he had a different daughter, one who was kinder, maybe he wouldn't need to drink.

"Kathleen's paranoid," he says. "She loves to be the victim."

She's not the only one. I'm like a rubber ball on a string bouncing back to the old familiar paddleboard. My father-the-paddleboard leans back and smiles. That look makes me want to punch him. "You shouldn't have started with Kathleen in the first place," I say.

His smile goes away. "It was the liquor."

"It was you and your screwed-up hormones."

He raises a graying eyebrow. "What do you know about hormones?"

"You and Kathleen spy on each other like two teenagers. She tries to run you over with her car because you mentioned a female customer by name. Very mature. Very loyal."

The word *loyal* gets lost in my throat. I'm my father's hypocritical daughter.

He stares at me. "What's got you so sour on love?"

The whine of a siren grows then dies. Red lights flash through the windows, bounce off the walls. "You better tell the ambulance men your heart attack is all better now," I say.

His chin ducks into his shirt. "You go."

"No."

His little boy smile is sheepish. "I'm just too weak."

"Why do I have to be the adult?" Still, the ambulance needs to be available from someone who really needs it. "Damn it, Mickey."

His chin comes out of hiding. He knows he's won.

I pat my hair, smooth my skirt. The crazier Mickey gets, the neater I feel compelled to be. I have tried to appear neat and sane as I've greeted the police, firemen, and priests who have all come on rescue missions to our home. Michael Patrick, "Little Red," "The Blazing Bantam" Carey is one taxpayer who gets his money's worth from local resources. I sigh my victim sigh and march to the door.

•

"I have a surprise for you in your room," my father says.

"What room?"

The man who was dying of a heart attack half an hour ago leaps out of his chair and pulls me toward the hall.

"I've never even lived in this house," I say.

He opens a door. "This is your new bedroom."

Kathleen's beauty chairs with the attached dryers are gone. The little studio bed has a new spread. "Took your rug to the dry cleaners myself." He hikes up his cabbie uniform pants and kneels by the hand hooked rug.

"Sandy and Andy." I sit on the rug and run my hands over the soft, wooly elephants. "It took Alice half a year to do this rug. Do you remember?"

"I knew you'd love my surprise," Mickey says.

"It's wonderful. "But I thought you gave all my things to Kathleen's niece."

"Not the rug," he says.

There it is again. I want to kiss him and kick him. Without my permission he gave all my belongings from the house on Hibiscus Street to Kathleen's family. I was sure I would never forgive him. Now, my rug has reappeared and I think my father is a saint. I slide my fingers in the thick yarn. Maybe he does care. But then, why can't I have my old bed and nightstand and my radio? Something pink and friendly sits in the corner. "You found my dresser too?"

"Would you believe it still has your school pictures in the drawer? Little Tina took good care of it. You got lucky there."

I walk to the dresser and smile at the decals of frogs in top hats and rabbits in aprons that Alice put on the drawers one rainy afternoon. My dresser, and my rug have come back from Never-Neverland and Kathleen's chairs are gone. "What's going on, Mickey?"

"I want you to come home."

"Home is Hibiscus Street where I lived with my mother. I have a place to stay."

"A boarding house with a bunch of females no one else wants is not a home. I want you to live here with me."

I've waited so long for my father to say these words. But I don't believe them. "What about Kathleen?"

"She's gone for good this time. Mi casa, su casa."

"What about Alice's books? Did they come back from Never-Neverland too?"

Mickey holds ups his hands as if blocking a punch.

"I wanted the books more than anything else," I tell him. "If you hadn't donated them to some mythical library I would know if Alice thought my namesake Pamela was pure and lucky or pure and a little sly. I would know if Alice admired or hated Mary Crawford. I would know. . ."

"How would you know all that?" Mickey says.

"She underlined her favorite passages. Without her copies of her books it will take me a lifetime to figure out what she thought. And even then, I might be wrong."

"Sweetheart, if I could get them back for you, I would. But isn't what you think about those books what's really important?"

"She was my map. I hate cutting through this jungle all by myself."

"Jungle? We live in Santa Monica."

I can't tell my father how Charlie has confused and hypnotized me.

There's a whine at the door. Mickey lets Skippy in. Alice's dog has grown thin and gray in her absence. "One big happy family," Mickey says. "You don't have to pay for rent or food. We can save up for your tuition at UCLA."

"You'd do all that for me?"

"You're my daughter."

He does love me. I don't have to fantasize about a television daddy. "We can take Skippy for walks together. I don't have to buy an ironing board. You already have one built right into the wall."

"Then, it's all settled?" He looks surprised.

I pet Alice's dog. His ribs stick out. "What time of day does he eat? I'll make feeding him my job."

"I feed him every morning. Duke eats better than I do."

"His name is Skippy," I say.

"You and your mother were always terrible with names. Duke was named after one of the greatest center fielders to play the game, Edwin Donald Snider – the Duke of Flatbush."

"Alice named him Skippy because he didn't walk. He skipped when she had the leash in her hand."

My father's eyes get sad. "That was a long time ago."

I want to make that sad look go away. "Daddy, who was Tom Heinrich?"

"Old Reliable? Right fielder for the Yankees."

"Is it better to be reliable than, say, to be Jackie Robinson?"

Mickey snorts. "Tommy Heinrich was a top-notch everyday player. But Jackie was Saturday night. You hungry? I made your favorite. Beef stroganoff."

Half-crocked, my father can still follow the *Grand Diplome* directions. He's eaten sandwiches for dinner for weeks so he can save up to make duck in orange sauce. His meticulous cooking is the only recent evidence I have that he might actually like himself.

"I'm still a little worn out from those pains. You don't mind heating it, do you? Just a low flame. You're not boiling hot dogs."

He pats the dog's head. "See, she loves our cooking. She's going to come home. She might even get your name right one of these days."

•

I sit on the rug my mother made for me and look out the window at the small peach tree in the back yard. I could live here in Mickey's house. Instead of warming my meals on a hot plate, I could eat Mickey's cooking. I might even put on a few pounds. Charlie wouldn't call me skinny anymore.

I walk to my dresser. Under an old sweater that never belonged to me, my fingers find a stack of slick papers. The photograph from my one year of Catholic School is smaller than the others. Mickey wanted me to go to Saint Monica's. He thought I'd get a better education. I remember Charlie's green and gold Saint Monica's High School ring.

I hold the picture of Sister Joseph's second-grade class to the light. The girls wear navy blue dresses. We stand with our hands behind our backs. We look as if any second we're going to sprout wings and fly off. I'm in the front row with ribbons in my braids. Broad-faced Sister Joseph kneels next to me. And in the back is my friend, the pesky boy who played tic-tac-toe and Hangman with me.

I loved Catholic school. The nuns smelled of soap. The classrooms smelled of polish. And the books told beautiful stories of ordinary people who had been touched by God to become saints. But Alice was afraid I would become a believer. "The nuns will tell you Jesus was the Son of God. He wasn't. Jesus was just a nice man. Keep it to yourself. It's our little secret."

Our little secret began to worry me. The stories about Jesus rising from the dead began to seem as real and wonderful to me as the shadows of Eucalyptus leaves dancing on the Church's stained glass windows. One Sunday morning, I sneaked off to Mass. Alice made me quit the school. Even now I remember how the thick and lovely wool filled my hands when I folded the uniform for the last time.

I squint at the second-grade class picture. Once, when I forgot my lunch, the pesky boy shared his sandwich with me. I study my friend's face. Even then he was generous.

Though both his front teeth are missing, the 7-year-old Charlie Fain is grinning.

4

I prop the school picture on the counter and tear lettuce for a salad. Charlie was gorgeous even then. Once, the most popular boy in second grade picked shy, freckled faced Pamela Carey to help him wipe the blackboard. All during second grade I wondered what it would be like to touch Charlie's hand. When I wiped the blackboard, I got my chance. I dropped my eraser and then, when I bent down to get it, my chalk-covered hand bumped Charlie's.

I smile at the hard-boiled egg I put into the mouth of the machine that looks like a pencil sharpener and gleams like a trophy. I crank the handle. The shell cracks in half and drops into a metal bowl. The egg comes out peeled. It was so sad for my father that no one could see the importance of his invention.

Something hisses. Mickey's delicate beef stroganoff is on full boil and flowing over the pot. There's another hiss and the gas flame dies.

If I keep thinking about Charlie. I'll destroy households with my scorch marks and overflowing sauces.

•

Propped by pillows, Mickey smiles at pictures in a scrapbook. The yellowing photos of the boxer with knobby knees make me proud. Little Red Carey was a small kid with a big punch. Sportscasters asked his wife what she fed him for breakfast. Mickey answered for her: "Mash potatoes" – getting all he could out of his somber Irish immigrant father. He hums, turns to pictures of his last fight, and returns his scrapbook to its hiding place.

I want to put my arms around him and tell him how proud I am of him. He jumps out of bed and kneels. The sneak isn't praying. He grabs a bottle of Jim Beam whiskey and gulps. Then he gargles and swallows mouthwash. Every time I believe we could be a real father and daughter, he ruins it.

Back in bed, Mickey looks up, sees me in the doorway. "How's dinner?"

I march to the bed and grab the whiskey. "You're killing your appetite." I open the window and pour the alcohol on the hydrangeas outside. "You're not even trying to make our plan work."

"I had a little tickle in my throat. Liquor's medicinal. Cure's the common cold."

I shake his shoulders. He waves his thick arms and bats me away. He smiles. The lunatic is enjoying himself.

I back away. "I can't trust you."

"I put a lot of effort into your coming home. That rug of yours cost me 30 bucks to dry clean."

"You found a cleaners next to a bar."

His small eyes glitter. He's guilty. Why do I keep believing he'll change?

He punches the mattress. "I didn't raise my daughter to live in a dive hotel with a bunch of unwanted females."

I look at my second-grade class picture: 7-year-old Pamela Carey had spunk. She dropped her eraser on purpose so a boy would pick it up and she could touch his hand.

I bend down. Mickey's breath reeks of whiskey and mint-flavored mouthwash. He needs a shave.

My hand darts under the pillow and grabs a second bottle of Jim Beam. "You didn't worry about where I was going to live when you sold our house on Hibiscus Street and moved in with Kathleen. You left me no place to go."

He reaches for the bottle, but I'm too quick for Little Red now. "You didn't worry about how I was when you disappeared right after Alice's funeral and went to Kathleen. I had just lost my mother." I can't stop my tears. "That's the kind of father and daughter we are."

I slam his bedroom door and hurry to my dresser. I grab my school pictures. Something thumps in the drawer. I reach my hand in. Alice's hook that she used for making rugs warms my hand. I open drawer after drawer. In a brown paper sack, I find scraps of wool she had saved. There's a houndstooth check from a skirt I wore in fifth grade, black wool from her favorite suit, and a narrow strip of blue wool she had kept when she had cut and hemmed my Catholic School uniform.

I look at the elephant rug. I wish I could roll it up and take it with me. But I don't have room for it at The Palms. "I'll see you later," I tell the two elephants. I grab my school pictures, Alice's hook and the wool remnants. In the kitchen, I turn off the gas flame, then leave my father's home.

•

I place the saucepan on the hot plate and wait for the water to boil.

My scholarship essay is due soon. I close my eyes. Images of Mickey and his heart attack, and Charlie at home plate cavort behind my lids.

I make myself open my eyes and stare at my notebook. If only Alice were here again to help me with my homework. Instant coffee warms my insides as I write.

> For Jane Austen and other women of her time, marriage gave women greater autonomy then living as maiden ladies in their more prosperous brother's or sister's homes. Yet in book after book, Austen portrays unmarried women as lively, self-directed, and autonomous.

I chew my pencil, then:

> Lady Russell, Mary Crawford, Anne Elliot, the Bates women, the widowed Mrs. Dashwood, even Elizabeth Bennet and Fanny Price, all have full inner lives independent of men.

I study the picture of Alice as a little girl with a big bow in her hair. I write:

> Inside the conventional romance novels, was Jane Austen secretly writing a tract against marriage?

•

I can't wait to see Charlie's face when I show him our school picture. Maybe he'll tell me, "I had such a crush on you I didn't know what I was doing."

I hum *The Girl from Ipanema* melody and gun my car's engine. My Plymouth almost sideswipes a gasoline truck. The driver makes an obscene gesture with his hand. I'm the one who still doesn't know what she is doing.

I fix my stare on the ocean.

Old Chartreuse, newly washed and waxed, beats my dusty Plymouth into the parking lot. Charlie runs and opens my door. "What a memory I have." He taps his head. "I figured out where I knew you from."

"I can show you where I know you from." I take the photograph from my skirt pocket.

The school picture looks small in his hands. His grin fades. "Probably took you two seconds to remember."

Wonderful. I've ruined his surprise and made him feel stupid. "You were the one who said we'd met before. I was surprised you remembered."

"Why? Because I'm dumb?"

I point to my picture. "Freckle face. Braids. Look at Kathy with her blond curls and perfect smile. She's the kind of girl people remember."

"I remember you."

Now he'll tell me how crazy in love with me he was. I fluff my pixie hair and wait.

"I used to copy word definitions off your papers," he says. "You caught me and said, 'You don't have to do that.' You showed me your dictionary and taught me how to look up words by using the alphabet."

He wasn't in love with me. He liked my dictionary. "Kids in public school used to call me *Pamela Carey, the dictionary*."

"They shouldn't have made fun of you for being smart. I owe you. I got A's in vocabulary up until fifth grade."

Should I ask him what happened to him in fifth grade? No. I'll sound like I'm interrogating him. "Once I forgot my lunch and you gave me half your sandwich."

"Bologna?" he asks.

I nod.

"My mother's idea of a good square meal."

"So what happened to your vocabulary in fifth grade?"

"My father left. The only word I could remember the meaning of was *divorce*."

I look at the picture of the 7-year-old with the missing teeth. "Why would anyone want to leave you?"

"You left. All through summer I looked forward to seeing you at school. You never came back.

He was crazy in love with me. The hills behind the restaurant could never look more beautiful. Anise waves like bright green feathers in the dusty chaparral. The 7-year-old Charlie loved 7-year-old Pamela. "My mother's worst fear was that I'd become a Catholic."

"You mean you weren't?"

"She wasn't. She was a sort of pantheist."

Charlie blinks.

"She thought God was everywhere. In us. In the ocean."

"Is she still worried the Church will get you in its clutches?"

"She died four years ago."

Dark blue eyes get sad. He is still the boy in the photo. He is still my friend.

•

I soap the sponge and glance at my Jane Austen essay. I scrub the stainless steel malt machine until it is so clean it sends back my reflection. I study my face and look for traces of the 7-year-old girl. I still have some freckles. The 18-year-old Charlie Fain suddenly appears in the malt machine picture.

"Why don't we finally have that coffee together?" He takes the sponge out of my hand. I reach for my notebook. I feel like a princess being led to the dance floor. He steers me to a table in the dining room where a woman is sitting across from Mr. Zimmer.

"New girl already?" The woman keeps her stare fixed on her freshly sharpened pencil darting across her account ledger. "I told you, Howard, it's more practical if you pay them better."

The boss, his skin still puffy from sleep, gulps coffee.

Charlie puts a chair next to the bookkeeper, and grins at me. "Sit."

Mr. Zimmer turns to me. "Didn't you come here to work?"

"She already cleaned the malt machine," Charlie says.

The bookkeeper looks up at me for a moment, frowns, then goes back to work.

"Pam, are you hungry?" Charlie says. "This girl never eats."

"If she never ate, she'd be dead," Mr. Zimmer says.

Charlie hands me a lemon jelly donut. My stomach grumbles.

"She is hungry," the bookkeeper says.

"There are those starved cats again," Charlie says. "Where have you been living anyway? A concentration camp?"

Charlie doesn't think I'm a princess. He thinks I'm a waif. I want to take my howling stomach and run out of _Immer's Cof_ee _hop_ and never come back. Charlie turns everything and everyone into a joke.

He pours coffee for me.

"I changed my mind about the coffee," I say in what I hope is my coldest voice. I pick up my notebook and stand.

"Even if you don't drink coffee," he says, "you can still meet my mom."

Not the bookkeeper, but mom, the lady who makes bologna sandwiches.

"Mom, this is Pamela Carey. Pam, my mom."

Mom's smile of greeting is small.

I sit and fold my hands in my lap.

"This is the girl I wanted to marry," Charlie says.

She looks surprised. "Not in this decade, I hope."

She can't be as surprised as I am. My elbow bumps my coffee cup. Coffee spills over the cup, off the saucer onto the table where it picks up speed and sloshes onto my notebook on my lap.

"We met in the second grade," Charlie is saying. "She was perfect."

Did he say wanted to marry or wants to marry? I stare at the Jane Austen essay, the puddle of coffee in my lap.

The mother of the groom frowns at the bride. The bride pours cold water on coffee staining her paper and her skirt. The puddle grows.

"What's that you got on?" Mr. Zimmer's eyes, able to focus now, stare. "Customers want white. Otherwise, they think you're hiding dirt."

"Brown is more practical, Howard." Charlie's mother's smile is back. Is it possible that she likes me? Usually, mothers of my friends sniff out my neediness and tell their children to stay away from me. Maybe they're afraid that losing a mother is catching.

I want to pay Charlie's mother back for the bologna sandwich and thank her for liking me. "My mother didn't believe in early marriage either. She said I should get my education first and I should know myself before I tried to know someone else."

Mrs. Fain's smile gets bigger. Her face loses its pinched look. Even without makeup she's pretty. Charlie inherited her eyes.

Mr. Zimmer turns to Charlie. "So tell me, he was there and you didn't get a contract?"

Charlie holds two slender fingers together. "Sometimes I think he's this close to signing me. But maybe I'm just fooling myself." He glances at me. "The way I fool myself about everything else."

Does he think because I said I was against early marriage I'm not interested in him? If only that were true. Napkins sopping up coffee and water turn to muddy wads in my lap. I will have to rewrite my essay in between work and studying for finals. The essay feels like a mountain too tall to climb.

"You do daydream too much," his mother says. "Close isn't a contract."

"He does have talent," I tell her. "Mr. Reisner told me Charlie is a natural."

"See, mom?" Charlie says.

Mr. Zimmer bites into a jelly donut. "Maybe you would have a contract if you'd ease up on the flash. Make Reisner see you're solid. Like Old. . ."

"Charlie could be reliable," I say. "Only. . ."

"Only what dear?" his mother asks.

All three of them are staring at me. If only I could have an answer that would please them all. I take a deep breath. "Charlie will stop trying so hard when he has more confidence," I say. "He needs to trust himself."

"With fans like you and Howie, how can I trust myself?"

When am I ever going to learn to keep my mouth shut?

"I've always told you a little constructive criticism helps everyone," Mrs. Fain gives me an encouraging smile. "This young lady may have some insight into your troubles."

I didn't know Charlie had troubles. I don't want to be in the middle of an ongoing argument between mother and son. Mrs. Fain seems so bright and hardworking. What would it be like to have a parent who solves problems instead of making them?

Something makes a popping sound. Charlie is cracking his knuckles.

"You don't believe you have talent," I tell him. "One day you try to be DiMaggio, the next Jackie Robinson. Some day you'll have the courage to be you."

Charlie frowns. But his mother is smiling at me. "You seem very wise, dear," she says.

Charlie's frown gets bigger. "A regular oracle."

"One should never fear the truth." Mrs. Fain slings the strap of her purse over her shoulder. "Remember what we talked about, Howard. Thank you for the coffee." She tucks a stray auburn curl behind her ear and picks up the ledger book. She nods at me.

Filled with lemon donut and the warmth of her smile, I'm cat-content.

Charlie stands at the window and watches his mother march in her Oxfords to a beige VW. "She's not going to believe I can play baseball until I'm in my uniform at Dodger Stadium."

"She's had more than her share of hard times." Mr. Zimmer is watching her, too. "She took good care of you for all those years. That has to count." He gets up from his chair and heads for the kitchen. "Time to make that potato salad."

Charlie and I are left alone in the dining room. Before I can find words for another apology, he says, "You did a great job of proving to my mom that she was right all along. I am a hot dog."

"I told her you had talent."

"You told her I thought I was Jackie Robinson." He stares at the table. "You probably wouldn't have wanted to talk to me even if I had gotten through last night."

"You called? How did you get my number?"

"Phone book. I got some weird guy who kept asking if I was a doctor."

The second he finds out that the weird guy is my father, any chance of a relationship with Charlie is over. Mickey has scared away every boy I've known – except Warren. Warren didn't care how crazy and insulting my father was. Warren is wonderful. So, why is my heart beating faster because Charlie called me last night? I can feel that awful, vain smile back on my face. "I live at The Palms Boarding House. I'm sorry I missed your call."

"Like hell you are. You didn't want to hear from a showboater like me. I won't bother you again." He pushes the cafe doors open. "OK, Howie. Let's get this show on the road."

It's over. I should be glad. I can go back to Warren and never think about Charlie again. So why do I want to run after Charlie and take back everything I said?

5

I place red geraniums in glasses and put a jar as a vase at the center of each table. I touch velvety petals. When Charlie sees how pretty the flowers are, he'll understand that I like to brighten up rooms and lives. He'll know I was trying to help him.

"You were hired as a waitress, not an interior decorator." Charlie's cold voice interrupts my reverie. Still angry, he's not used to criticism. Other girls must tell him how wonderful he is. I slap the sponge on the table. Whatever made me think I could be honest and still get a boy like Charlie's attention?

"Nice flowers," Mr. Zimmer says. "Charlie, your friend really knows how to fix things up."

Charlie glances at me. "She's Betty Crocker with a dagger."

He hates me. That shows how immature a person he is. He's not interested in improving himself. Warren always values my opinion.

"I think the flowers make the room look friendlier," I say in a very unfriendly tone.

Charlie turns his back to me. Mr. Zimmer stares out the window at the Gray Line tour busses and surfers in their Woodies and the Tonga Lei restaurant with a bamboo roof and ragged banana trees. Next to the restaurant: white sand and the sea. "Whoever thought a North Dakota farm boy would have property at the beach?" Mr. Zimmer says. "I designed the building myself. Bet you didn't know it's a trapezoid."

"The building's trapezoid shape is the most attractive thing about this place." I glare at Charlie. "Mr. Zimmer, your chili is wonderful. I love the cumin and just that dash of oregano." Betty Crocker with a dagger can't keep her mouth shut. "The chili could make you famous. You could call it Zimmer's Texas-North Dakota chili."

Mr. Zimmer nods. "Maybe someday when the kid becomes a rich and famous ballplayer, we'll have a chain of Zimmer-Fains up and down the coast."

Charlie puts his chef's hat on. "With Howie's cooking and my name, Fain-DiMaggio-Robinson, we'll have dozens of coffee shops." He eyes the flowers. "I mean, Pacific Coast Eateries."

The screen door squeaks open. A man in a bloody apron nods at the two cooks and takes a table by the window.

"Why, here's one of our clients now," Charlie whispers. "Luckily, he left his cleaver in the car." Chin jutted out in imitation of a snooty waiter, Charlie pretends to balance a tray and minces into the kitchen.

Eateries. Charlie could still get an A in vocabulary. Why does he think he's dumb?

I put a menu in front of the man with a bloody apron, then wave a warm-handled pot. "Coffee?"

"Do you want to kill me?" the man asks.

The little butcher must be some kind of nut, someone who thinks the Russians are poisoning our water. "May I take your order?"

For some reason the man looks even angrier. "Three eggs fried, sunny side up, hashed browns, wheat toast. But forget the jelly. Those things in packages aren't real jelly. They're squares of boiled rubber."

I step to the counter. Charlie has his back to me. He pretends to be very busy. I can play that game too. I clear my throat and tell the Zimmer-Fains, "The customer wants a Number 6, but hold the jelly."

Something is hissing. I peer over the counter. Mr. Zimmer turns hashed browns. Three eggs bubble on the grill. His accomplice, fighting a grin, pulls wheat toast from the toaster. "You both already know his order?"

"When he comes in, just holler, Sam, and I'll know what to do." Mr. Zimmer can't stop laughing at me. "And never give him coffee." Mr. Zimmer hands me the platter of food. "Cucamonga Sam hasn't changed his order in 10 years."

Charlie doesn't even try to hide his grin. They are both so smug.

My fingers curl around the platter. How would the Zimmer-Fains like to start off the morning with a fried egg shampoo?

I give Cucamonga Sam his order and hurry to a nicely dressed woman who has picked a seat as far away from the butcher as possible. "I like your hair," I tell her.

She smoothes her perfect bee hive.

"Do you live in Santa Monica?" I ask.

"San Diego. Is it a requirement to live in Santa Monica to be served here?"

I know I'm a jerk to be using this poor woman this way. I lean closer to her. "We're just taking a little informal survey of how many out of town customers we have."

Her look says we'll have one less customer if I keep bothering her. "I'll take the Number 4," she tells me. "I like the eggs over easy and I want the cottage fries, not the hash browns."

I look up from my pad and try a smile. "It's nice to meet you. I'm Pamela and you're. . .?"

"Sue. It's not nice to meet you."

"I'll be right back with your breakfast, Sue." I hurry away from those angry eyes.

I march to the counter and holler, "Sue."

Charlie squints at me through cigarette smoke. The boss, bent over the radio, turns down the sound. "What?"

"Sue is here," I say. "San Diego Sue."

Both cooks peer over the counter at the woman with the bee hive. She glares at them.

Mr. Zimmer snorts. "What the hell does she want to eat?"

"Sue," I yell again.

Mr. Zimmer blinks, still confused.

"It's a joke, Howie." Charlie is smiling at me. "Cucamonga Sam – San Diego Sue?"

I smile back. "San Diego Sue wants a Number 4. Cottage fries."

•

The back door slams. In jeans and his red baseball cap, Charlie walks across the lot. He didn't even say goodbye.

"Could I take my break now?" I ask.

Mr. Zimmer stirs chili and nods.

I run out into a morning that smells of anise. Charlie is sliding into the driver's seat. "Wait," I shout over the groans of Old Chartreuse's engine. I pound the window. "I thought we were friends all the way back from second grade. Shouldn't friends be able to tell each other the truth?"

Charlie stills the motor.

"I wasn't trying to hurt you," I say. "Reisner says you're major league – "

"Log." Charlie almost smiles.

"Timber. He says you take too many chances."

Charlie is nodding. "I do try too hard. With everything." He studies me. "Everyone."

He's looking at me so intently I have to turn away. "Twelve assists," I stammer. I'm not really sure what an assist is. "He said you were all over –"

"Yeah, yeah, all over the field. He also said I could do anything against this competition." Those dark blue eyes are still staring at me. "But can I beat out the real competition?"

A little Fourth of July sparkler goes off inside me. Is Charlie talking about baseball or love?

Now he's smiling. "At least you want to be my friend."

"I was going to call you when I found our picture," I say. "But something came up."

"Something like Warren. You've made it clear who you would rather be with."

If only it were clear to me. "Warren is my boyfriend. But I was with my father last night."

"Right," Charlie says. "You were with your father for the whole evening and even though you found the picture you couldn't take one minute to call me."

"My father has problems," I say.

"He's a fruitcake. " Charlie laughs. "I almost told him I was a doctor to get a word in."

I step away from the car. It's one thing for me to complain about my father, but I don't like it when anyone else does.

Charlie's eyes look concerned. "We are friends, right? We should be able to tell each other the truth."

"My father's not so bad."

"He told me you were living with a bunch of female losers. He thought I was one of those doctors for ladies and he asked me if I like looking up women's. . ." Charlie turns away, then looks at me again.

I want to run inside the restaurant and scrub some tables. I'd rather do anything than have this conversation. But something makes me stay with my feet planted in the parking lot. My awful secret, the one that I've always kept inside me, suddenly feels like a gift, like something precious I can give to Charlie. I whisper, "My father drinks."

Charlie gets out of his car, wraps his arms around me. The nubby lining of the sweatshirt that he's wearing inside out is soft against my face.

I feel safe and warm in his arms.

"Does he hurt you?" Charlie asks.

"He hit me in the face with a dishtowel. Does that count?"

Charlie sucks in his breath. "It counts."

I can still feel those blows from the cloth against my cheek. I rest my face in the sweatshirt lining. It feels as soft as a teddy bear. "He and my stepmother are both crazy. Once, when he passed out in her backyard, she beat him with a broom and broke three of his ribs. And she tried to mow him down with their car. And they chase each other around the house – with knives."

"My parents used to fight," Charlie says. "It scared me because they were so angry. I thought it was my fault. But they didn't hurt each other physically."

"My dad and stepmom say their behavior is proof they're in love."

Charlie hugs me tighter. "That's not love."

I step away. "I've never told anyone some of this stuff. Not even Warren."

"You had to tell someone." Charlie steps closer and holds me again.

•

I rest my warm coffee cup against my cheek and imagine that the cup is Charlie's sweatshirt lying soft against me. But it's Warren, not Charlie, who is talking to me.

"We do our undergraduate work here, so I can live at home and save money for graduate school. Then, I could do the Master's program in writing at San Francisco State. That would put 400 miles between us and our parents."

Warren's melodic voice is wonderful background music for the picture I'm trying to keep in my head. I shut my eyes and take myself back to that parking lot and Charlie and the air that smelled of anise. I even heard his heart beating.

"If we both got TA jobs, we could even get married while we were still in grad school," Warren says.

Just thinking about that sweatshirt and Charlie's arms around me sets off a thousand Fourth of July sparklers inside me.

"Pamela, are you listening?" The sharp tone in Warren's voice brings me back to the school cafeteria and my untouched sandwich. "Are you all right?"

"It's hot in here." I take off my sweater. Even with Warren staring right at me those Fourth of July sparklers are still exploding. I'm surprised that Charlie's name isn't flashing on my forehead. I'm afraid to look at Warren, so I stare at his wrinkled shirt. His mother, The Bitch, doesn't believe in ironing shirts for her only son. Since he works so he can pay his mother's rent, well-pressed shirts are a low priority for him. "If you give me your shirt later, I'll iron it for you."

He eyes the scorch mark on my collar, but says nothing. I had promised myself to keep my sweater on all day to hide the mark.

"Did something happen with Fain at the restaurant this morning?" Warren asks.

I gulp water. Maybe the word *Charlie* is flashing on my forehead. "I told him you were my boyfriend."

"If I over-reacted," Warren says, "I'm sorry. But you were paying so much attention to him. Or at least to his career. Forgive me?"

"There's nothing to forgive."

Actually, there is a lot for him to forgive me for. "You're wonderful," I tell him. "Smart and kind and loyal."

There's that word *loyal* again. I'm surprised I can say it without buzzers going off all over the cafeteria, rattling windows and knocking food off of tables.

Warren pats my knee. "I put myself in your place. You were sitting next to a scout, maybe the very scout who will make Charlie famous. In spite of his mouth, Fain is a joy to watch. I can see us some day in front of the TV. I'll tell our kids, I played ball with that guy and your mama talked with the scout who discovered him."

He is so dear. I just need a little will power, a little discipline, and this temporary Charlie-itis will be gone. Already the sparklers inside me are losing their warmth. "The picture of you in front of the TV with our children is so charming." I stir muddy coffee. "I didn't realize there was more than one scout watching Charlie."

Warren stops smiling. "He draws a lot of interest."

"Not from me," I say. "I don't even like baseball. I wouldn't even be at the game if you weren't playing. A silly game. Boys with sticks, making a big deal about running around a bunch of sand bags."

Warren's gray-green eyes look worried. He doesn't believe me anymore than I believe myself. Baseball season is over and if I quit my job at the restaurant, I'll never have to see Charlie again. I take Warren's hand. "Everything is going to be all right."

"Is there anything you want to tell me?" he says.

"Maybe we should go up north for our undergraduate work too. San Francisco. Seattle. Alaska. Maybe there's a College of the Arctic. No telephone. We could get to school by dog sled." There would be nothing except the odd blue eyes of the huskies to remind me of Charlie.

Warren frowns. "Did something bad happen last night?"

"Last night?" I squeeze my eyes shut. "My father thought he was having a heart attack."

"Thought?"

"It was gas from Waldo's cheeseburgers. But meanwhile I had called an ambulance."

Warren is nodding. "It must have been so hard for you. You thought he was going to die the same way your mother did. Ever notice how your dad times his little events during mid-terms and finals?"

"He asked me if I wanted to live with him. He would help me with tuition for UCLA."

"You don't need any more of your father's antics. Besides, you might win that June Wells scholarship." Warren's lilting voice makes even a lecture sound like poetry. "You didn't have much time to study for finals."

"I didn't study at all."

Warren shakes his head. "He always finds a way to distract you. And you always fall for it. I think he wants you to fail."

"I don't want to talk about Mickey anymore."

"You're smarter than I am," Warren says gently. "You should be at the top of every class. What about your scholarship paper?"

"I sort of did it." I sip the rocket-fuel coffee and smile. "I wrote about Austen's heroines sense of self. How even if all them had remained unmarried, they still would have purpose in their lives and things to interest them. They would live the way Jane Austen did."

Warren cocks his head. Is he going to be as puzzled as Professor Malcolm will be by the topic?

"Not very academic." He smiles. "But interesting."

Poor Warren. He only wants what's best for me. His mother still complains about the hospital bill she had to pay when he was born.

I take his hand. "I won't let Mickey or anything else distract us from our goals."

6

Ocean air wets my face. I hurry across the restaurant parking lot. It's Saturday night. I have one day and two nights to study for finals and rewrite my Austen paper. So why is my stupid heart beating so fast?

My hand shakes. I have to slide the car key in the lock and slip inside the Plymouth before Charlie comes outside. But maybe, he's no longer interested in me. The mercurial jerk has hardly spoken to me all day.

Charlie shuts the restaurant door. He glances at me, then gazes across the highway. Lights from slow-moving fishing boats look like they're dancing on the dark sea. "Sure is pretty tonight," he says.

"Sure is." My deceitful heart beats faster. The Plymouth door pops open. I listen to the traffic on the highway and the waves breaking on shore. Saturday night is date night. Charlie must have a girl waiting for him and Old Chartreuse. *"Get in the car,"* I tell myself. I grip the door handle.

"How about going for a coke?" Charlie says.

His voice was so soft I'm not sure I heard him correctly. I wait a minute. "Did you say something?"

He cups his hand around his ear. "Say what?"

"Did you ask me out for a coke?"

He stares at the sky, then slaps his knee. "By golly, I did." Charlie Fain thinks he's funny. I look at his expectant face. He's sure I'm going to say yes. Already, a few sparklers are setting off inside me. "I have to study."

"Coke will help you concentrate. Besides, no one but wallflowers, nerds, and greasy grinds spend their entire Saturday night studying."

Just looking at Charlie makes me feel as if I've had a hundred cups of coffee. "Don't you ever study?"

He stares down at his sneakers. "You just don't want to be seen with a dumb jock like me?"

Who could have made Charlie so self-doubting? At Catholic School, the only way celibates like Father Callahan could keep the boys' respect was to talk down to them and tell them they were stupid. I study Charlie's hurt eyes. Why couldn't he see their cowardly game?

"Everyone has to study," I say softly. "No one is born with knowledge of American history or English Literature."

"Yeah, well." His voice is cold now. He takes out his car keys. "Don't want to keep you."

"Maybe I have time for a small coke," I say.

"Hop in." His hurt look has vanished. He's grinning. Could he have planned this whole Poor Me drama all along? "The best place for cokes is the Santa Monica pier."

•

The little round Skee Ball ball feels cold and hard in my hand. Charlie puts his hands on my shoulders and turns me. "Face the center. Stand with your feet apart, then aim, and let your arms drop. It's all one natural action. Skee Ball is a lot like bowling."

"I flunked bowling," I tell him. "It's the only class I ever got an F in."

"It's not possible to flunk bowling."

"It is for a greasy grind like me."

Charlie puts his hands more firmly on my shoulders. "Now, you have Fain power. You can't go wrong."

My hands feel hot as firecrackers. I aim the ball at the center circle and let go. The ball arcs up and lands in the smallest circle.

"We have a winner here," Charlie shouts over the racket of rock music and pinball machines. People turn and stare.

"I can't believe I did it," I say.

Charlie squeezes my shoulders. "What I say works."

The game owner with faded eyes takes a winning ticket out of his apron.

Charlie's arms, soft and wooly in a wine-colored, V-neck sweater surround me. "See, winning is better," Charlie whispers in my neck. "If you're a winner, Brownie troops will march in a parade in your honor. Shortstops with a .430 batting average will hug you. If you're a loser, you can't get someone to buy you a second cherry vanilla coke."

I sip my second cherry vanilla coke and look up at Charlie and the bright lights of the arcade. Music from the merry-go-round fills the air. This is a perfect Saturday night.

•

"How about some pictures of us?" Charlie says. "They're cheap. Four for a quarter."

A man with big ears and a big belly leans against the photo booth. He puts his arms around a small woman in bedroom slippers. Together they study a narrow strip of shiny black and white photographs. The man and woman are in love. If we take our pictures does that mean Charlie and I are in love?

"I have to go home and study," I say.

Charlie pulls me into the dark, curtained booth. "Pictures just take a minute."

We're alone in here. Charlie puts his arm around me and lights flash.

He slides our wet photos from the slot. There it is – documentary proof that Charlie and I were together. The photo company even kindly provided the date stamped on the back. Now, there's no doubt that I'm a two-timing Jezebel.

"Want to see?" Charlie holds the pictures by their edge. He doesn't want to smudge the image.

"You have me so mixed up."

Charlie's eyes widen.

"A simple cherry vanilla coke turns into a night of Skee Ball and picture taking," I tell him. "I haven't thought about American History for a second."

"As soon as we turn in our winning tickets and get your prize, I'll take you home."

"Prize?" I shriek. "I'm going to get a B on my exam and hurt my chances for a scholarship."

Charlie looks at me for a long time. Is he going to yell or rip up our picture? "I don't know the rules for this," he says. "It's not like baseball where there's a strategy for every situation. Maybe it's more like golf. You have to play it where it lays."

Golf? Baseball? And they say women are illogical.

"You walked into Zimmer's and *blam*, everything fell apart," Charlie says. "You don't fall for my usual tricks, and I don't want you to. You get me talking about things I don't want to talk about, like my Dad. And you get me thinking about things I don't want to think about, like my showboating. Pretty soon, even though we're both supposed to be home studying, I'm standing here at 11 o'clock at night on the Santa Monica Pier having my first fight with you."

He brushes past me and marches back toward the pin ball machine. I tag along behind.

•

"Pick a prize," Charlie tells me.

Kewpie dolls and stuffed animals hang on hooks in back of the blond cashier. She wears a scoop neck blouse with rhinestones. She has a freckle on her right breast. On a rafter above her, a ginger colored lion looks at me with hopeful eyes.

"Do I have enough for the lion?" I ask the cashier.

The cashier glances at Charlie, then examines my fistful of tickets. She stands on tiptoes. Her hands can't quite reach. Charlie leans over, next to her, and grabs the lion.

"That was nice," the cashier says.

All night, girls have been glancing at Charlie. Some of them have been bold, smiling trying to get his attention. He hasn't noticed them, but he is looking at the cashier. "How you been Sara?" he asks.

"Better now," she tells him.

I want to throw the lion at both of them.

•

"Now I know your game," I tell him. "You have some kind of hollow leg when it comes to girls. You have to get every last one of them to love you. And if one of them isn't completely out of her gourd in love with you, you feel like a failure."

"You think I'm some kind of a Don Juan or whatever?" Charlie doesn't look pleased with my portrait of him. "Sara's a friend of mine. I've known her almost all of my life. Her brother, Randy, played Little League, Pony League and American Legion ball with me. He was a wonderful athlete but he got hurt in a car accident."

I turn my head and look out at the inky black ocean.

"You don't believe me? *The Evening Outlook* wrote an article about Randy."

"Monday, I'll go to the newspaper and check on your story."

"Good," he says.

He doesn't sound angry anymore. He sounds relieved. Maybe he's telling the truth. It's not his fault if Randy's sister thinks a neckline starts somewhere down near her navel. But why isn't he angry at me for insulting him, and calling him names? He's used to girls being out of their gourds over him.

Wind from the ocean blows the colored lights overhead. "I'm sorry," I say.

"That's not a proper apology."

"I said I was sorry."

He puts his fingers on my lips, then leans down and kisses me.

•

In my room at The Palms, I plug in the iron. Maybe I can iron the still-wet paper dry. The paper crinkles and sticks to the iron. I set the saucepan on the stove, take the instant coffee from the cupboard. I open my notebook and begin to write.

A voice says, "Fog. No customers. Just seagulls. They're all over the parking lot. It looks like a god damn convention."

I press the telephone receiver closer to my ear. "Mr. Zimmer, is that you?"

"Unless you're real hot to clean up bird shit, there's no point in coming in today."

"What about tomorrow?" I ask.

"I think it's coming," he says.

"I mean should I report to work?"

"What am I – the weatherman?"

There's a whirring noise and then silence. Did Mr. Zimmer hang up on me?

I listen for a long minute. Did Mr. Zimmer tell Charlie not to come in today, too? I can still feel Charlie's lips on mine. Maybe, Charlie and I could spend the day together.

Behind me, Shirley pounds on the bathroom door. "Damn it, Luna. I want you and your wheelchair out of there. I'll be late for church."

Every Sunday, Shirley shows the rest of us poor sinners how she's the holiest of us all. She bullies her way into the bathroom, hogs the full length mirror in the hall. Then, she's off to United First Methodist. I can just picture her barreling down the aisle, shoving past her fellow worshippers so she can get the best seat, smack in front of the reverend, presumably closest to Heaven.

The bathroom door squeaks open. From her wheelchair, Mrs. Livingston looks up at me. "Why don't you come to Mass?"

She's right to be worried about my soul. I've turned into a two-timing Jezebel, a slut. I don't need a neckline down to my navel to be a tramp. I'm a tramp in a white blouse with a Peter Pan collar and a pleated skirt. I'm going out with two boys. I'm kissing two boys. If I went to church with Luna, everyone would turn in their seats and start throwing their Bibles at me. I'm acting like my sneaky, lecherous father. Maybe an inability to be faithful is a genetic trait.

I tell Luna, "My soul does need a lot of work. I'll go with you tomorrow, I promise. But today, I have something else I have to do."

"Let me get this straight." Grinning, Charlie pulls me into a tiny living room. "You drove all the way here to scenic Lemon Avenue, the so-called bad part of town, just to tell me you couldn't see me? You could have told me on the phone. That must means you're dying to see me again."

"I just can't date two boys at the same time," I say.

"Absolutely not," he says with a smile.

"Then, you agree with me?" He's certainly in a good mood for someone who's being dumped.

"Absolutely. You have to tell Warren about us." He pulls our picture out of his pocket. "We look even better in the morning light, don't you think?"

Charlie looks even better in the morning light. In his pin-stripe Oxford shirt and khaki pants, he looks as if he could be a scholar, an Ivy Leaguer, the kind of boy Alice in one of her rare, pro-marriage moods dreamed of for me. But what does Charlie know about science or literature or philosophy? He probably thinks Plato is some kind of modeling clay for nursery school kids. "I can't see you again," I say. "I'm supposed to be going with Warren."

His grin dies. "So Ashburn wins?"

"I'm sorry."

"I meet the girl of my dreams and she wants someone else." He cracks white knuckles. "If you like him more, there's nothing I can do about it."

"Well, that's settled," I say. "This is easier than I thought it would be."

Charlie holds his hands up. "Hey, I know when to quit."

I've seen him get more upset about missing five points in a Skee Ball game than he is about losing me. But if I am the girl of his dreams, why doesn't he fight for me?

"I'm sure you know what you're doing," he says in that maddeningly calm voice. "And hey, even if someday I'm going to be a Major League ballplayer, that's someday. What we got right now, is Ashburn, who's smarter than I am. He doesn't live on picturesque Lemon Avenue where the bullet shells and lemon peels mingle. He drives a better car. One that actually starts. And it's a nice refined gray instead of a putrid Chartreuse. And he has a father."

Just because I wish I still lived on Hibiscus Street, does that make me a snob? Lemon Avenue doesn't look so bad. Charlie's little house is neat.

"The problem is we live in different worlds," I say. "You're an athlete. Warren and I both want to be professors. I've applied for a scholarship at UCLA."

"You think I don't understand you because you want to teach?"

"Not just teach. Be a professor."

"Right. I heard you the first time. I can hear the difference between a 90 and a 92-mile-an-hour fastball." Charlie's grin is back.

"Some women do become professors these days." My voice sounds cold. Why am I being so hard on him? I should be grateful that he's accepted my decision. Instead, I feel like kicking him. He is glad to be rid of me. He agrees with me that we are a mistake. I close my eyes and shut out his smiling face.

"So this isn't about crummy neighborhoods, or chartreuse cars, or lack of fathers?" the chirpy voice says. "This is because you want to teach?"

It's a mistake to open my eyes. The jerk is grinning. "Not just teach. Be a university –"

"– Professor," he shouts and dances toward me. "And there's no way I would understand that, right?"

"If I knew this was going to make you so happy, I would have broken off with you earlier."

"Broken off? If you think we're breaking up, then that means there's something to break." He grabs my hand. "I have something to show you." He pulls me through a hall into a small room with a bed and more books than I've ever seen in a person's home before.

"I tell you I can't date two boys and your answer is to drag me into a strange bedroom and show me a bunch of books?"

Charlie pushes me toward a shelf that is painted the same pale yellow as the room. "Look at the titles."

I'm in the kindred spirit business. Every time I see books that someone has taken the time and love to collect, I hope I'll find that one someone who chose the books I would choose if I had the money.

I'm always disappointed.

Other people's shelves hold romance novels, cookbooks. Even Warren has too much science fiction for my taste.

Now, Charlie warms my shoulders with his hands and steers me closer to worn, gray, brown, black, and faded green and blue hardbacks that look promising. I see Flaubert's *Temptation of St. Anthony*, the familiar, boxed Proust, Tolstoy's *War and Peace* in the same rose and black cover that Alice had.

These are the books I would choose.

But they can't be Charlie's. On his day off from playing ball and flipping burgers, he doesn't come home and curl up with Proust. The Fains must rent this room to a college student.

"She graduates from UCLA on Friday," he says.

"Who?"

He blinks, surprised. "Mom. Who did you think we were talking about?"

The bookkeeper is also a student. "But, she's so old."

"Forty. And not a bit decrepit." He winks. "She's an English Major." He kisses my forehead. "Just like you."

Running his finger along the spine of a book of Gerard Manley Hopkins poems, he sighs. "Just about killed her. Working and going back to school full time. She studied everywhere. Even at my games. The score could be tied and people shouting all around her. There she was reading her Chaucer." His eyes shine with pride. "In Middle English."

No wonder he noticed me in the bleachers. I was the only one not cheering, the only one like her. "What is she going to do now that she has her degree?" I ask.

"Graduate school. She wants to be a – professor. I'll be surrounded." He pauses for breath. "All I can do with books is put one on my head and walk across the room." He picks up *Anna Karenina* and demonstrates. "I wanted to find someone just like her, so I could get smart, too. And here you are, an A student."

"A minus," I tell him. "I'm not always the top person."

"And your father's a drunk," he says this as if Mickey's drinking gives me extra points. "You live in a boarding house. You want to go to school so badly you ignore the obstacles." He pats the Tolstoy on his head. "You really love this stuff." His eyes are shining with pride for me.

I turn from those dark blue eyes, and look at the Hopkins book and think of the tormented, humble Priest who still had the joy to write, *Glory be to God for dappled things.*

Charlie is right. He does understand me. Maybe he loves me. Why should suspecting that he loves me make me so damn happy?

"See, we were made for each other." He tugs my hand. "Let's go."

Where? His bedroom? His hand feels so warm. I let him lead me through the dark cave of a living room, past a small fireplace, and a mantle with the statue of the Virgin.

"Your stomach was growling again."

I feel my disappointment. Not his bedroom. Her kitchen.

Maybe he doesn't love me. He just likes to feed people. But that's good, isn't it? He won't give me a chance to be a two-timing Jezebel. He slips on a dotted Swiss apron. "You look cute in ruffles," I say.

"I look like a sissy, but all my aprons are at Howie's. Tomato soup or tomato soup?"

I blink at sunny yellow walls. It's too bright in here. Too warm. Too happy. "I have to go," I tell him. I wink at him. "While I still can."

He doesn't see my wink. He has his nose in a cupboard. "We have Saltine crackers. A whole big box of them." Charlie steers me toward a chrome table with a Formica top. "When was the last time you had a home-cooked meal?"

I don't answer. I want him to talk about love, not food. But he's opening another cupboard. This one has three cans of Campbell's soup and six boxes of Kraft Macaroni & Cheese. Are canned soup and boxed macaroni Charlie's idea of home cooking?

With a stainless steel spoon he prods a tomato red lump into a saucepan. He adds water, stirs. He drops white bread into a toaster and asks, "You ever eat at Warren's?"

Strange. He's not worried that Warren loves me. He's worried that Warren feeds me. "He's not allowed to boil water in his mother's kitchen."

Charlie nods. He looks cheerful. "Do they serve meals at your boarding house?"

Would it bother him if they did? "I have a hot plate."

Whistling, Charlie puts placemats on the table. His has a

photograph of Santa Monica's palm-lined bluff overlooking the highway and beach. Mine shows the pier, merry-go-round and harbor. I study the pier in the picture and try to find the place where we were standing when Charlie kissed me.

"What can you cook on a hot plate?" Charlie slathers butter on toast. "You should have asked for a stove in your room. Or at least kitchen privileges. Didn't Warren give you advice about the stove?"

"Warren and I have never talked about stoves," I tell Charlie, who looks adorable in his fluffy apron. What would he do if I jumped up and kissed him?

Charlie waves the stirring spoon. "I would have gotten you use of that stove."

He places a bowl of soup in front of me, then gets a bowl for himself.

"Of course I don't know why I thought Warren would help you. The guy can't iron his own shirts. Every day he either has on the wrinkled brown and white stripe or that sad, little green plaid. How long does it take to iron a shirt?"

I put down my spoon. "Warren has other priorities."

"Eat," Charlie says. "Tomatoes have Vitamin C."

I swallow sweet tomato soup. Charlie is staring at me. Do I have soup dribbling down my chin?

"Where do you shop?" Charlie asks.

"Shop?"

"Grocery shop."

"Safeway or Vons."

"I knew it. And you probably go to that ritzy Fireside Market too. You should be shopping at Lucky's."

I chomp on buttered toast and try to make some sense out of Charlie's words. Charlie is mad because Warren doesn't iron his own shirts and I shop at the wrong grocery store. "Are you saying I don't take very good care of myself?" I ask.

"Well, do you?"

"I've been on my own for a very long time."

"That doesn't mean you're doing a great job of it," Charlie says.

I put down my spoon. I'm not hungry anymore.

"You bring your school books in when you apply for a job. You flunked bowling. You don't eat enough. You hardly touched your soup. Five minutes from now those starved cats will be serenading in your stomach again."

I stand up. "I'm going now."

He looks bewildered. "What did I say?"

"You have an odd way of letting someone know you care about her. You tell her how messed up she is."

"You're not messed up. You're wonderful. A real fighter. But Wrinkled-Shirt Warren doesn't help you." Charlie points his soup spoon at me. "That's why you and I are a better combination. You're educated, but I'm street wise. If you make it to 16 on Lemon Avenue without being knifed and chopped up into bite-sized little pieces, you're a real survivor."

Charlie struts across the kitchen in his dotted Swiss apron and dishes out more soup. "So, what do you say? Is it me or Warren?"

I whisper to the ruffles. "I need more time."

8

This is my first trophy." Charlie picks up a golden loving cup. "My dad was still with us when I won it. I was the team MVP."

"Very nice." I smile and try and remember what a MVP is. Masculine Very Perfect person? When is Charlie going to kiss me?

Outside Charlie's bedroom window the gray day suddenly shines. Pine needles and branches wet with fog glow like the Fourth of July sparklers that are going off inside of me.

Just standing in Charlie's bedroom, makes the nipples on my breast stand at attention and my vagina get as wet as the Everglades. Even though Charlie doesn't have one finger on me, I'm picturing the two of us in a beautiful alpine meadow, and we're lying in a field of flowers and he's kissing me on my neck and shoulders and back.

"I called my dad and told him about you and about what Reisner said about maybe signing me. My dad said he'd try to come to one of those Semi Pro games. Will you come to one tomorrow night?"

"I don't know what my schedule is," I say politely. Behind my eyelids, we're back in that field of flowers and Charlie has his tongue on my belly. If I blow my finals tomorrow, I can get a job writing one of those sleazy romance books.

"Here's something that might interest you." He opens a drawer of a rickety chest.

Charlie's taking off his clothes would interest me. I could help him by giving the zipper on his khaki pants the tiniest of tugs. My face gets hot. When did prim little Pamela turn into the whore of Lemon Avenue?

Charlie takes a picture from under a pile of socks. In the wedding picture Charlie's mother is young. A round-faced girl in lace. Her groom has Charlie's blond hair and cocky grin. He looks innocent, waiting for life to start. Charlie smiles. "Dad said Mom was like a pioneer woman, a rifle under one arm, a baby under the other."

Mrs. Fain a pioneer? She buys macaroni and cheese in a box. People in love are deranged. I should know. I'm getting more and more unhinged as the minutes on my watch tick by. To get my mind off Charlie, I study the photograph. Mr. and Mrs. Fain look so young and full of hope. My parents once had hope, too. Why did Mickey go looking for love away from home? Charlie slides the picture back under boxer shorts. I stare fascinated by his underwear and then the drawer closes.

Why did my father stop loving my mother? I look up at Charlie's and my second-grade picture framed on the wall. I step closer. "Why do people leave each other? Why did your dad leave you?"

"I don't want to leave you." He leans down and kisses me.

We kiss for a very long time. "You feel so good," I tell him.

"You feel wonderful." He slides his hand down my back, and kisses me again.

Everywhere he touches me, he lights a fire under my skin. I close my eyes. I see Charlie and me in that field of flowers. He slips his hand under my blouse. His fingers glide inside my bra. Behind my lids, that field of flowers goes dark. Warning lights flash, stop signs rush toward me. A dark hall opens to a room where unwanted babies cry on the floor. The door shuts. Then, I see Mickey in an overcoat and black hat sneaking down the alley to Kathleen's back door. I open my eyes, and see Charlie kissing me. I pull away.

"What's the matter?" Charlie says.

"I feel so out of control." I hug myself and look up at the wall above Charlie's head where a pale Jesus clasps his hands in prayer. Watercolor-blue eyes plead with me to stop before it's too late. I tell Charlie, "Mickey nailed a crucifix on my bedroom wall. He said, 'Jesus died for our sins. Don't touch boys and add to His troubles.' My father is a hypocrite, but still he has a point. We shouldn't be doing this."

"What we have is special," Charlie tells me. "The Church says love and sex are a sin. But I think love is beautiful."

Is Charlie saying he loves me? But how do I know for sure that he does? Mickey said he loved Alice and then he slinked off to Kathleen's.

"Sex makes people crazy," I say.

Charlie's eyes get wide.

"It's a theory I have."

"Sister Michael used to say if people French kissed, their teeth would fall out," he says. "During recess all us fourth graders hid behind the backboards and French kissed our brains out." Charlie taps his fingers on his shiny white teeth. "So much for theory."

"You said my father was screwy. It was sex that messed him up."

"You told me it was alcohol," Charlie says.

"He cheated on my mother. He drinks because he feels so guilty."

"He drinks because he drinks," Charlie says. "Besides, I'm not your father and I don't have a wife somewhere."

"But I have a boyfriend somewhere. I'm just as bad as my dad. I'm a cheat and a sneak."

Charlie sits on his bed and pulls me next to him. "I know you don't want to hurt Warren," Charlie tells me. "But you have to be true to yourself. What do you want?"

I lean over and kiss Charlie. "I want you."

"You have me." His tongue touches mine. My fingers touch his face, his neck, his shoulders, but that's not enough for me. My sneaky, eager little hand reaches for his zipper. Charlie's hands struggle to unsnap my bra. He touches my breasts and discovers those traitorous nipples that have been waiting for him. He grins and lifts my bra and blouse. Now, my blouse covers my eyes and is halfway over my head. My hand tugs on his zipper. It makes a wonderful little whirring sound.

"Are you sure?" Charlie says.

"Yes, yes," I say, then I wonder what does he mean? What am I supposed to be sure of?

He has my underpants in his hands. He smiles and drapes them on the bedpost.

He sticks his finger inside of me. His finger feels like a tiny, brave little toothpick of a boat sliding around in the big, swampy Everglades. "Warren never touched me there," I say. "This is amazing."

"Amazing," he says and drops his pants.

He's beautiful, but he's so big. I pull my blouse off my head so I can get a better view. It's not possible but his penis is getting even bigger as I watch. Just what am I supposed to do with him?

Outside the bedroom window something squeals. A VW brake. Charlie peeks through a frayed curtain. "Mom's home."

His mother is here?

He jumps up, and searches for his pants. He hands me my bra. I slip it on, but I can't find the snaps. My bra is inside out, but at least it's covering my breasts. Luckily, my skirt still hangs halfway down my knees. I pull my skirt. "Where is my blouse?" I ask Charlie.

Charlie looks under the bed. He bumps his head. I spot my blouse next to a pillow. Charlie buttons his shirt. I slip my blouse over my head. It hangs like a wreath around my neck.

"Charlie," a voice calls. The door creaks open. "I got your favorite German chocolate cake with crumb frosting."

Holding a square pink box and dressed for church – Jackie Kennedy pill box hat, suit, gloves – Mrs. Fain steps into the room. Her jaw drops. Her eyebrows frown. "What's going on in here?"

If she didn't remember me before, she'll remember me now.

She grips the string on the cake box as if it were a life raft. Her stare is fixed on my stained underpants that dangle forlornly from the bedpost.

"We weren't doing anything wrong." Charlie's smile fails. He can't keep looking at his mom, so he turns to me. "I told you about Mom graduating. Tonight, we're going to celebrate with chicken fried steak, ranch potatoes, the whole works."

Is there a tear in the corner of his eye?

I don't know where to look. Each part of the room holds its own special horror: angry Mrs. Fain, nervous Charlie, my underpants, and reflections of myself in the mirror with my blouse around my neck. I've ruined the Fains' celebration. I was right the first time. The harvest of love and sex is shame and disorder.

I turn my back to Charlie and his mother and put on my blouse. When I turn back, Mrs. Fain is weaving string through her fingers. She tells Charlie, "You promised me you would keep your sex life out of this house."

Charlie's sex life? Does that mean he has lots of incidents like this?

"But Pam is special. I told you everything about her. Second grade."

"You don't know what you're doing. Either of you."

"Pam's a virgin," Charlie says.

"Not for long." Mrs. Fain glares at me and then slams the door.

"But she's an English major," Charlie shouts at the closed door.

I can hear her crying in the hall. Now would be a good time to grab my underpants. Why did I have to wear the one pair that is stained? I step closer to the bedpost. Before I can grab my pants, the door opens.

Mrs. Fain's gloves and Jackie hat are gone. Her cheeks are red. Her curls are wild. She is crying like a lost little girl.

"Don't blame Pam. I'm the one who started this," Charlie says.

"It's my fault," I cry.

Mrs. Fain looks at Charlie, then at me. "You're both babies."

I can't believe it. She's not blaming me. I want to throw my arms around her and kiss her.

"But I should be able to do what I want in my room," Charlie yells. "I love Pam. You don't know what it's like to be young."

"Right. I was born middle-aged," his mother shouts back.

Did Charlie say he loves me?

"You're babies who will wind up having babies." Mrs. Fain is talking and crying at the same time. "You'll end up just like me – having to take care of someone else before you have a chance to know who you are. You're making a big mistake."

"Are you saying that I'm a mistake?" Charlie looks horrified.

"I'm saying sex is wrong. You need to be mature. You need to take responsibility for your actions." She darts across the room and grabs my underpants. "I'm sure your mother would tell you the same thing. You don't know what love is." She throws my underpants at me. "Love isn't sex."

My underpants land on my nose. I take the pants from my face and blot my tears. Like the mature, responsible girl I am, I run sobbing to the door.

•

No Charlie. But he's here somewhere on campus and he'll be looking for me. He'll want to tell me how much he loves me. He can't wait for me to ruin his life. I walk fast down the hall of the Humanities Building and knock on Mr. Malcolm's door.

•

Mr. Malcolm looks up from my paper. "This isn't what I expected. It's more of a psychological study than a critical essay."

The bright office light hurts my eyes that are already tired. My fingers tremble from the coffee I drank at three in the morning. "You told me to be as original as I could be."

"Within the literary critic framework." Mr. Malcolm smoothes neat blond hair that wants to curl. "We Lit Crits are a rare breed. We only love metaphors and symbolism and irony. We like to compare one work to another." He points to the books of criticism he has written. They sit on a shelf next to books by Edmund Wilson and Alfred Kazin. "Last time we met you said you were going to write about the different ways Charlotte Brontë and Thomas Hardy have used their sense of place."

"That was several essays ago. This scholarship is so important and I keep changing my mind about what I should write about."

"I'm afraid we don't have time for you to write another essay, I need to turn it in for you today. I can't say I'm entirely pleased."

I reach for the paper. "Maybe I shouldn't enter it at all."

"Nonsense. It is well written. I'm only reluctant because when I was younger I tried to be a little too independent." He glances at framed diplomas from Harvard and Yale. "That's why I'm teaching here at a junior college."

"Independent in what way?"

His face pinkens. He stares at his shiny fingernails. "I wrote a paper on E.M. Forster."

"But Forster is wonderful?"

"The professors thought my paper was too personal, too psychological, too. . .Lit Crits are an Old Boys' Club. Be wary and good luck, Miss Carey." He shakes my hand and opens his door for the next student.

•

Warren's voice chases me down the long corridor. "What did you put down as the importance of Father Time in *Jude the Obscure*?" he asks.

I skid to a stop. "Doomed."

Warren looks puzzled. "What do you mean?"

I feel tears building behind my lids. "Father Time shows that Jude and Sue are a doomed pair."

"But there's more to it than that," Warren says.

"I didn't get more." Tears roll down my cheeks. Are Warren and I a doomed pair? I close my eyes and see my underpants on Charlie's bedpost.

Warren wipes my face with a handkerchief. "Don't worry about the test. I'm sure you did a splendid job."

"That's because I'm such a splendid person," I say.

Warren shows me a blue smudge on the handkerchief. "This Christmas I'm going to find you a pen that won't leak even if you bite it."

"I have to leave." I kiss Warren.

"Are you going to work?"

I could be like my father and lie, but I don't want to be more of a cheat than I already am. "I quit my job. Mr. Zimmer won't be expecting me today because of the fog and tomorrow he'll get my letter of resignation."

Past bike racks, Old Chartreuse sits two aisles over from my Plymouth in the parking lot. The strong June sun breaks through the mist. Beyond tennis courts and the track, the gym door swings open. A tall boy, his blond hair catching the sudden light, steps out.

I take my car keys from my purse. "I need to get away for a few days." I sprint toward my car.

"What about summer school? Your class starts tomorrow." Warren runs behind me.

"I'll make it up," I pant.

"If your father upset you, we can talk. It's not like you to escape your problems," Warren says.

Nureyev is dancing down the gym steps. "I have to get away," I say.

"You never wanted to be away from me before," Warren shouts.

I stop and let Warren catch up with me. "I don't want to be away from you now."

Warren studies me. "You're not leaving because of that hot dog are you?"

I turn my head so Warren won't see my tears.

Warren grabs my hands. "Where are you going?"

"You can't tell anyone if you don't know."

"Tell who? You said you would never keep secrets from me."

I rip paper from my notebook and write down an address. "Tell no one. Our future depends on it." I give him his ink-stained handkerchief. "I just need time."

I run, putting asphalt and rows of cars between us. A book falls from the stack under my arm. I look at the red cover, with the black and white drawing of Yeats. I can't just leave the book there. A Chevrolet with a dented bumper backs out toward the spot where the book lies. I sprint, swoop down, then jump out of the way of the car.

"Whatever is bothering you we can work it out," Warren shouts over a row of cars.

"We're going to be fine." I wave the book. "I have the Yeats."

Tears blur my eyes. I open my car door, yank a knob on the dashboard. Headlamps light the fog.

In my rearview mirror, Warren, still waving, gets smaller and smaller. On a strip of lawn next to the gym, Charlie is talking to a coach.

I'm safe for now. I turn left on Pico Boulevard. My Plymouth bounces down the hill toward the highway and ocean.

9

The sign reads, *Welcome to the Avocado Capital of the World.*

I'm almost there. Her eyes will light up when she sees me. She'll open her arms wide and let me in. All my troubles will disappear. She'll make me Postum and her gypsy stew. We'll walk the dogs and pick her fruit. I'll be completely happy. I'll be home.

I can hardly wait. To calm myself, I study the mountains. Farmers in jeeps and pickup trucks drive up inclines of rock canyons and cliffs to tend trees planted in rows. Squares and rectangles of irrigated lands are green. Patches of thirsty chaparral are brown. The mountains look like crazy quilts.

Charlie would be thrilled if he were here with me. One of his heroes, a ballplayer, turned farmer, has made avocado country famous. Duke Snider lives somewhere in these hills. I sit up in my seat. What's the use of driving 90 miles to get away from Charlie if every few minutes I'm going to find some new reason to think of him?

Letters on the window of the Alligator Pear Cafe read, *Air-Cooled.* There's a picture of a penguin in a pink parka sitting under a dripping icicle. I smile at Patty Penguin. She is an old friend. My Aunt Lottie painted her. Little Valley of the Oaks is the only place that's felt like home since Alice died.

I roll down the window. Waist high cattails and yellow prairie grasses blow in the hot wind. Every inch of me is wet. Where I'm going won't be much easier to take. The creator of Patty Penguin doesn't believe in air conditioning. She says it makes her sick.

Her road is past the feed store. Today's newspaper, its edges already curling in the sun, sits on top of her log-shaped mailbox. I should get her paper, but now that I'm almost there I can't wait any longer. The car bounces over ruts.

I stop in front of yellow roses. Her Jenny Lee's.

My feet kick up puffs of dust on her walk. The porch across the front of the house still sags. Big wooden chairs, painted in her Wedgewood blue period, have faded to a battleship gray. The shades are down. She's home. To trick burglars, she puts the shades up when she goes away. Before doorbells chime, the dogs start yipping. I peer through the peephole. A circle of light opens into an empty hall. The lump that's been in my throat since yesterday afternoon feels big and sour. I was wrong. She's not home.

Dogs hush, the door opens. I see a flash of yellow, the bow in her hair. Big arms open wide. "Baby," she says, and I'm wrapped in a cocoon of cloth and flesh.

She keeps hugging me. I breathe in the smell of her oil paints and pretzels. (Once I made a list of Aunt Lottie smells: licorice, garlic, glue, clay, Mason Dots, peat, home cooked beans, onions, and crayons.) Why do I stay away so long?

I was right to come.

She puts an arm around my shoulder. "Let's get out of this furnace."

Mugsy and Tuffy, fat black Scotties, paw my legs, lick my ankles. The house is 10 degrees cooler. Not enough. Lottie leads me to the living room. "Let me get you your drink," she says.

"Don't go." I hold onto her hand.

She looks puzzled. "I'll just be a minute."

I sink into a couch. She disappears down the hall. Drawn shades, thick curtains block the sun. But light and heat seep in a space under the French door and through a strip of window left uncovered. I lean against cushions. I close my eyes and see Charlie's face.

"Postum." Lottie has my mug on a tray.

"Can I stay here forever?"

She laughs. "Any Carey in trouble can stay here for as long as they need too. You know that." She settles into her easy chair. The chintz cover has tiny pink hearts and blue flowers. "How's my brother behaving?"

"Badly. He thought he was having a heart attack. He made me call Alice's gynecologist."

"Dr. Cade?" She grins. "Honey, he needs help. He's an alcoholic. It's a Carey disease."

"He went to AA. But he was drunk."

"I don't know what any of us can do, except put him in a hospital."

Now, I remember why I stay away. She's going to tell me how Mickey is neglecting me, how selfish he is. Even though I agree with almost everything she says, I don't want to hear her run him down.

Her eyes narrow. "How are your grades?" Then, she laughs. "I'm asking Alice McMullen's daughter if her grades are good."

Back in Kelso, Washington, the town fat girl and the town brain were best friends. "But they are good?"

I nod.

"How is your cute boyfriend with that wonderful voice? Is he still writing poetry?"

Mickey. Grades. Boyfriend. The third degree. She knows I'm in some kind of trouble. I stare at the frayed strap on my sandal. "Warren and I are going to be fine."

"Did you get that job at the coffee shop?"

She'll think I'm terrible for leaving the restaurant. She never quit anything. Except housework. Even in the rosy afternoon glow I can see the dust. Dust on knickknacks and furniture. Dust on Paper Mache donkeys and Wise Men who have been waiting on the hearth forever. "Mr. Zimmer makes a great chili."

She fishes a bag of potato chips from under the coffee table. "My brother needs self discipline." She pours herself a coke. Varicose veins marble her white legs. She promised her doctor she'd cut down on salt and sugar.

What would Charlie think of my 270-pound aunt? Would he just notice her weight or would he also see how good she is? What would he think of the dust? What would he think of the Wedgewood blue piano?

Damn. I'm wondering about Charlie again. But I couldn't love someone who didn't love my aunt. I should bring him here. He'll hate her and I'll stop caring about him. I sweep my hand across the cherry wood end table. Alice used to write *dust me* on this table. Now, dust clings to my palm.

Dust gives Lottie asthma. She promised she would dance at my wedding. She will never make it.

"It's good you took an afternoon off," she is saying. "Away from my brother."

Does that mean she doesn't want to me stay here forever? How can I tell her I want to stay for as many days as it takes to get over Charlie? Those days might take a lifetime. I look at my Uncle Jacob's empty chair. The matching easy chairs have backs that look like wings. She loved her husband, and she reads romances. She'll think I'm stupid, even crazy, for running away from love.

"How's that Postum?" she asks.

"Perfect." When I was a girl in braids, I sat with Lottie and Jacob in their breakfast nook in Santa Monica and pretended I was grown up and drinking morning coffee. Now, I'm pretending I can go back to being that girl in braids and back to a time when my aunt could hug me and make my problems disappear. But I forgot what my aunt was really like. She never let me run away from anything. When I was scared of the water, she threw me in the pool and made me dog paddle to the side. I breathe in fumes from the kitchen. "Onions. Beans. Corn. Are you making gypsy stew?"

"It's on the stove. So everything is fine with you?"

I nod. "What could be wrong now that I'm here with you?"

"Any number of things. But you are all right? I was going to call you. But, now I can tell you my news in person." Her eyes glitter. "I may have a house guest."

She will. Me. But whom does she mean? Another broke, drunk, diseased, Carey is coming here? I don't want to share her with someone else. After all, I'm her favorite person in the whole world. "Who might be coming?"

"Rose."

Impossible. She hasn't seen Rose for years. I'd almost forgotten about her. But if Rose is around, I'm only Lottie's second favorite person. I look up and find Rose's picture. Framed in oak, the only portrait Lottie ever painted, the little girl with gold curls and pink and cream colored skin sits in a bathtub and clutches her purple turtle. The girl is smiling at the painter, her mother.

Lottie and Jacob spent their savings on fees to adopt Rose, pay for a crib, playpen and high chair. When the natural mother changed her mind and wanted Rose back, she took Lottie to court. The wrong mother won.

She was an untidy woman in a gray coat. She grabbed Rose out of Lottie's arms. Rose clutched Lottie's hair. When the woman started for the door, Rose cried, waved her arms and tried to swim back to Lottie.

"Pam, she's a beautiful, young lady now," Lottie tells me.

"How did you find her?"

"Didn't you ever wonder why Jacob, who was a garment salesman, moved out to the country? A detective we hired told us Rose's family lived in Fallbrook." Lottie is smiling now. She rolls up the potato chip bag, and tucks it under her chair. "Remember how I taught Rose how to swim? I taught you, too. She's very good. She swims in competitions. I go to her meets."

I can picture Lottie trying not to be conspicuous, a hulk in a raincoat sitting in the back of the stands. A sad moon face in the bleachers.

"Does she notice you?"

Lottie snorts. "I'm hard to miss. But she doesn't know who we are to each other. She probably thinks I'm someone else's mother.

Someone else's mother. It's not fair. Rose doesn't know how much she owes to Lottie, how much Lottie loves her.

"I bumped into her once," Lottie is saying, "accidentally on purpose at the hot dog stand. She apologized as if it were her fault. She looked at me for a long moment and I thought she knows. Then, she stepped away. Do you think something about me reminded her – just for a second – of something nice? Something she couldn't quite remember?"

The smell of pretzels and oil paints, someone soft holding her close. "Yes. I'm sure of it."

If Rose remembers Lottie, she'll want to know her. What if there won't be room for me? "You said Rose might stay here?" I ask.

"I read in the paper her mother died."

The woman is the gray coat is dead.

Lottie pats my hand. "Now, both my girls have lost their mothers."

I hold onto Lottie's hand.

She stares at the painting of the girl in the bathtub. "She has three younger brothers. Her father works at a packing plant. They're short on money. I thought I could offer to take Rose in, to help them out."

"That's a wonderful idea." I smile at my generous aunt who has room to love both Rose and me. The yellow fabric of Lottie's dress strains over her mound of stomach. Her wiry curls are black at the roots, red at the tips. What if Rose turns her down?

"I know what you're thinking," Lottie says. "A perfect girl like Rose might not be happy to know that a person like me, bathed her, fed her, changed her diapers."

"She was lucky to have you." My foot kicks a box of pretzels. I set the box on an uneven stack of newspapers. There's a hole in the Oriental rug. "She may think you're not in a position to help her."

"I sold a couple of paintings. The one of the fence, wood pile, and old threshing machine you like, and another one you haven't seen, of an empty barn. I'm working part time at the Mission School at the Pala Reservation. I'm giving the Indian kids art lessons."

She's telling every one of them who can clutch a pencil that they have a chance to be another Van Gogh. Rose is still lucky.

"I just hope you don't get your heart broken," I say.

She leans back and looks at me through half-shut eyes. "Who is breaking your heart?"

You can't fool the people who raised you. "I'm breaking my heart and hurting other people. You did say any Carey in trouble has a home here. Even if Rose does come, can I stay for awhile?"

"You'll always be my little girl." She sits forward. "So, why is your heart breaking?"

"I don't think you'll understand."

"Try me," she says.

"I'm afraid I'm falling in love."

"But that's wonderful."

"It will ruin my life," I say. "The boy is unsuitable."

"The boy is unsuitable?" Lottie laughs. Her pink mules fly up. Her stomach jiggles. She laughs until tears come. "Oh God." She is wiping her eyes with her sleeve. "He picks his teeth? He's a thug? Unsuitable how?"

"He's a ballplayer."

"Ballplayer?" she gasps. "Oh, my God. Not a center fielder?"

"He's a shortstop. This isn't a joke, Aunt Lottie. This is my life."

Her slippers thud on the carpet. "And it's been terrific so far. You live in a room with a hot plate for company and you work with roaches."

"I left that job, remember? Quitting the movie theater and going to Zimmer's is what started the trouble. Don't you trust my judgment?"

"Yes. But it's your living your life according to the Gospel of Alice that I don't trust. Falling in love with a shortstop is probably the first original thing you've done. This is your first act of judgment. You're unhappy because the timing is wrong." She shakes her finger in my face and starts grinning again. "You're not supposed to fall in love until you're a college professor, and you own your own house with a picket fence. That was your mother's prescription for a happy life."

"A life with Charlie wouldn't work," I tell Lottie. "I know me. I'm bossy. I'll start telling him what to eat so he'll play better. I'll tell him what books to read. I'll run his life for him and forget about my own."

"Besides leaving the Church, can you name one original thing Alice ever did?"

"You're not listening," I say.

My aunt wags her finger at me. "You're not listening. Where did all of Alice's ideas about independence and all of her intelligence get her?" Lottie's eyes look sad. "I've never said this before, but who of the two of us ended up doing something, accomplishing something?"

My mouth snaps shut.

"Who was more successful, the sloppy romantic or the disciplined intellectual?" Lottie looks ready to cry. "I'm not bragging. I'm stating. Who does my niece call the Almost Celebrity?"

"But you have talent. You're good at what you do."

Lottie takes Jacob's photo off the table. The glass gleams. She keeps his picture dusted. "He was always there to encourage me. Does a hot plate encourage you?"

"Warren does."

"He's a fine boy. But you don't love him enough or we wouldn't be sitting here talking about shortstops."

"Charlie is gorgeous. He's sensitive. He's as graceful as Nureyev. He makes baseball look like ballet."

"My favorite uncle was named Charlie. He was your grandfather's brother."

She will be my Charlie's fan forever now. "Aunt Lottie. It's just not that simple."

She puts her hands on the arms of the chair and pushes herself up. "Pamela, dear. It's just not that hard." She walks to the kitchen. In a minute she's back, waving the ladle. "Do you think that loving anyone for any reason is so frequent? You have to grab love where you find it." She steps back to the stove.

Living out in the country, alone with dogs, of course she'd feel that love is rare. I shouldn't have told her about Charlie.

I pick up Jacob's photo, and look at his kind eyes, and his sad mustache. Even in this touched up photo taken at Sears on his day off, his smile is tired and his shoulders sag. Because he loved her, Jacob worked hard for Lottie.

Just because Lottie was lucky in love, she shouldn't assume love would work out for me. I trail my fingers through dust on the end table. Just because Alice was unlucky in love, she shouldn't assume I would be unlucky, too.

Aunt Lottie, with bowls of gypsy stew in her hands, steps into the living room. "I think I understand you and your Nureyev. You always liked my yellow roses and Alice's hollyhocks."

"What does that have to do with Charlie?"

"You liked my paintings and Warren's poetry. You said Warren's deep, rich voice put you in a trance. Now, it's baseball and ballet. Don't you see? You've been in love with beauty all along."

10

The phone rings and my heart does a little dance. Even though I've only been gone 24 hours and even though Charlie doesn't know where I am, my stupid heart starts beating faster. Charlie could be calling me.

Lottie, taking groceries from a bag, makes a face. Being an Almost Celebrity is inconvenient. People expect her to answer her calls. I can't stop myself I reach for the phone. "Klein residence."

"Pamela Catherine Carey. What the hell are you doing down there?"

"Daddy?" I wrap the cord around my wrist. "Did you want to talk to Aunt Lottie?"

"No." He minces his word in imitation of me. "I want to talk to you."

How did he know I was here? Warren wouldn't have told him. My face gets hot. There's no way he could know about me and Charlie and what a shameful fool I made of myself.

"We had a little commotion at the house last night. Kathleen and I were having a reconciliation dinner. I made Chicken Vichy and those carrots you like in the Béchamel sauce. Then, this lady in linen and gloves and a hat shows up."

"Mrs. Fain came to your house?"

"Naturally Kathleen thinks she's one of my babes. And she was cute. A freckle face."

I sink into a chair. Mrs. Fain came to my father's house and told him I was a slut.

My father's voice keeps going. "Kathleen starts screaming, 'A tramp like you should be ashamed.' Then, Kathleen beats the linen lady with her dinner napkin."

Wait a minute. Kathleen called prim Mrs. Fain a tramp? But I'm the tramp. I shut my eyes and see the stained underpants on Charlie's bedpost. Poor Mrs. Fain. First, she has to be exposed to me naked with her son and then my father's wife calls her names. She will tell her son he is well rid of me.

"Kathleen was a fireball. But the linen lady had guts too." Mickey is chuckling. He finds the grotesque scene funny. "She grabbed the napkin and told Kathleen to behave. Even said please! Is she a schoolteacher?"

"She's a rational human being," I say.

Behind me, Lottie starts to hum.

"Don't get on your high horse with me, young lady. She said you. . ." His voice drops an octave. "She said you and her son were," he clears his throat, "naked in her home."

"She's telling the truth. Though I did – I had my skirt on, sort of, and my bra was. . .Daddy."

Lottie hums louder. Puffing her cigarette, her raincoat flapping around her legs, she is standing on tiptoes and putting cans of tomato paste and bags of lentils in her cupboard.

"Kathleen told the linen lady, 'That doesn't sound like our Pamela.' She used the word 'our.' She wants me back, see?"

Poor Mrs. Fain. Yelled at. Hit. Not even believed. Until now their Pamela has always been so virtuous. "What did Mrs. Fain want?"

'She wants the Pope to construct a Berlin Wall between you and her son. I thought we raised you right."

Yelled at. Hit. But believed. Their Pamela has the morals of a slug. "I made a terrible mistake. That's why I'm never going to see Charlie again. That's why I'm here."

"Naked in a strange boy's bedroom. I taught you to be good. Besides, you already have a boyfriend. Warren what's his face. How many guys do you need?"

"I don't know what's the matter with me."

"You embarrass me in front of my wife. Kathleen stood up for you. But she was shocked."

I start to cry. "I'm so sorry," I sob. "I love you."

"Jesus Christ in a jockstrap," Mickey says. "You're 18 years old. Where did you learn to behave that way?"

"I don't know. I guess I'm a tramp."

Suddenly, Lottie grabs the phone from me.

"There is such a thing as standards," Mickey is yelling now.

"Standards like cheating on your wife?" Lottie says softly into the phone.

I gulp air and listen to the sudden silence.

"I'm not talking about me," Mickey shouts. "I'm talking about Pamela."

"Only those who have never sinned should cast the first stone," Lottie says.

"Don't get Biblical on me," her brother tells her. "Besides, young Romeo still has pimples. He's just a baby."

I grab the phone from Lottie. "Did Charlie come to the house too?"

"He's just like you. He can't wait to get into more trouble."

"Did you tell him where I was?"

"I didn't know where you were. He had already tried those losers at The Palms. I didn't think of Lottie's until just now."

Outside the kitchen window, jagged hills look sharp against a gray sky. Why am I so disappointed? My hiding place is still a secret. I should be relieved. "Did he look sad?"

"I already told you. He's a good looking enough kid. But he's a baby. You were right to go to Lottie's and get away from temptation."

"Do you forgive me for what happened at Mrs. Fain's?"

There's a long sigh. "Nobody's perfect. Not you. Not me."

"Thank you, Daddy."

There's another long silence. Then my father says, "The kid did say he was going to look for you at the pier. He said something about Skee Ball. He was going to go back there and think things over." There's a pause. "He did seem pretty downhearted. Can I talk to my sister now?"

I hand the phone to Lottie and sit on the window seat. Mickey's words bounce off the grimy walls. *He did seem downhearted.* He does care for me. A little sparkler lights up in me again. But he's going to the pier to look for me and think things over. While he's thinking, Sara with her scoop-neck blouse down to her navel will be there to comfort him.

I press my face against Lottie's kitchen window. Clouds from a tropical storm dump sheets of unseasonal rain. Rain will keep customers away from the pier. The cashier and Charlie can stay warm in her apartment. She will make Charlie forget he ever knew me.

•

Dawn. The sun rising over the mountain brings a new day. Lottie is singing, "Oh what a beautiful morning" to the cottonwood trees hugging the banks of the Santa Margarita River. How can my aunt be so cheerful when there is an entire day to get through?

The Studebaker bounces, and jumps over a small ravine. My stomach churns. It wants food. Food I don't want and can't keep down. When I was at The Palms I used to dream about Aunt Lottie's meals. Now, I can't look at an apple without getting nauseous. I blink at farmhouses on green hills. I've lost my appetite.

"Those cottonwood leaves are dancing," Lottie sighs. "I'd like to sit on a flat rock, dangle my feet in the river, and watch the day go by."

"I could never spend a whole day sitting," I sound prissy and old.

She looks at me and says nothing.

Dust on the dashboard makes me sneeze. I push stuffing back into the ripped seat. "How old were you when you met Jacob?"

"Your age – 18. He was 28. But you knew that already. My family thought his coming was a miracle, an answer to my mother's prayers."

I look out the window at cornfields. "Alice said any boy can fall in love with any girl if he's needy enough." Could Charlie, hurt that I've run away, fall in love with Sara?

Lottie spots the cornfields, smiles, and starts humming that awful song again. Just how high is an elephant's eye? "Did it worry your family that Jacob was a Jew?" I ask.

She snorts and pounds the steering wheel. "He was a man. He loved me."

"What about the Church? Didn't your family want him to convert?"

"Of course. They wanted him to marry me as soon as he was confirmed." She sighs a happy, lovesick sigh. "Jacob had to learn a lot about Catholicism mighty fast. Father Ryan was worried we would fall into sin. When people are in love," she looks at me, "they are so lustful they do crazy things. The Church doesn't mind a little lust just so long as people get married right away. Is your Charlie a Catholic?"

I nod.

"You see, things work out. Warren is a lovely person, but he's not a believer in our faith."

I frown at the blue sky and at hills rolling out to the sea. "Aunt Lottie, do you think the Church pushes people into marriage?"

Her answer is a grin.

"But just for argument's sake, say I got married early the way you did. How could I keep up with school? What if I had gobs of babies?"

"You can count, can't you?" Lottie says. "You have a calendar? You don't have to have babies unless you want to. Marriage isn't an end. It's a beginning."

•

We load bags of fruit into the trunk of her car. In the back seat, the Scotties bark and paw the windows. "What a harvest." Lottie smells a peach. "Peaches are Rose's favorite fruit. Maybe, if I get very lucky, she'll eat one we picked this very day. I'll make a cobbler."

I brush grass off my legs. "You already talked to her and told her who you were?"

"Only in my mind. Every time I pick up the phone to call I get butterflies, big butterflies, Monarchs, Swallowtails. You didn't know I was such a coward."

"I thought I was the only one," I say. She studies me. "Charlie must be so hurt," I tell her. "I left without saying goodbye."

"You do owe him an explanation. Particularly since the two of you were so. . .serious." She straightens the bow in her hair. "Lord, what a morning."

Rivers of yellow light run across tree trunks and meadows. I rest my cheek against a soft, fuzzy peach. If I had known that afternoon was the last time I'd see Charlie, I would have been bolder. I would have touched him more and kissed him more. I would have made sure I had even more to remember. I smile. Maybe prim little Pamela isn't so prim. If everyone, including me, is going to call me a tramp, I should have acted more like one. I should have had more fun.

"Those can't be asters," Lottie squints. "Not this early?" Like a big cat, she scrambles up a hillside. "Not asters," she calls. "Lupines." Her face rises from the grass.

She's beautiful. My aunt is beautiful. Almond-shaped eyes, chiseled nose, pink lips, she is still the girl Jacob fell in love with. She clutches a flower and slides down the hill.

She is so daring. If only I could be just like her.

•

What if Rose drinks or is wild with boys? I picture the baby she once was with a child's birthday hat on her head and a glass of champagne in her hand. She could ruin Lottie's life. "You're getting in touch with Rose could be a mistake," I say.

Lottie stops pacing the kitchen and cocks her head.

I clear my throat, just the way my hypocritical, sanctimonious father does. "Maybe she doesn't like dogs."

"Dogs?"

"She could be allergic to them," I say.

Lottie blows a pink gum bubble. It pops on her nose. "You don't want me to meet her because she might not like dogs?"

"We don't know anything about her."

Lottie stands very still. The grandfather clock in the hall ticks.

I clear my throat. "Maybe she doesn't like. . ."

"Fat people." Hugging herself, Lottie squeezes onto a kitchen stool. "She'll think I'm a freak." Lottie's face softens. "You want to protect me from that disappointment."

"Painters, I was going to say. Maybe she doesn't like painters."

Lottie starts drawing Elsie the Cow on a notepad by the phone.

"Some people think artists are strange," I tell her. "Maybe you won't like her. Or she's not who you think she is."

Lottie's eyes get dreamy. "I know who she is." Lottie gives Elsie full udders. "There's only one thing wrong with my plan."

Just one? I sit on a stool next to Lottie.

"But it's a biggie," she says.

Biggie. My adolescent aunt doodles, blows bubbles, and talks like a character in a comic strip. Should she even be in charge of a teenager?

"When I tell her who I am," Lottie says, "she'll know her own mother didn't want her."

Biggie.

"It almost killed Charlie when his father left." The words are out before I can stop them. Oh, what a help I am.

She looks at me. "His father left him?"

"He's never gotten over it."

"Poor boy." Her eyes mist. "What could be worse than finding out someone you loved didn't want you?"

Now, someone else he cares about has left. Did a little of him die all over again because of me? "He and his mother are very close. Or at least they were until I came along. I caused a fight. Mrs. Fain told Charlie he was a mistake. Because of him, she had to get married too young."

Lottie nods. "Rose will hate me for telling her the truth."

"Just leave things the way they are. That's what I'm doing with Charlie. I'm not going to see him anymore. At least you can go to Rose's swimming meets. You'll know she's all right."

Lottie stares at something across the room. Her wedding picture sits next to a stack of dusty dishes on a hutch. She and Jacob smile over their cake. When, I was little, the photograph was black and white. Now, the white has turned to egg shell, and the black is toast brown. "But I could be a comfort to her. God knows she could be a comfort to me."

Not if Rose is a party girl or a shoplifter. But maybe Rose is a boring Goody Two Shoes like me. If Lottie hadn't helped raise me, and if I had just met her, she would be the last person I would want to know. It makes my toes turn cold, just to think how much I might have missed.

Lottie eases herself to her feet. "If I'm not going to find out what Rose and I could be to each other, I may as well die." She snaps a bubble. "Why don't I just crawl in the grave with Jacob or Alice?" She looks so big standing there, daring me to refute her.

Living alone with avocados and Scotties has turned her morbid. I whisper, "What if she blames you?"

"At least I'll have tried. I'll let her know I care. That has to count." She picks up the receiver. "You want to stay or. . ." She looks doubtful.

"You're going to call her right now?"

"I thought that's what we're discussing."

"She's going to pick up the phone," I say, "and you're going to say, 'Oh, hello. I raised you until you were two and a half, and then your mother took you away from me. I've been spying on you all these years and now that your mother is dead, I want to know if I can be of any help.' "

Lottie waves the receiver. "Maybe you should just wait outside."

"Losing her mother wasn't bad enough. You're going to shatter her." My voice gets loud. Tears trickle down my face. Three days of being sensible and staying away from Charlie and I've turned into a maniac.

"I'll be tactful," Lottie says.

The doorknob turns in my hand. "I'll be outside if you need me."

The door slams behind me. Outside, it's an inferno. I blink at the thermometer nailed to the side of the house. It's 92 horrid degrees. A rabbit sees me, freezes, then darts behind a rose bush. A road runner lifts its head from a pan of water and flies to the roof.

Pam the Pariah.

But I don't scare the lizards. They do pushups on the rocks. Where did they get their energy? One lizard, its tail swishing, jumps on top of another. Mating? Or murder? I turn away, then look back.

Mating.

Feeling sick to my stomach, I lean against the screen door. A warbler with a yellow throat lands on a juniper branch. Next to him is a nest of eggs. The wind blows, the branch sways, the nest rocks. As if he has nothing to worry about, the little warbler starts to sing.

Inside the house, Lottie is on the phone. Her shoulders sag. Something awful is happening. I don't want to add spying to my list of sins. Shielding my face from the sun, and telling Baby Rose in the party hat, the baby I once loved, "Give Lottie a chance," I walk across the patio. My foot kicks a rock. Just as I gave Charlie a chance?

Garish Ozzie Nelson darts above me. Ozzie and Harriet Oriole, Lottie's favorites, return every year to weave their nest from palm branches. Ozzie's orange head and yellow breast match the blinding light of the sun. His love call, a shriek, makes my ears ring.

I duck under the shade of a lacy jacaranda tree. Oranges from the grove fill the air with their sweet fragrance and make the yard smell like a bride's bouquet.

Bride.

I should have known better than to visit the California heartland in June. Nature goes berserk. Ozzie and Harriet Oriole squabble and multiply. Lizards do pushups in the heat. Even my middle-aged aunt slides down hillsides on her bottom.

I should have spent my summer in a convent, maybe joined the order of nuns who sleep in their coffins. But the nuns hide from the world for a reason. They want to show their love for Christ. Now that I'm hiding, I don't feel love for anyone or anything.

The screen door opens. Lottie holds a box of tissues. I start to run to her, then stop. Maybe she won't want me near. Maybe she's afraid I'll say I told you so. I wouldn't. I may be mean these days, but I'm not spiteful. "What happened?"

She grips my arms. "I couldn't do it."

Thank God.

She drops the box, lets tears come. "I talked to Father Timothy. You don't know him. He just came from Ireland a few months ago. He told me to pray for guidance."

"He studied theology, traveled 6,000 miles and all he could come up with was 'Pray for guidance'?"

Lottie shakes her head. "Don't be a cynic." The glint of belief lights her eyes. "You should talk to him."

She told the young priest, a stranger, about her cynical, troubled niece.

"He's so understanding," she says. "He's just a little older than you."

"He knows as much about love and sex as I do. Nothing."

"Father Timothy knows about people and about God's will for them. He says when people are in love, it's God's will for them that they get married." She looks ready to cry again. I'm hurting her more than Rose ever could. "You've never shouted at me before. Never."

How can I be so mean to someone I love? "I'm sorry."

"Leaving Charlie can't be right if this is how you act."

Sweat trickles down from behind my ears. I take a tissue and blow my nose. I'm not just crying. My whole body seems to be leaking.

"You're not supposed to get over people," she tells me. "When Jacob died, and when your mother died, well-wishers told me I'd forget, that in time my wounds would heal. I said I didn't want to forget. Why should I want a world without my husband or my best friend?" She bends over a faucet and washes her face. She shakes her head. Warm drops shower me. "You can choose not to be with him. But don't try to forget. You'll only be fighting yourself."

"You mean I shouldn't try to stop loving him?"

"That's a start. But what's so wrong about loving him. What are you so afraid of?"

"He's impatient. He wants everything yesterday. When I'm around him, I forget what I'm doing. I was supposed to study Saturday night. Instead, I spent the whole night with him playing Skee Ball on the pier. The next day I went to break up with him and I ended up. . ." My face gets hot. I blow my nose. "Well, you heard where I ended up."

"So it isn't really him you object to," she says. "It's how you behave around him. So if you could change your behavior – ?"

"I can't. All I can do is stay away from him."

She looks at me for a long time. "At least if you let yourself love Charlie from a distance, you'll stop hating yourself and everyone else."

Ascarlet and green hummingbird hovers next to my nose, then darts at the rushing water. I wear Lottie's straw hat and canvas garden shoes, and water the Jenny Lee. Lottie has always loved roses. Back in Kelso, she and Alice grew them together. When Lottie adopted a baby, she named her Rose. She wanted to give her baby something beautiful. She did. Rose probably doesn't know who named her or why. Lottie's gift is a secret. Love can be a secret.

My hand brushes against a yellow rose. Years from now, Warren reading the sports page will say to me, "That egomaniac is still playing." He'll tell our son, "Fain used to have a crush on your mother." Our son will say, "You told me, Dad." Warren will wrap his arm around me. "Thank God nothing ever came of it." I'll tell my lie again. "There's been no one but you."

When they've left the room, I'll open the paper and check Charlie's statistics. I'll have memorized his batting averages, and what the press has written about him. The veteran ballplayer will never know he had a secret fan, a fan who loved him.

I move the hose, tilt my face and look up through oak branches at the blue sky and sun. For the first moment since I walked into Zimmer's, I feel at peace.

Down Lottie's road, a car coughs and wheezes. The car has a hole in its muffler. It sounds like an army tank. It sounds like Old Chartreuse. My heart races. I shoot water at my foot. A yellow-green Ford with a bashed-in side lurches to a stop at Lottie's gate. I turn my head and look for a place to hide. I could just squeeze behind the camellia bush.

The driver, a boy with blond hair, is watching me. I raise the hose in greeting. Charlie's angry glare makes my "hello" die in my throat.

Charlie slams the car door, shoves open the gate. "So this is where you're hiding?"

He looks so beautiful. To keep myself from running up and hugging him, I dig my heels in the grass and lock my hands behind my back.

"I came to say goodbye," he tells me. "Saying goodbye is a common courtesy and something you do for people you claim to care about when you're planning to leave town."

A foolish inappropriate grin spreads across my face. "You drove 90 miles to say goodbye?"

He slams the gate. "I'm leaving town. I figured I might never see you again. Not that you care. You couldn't get away from me fast enough."

I look at my soggy shoes. I've broken his heart and he's given up on everything and he's just going to wander around until he can heal his terrible pain. He's out of control. I have the same awful effect on Charlie that he has on me.

"I'm so sorry," I say. "I should have come to say goodbye. But I was afraid if I did I wouldn't have the courage to leave."

His face softens. "I guess you had your reasons." He lifts up his sunglasses. "Of course, I don't think running away solves anything."

So, then why is he running away?

"Aren't you going to wish me luck?" he says.

He wants me to wish him luck in running away. "Good luck," I whisper.

He looks at the road cutting through the patchwork quilt mountains. "When I called The Palms and they told me you left, I felt seven years old all over again. How could you do that to me? I said I loved you. The least you could have done was tell me where you were going."

"I didn't think it would hurt you that much," I say. "I'm not used to people caring that much what I do."

He studies me. "You're not used to people caring about you, period." He steps closer, then stops. "I've got a long drive ahead of me." Fishing keys from his pocket, he turns and starts walking to the car.

"That's it? You drive 90 miles and all you're going to do is say goodbye?"

His face turns sour. "You're the one who left me, remember? Besides, I'm not on my own schedule anymore." The sour look disappears and now he's actually smiling.

He's strangely chipper for someone with a broken heart. And what about all this talk about schedules and drives?

He pauses at the gate. Maybe he's had another change of mood. Maybe he's going to say he didn't really come to say goodbye. He came to tell me he can't live without me.

He says, "Did you know Duke Snider lives here?"

I sigh. "It's common knowledge."

He fiddles with the gate latch. "Aren't you even going to ask me where I'm going?"

"Where are you going?"

"Cotton Valley."

It sounds far away.

"It's only Class A, but Reisner says it's a real good team and I'll get a lot of playing time."

"You got signed?"

He looks surprised. "What did you think we were talking about?"

I run to him and hug him. "Congratulations. You're going to have a wonderful career."

"See, I was the right bet all along. I really am who I say I am. You didn't have to run away from me."

"I'm so sorry."

He looks down at me. "Things would be perfect if. . ."

His face looks wistful. Then, he straightens his shoulders and frees himself from my grasp. "If I can make the transition to second base." He climbs into the car.

For the first time since I've known Old Chartreuse, the motor starts at the turn of the key. Charlie pokes his head out the window and calls, "See you." He frowns. "Well, I guess I won't see you. Have a good life."

Tears prick my eyes. He's really going. But what did I expect him to do? I ran away from him. I kept my love for him a secret from him and even from me. Did I think he would stay and beg me to love him?

He could have tried.

What a mean hypocrite I am. I claim to care about him, but I don't. I was happy to see him, but I still didn't want him to know I loved him. He was so hurt and he thinks I turned him down because I thought he couldn't make it as a ballplayer. So why did I turn him down? Do I love Warren more? Or am I afraid of Charlie's power over me?

I blink at the whale-shaped car. Booming, drowning out birdsong, Old Chartreuse turns.

If I marry Warren, I'll be kissing Warren, and I'll see Charlie's face. I'll dream about Charlie and in my waking moments, I'll wonder what life with Charlie would have been like.

I dash past the open gate. Waving my arms and shouting, I run down the road.

Yellow green tail fins gleam in the light and move on.

Why doesn't he look in the rear view mirror and see me? My lungs squeeze. I keep running. At the crest of the hill, I jump up. My arms beat the wind. My legs kick the air. I call, "Wait."

Half way down the incline Old Chartreuse stops. I skid down the hill.

He opens the car door. "What is the problem?"

I'm out of breath. Tears stream down my face. "I don't want to live without you."

He lifts his sunglasses and looks at me. "That's not a problem."

•

The road curves through the hills. Live oaks replace the avocado trees. Then, the hills get browner and the trees get smaller. Charlie leans over and touches my shoulder. The sweet smell of tobacco crumbs comes from his shirt pocket. "So I was right all along? You do love me?"

Over the roar of Old Chartreuse I shout, "I do love you, but no one was supposed to know."

"Not even me?"

"Especially not you." I put my fingers on his lips. "It was a secret."

First he smiles, then his eyes get wary. "But it won't be a secret now?"

"As soon as we get to L.A. I'll tell everyone we know."

"L.A.? Are you crazy? I have to be on Rolly Wynn Field at 10 tomorrow morning."

"We're going to Cotton Valley right now? I thought I could talk to Warren and my father and your mother. We need to clear things up."

"What could be clearer?" Charlie says. "We're together and we're going to the major leagues."

I look down at Lottie's soggy garden shoes. Just exactly what am I doing? I'm wearing my aunt shoes that are two sizes too big, and I'm racing off with a boy I hardly know to a place I've never heard of.

I've never been happier.

•

Wildflowers carpet the hills. A warm breeze blows through the almond trees. We should be tangled in each other's arms. Instead, Charlie is studying a map. I move closer to him. "Where are we?"

"Frenchmen's Rock." Charlie points to a small dark circle on the map, then frowns at a cafe with peeling paint, a market with fresh peaches for sale, and a tiny gasoline pump. "I think we made a wrong turn back at Ridgeville." He scowls, cracks his knuckles, then opens a bottle of warm coke. He tilts his head and looks at me. "So how come you ran away?"

If only I could wrap my arms around him and tell him how sorry I am. Will he think I'm too forward?

"I was scared. I was supposed to be with Warren. Did he tell you I was at my aunt's?"

"Warren knew where you were? I was the only one you were hiding from?"

I put my hand out to comfort him and then pull it back. "You were the only one who hypnotized me and made me forget what I was doing."

Charlie smiles his cocky smile. Then, his face gets still again. "I never felt so rotten before, except when Dad left. At least he told me he was going. After I found out you were gone, I didn't want to go to the ballpark. I ended up playing the worst game in my entire life. Of course Reisner was there. He said I looked lousy. I told him I had the winter flu. He said, 'It's the middle of June.' Then he laughed and said, 'Son, you're going to have to learn to play hurt and sick. You're a professional now. And he handed me the contract."

"That's when you decided to try and find me?"

"I knew where you were. I just wasn't ready to see you."

"You knew where I was and you didn't call?"

Charlie's face looks stony. "You didn't want to see me and I wasn't going to beg. I only came to say goodbye."

If Charlie hadn't come to Lottie's, I might never have seen him again. If I had the courage, I'd grab onto his knee and hold on.

"I thought I was bad for you," I tell him. "I made you and your mother fight. You were wrecking Warren's and my five-year plan."

"You have a five-year plan?"

"We were going to get married after our first year of graduate school. I wanted to have at least a start on a Master's Degree."

"Now the wedding's off?" Charlie says.

"That wedding, yes." I lean over, take a deep breath and kiss Charlie's cheek. His skin is soft and sweetly fuzzy. "So, did my aunt call you?"

Charlie puts down his coke and stares at me. "Would she do that?"

"She promised not to." Should I kiss him again or should I wait to see if he kisses me? "She always keeps her promises."

Charlie sighs and looks intently at his sneakers. "Standing in your aunt's yard, you were even prettier than I remembered. You broke my heart all over again." He bends over the map. "Highway 99 goes right through Frenchman's Rock. We're not lost."

He's never going to kiss me. "It had to have been my dad. You got him drunk and made him talk."

Charlie shakes his head. "I don't think he'll ever talk to me, drunk or sober. Even if we give him 10 grandchildren."

He just said he wanted to have children with me. A bird with waxy black and white wings that look like windowpanes soars to the top of a nearby tree. I tell Charlie, "Birds. Flowers. Trees. Everything I see reminds me of you."

"Birds?" Charlie looks puzzled.

"That bird flies with the grace of a shortstop."

Charlie says, "Shortstops don't fly."

A song by the Teddy Bears comes from the jukebox of a small cafe. I hum along: *To know, know, know him is to love, love, love him.* What was it Alice said once? *You know you're really in love when mushy lyrics suddenly sound true.*

"Do you really love me?" I ask.

Charlie sputters coke.

"Is that a 'yes'?"

He leans over and kisses me on the mouth. "Yes."

I lick coke from my lips. I can feel my smile. He kissed me without me having to kiss him first.

A ripe almond plunks on Old Chartreuse's hood. What if I had never gone to Zimmer's to ask for work? I would never have been sitting here at Frenchman's Rock. I would never have known that Charlie Fain could love me. "I'm never going to leave you again," I say.

"You better not," he says.

I put my arms around Charlie's strong shoulders. "I hope I never hurt you again." I kiss him so hard he leans back and stares at me.

"Was that too much?" I ask.

He leans forward and kisses me harder than I kissed him. He puts his arms around me and pulls me down to the grass. We're tangled together in a field of flowers.

•

The phone rings in her kitchen. I hear the dogs barking before I hear her voice. "I tried calling you from Frenchman's Rock, but you weren't in. Now, we're at Smithfield."

"Pam, is that you? I was worried."

"I'm with Charlie."

"So, you're fine? Nobody kidnapped you?"

"I'm going to watch Charlie's major league debut."

"Nureyev got signed?" my aunt says.

"He's wonderful. Everything is wonderful."

"The roses have never looked better," she says.

"That's wonderful."

She giggles. "You left the water running."

"If Warren or Mickey call would you tell them I'll be talking to them soon? I want to tell them about Charlie. He's wonderful."

"So, you and Charlie are getting married."

"All I know is, we're wonderful. We're going to Cotton Valley. It's somewhere in the San Joaquin Valley. Oh, and I left my purse in the guest room. And I have your garden shoes. I'm wearing them right now and they're. . ."

Lottie is laughing. "Wonderful. My garden shoes are wonderful."

12

The kid in the straw hat who worked the counter of Valley View Grocery told us Rolly Wynn Stadium was on the east side of town, near the aviary with exotic birds and the feed store. We couldn't miss it.

We missed it. Twice.

The park behind the aviary has slides for children. Charlie slams Old Chartreuse's door and runs into the store. I follow him.

Parrots screech. Canaries sing. "The ballpark is at the north side of town next to the grist mill," a pretty lady with brown curls and smudges of rouge on her cheeks says..

Charlie dashes to the door. I run after him. The pretty lady calls to him, "Today should be a very good game. The Pickers are in first place and our new second baseman is here."

Charlie's face lights up. Then, he glances at the clock on the wall. "The new second baseman is already three minutes late. Which way is north?"

The lady is staring at him with awe. "You're Charlie Fain?"

He nods.

She bats long, mascara-clumped lashes at him. "We're so glad to see you."

I take Charlie's hand. "We're glad to see you, too."

She keeps smiling and points a finger that has a perfect red nail. "You just go back to the corner, turn left and drive through town."

I tug Charlie's hand and pull him past a brightly feathered parrot who cocks its head at Charlie and says, "Pretty boy."

We jump into the car. Charlie guns Old Chartreuse's motor. "What do you suppose a grist mill looks like?" He turns the car onto a boulevard. We drive past a drug store, a dime store, a hardware store. Many of the stores have signs that read *Go Pickers* in their windows. Charlie checks the position of the sun and mutters, "I think we're going north. Or south. All I know is we drove down this damn street once already."

"Why don't we stop and ask someone else?"

"You ask three different people in this town and you get three different answers," he says.

There's a Picker sign in a liquor store window. "Stop here. I'll just make sure we're going in the right direction."

The car bumps over a rut in the lot. Charlie keeps the motor running.

Inside the store, I step on a worn welcome mat. A buzzer dings. A bald, wide-faced man behind the counter looks up from a sports page. I get a glimpse of myself in the mirror. I have dark circles under my eyes. The blouse that was fresh when I put it on at Lottie's yesterday is now wrinkled and stained. I run my finger through my hair. "I wonder if you could please tell me where Rolly Wynn Stadium is?"

"Where who is?" The man's grin reveals a row of uneven yellow teeth.

"Not who," I say. "What. Rolly Wynn Stadium. It's the baseball field."

He burps. "Turn left at Pepper Tree. Two blocks down to Cottonwood." He burps again. The second burp is louder than the first.

"Thank you," I say.

"Thank you, Mr. . ." he says. "Remember your manners."

Mr. Belch is telling me about manners? "Thank you, Mr.– ?"

"Wynn." He points to an ugly pink and purple sign. It reads "Rolly Wynn Liquor."

"You're Rolly Wynn?"

"Before there was a field, there was a man," he says.

It must be a horrible mistake. No one would name a park for a man who can't remember to say, "Excuse me" when he burps.

•

A door marked *Office* in a low, shabby building swallows Charlie. I'm left alone. I glance at the blur of excited faces in the bleachers.

Strangers.

In a moment they are going to get the thrill of their lives. They are going to witness the debut of Charlie Fain. Today, in baseball history, a new star will be born. I smile at the field. In a moment Charlie, in uniform, will be out there.

The field looks bigger than the college diamond. There are long distances between the bases. The outfield goes on forever. There are so many places a ball could go. But Charlie is so good he will dominate any field that he plays on.

Men in white uniforms with blood-red caps run onto the field. A tan, gray-haired man, too old to be a player, bats balls onto the field.

The players warming up are fast. They field most everything that comes their way. Balls hum, slap into gloves, and then hum again. Next to the college players I'm used to seeing, these guys look like speeding giants. In a moment, Charlie will be one of them.

Standing in my shorts, old shirt, and aunt's garden shoes, I breathe in the friendly smell of warm-buttered popcorn and hot dogs. I should sit with the home fans. After all, I'm a Picker fan, too. But I don't know which bleachers are for the home team. Then, I see them: a troop of Brownies waving little orange and brown flags. The team leader, a plump woman in a Brownie t-shirt and slacks, waves a banner that says, *Go Pickers.*

I press my way past people's knees, and squeeze myself into a free spot. A man next to me makes a slurping noise. "Excuse me," he says.

At least someone in this town has manners. "You're excused," I say.

He nods, amused. "Guess that's why they call them Slurpees."

He's very neat. Too neat. Every thin, sandy-colored hair is in place. His jeans look stiff and new. His blue shirt, washed often, is clean. His nose is the giveaway. The veins are a little too big. The skin is a little too red. I would bet if I looked down at his hand it would be shaking ever so slightly. It must be a knack. Or fate. I'm in town five minutes and I've already met someone who has a drinking problem.

"The team working out," I say, "they're the. . .?"

"Butchers."

"What an awful name."

"They're from Manteca," he says.

"Oh. That explains it."

"Manteca is famous for its slaughter houses."

"Famous?"

"Of course they have a sugar packing factory, too. Spreckels Sugar." The man's nervous eyes brighten. "But Manteca Sweets wouldn't have the same punch to it."

"Are the Pickers as . . .imposing as the Manteca Butchers?"

"We have Tank. He's big. And Kahlil Gibran, the catcher. Rusty, he's big for a third baseman. And Fain."

"Fain?"

"The new second baseman. He's 6-foot-3."

How did Charlie grow three inches?

A man in a red and white checkered shirt and a brown and orange Picker cap taps my neighbor on the shoulder. "Walt, have you seen the second baseman yet?"

Walt turns, looks at the field. "He should be coming out right about now."

Charlie must have heard Walt's words. Charlie, in a brown uniform and pumpkin colored hat, trots out on the field with the other Pickers. He's beautiful.

"I don't think he's 6-foot-3, the man in the checkered shirt says.

"But he's well built. Solid," Walt says.

"Well built." I hear the smugness in my voice. The well built new fielder studies the crowd. When he sees me, he nods. The well built new fielder loves me.

"He's supposed to have pretty good range," Walt says. "But the problem is he hasn't played second since he was in the eighth grade."

Walt knows more about Charlie than I do. Are all fans such experts? Charlie shouldn't have a problem changing positions. After all shortstop is next door to second base.

"Have you been following the Pickers long?" I ask Walt.

"Since '54. I missed their last great season 10 years ago. Of course, it's only June, but this is their year."

If they're already in first place and now they have Charlie, they can't miss.

"Walt's usually right." The man in the checkered shirt has white goop, (some kind of medication?) in his left eye. "Last year, Walt said we'd come in third, four games back. I don't know how he did it. Everyone in town said he was crazy. We always finished last. But he called it right — third place. Maybe it's voodoo."

"It's baseball," Walt tells the older man. "Baseball is numbers. Look at Gibran. The kid's built like the side of a barn and he hits .400. How can you come in last with a kid like that on the team?"

A band in a brown and orange uniform, probably a high school band, marches onto the field. A voice from a loud speaker says something incomprehensible. Everyone gets to their feet. Many sing along with *The Star Spangle Banner*.

The game, Charlie's first game as a professional ballplayer, begins.

The Manteca lead-off man hits the first pitch right through Charlie's legs. The sun must have gotten in Charlie's eyes. He just didn't have a chance to see the ball. A boy in front of me, with a propeller on his cap, and a squirt gun in his hand, boos Charlie. He isn't even going to give Charlie a chance.

"Hey, Walt, you sure this Fain kid is good?" the man with goop in his eye, asks.

"Second base is a whole different world than shortstop," Walt tells him. "It's going to take some getting used to."

I look at the infield. How could a few feet between positions make so much difference?

The next Manteca batter hits the ball straight to Charlie. Charlie scoops it in his glove. Fans cheer. Charlie drops the ball. The cheers change to boos. What is the matter with Charlie? I've never seen a ball just dribble out of his glove before. Maybe his problem is lack of sleep. We drove Old Chartreuse off the road and took a nap. We tried curling up in the back seat together. We both got stiff necks and averaged about four minutes of sleep each. If Charlie hadn't driven 200 miles out of his way to come and say goodbye to me he would be fielding balls faster than anyone and the sweet-faced little Brownie in front of me wouldn't be booing him. I wait for Walt to say something encouraging, something in Charlie's defense. Walt says, "The kid does look nervous."

"I'd be nervous, too, if I was him and knew I was going to stink up the joint." The older man rubs his bad eye and then shuts it.

The third batter hits the ball right to the center fielder's glove. I swat at a fly on my knee. Maybe, if I get really lucky, another ball won't go to Charlie for the rest of this inning. I used to hope the ball wouldn't go to Warren. It can't be possible that Charlie is the Warren Ashburn of this team.

The next ball is hit to the third baseman. A stocky guy with red hair (Rusty?) makes the long throw to first. Two out. Charlie may get out of this inning without another error.

I get my wish. The next batter sails the ball to center field. Charlie is temporarily out of danger.

.

Charlie's first up. If there's one thing Charlie can do, it's smash the ball. He looks more confident now that he's at the plate. But his knees seem to bend more than usual. His hands grip the bat an inch or so higher than they have in the past.

The pitch is fast. Too fast. I shut my eyes. Something cracks. The sweet slap of the bat against the ball. A hit for sure. At least a double. So, why isn't anyone cheering?

A voice behind me says, "Kid's been here 20 minutes and he's already cost the team money."

I open my eyes. Charlie holds half a bat in his hands.

A little kid in a Picker uniform gives Charlie a new bat. Charlie uses the bat to hit the ball back to the pitcher.

"The kid's rattled," Walt shakes his head. "The problem is he could get the rest of the team rattled."

Charlie turns and looks at me, then he slumps his shoulders and slinks back to the dugout.

"Maybe the Butchers sent him here," the older man says. "Fain is a Butcher spy. He's here to shake up the Pickers."

How can fans like Walt's friend be so cruel? Doesn't he know ballplayers don't fail on purpose?

Back out in the field, Charlie's jaw is clenched. He looks as if he's waiting for the next disaster. It comes. A batter hits the ball in the hole between first and second. Charlie charges, and scoops up the ball and aims it toward first base. He hits the runner on the shoulder.

Walt's friend clucks his tongue, then sighs. I should tell him that I love Charlie Fain and I'm proud of him for even being out there. "Charlie Fain is. . ."

"Pathetic," the critic, with the bad eye, says. He turns to Walt. "This is who you told me to come out and see? I should have stayed home and watched the wife vacuum."

"The kid is just scared. It's his first time out there," Walt says.

I look at Charlie. His baseball uniform is too short. "It must be hard to play for a new team when so many so-called fans are watching and waiting for you to make a mistake."

The Picker's first baseman steps over, puts a hand on Charlie's drooping shoulders and straightens his cap.

"See, now you're both defending him," Walt's friend says. "You get some new Bozo out there and people start feeling sorry for him. Three errors in less than two innings?"

The kid with the propeller on his hat doesn't feel sorry for Charlie. He squirts water toward the field and yells, "Get him out of there."

The new Bozo out there must feel terrible. He keeps looking over at me, checking to see that I'm still here. He's afraid I'm going to disappear.

Just the way his talent has.

When we were driving to Cotton Valley I couldn't wait to see Charlie play. I never dreamed I would start wishing he and I were somewhere else. With Walt and the old man with a gooey eye watching, I stand up and wave to the Picker's new second baseman.

•

"Don't I know you?" The television daddy, a clipboard tucked under his arm, a box of popcorn in his hand, smiles at me.

"Mr. Reisner. What are you doing here?"

"That's the very question I was going to ask you. This is where I live."

"You live at Rolly Wynn Stadium?"

He smiles up at the white sky. "Cotton Valley is my home town. But you're a long way from yours."

I use the napkin I got at the snack bar to dab at perspiration on my chin. I swat at a fly, then quickly scratch my red ant bite. "I came to watch Charlie. He's not doing very well, is he."

"I see you're getting to know our local insects." Mr. Reisner is still smiling at me. "Fain isn't doing so bad."

"You call no hits and four errors not so bad?"

"Your boyfriend's just not used to winning."

I try to fluff my short strands of hair. Mr. Reisner thought Charlie and I were together way before we thought we were.

"He isn't winning," I say.

"He's here, isn't he? He's playing pro ball. He's probably in shock." Mr. Reisner smiles. "It hurts to finally get where you've only dreamed of going."

"My father always said winning was wonderful."

"Oh and what did he win? The door prize at the plumber's convention?" Mr. Reisner stuffs popcorn in his mouth to keep from laughing.

"My father was pugilist," I say. "A boxer."

"I know what a pugilist is. He did a little boxing in the army, right?"

"No, it was awhile ago, but my father, Little Red, was a professional. He was a champion."

"Little Red?" Mr. Reisner struggles to swallow the popcorn. "Carey? No way."

"He said winning was fun. He made it sound exhilarating."

Mr. Reisner flips up his sunglasses and stares at me through bifocals. "It's hard to imagine a bulldog like that even having a daughter."

"Sometimes it's hard to be a bulldog's daughter."

"Winning probably was fun for him. God knows he made it look easy. My buddy and I used to drive to San Francisco to see him. He was gutsy. You must be so proud of him."

"I'm very proud of Charlie, too. He's come all the way up here on almost no sleep and he's playing on an unfamiliar field."

"Little Red Carey. Wait until I tell Willie – my buddy." Mr. Reisner grins at his hometown sky. He's forgotten all about Charlie. He's picturing my father knocking some poor opponent into the ropes.

13

I want to hold him and kiss him until all the hurt has gone away. But Charlie is hugging himself. His eyes look wary. He doesn't want to be touched. Still, the cut on his cheek is covered with blood and dirt. Someone should clean it before it gets infected. I dab his cheek with a napkin.

"What are you doing?" he asks.

"Your cut is terrible." I scrape off a chunk of dirt. He winces. "I was so proud of you out there. You looked –"

"– like hell. I looked like Ashy." He drops the car keys in my hand and slumps into the passenger's seat. "Get me out of here before they decide to beat me to death with a baseball bat."

"That bare-handed catch you made in the seventh was gutsy."

"It was stupid." He sits up, looks behind him, and then slinks down again. "The rest of them are coming. Let's go."

I want to tell him I'm not good with strange cars. It takes me awhile to figure out where everything is. But he doesn't look as if he can take any more bad news. He slides his glove under his head and uses it as a pillow.

I gun the engine. Old Chartreuse lurches forward, and then dies. "You have to keep pumping the gas pedal," a grumpy voice says.

I start the car again. We bounce toward the street. "Where are we going?"

"Anywhere but here."

I turn left on the street, then make a right at the corner. I drive down three blocks, then make another right, and stop in the middle of the block. "We're here," I say.

Charlie sits up and blinks at a trim little house with a girl splashing in a wading pool. "Where are we?"

"Anywhere but there."

"I meant a motel. Someplace where we can get some sleep." Charlie bats a bruised eye. "Someplace where you can ply me with liquor and love."

Motel? Liquor? Love. It sounds nice. "I'm not that kind of girl." I lean over and kiss him. "Or at least I wasn't until I started hanging out with you."

"I was joking. I'm beat. I couldn't do anything even if I wanted too. Well, of course I want to." His voice trails off. "I just need to be near you." He sits up. The glove slides to the floor. He reaches for my hand. "This is one of the worst days of my life. It helps to have you with me, honey."

He called me *honey*. The sweet word warms me. "You just had a rocky start," I tell him. "You'll do better tomorrow."

"Who was that man you were talking to?" Charlie says.

Is Charlie jealous? Jealous enough to forget how tired he is and take me in his arms? "He was a fan," I say.

"What color were his eyes?"

Good. Charlie is jealous and this is a trick question. "He wore sunglasses."

"Could his eyes have been hazel, with maybe a little yellow in them?"

I shrug.

"Did he ask a lot of questions about me?"

Is Charlie trying to figure out if I told the man I had a boyfriend?

"No." I tell him.

"But did he know a lot about me?"

"Well, yes. He knew you played second base in eighth grade. He knew your college batting average. Do you think he was a scout from another team?

Charlie's face is suddenly brighter. "That man may have been my father. He had the same color hair and he was the right height and build. Dad said he would try to come. Just my luck today's the day he'd actually show up."

"I don't think he was your father. The man I was talking to was named Walt."

"He could have used an alias. He didn't want people to know he was related to a disaster like me."

"Walt said he'd been living in Cotton Valley for nine years."

Charlie shrugs. "He looked like my dad."

"Walt said you're going to be fine. You're just going through a period of adjustment. That's what Mr. Reisner said, too."

"Reisner was here? Was there anyone besides my father who missed seeing me make an ass of myself?"

"Mr. Reisner said he lives here."

"You believed him?"

Charlie is so hurt he's not rational. "Why would Mr. Reisner lie to me?"

"He really came here to check up on me. He wanted to make sure he didn't make a mistake in signing me. Which he obviously did."

I take his hand. "Mr. Reisner said he grew up here. His father is a newspaper editor. There's a coffee shop named Clara's that has great chili. It gets so hot here you can scramble eggs on the sidewalk. There's a Norge do-it-yourself dry cleaners and a new Chicken Delight place. He told me these things because he knew you would be here for a while."

"Since we're going to be here long enough for us to order a Chicken Delight, maybe tomorrow you should find us a place to live."

"We can't live together unless we're married." I sound harsh and prim. "That doesn't mean we can't see each other for liquor and love. Well, we shouldn't drink either. Or. . ."

There's a long awful silence. Charlie sneezes. Did the word "marriage" make his nose itch? He says, "I dragged you all the way up here. You don't even have your purse or a change of clothes. I can't hit the ball out of the infield. This is not the time to talk about long range plans."

He tosses his fielder's glove with frayed webbing onto the back seat. "Tomorrow, while I'm making an ass of myself at the game, you can look for temporary places for us to live. Separate places." He yawns, then closes his eyes. "Meanwhile, see if you can find us a motel so we can sleep in a real bed. Make that two real beds. Separate."

He doesn't want me to ply him with liquor and love. He doesn't want us to live together. He doesn't want to even talk about marriage. Mrs. Fain and my father have nothing to worry about. All Charlie wants is a good night's sleep.

•

The house could be beautiful. The wood frame is painted farmhouse red and trimmed with white. It looks crisp. A bright orange cape honeysuckle cascades out of a window box. Morning glories trail up a lattice. Once, someone loved this house. Someone could love it again. I could paint the brown, rickety fence white. I could make this house Charlie's and my home.

Behind me, Charlie sighs. "This place is a shack."

I picture wind chimes hanging from the eaves, and potted geraniums sitting on the patio. "It has charm."

"It has termites." He shades his eyes and looks at brown grass and a strip of pockmarked cement surrounding a scraggly palm tree. He shifts his glance beyond the fence to cotton fields and railroad tracks. "Termites and trains."

"There's a sign for a room for rent just around the corner. There's a college in town. I could come over and work on your house when I'm not studying or working."

Charlie brushes dust off his uniform.

"This house has a washing machine. I could do your uniform for you right now."

"I don't know how long we're going to be in town," Charlie says. "So far the only thing the Pickers know I can do is break their bats. I busted two today."

I close my eyes and shut out the rose bush that with a little attention could be blooming again. "You asked me to find you a place to live. I did my best."

Charlie frowns at the railroad tracks. "This is an agricultural center. Every head of lettuce, every tomato, every ear of corn that is going anywhere in this state has to pass by this house."

"The house is probably beautiful inside," I say.

"The house is probably gutted."

I pull his arm and tug. "It won't hurt you just to look. I told the landlady we were coming. Her name is Mrs. Gooth."

"Gooth," he echoes. "Sounds spooky." He's brushing dust again. "I could use the machine, huh?"

He tags after me up the walk. In the living room we find a stone fireplace, knotty pine paneling and Mrs. Gooth. Her gray hair is bunched in a bun, but a few strands have become loose. The cameo pin on her white blouse has just lost its mooring. Long sleeves with lace edges flap at her wrist. She looks as if she's wearing her big sister's clothes. She could be our very own petite fairy godmother.

"This is Mr. Fain," I say. "I'm the one who called you."

She looks Charlie up and down, then smiles. "I'm not one of those who minds renting to ballplayers," she says. "Especially if they're married. You are married?"

Charlie sniffs, and then sneezes. I look down at Aunt Lottie's garden shoes and silently ask them, "Why does the word marriage make him sick?"

He is staring at the ceiling.

"The fireplace is lovely," I say. "I wonder if the chimney has been cleaned lately?"

Mrs. Gooth is studying me. "Of course you're married. You act like a player's wife. Pushy, but well meaning. Plus, I should do this as a favor to Grace Everett. She's in my prayer group, you know."

Charlie pats dust from his uniform pants. "Pam said there was a washing machine."

"It's right this way." She heads toward the kitchen.

I stop him from following Mrs. Gooth. "Who is Grace Everett?" I whisper.

"I never heard of her," he says.

"Why didn't you tell her we weren't married?"

"I thought you wanted me to have this place." He leaves me standing there. I run my finger along the wood mantle. I can see Charlie and me holding hands and watching the flames in a winter fire dance.

In a moment, they're both back. Mrs. Gooth waves a sheaf of papers. "Do you want to sign a rental agreement."

Charlie is gazing at a dent in the ceiling.

"The mark is from a champagne cork," Mrs. Gooth says. "The former tenants were celebrating their good luck. The man got moved up to Double A. They opened the champagne and poof went the cork."

Charlie slumps and rubs tired eyes. He hates this house I love. He doesn't want to live with cork dents. But the apartments I showed him earlier were smaller and shabbier.

"You, we can move in right away," I say.

"Well." He looks uncertain and ready to give in. "The bedroom was nice," he tells me. "Do you want to see it?"

Eyes narrowed, our fairy godmother is watching us. I wink. "The bedroom is the most important room in the house."

I follow him through a kitchen filled with late afternoon sun. The bedroom is cool and dark. It has knotty pine walls and a big bed. I bounce on the bed. "Not too hard. Not too soft," I say in a loud voice. Charlie and I could have wonderful times on this bed. I whisper to Charlie, "Mrs. Gooth is doing you and Grace Everett a favor."

He sighs. "How can I be paying for a house when I don't even know if I can stay on the team."

He pulls a checkbook from his pocket. The house will be his. I smile at the honey-colored paneling and think, "Thank you Grace Everett, whoever you are."

We follow Mrs. Gooth back to the living room. Charlie glances at the dent. He isn't going to change his mind, is he? He dates his check.

A train whistle blows. Wheels clack along the track. The train grumbles, and then roars. The house's windows start to shake. Charlie stops writing. He looks at me. "Trains. Did I tell you? How do you expect me to sleep through that racket?"

"That's the San Joaquin Daylight," Mrs. Gooth says. "It only comes through once every afternoon."

"Just once a day," I say.

Charlie presses tight lips together. "$90?"

"$180," Mrs. Gooth yawns as if $180 were nothing. "That's the first and last month's rent."

"$180." He shivers and starts writing again. "The first and last may wind up being the same month."

I step to the window, and stare out at the empty tracks. Please don't let another train come by.

"Plus a cleaning deposit," Mrs. Gooth says. "That's $50."

He glares at her. Her thin, high voice tossing numbers at him is getting on his nerves. He tears up his check and starts a new one. "So, that's $230?"

She pats the arm of an easy chair, the only piece of furniture in the room. "And $25 for the chair."

Charlie lifts his pen off the check, and stares. "We have to rent the chair separately?"

"I thought you might like to buy it."

"I, we don't need a chair," he says. "I thought this place came furnished."

"Everything but the chair," she says.

I look at the chair. It's a lovely powder blue. The chair's back and arms look like wings. Charlie and I could cuddle in the chair together. "I'll take it," I say.

Charlie pulls me aside. "It's a scam, don't you see? Prayer group. Grace Everett. This Gooth lady pretends to be batty, just to throw us off. Then, she sells us a chair. She sells this same chair to everyone of her tenants. They're probably all farm workers or ballplayers who just come and go. Who's going to bother to rent a U-Haul trailer to move one lousy chair?"

"I will," I say. "It's for us."

He looks at me and his face softens. "I'll buy you the chair. It's my treat."

•

I sit in our chair and listen to the rumble of the washing machine. In the kitchen, Charlie is making sandwiches. I snuggle into the chair and rest my eyes.

Curtains would look lovely against the diamond pane windows. I could put my Sandy and Andy elephant rug next to the fireplace. We could put Charlie's trophies on the mantel. We will build a home together.

Will it still be a home if we live together and we're not married? I open my eyes and stare at naked windows. This wouldn't be a home. It would be a shack.

Charlie and I would be shacking up.

Lottie and Alice used to talk about a girl back in Kelso who shacked up. She wound up working in Woolworth's and had to raise a child on her own. *She got what she deserved.* Tomorrow, I'll go to the house around the corner and find out about that room for rent.

I curl into the chair. I can picture flowers in a vase on the mantle. A hand on my shoulder wakes me. Charlie leans over and kisses me. "Dinner," he says.

14

Aren't you coming to bed?" Charlie stands in the living room. He's wearing just his shorts and undershirt. In the moonlight shining through the window he looks like a Greek God.

"Well," he says.

The Greek God wants to be with me. Those now familiar Charlie Fain sparklers run up my spine. I want to grab him and pull him into the bedroom. But what about that girl from Kelso who was shacking up? It takes all my courage to say, "I thought I'd sleep in the chair."

"I didn't buy you the chair so you could sleep in it," Charlie says.

"I can't sleep in your bed," I say.

His breath on my neck heats me even more. "Why not?"

We could just lie in each other's arms, I tell myself. Nothing has to happen. So why is my vagina as wet as the Everglades again?

"We love each other," Charlie says. "How can it be wrong?"

"We're not mar. . ." Before I can say the word he is sneezing again.

He looks at me with watery eyes. "You came all this way with me just so you could sleep in a chair?"

He slaps the chair's arm. "If I knew that that's what you were going to do, I would never have bought the damn thing." He leans against me. He feels heavy, and inviting. "Just come to bed with me. I won't do anything. I promise. We'll just sleep together. That's all."

We can lie in each other's arms all night, and we can even kiss and touch each other and still stop ourselves from going all the way. After all, we're mature.

I let him take my hand and lead me to the bedroom.

He turns on the overhead light. "It's a good thing I brought our camping gear," he says. Two single sleeping bags sit on the double bed. "My mom and I go to Arrowhead. We love it up there." He unzips the bags, shows me the linings. "The only thing is, I thought I was just taking one bag. I didn't know they were rolled together. Now, she won't have a bag if she wants to go camping on her own."

Do the two bags open up into one so that we can snuggle together? Or, is Charlie unfortunately, a man of his word? He really meant we should just sleep together and in two separate bags?

"Do you want the ducks or the Scotch plaid?" Charlie asks.

"The ducks," I say with a sigh.

Charlie hands me a big blue shirt. "You'll want this, since you don't have pajamas or whatever it is that girls wear."

Charlie does want me to cover myself up in a shirt and zip myself into a cocoon of a sleeping bag. My vagina gurgles. My face burns. I grab Charlie's shirt and run into the bathroom.

I turn on the light and take off the clothes I've been wearing for more days than I can count. My nipples stand at attention. My body keeps giving me away.

I button Charlie's shirt and march into the bedroom. Charlie is staring at my legs. I can't stop myself. I lean over and kiss him. He feels so good. My hand keeps wandering. I want to touch every part of him. We sit on the bed. His shorts press against me. He feels big and soft at the same time. He feels wonderful.

"I want you," he says.

"I want you too."

Charlie reaches for my underpants and pulls them off. He puts his finger in me. He makes me burn.

"Don't stop," I say.

"Are you sure?" he asks.

He feels so good, but I can't be sure this is the right thing. What about that poor girl from Kelso who ended up pregnant and unwed? Charlie looks so appealing in the moonlight. If only I had some sign, some indication of what I should do.

A voice says, "Does Chekhov want a drink?"

Sexual desire really does drive people crazy. Now, I'm hearing things.

"What did you say?" Charlie asks.

"It wasn't me." I point to our window. There's a silhouette on the shade of the house next door. Charlie's neighbor has nice hair, a bouffant with ends turned up in little girl curls. "Do you want crackers?" The woman's voice is husky. "They're Ritz."

"Anton Chekhov never had a Ritz cracker in his life," I tell Charlie.

"If we can see her, she can see us too. How about going to our chair in the living room?"

My breasts have stopped tingling. This nutty woman may be the sign I wished for. I don't want to wind up a woman alone who has only a dead Russian writer for company. "I don't think I'm ready," I tell Charlie.

He glares at the silhouette on the shade, and then turns to me. "We aren't hurting anyone."

"We can still hold each other and just go to sleep," I say.

"Right," he sighs. He gets up and goes to the bathroom.

He turns on the shower full blast. When he turns it off, the lady next door is saying, "Cheese and crackers."

Charlie steps into the bedroom. He glances at the window shade next door. "Tomorrow we'll get some curtains." He strokes my hair. "The bags open up to one."

We snuggle together. I rest my head on Charlie's silky shoulder. He shuts his eyes. His hand drops. His breathing gets more even. He feels so warm and safe.

The voice next door says, "Camembert."

Charlie and I are at a lovely party on a Russian country estate. I drink tea in a glass and have Camembert cheese on bright orange crackers. In the distance, a train whistle calls. The Moscow Express? No. The San Joaquin Starlight. Soon the house will be shaking again. I curl deeper into the sleeping bag and hold onto Charlie.

•

I step into the kitchen and yawn and stretch. I hum a few bars of *Oh, What a Beautiful Morning*.

"Can you believe it? It's flannel," Charlie frowns at his uniform.

"It was wonderful being so close to you last night," I say.

Charlie stops tugging at his uniform and smiles.

"I wish we could be that close every night, but I really should see about that room for rent."

"We'll get curtains for the bedroom window. That will take care of Wild-eyed Wanda next door."

"I can't live here unless we're married."

Beads of sweat form at his neck. He fights a sneeze. "Flannel in this weather?"

He glances out the kitchen window. The thermometer nailed to the siding reads 96. In the fields, discouraged cotton leaves curl like fists. Heat rises in waves from the red brown earth. "Friggin' flannel," he says.

"I'm sorry you're uncomfortable." I pat his shoulder. The flannel feels stiff as cardboard. Charlie must have put in too much starch.

He slides his hand under the fabric, then flaps a sleeve that dangles to his knee. "Maybe it isn't really flannel. It feels more like a hair shirt." He pulls down the too short pants' legs. "I wonder how many guys have worn this uniform?" he says in a soft voice. "I wonder where they are now? In some special cemetery just outside of town for ballplayers who were almost good enough? At night, they come out of their graves and haunt guys like me, and they say, 'You're going to join us soon.'" Charlie slumps against the wall and pokes at a loose button. He stares at a curl in the linoleum that looks like a stalagmite. "Second base. I haven't played the position since I was 13."

"You'll get better," I tell him.

He rubs his sleeve. "This is a hair shirt for sure. It's perfect. If I play another game like yesterday's or the day before, the fans will kill me." He grins. "Bizarre murder. Ballplayer martyred at second. At least my mother will be happy." He snaps off a dangling thread from his shirt. "Her son will have a shot at being a saint."

•

Carrying a grape Slurpee, Walt bumps my elbow. "Excuse me." Then, his eyes brighten. "Oh, it's you." His smile gets bigger when he sees Charlie step behind me, and wrap an arm around my shoulder.

He grabs Charlie's hand. "Don't let the doubters get you down. You got what it takes."

Charlie looks at Walt's brown eyes, then nods his head. Walt steps up the bleachers.

I turn to follow Walt, but Charlie grabs my elbow. "That's not where you're supposed to sit."

"But I like Walt."

"You should be with the others," he says.

"The others?"

"The wives," he sniffs, "and girlfriends."

He steers me past old men in Dodger caps and women with wrinkled elbows and laps filled with yarns. He nudges me toward a group of younger women.

A broad-faced girl with freckles rocks a stroller and eats a corn dog. A sallow-faced woman in pin curls reads a movie magazine. A pretty blond with Sandra Dee bouffant hair polishes her nails. They all wear wedding rings.

Alice wouldn't like these baseball wives. "Don't eat, do your nails or wear curlers in public," she told me. Her rules of female etiquette insisted that a woman should always be well groomed and well nourished, but how she got that way should remain a mystery.

They look up at me. There's no wedding band or even nail polish on my fingers. My hair is too short to put in curlers. I have no baby, movie magazine or even purse to hold. In my wrinkled shirt and aunt's too large garden shoes, I look as if I've just dropped off from another planet. I tell Charlie, "I think I'll freshen up before I face them."

•

She wears a black armband. She is leaning over the bathroom sink and pulling down her lower lip. "Gum disease," she says.

"Vitamin C is good for that."

She squints at me. "I saw you in the stands the other day. You're. . ?"

"With the second baseman."

"Jesus," she says, "do you have a name? Or is that it? With the second baseman?"

"Pam."

"Well, Pam, nice to meet you, I think." She takes out a small, round case from her purse. The case looks like a wheel. Each spoke has a white pill. Neatly glued fake eyelashes flap at me. "Vitamin C. One for every day of the month."

I step closer. "Are those birth control pills?"

"Insurance." Then, she laughs. "I'm the catcher's wife. But I don't want to get caught."

I look at the pills. Amazing. Pop a pill in your mouth, swallow, and your body changes. You don't have to make babies if you don't want to. Maybe if I had those pills I wouldn't be so scared of sex. Maybe I wouldn't end up like the girl from Kelso.

- 114 -

"Where do you get those?" I ask.

"Just go to a doctor and ask him for a prescription. They give them to you if you're married." She looks at my ringless hand. "Or if you say you're married. They don't check. Or you can tell them you have an irregular period. That works, too." The catcher's wife smiles at herself in the mirror, and runs a comb through dyed-orange hair, then puts on white lipstick. "I'm Mrs. Kahlil Gibran. You can call me Mrs. G. for short."

"Gibran? He's a writer. A prophet."

"Folks, we have a live one here," she tells the air. "My husband's name is Barry Silver. They call him Gibran because he reads *The Prophet* in the dugout. They're not used to seeing anyone read anything. You do read, don't you?"

Mrs. G. likes to make people feel small. "I've read Gibran. Do you have a name? Or is that it? Mrs. Barry Silver Kahlil Gibran?"

"I'm Raquel."

"As in Raquel Welch?"

"As in Raquel. Have you met the nasals?" she asks.

"Who?"

"The wives. The M.H.H. club. The My Husband He's. . ." She holds her nose. "My husband, he was swole up so bad. My husband. he tore a ligament. My husband, he spit up his Swiss Cheese omelet." She stops smiling. Her shoulders droop. "I love my husband, but being married isn't everything. So," she glances at my left hand, "if I happened to be unmarried and I still wanted romance in my life, I'd just enjoy being a free woman. We've got the pill. Why not use it?'

She picks up a silk parasol with large lavender roses on it. She twirls it. "Ah hell. We got a game to watch." She opens the bathroom door, flaps her lashes at the bright light. "And it's a thousand degrees."

I follow her over the grass. She stops just short of the bleachers, points to the wives, then stage-whispers. "Look at them huddled together. Primitives. It must be wash day at the river."

"The armband," I ask. "Who died?"

She snickers. "Me. We interrupt this life, this marriage, to bring you the 1963 baseball season."

15

I look at the group of girls who are looking at me. I never fit in with my Brownie troop. Alice called the Brownies "Little fascists in little brown uniforms." Mickey came drunk to our picnics. Now, there's no one in my family here to embarrass me. I have a chance to belong.

Mrs. Kahlil Gibran, alias Raquel Silver, points to me. "Ladies, this is Pam. She's relatively alert."

The woman with three pin curls on her forehead looks up from her magazine. The magazine cover shows Marilyn Monroe's face shrouded in a cloud. She is looking down from heaven at Joe DiMaggio. The woman reading about Marilyn's haunting of Joe gives me a sour look. "You're the Magnet's wife?"

"Wife?" I sneeze. "Magnet?"

She looks out at the Pickers on the field. "Does that second baseman belong to you?"

Next to her, the pretty blond woman stirs. She looks embarrassed.

"Someone called Charlie a magnet?" I ask.

The freckled face young mother rustles through diapers and bottles. Handing me a newspaper, she says, "I'm sorry, Mrs. Fain."

I should take the time to explain that I'm not Mrs. Fain. But I want them to like me, so I say nothing. My eyes scan the sports page:

> Now you see it, now you don't. Something happens when the ball crosses Charlie Fain's, the newest Picker, magnetic field. The ball never comes back into play. The ball never leaves second base.

I give the newspaper back to the young mother. "That's cruel. Charlie makes lots of good plays."

A voice at my elbow says, "Neil gives everyone a hard time at first." The pretty blond smiles at me. "But then' he'll ease up."

"Don't believe Pollyanna," Raquel says. "Nordstrom eats Little Leaguers for breakfast."

"He has no right to call Charlie names," I say.

The girl with pin curls squints at the field. "The scorekeeper's hung over again? How are we supposed to know what's going on?"

"We're supposed to watch," Mrs. Gibran says.

A bat cracks. A ball sails over the fence toward the trailer park. At least Mr. Nordstrom can't blame Charlie for the home run. The woman in pin curls is shaking her head and staring at Charlie. "Who does he think he is? A parking lot valet?"

Charlie is swinging his arm and waving the Manteca Butcher past second.

This is how I got in trouble in Brownies. Some little Brownie said something dumb and I couldn't wait to let them know just how dumb they were. If I want to fit in, I need to keep quiet. I try to swallow my words, but they come anyway. "Charlie is just trying to keep the other team off balance."

The lady in pin curls honors me with a smile. A new batter steps to the plate. "He is cute," the pin curl lady says.

"Who?" I ask.

"Your Charlie. He could be a movie star, like my Rusty. He's the third baseman." The big man at third has orange hair and the dustiest uniform I've ever seen. "Rusty's handsome, don't you think? Of course we all think our husbands are the cutest."

"Jesus," Raquel says.

Rusty's wife stares at her. "You shouldn't use His name in vain."

"Norma, if Jesus were playing for the Pickers, you'd be telling everyone how cute He is. 'Ooh, look at those curls.'"

"Jesus doesn't have curls," Norma tells Raquel. "He has straight hair. If you'd go to Church once in awhile you'd know that."

"He caught one." The pretty blond nudges me. Charlie scoops up the ball. The batter is out, but the runner from first base keeps coming. Doesn't he see Charlie standing in the baseline? Charlie turns, points the ball, but the runner doesn't stop. Before Charlie's foot tags second, the Butcher slides into him and knocks him down.

I get to my feet and start for the field. Raquel and the blond girl both grab me and pull me back toward the bleachers. Raquel's fingers squeeze my arm. "He's all right."

"He's flat on his back," I say.

The ball dribbles out of Charlie's glove. The runner is safe. Charlie stands. Fans boo. Someone in the crowd yells, "You never heard of a pivot?"

I free myself from Raquel's grip. "I've got to see if he's all right."

"He's just embarrassed," she tells me.

"We don't go on the field," the mother, burping her baby, says. "They don't like it."

"It's kind of an unwritten law," the blond says.

"They see themselves as soldiers on a battlefield." Raquel's smile is contemptuous. "They're out there fighting the good fight. They don't like their womenfolk around."

Norma, pulling bobby pins from her hair, mutters, "Magnet." She stares at my left hand. "No ring. Are you sure you're married?"

"Well, actually. . ."

"Of course she's married," Raquel says. "You think anyone would watch that second baseman's performance voluntarily?"

•

Out of the corner of my eye I see her: a woman with golden hair combed in an upsweep. She wears a royal blue suit with handsome wooden buttons. Her perfume is Chanel No. 5. Alice, my mother, has come here to comfort me and take me home.

The glare from the field is silver white. Pale clouds overhead have angry purple undersides. Though it's over 100 degrees, I have goose bumps.

"The heat's murder," a voice says. I feel something cool on my lips. Sandra Dee is offering me a coke. "You looked like you were going to pass out."

Ice wets my mouth. The wives' faces stop shimmering and come into focus. "I'm Bonnie, by the way," the soft voice says.

I swallow coke. She isn't my mother or a movie star. She's Bonnie, with kind, grape-green colored eyes. I must still be light headed because I hear myself say, "You're beautiful."

The wives titter, then giggle. Girls don't give other girls compliments. Another unwritten law.

Bonnie blushes. "I'm not beautiful." She points to her hair. "Dyed." She taps her nose. "Bobbed." She points to her teeth. "Capped."

Raquel stares, then snorts. "I knew about the hair. I suspected about the nose. But the teeth?" She tugs her orange hair. "Why do we do it?" She nods at the field. "Just so those clowns will notice us once in awhile?"

Bonnie smoothes her straight, pink skirt. "I do it for me."

"Sure you do," Raquel says.

•

Charlie has a chance to redeem himself. The score is Butcher's 4, Pickers 0. The bases are loaded. Charlie is the tying run. I shut my eyes and picture Charlie hitting the ball out of the park.

"Is your hubby a clutch hitter?" Beth, the girl with the baby, asks.

"I bet he chokes," Norma's voice cuts me off before I can answer.

Back in Santa Monica, he was so much better than everyone else. And he knew it. He never choked then. But now fans boo him and writers call him names. Would that make him forget how to hit a ball? "He's a wonderful hitter. They may just pitch around him." Smug little Pamela, the servant girl, is back.

"And walk a run in?" Beth's glance at me is sad. She feels sorry for me. She thinks I 'm married to a loser. Well, I'm not married, and Charlie isn't a loser.

"Strike," the home plate umpire says.

Norma's head swivels. She glares at me. "He didn't even swing. My Rusty's at third and he didn't even swing."

"Jesus, Pam's not at the plate," Raquel says.

Charlie swings and misses. Butcher fans clap, and cheer. They love to see the parking lot valet fail.

Charlie hunches and his knees curl. He looks as if he'd like to be somewhere else. But he's at the plate with two strikes against him.

The pitch, a perfect strike, sails over the plate. He doesn't swing. He just watches the ball go by. He choked.

Norma's Rusty rushes to the plate from third. Her Rusty is going to kill my Charlie. The Picker first baseman jumps up from the bench, runs to the field and pushes himself between Charlie and Rusty. Rusty backs off. Charlie is OK.

Bonnie is looking at the first baseman. "Every day he does something to make me proud of him."

"The first baseman is your husband?" I ask.

She nods. "I'm sure Charlie is very grateful," I tell her. He doesn't look grateful. He throws down his bat and heads for the dugout.

I glance at Bonnie. "It must be nice to be proud of the man you love."

"Didn't I tell you he'd choke?" Norma is glaring at me.

"It takes awhile to get used to a new level of competition," Bonnie says.

"Nordstrom's going to have a field day with Mr. Magnet," Norma says.

The coke tastes sour in my mouth. Maybe the sportswriter missed today's game. He probably has other things to do besides watch the Pickers. "Does he come to all the games?" I ask.

"Every one." Norma applies fresh lipstick, then smacks her lips together. "It's his job."

"To be mean?" I ask.

"To be honest," she says.

He must be a frustrated athlete, some puny little guy with glasses who can't hit a softball. I lean back in my seat. What's happening to me? I'm starting to think like Charlie. I'm starting to divide the world into wimps and jocks. All my life I've always been on the side of the so called wimps my father made fun of. I look at the faces in the bleachers. "Where is Mr. Nordstrom?"

"In the beach chair," Bonnie points. "Behind home plate."

Next to a card table where a thin, sad-looking man sits and plays with a sign that says, *Pickers Booster Club*, there's a yellow and green striped chair.

Sitting in the chair is a man with broad shoulders and a broad back. He could be an shot putter, like Parry O'Brien. Maybe he wanted to be like Parry and couldn't make it as an athlete. His blond head bends over a notepad. He's writing something down. He looks out at the field again. The Pickers run to their positions. Mr. Nordstrom is staring out toward second base. He's probably thinking up more vile things to write about Charlie. Soon, Charlie will read those awful words. If he chokes now, what will he do after her reads the next Nordstrom report?

•

I stand on tiptoes, and wipe Charlie's bruised chin with a napkin.

"Stop it, will you?" Charlie tosses the napkin in the trash. "They'll think I'm a baby who still needs his mommy."

In the parking lot, horns blare, brakes squeal, players and their fans are going home. No one is watching us. We have the grass and trees to ourselves. "You'll do better tomorrow," I say.

"Tomorrow. I've got to go through the whole damn thing again tomorrow. I choked. No hit. No field. No nothing." He kicks the trash can. "Even Ashburn, your ex-boyfriend could do better." He looks up at the sky, and squints at high, white clouds. "Cumulus, cumulus, cumulus, something. I bet their laughing their asses off."

The clouds? "Clouds don't have. . ." I swallow.

"Those sons of bitches are rubbing their asses and laughing at me. "Look at that Fain kid. He can't even catch a ball. He should go back to flipping burgers."

The breeze picks up. Branches sway. Notepad in hand, a broad shouldered man in a golf shirt is leaning against a thick Eucalyptus.

"Charlie, we should go. You need your rest."

"Yeah, I got to be in shape to make an ass of myself tomorrow."

I tuck my hand under his elbow, and start to steer him toward the car. He takes three steps, then turns. "What the hell?" He tosses his fielder's glove into the trash can.

He squares his shoulders. He looks happy now. Free. He marches to the car. Old Chartreuse's door slams.

My heart is pounding. I know the ex shot-putter is watching me, but I don't care. I have to get the glove.

It sits on a mound of mustard-smeared napkins, half-eaten hot dog buns and crushed soda pop cans. I bend down but my hand can't quite reach the glove. I stand on tiptoes, arch over the can. My feet almost leave the ground, but my fingers find thick, leather fingers, the rawhide lacing of the glove.

Under the tree, the sportswriter is taking notes. I can see tomorrow's papers: second baseman throws tantrum, his girl friend (wife?) goes fishing in a trash can.

I hold the glove up high, and turn and face him. For a man who writes such awful things, he has a sweet face. I clear my throat. In my best schoolgirl voice I say, "Good afternoon."

•

"Here's the rent money for your room." Charlie hands me three crisp $10 bills. "Did you ask your landlord about phone privileges? We can talk to each other right before we go to sleep at night."

I don't want to ask a stranger about phone privileges. I don't want to go. I want Charlie to beg me to stay with him. I want to march to the nearest doctor's office, get a prescription for birth control pills and shack up with Charlie.

"Thank you for the money," I say. Or I could take the money and buy a black sexy nightgown. Or I could take the money and buy a business suit, and get a job and apply to the nearest college. Then, I could get my own place and only see Charlie on my days off from work or school. That would be sensible. "Wait a minute," I tell him. "You don't have a phone."

The doorbell rings. "I do now," Charlie says.

Charlie opens the door. "Good morning folks, the man on the porch says. "Is this the C. Fain residence?" There's a white panel truck parked in front of the house.

Charlie leads the man in, then turns to me. "If you wait just a little bit you'll be able to call home."

Right now, Charlie's house is my home. "I'll call Lottie and ask her to send me my things."

Charlie glances at my aunt's garden shoes. "Maybe you should use the money I gave you to get something new."

I breathe in the sweet summer air. Is this Charlie's way of asking me to stay?

"Where do you want the phone?" The big man with the black mustache and curly hair has the phone tucked under his arm.

"There's a jack in the kitchen," I say. "But of course, it's Charlie's decision."

"The kitchen is good," Charlie says.

In the kitchen, the man places the phone on the counter I just finished cleaning. The phone, squat, black and shiny with a silver dial, looks friendly.

"I've got to check to see if my uniform is dry," Charlie tells me. He steps out the back door. Outside, he hooks an old hose to a faucet. He squirts a dying rose bush. Charlie is starting to like this place he calls a shack.

"This is an old house," the phone man tells me. He looks at the pantry shelves. "There's lots of storage room. They don't make them like this anymore. You're connected," he says. "Could you sign for this, Mrs. Fain?"

Mrs. Fain.

I start to call to Charlie. But he's on his hands and knees pulling out weeds by a pomegranate tree. It hurts that Charlie is caring for the house only now that I'm leaving. The phone man is waiting. I take the paper he gives me. I hesitate, then write, *Pamela Carey Fain.*

I watch the man leave, then I sit on the wobbly kitchen chair. Why do I keep pretending to be Mrs. Charlie Fain?

I could have just called Charlie into the house and have him sign for his own phone. The truth is, I was curious to see how the name looked on an official piece of paper.

I must be completely out of my gourd. Three weeks ago, I was semi-engaged to Warren Ashburn. Now, I want to be Mrs. Charlie Fain. Why isn't being Pamela Carey enough for me? Why do I have to be Mrs. Anybody?

16

Carrying his dry laundry, Charlie walks into the kitchen. "My mother bought me these right before I left." He holds up pajamas. They have green bicycles printed on blue fabric. Pajamas with bicycles are for little boys who are too young to get married. He presses the pajama top against his cheek. It's a hug from home.

"I can't wait to tell her how beautifully they laundered," he says.

"You can call her right now," I say.

"Before you go rent your room you can phone your aunt." He picks up the receiver, and talks to a long distance operator.

I pour orange juice into a paper cup. Charlie doesn't need me to stay. He has his telephone, his rose bush, and even his damn little-boy pajamas. I gulp orange juice. I should leave the kitchen and give him his privacy.

"Hi, Mom," he says.

I tap Charlie's arm. He puts his hand over the receiver.

"I'm going to sit on the steps," I tell him.

He nods. "It's good to hear you, too," he says into the phone.

Sipping orange juice, I tiptoe into the living room. Why am I tiptoeing? Why do I suddenly feel as if I'm not supposed to be here? I feel like a guilty back-street girl. I finger Charlie's money. I will rent the room. Or maybe I'll just leave town. I miss my room at The Palms. It wasn't much, but at least it was mine. I miss school work.. I miss me.

"I just washed those pajamas," Charlie says into the phone. "They came out great."

I open the front door. A blast of sunlight and hot air greet me. I shut the door quickly, and sit in the blue wing chair.

In the kitchen, Charlie says, "It's rough, Mom. I may be out of my league. I did better yesterday. I got a single, but I act like a clod out in the field. Dad never did show up." There's a pause, then Charlie says, "I'm lonely, too."

I sit up. He's lonely? I've been here all this time, doing everything I can to make him feel better, and he's lonely?

Charlie tells his mom, "I didn't think it would be so hard to be without you."

Far away, I hear the rumble of a train.

"At least we can talk to each other now," Charlie says.

The San Joaquin Morning Express rattles down the track. The house shakes, and then gets still.

"I love you, too, Mom." Charlie hangs up the receiver.

I step into the kitchen. "How could you tell her you're lonely?"

"But I am homesick."

"Homesick isn't the same as lonely. You're with me every minute you're not playing ball. How could you be lonely?"

"I can be lonely for her and still be happy with you," he says. "My career is hanging by a thread. My dad never came."

"You make your life sound awful. Wouldn't your mom feel better if she knew you weren't alone?"

"She'd rather have me lonely."

"Maybe you'd rather be alone."

"Of course not." He looks hurt. "What's got into you?"

I don't answer.

"I know what I'm doing," Charlie says. "My mother makes a career of worrying. I probably shouldn't have even told her I was having a rough time. But if she knew about you, that would finish her off. She has such a great imagination. She could figure out hundreds of things that could go wrong."

"I thought you were glad that we're together."

"I am glad. I don't want you to even go and live around the corner. But I know that that's what you want to do." He grabs his car keys, and starts for the living room.

"Where are you going?" I ask.

He's so anxious to get out of the house that he puts on his sunglasses while he's still in the living room. "I'm going to get us some coffee and some real cups. We can celebrate my phone and you're renting the room."

He kisses me on the forehead. I shut my eyes so he won't see my tears. "See you later, sports fan," he says, and then he's gone.

•

Her "hello" warms my insides. Help is here. My aunt will give me courage. She'll tell me to trust my heart and everything will turn out right.

Lottie coughs into the phone. "He was standing on the stoop when I opened the door to get my milk."

It was a mistake for me to call. I'm only going to hear more bad news. My father came to check up on me.

"Where could I say you were at 7 a.m.?" Lottie asks. "Your Plymouth was sitting there in the driveway. Pam, Warren looked so sad."

Not Mickey. Warren. So many days have gone by and I still haven't gotten in touch with him. How can I be so cruel and cowardly?

"I offered him breakfast," my aunt tells me. "I tried to stall. I said you were on a walk. When you didn't come back, he got suspicious."

Orange juice turns sour in my stomach. I stare out at cotton plants wilting in the sun. "So, you told him I was here with Charlie?"

"You should have told him yourself. You said you would. You owe him that. He loves you. You've always been so honest."

I've betrayed my best friend and I've disappointed my aunt. Love has made me a monster. I look down at my aunt's shoes. I don't deserve to wear even her oldest, most holey shoes. Over the telephone lines that connect us something crackles. "Are you still there?" she asks.

"I'm sorry," I say.

"And is Charlie still wonderful?"

"Yes."

"Is marriage in your future?"

"Charlie rented a house. He bought me a chair."

"You're not living together are you?" The question sounds like an accusation.

"Of course not." I sound indignant. But why couldn't I be a free woman and buy my little wheel of birth control pills and shack up with a man? "I'm getting a room nearby. I'll find a job and enroll at the college here."

"Honey, the college there won't be UCLA. He hasn't mentioned marriage?"

"The word makes him sneeze." I stare at my signature on the paper on the counter. Pamela Carey Fain.

"When people are in love they think about marriage. Warren would marry you in a second."

"Warren and I both agreed we should wait, remember?"

"That was before Charlie. Have you talked to your father? I won't be able to cover up for you in front of him. He knows me too well."

Behind me paper rattles. Charlie is standing in the kitchen with a sack of groceries.

"I'll talk to both of them just as soon as I have a chance." I hang up the shiny new telephone receiver. Why did Charlie ever get this phone? All it does is let me know how much trouble I've caused.

•

"I got some real cream to go with the real coffee," Charlie says. "And a real cup." He pulls a lovely yellow mug from the bag.

Seeing that mug makes me swallow hard. It's so solid and friendly. It brightens the kitchen and makes the curling linoleum seem as if it's part of a real home. If only Charlie had bought a mug for me. But he doesn't expect that I will be here in the mornings.

I sit at the card table with my back to Charlie. The folding chair wobbles.

"The coffee's ready," he says. "Do you want some?"

I hold out my paper cup. Charlie grins and takes a second yellow mug from the bag. I can feel my smile. The coffee warms me. I tell the steam, "Coming here was the first thing I've ever done on impulse and now everybody hates me."

Charlie clinks his mug with mine. "I don't hate you."

His new blue Bermuda shorts show off his tan legs. He looks like a model and I look like someone who has been wearing the same clothes for almost a week. I look like someone who would let her best friend and her family down. "I don't even have my own toothbrush," I tell him. "Or a comb."

He looks surprised. "I was just at the store. I could have got you a toothbrush."

"I miss my purse. I feel naked without it. The shoes I'm wearing belong to my aunt and they have holes."

"Did you ask your aunt to send you your things?"

"I thought falling in love was supposed to make things easier, make things fall into place. My aunt is disappointed in me. My father thinks I'm at my aunt's. Warren knows I 'm here. Your mother thinks you're lonely. I have no money, no job, no school. I'm no use to anyone. Not even myself."

"I need you."

"You told your mother you were having a rotten time."

"It would be a lot more rotten without you. I don't know if I could keep going out there every day making an ass of myself if you didn't still believe in me. Sometimes at night, I'm scared to shut my eyes because the minute I do, I 'm right back in that field watching the ball sail past me."

"I really help you?"

"I'd be a total basket case without you. At least when I open my eyes at night, I know you're here."

"Then why do you want me to rent the room around the corner?"

"I don't. I want you to stay here with me. Please just for one or two nights. Until things with the team straighten themselves out one way or another."

I smile and wrap my fingers around the handle of the mug. Tomorrow, I'll be here for morning coffee.

•

The bed sheet on the window keeps Charlie's room dark and private. No one in the entire world knows what we're doing but Charlie and me.

But I keep thinking someone's knocking at the front door. I picture Mickey and Mrs. Fain, "the linen lady," standing on our porch. The lady from Kelso, who shacked up with a man, stands with them. I shut my eyes and wish I were someone else – Pamela, the barmaid with bouffant blond hair and a push-up bra. That Pamela would pop her birth control pill with her afternoon martini. She would rip Charlie's clothes off. She wouldn't make him sleep in his under shorts.

"I don't know how much more of this I can take." Charlie groans beside me. "If I just reach over to pat you good night, we'll start kissing again. Then, I'll touch you and I'll have to go and take another cold shower."

"I'm cruel," I whisper. "I shouldn't put you through this."

His hand squeezes my breast. I press against him and whisper, "I love you."

"You can help me out." He takes my hand and puts it against him. "Touch me," he says.

I let my finger touch the cotton under shorts. It looks as if there's a big dill pickle under the material.

"Not so soft," he complains. "Really rub me."

I put my palm on him. He grabs my hand and moves it up and down on the bump of his shorts. "Harder," he says. "Much harder."

He starts writhing and gritting his teeth. "Oh God," he gasps. I take my hand away.

He sits up. "Why did you stop?"

"You looked like I was killing you."

He puts my hand back on him. "Keep killing me," he says.

I get on my knees and bend over him so I can get a better grip. I move my hand up and down. "Harder," he says. My fingers are starting to get tired. I lift them up and give them a little rest. "Oh God, don't stop," he says.

He looks so helpless down there. He even looks a little silly. My fingers begin to ache. To distract myself from the pain and help pass the time I start to hum *A Hundred Bottles of Beer on the Wall*. When I get to 87, Charlie gasps, grabs me around the waist and hangs onto me. "Thank you," he whispers. "Thank you."

Whatever I did, it must have been the right thing.

He lies down and pulls the sheet over him. I smile in the dark. I am Pamela the blond barmaid who knows how to make her man happy.

•

I listen to the phone ring and I have a conversation with my father in my mind:

"Daddy," I tell him. "I'm so in love. I can't stand to be away from Charlie for a single second."

My father clears his throat. "Are you living with this boy?"

"I just can't leave him," I say.

"Well," the father I imagine tells me, "If you love him as much as you say, how can it be wrong?"

Mickey, my real father, answers the phone. "Daddy, this is Pam. I wanted you to know where I am."

"Lottie's right? We've had this conversation."

We've never had this conversation. "A few days ago I was out watering the roses."

There's an impatient sigh on the other end of the line.

"Charlie, the boy you met, came and told me he got signed. He's a ballplayer. I didn't want to be without him, so I jumped in the car and came along."

My father makes a keening sound. "Where are you?"

"Cotton Valley."

"Jesus H. Christ."

"I love him, Daddy."

"This is really Pamela Catherine Carey?"

"Yes."

"My daughter doesn't whine, 'I love him, Daddy.' And she doesn't have her head between her legs."

I frown at the yellow coffee mug. "Why do you have to make everything so coarse?"

"My daughter doesn't chase a boy halfway across the state."

"He asked me to come." Did he ask? He opened the car door. He lifted his sunglasses. He said it wasn't a problem if I wanted to be with him. That's almost the same as asking, isn't it?

"So are you two shacking up? The jerk's just taking advantage. I should know."

He should.

"Charlie loves me. He wants me to be with him."

"Did he ask you to marry him?"

"No."

"Then, he doesn't love you. You're throwing your life away. Ever since I can remember, you wanted to be a teacher. Not once did you say all you wanted to do was sit around and watch some guy play ball."

"Of course I'm going to stay in school."

"Of course nothing. Aren't you supposed to be in summer school right now? Aren't you blowing that scholarship you were so sure you were going to get? Charlie will be going to Mexico or South America to play winter ball. And you can't leave him, remember?"

"How long does winter ball last?

"Jesus in a jockstrap, how long do you think?"

I sigh. Why do I become brain dead when I talk to my father?

"You should get on a bus right now and come home. The longer you stay with him the harder it's going to be to leave."

There's an awful sloshing sound. Some liquid, beer? whiskey? It's being poured into a glass. I hate all those sounds: ice clinking glass, the rasp of a beer can being opened, the twist of a cap on a beer bottle. I'm driving my father to drink.

"It's only Seven-Up," he says, before I have a chance to ask.

I almost believe him.

"Do you have a hat?" he says.

"A hat?"

"I was in that hellhole when I was a bat boy. The field is a wreck. The big ants bite. The horse flies suck blood, am I right?"

He has been here.

"You sit in those bleachers without a hat you'll get sunstroke. Just come home. You won't get sunstroke in Santa Monica. You won't get pregnant either. Go to school. See Warren what's his face. Find out if you still feel the same way about the ballplayer in a year."

"A whole year? I can't be away from Charlie for a single second."

"Just come home before you end up barefoot and knocked up," Mickey shouts.

There's a pause, whispering and then something muffled that could be sobs. Have I made my father cry?

"Daddy, I'm so sorry," I say.

"Pamela." Kathleen's sultry voice comes on the line. "Your father's taking the news very hard right now, but as soon as you and your young man have things worked out, Mickey will be the first to cheer."

"I don't want my father to be hurt for a single second," I say. "I'm not trying to hurt anyone."

There's a tapping sound. I can picture long red fingernails dancing on the receiver. "Running away with the boy you love is so romantic. Your young man is so handsome. Those penetrating blue eyes. Naturally, I was happy to play Cupid."

"Cupid?"

"I told Charlie you were at your aunt's and I drew a map for him."

"That was very kind of you, Kathleen."

"I was only trying to do what your own mother would have done."

Alice would never draw a map for a boy like Charlie.

"As soon as you firm up your plans let me know," Kathleen says. "I, of course, prefer Father Connors, but I know Lottie will be pushing for her Father Timothy. The ultimate decision is yours and your young man's. It's too bad that June is almost gone. It really is the nicest month for weddings. Do you have a tentative date in mind?"

I twist the phone cord around my finger. "Well, I. . ."

"Jesus, Pam." My father, who will be the first to cheer, is back on the phone. "Just get your ass home."

17

I sip coffee from my yellow mug. I still feel dreamy. Sunlight streaming through the window makes a lacy pattern on the floor. I stir cream into my coffee with a spoon.

Spoon. June. Moon. Honeymoon. June is the best time for weddings.

Cupid Kathleen, who wants a wedding for me, is nothing like my mother, who dreamed of a teaching credential, an independent income, and satisfying work for me. Alice made fun of 10-year-old girls who had hope chests. She said they had dishtowels for brains.

I sip sweet cream and half shut my eyes. I see me walking down an aisle past Aunt Lottie and Kathleen to where Charlie – and two priests – wait for me.

Charlie, carrying a sports bag, bangs open the bedroom door and squints at the lacy sunlight. "Do you still have the rent money I gave you?"

Aunt Lottie, Kathleen, and the two priests disappear. I am not getting married. I am living with someone. I am shacking up.

"The money's under my sleeping bag, but I'm going to need it to rent the room when you're ready for me to go."

"You don't want me to starve to death do you?" he says. "I need some of the money for food. We're going on the road."

Coffee warms my stomach. He doesn't want me to go. He wants to find some excuse to use the money so I can't leave him. "Where are we going?"

"Not you. The team. We're playing Modesto, Sacramento, and a doubleheader in Reno."

Charlie's leaving me. "Can't I come?"

"The team goes on the bus. There's no room for," he sniffs, "wives." He puts keys in my hands. "I know it's going to be hard, honey. We haven't been apart for a minute. I'm going to miss you like crazy. But you can drive Old Chartreuse. You can get to know the town. You can visit the other. . ." he coughs.

"I don't have my driver's license. My purse. My clothes."

Charlie blinks at me. It isn't his fault, I jumped in a car and drove off without any of my belongings.

"Maybe you can get together with one of the wives and drive to Modesto. I can sneak you into the motel."

"I don't know where Modesto is." I sound like the helpless female I've always detested. "I can use this time," I tell him, "to call Lottie and have her send me my things."

"Now, you're cooking." He kisses me. "You can look Modesto up on the map." He disappears into the bedroom. "You can go to the DMV and get a duplicate license." He comes back waving a $10 bill. "I'll be able to eat like a king. You can eat like a queen. You can stock up. Maybe even buy us a frying pan."

First the coffee mugs, now the frying pan. He definitely wants me to stay. But is it the right thing to do?

"If I use the money for food, and a pan, I won't be able to rent the room."

"You won't need the room. I'm not even going to be here for seven whole days. When I come back, maybe we'll find out we won't have any use for that room at all. I may have a big surprise for you. I had a great dream last night. I was at the plate. The ball coming at me looked like a big white volley ball and I whacked it out of the park."

He's going to be gone for a whole week and he couldn't be happier.

"Don't you see? It's great news for us." He leans down and kisses me. "Our luck is changing. I had a good dream, not a nightmare. Yesterday, I went back to chewing Wrigley's Doublemint. Maybe that Dentyne jinxed me. If I start hitting, they'll keep me in the lineup even though I can't play my position." His face gets still. "It was even bigger than a volleyball. The ball was a big, white, round moon. From now on, it's Doublemint."

Outside, a horn honks. "That's Steve Willis." Charlie grabs his gear bag, kisses me on the forehead.

"Are you going now?"

"He's picking me up so you can have the car. See, I think of everything." Over his shoulder he shouts, "Just try to guess what my surprise might be. You're going to love it, if it happens. It's what you've been waiting for."

The front door shuts behind him. In a second it opens again. Charlie races in, hugs me hard. "God, it's going to be terrible without you." Whistling, he skips through the house and down the steps.

I run to the window. Charlie doesn't wait to open the door of the little sports car. He climbs over the side and curls himself up into the front seat. Steve Willis guns the engine. The little Austin Healey sounds like a big jet. The car lurches forward. Chewing his Doublemint and taking the $10 bill he said belongs to me, Charlie is off to Modesto, Sacramento, and a doubleheader in Reno.

•

In the kitchen, I sit at the table and blink at the three Dolly Madison donuts left in the box. Winter ball. Away games. There's no way I can be with Charlie all of the time. I should be happy. I should be calling school and legally dropping my summer school classes so I won't be given a bad grade.

I shut my eyes, see my schoolbooks neatly stacked on the desk at Lottie's. Just picturing the books makes me feel happier, stronger. So, why am I reaching for the local phone book so I can call up one of the wives and invite myself along on a trip to Modesto?

The phone rings. Maybe one of the wives is calling me right now.

"Hello," I sing into the phone.

"Is this the Charlie Fain residence?"

"Why, yes it is." I sound too eager.

"This is Charlie's mother. To whom am I speaking?"

My stomach jumps. I squeeze my eyes and try to shut out the picture of the dirty underpants on the bedpost. "Charlie's on the road," I whisper and hang up.

The phone shrieks again. Coward that I am, I let it ring seven times before I pick it up. Mrs. Fain says, "To whom am I speaking?"

"This is the landlady."

"When will Mr. Fain be back at his residence?"

"In a week."

"Could you please give him a message for me Mrs. . .?"

"Gooth," I say.

"Mrs. Gooth." There's a funny choking sound. Is she laughing at me? "Would you please ask Charlie to call home?"

"I'll give Mr. Fain your message."

"And would you tell him not to do anything dumb. Like marry his landlady." She slams the phone down.

•

At the dime store, I bought a new notebook and pen. I checked the Austen novels out of the library. Lady Russell is my favorite. True, she's a widow who misses her husband. But she faces her reversals in circumstances with grace.

I study the lacy sunshine streaming through grimy kitchen windows. I picture a white tablecloth on the cardboard table, fluffy curtains on the windows. I haven't had a home since Alice died and my father sold our house on Hibiscus Street. If Charlie and I were married I could make this place a home for us.

I put the new frying pan on the stove and make myself a quick breakfast. I think a little bit about Miss Bates in *Emma* and then I attack the windows. I squirt blue liquid on the glass and wipe off months of grime. I finish a second pane and then a third.

I make myself a cup of coffee and take it out into the backyard. I find a geranium bush choked by weeds but still in bloom. The flowers will brighten the cardboard table. I snap off pink flowers and head back inside.

Someone is standing in the kitchen. Warren. My fingers clench flower stems so hard the juice seeps out of them. I step closer to him, so close that I can see the hurt in his eyes. I back away and say, "I've missed you."

He glances at the shiny new phone. "That's why you called me so often?"

"I didn't know what to tell you."

"How about the truth?" He puts two sacks on the table. "You owe me that much after everything we've been to each other. So, what did you do, just run off and get married?"

"No."

He shuts his eyes, sighs. "Thank God."

"I came with Charlie on an impulse. I jumped in the car."

He starts to smile. "Do you mean you're ready to come home with me?"

"I mean I didn't plan to go away with Charlie, and I'm not Mrs. Charlie Fain."

Warren's smile dies. He stares at the roll of paper towels. "You just clean his windows. I had to come and see for myself. But I still don't believe you're here with him. Just what the hell are you doing?"

I don't answer.

"I thought you loved me," he says.

"I do, but I love Charlie, too." I point my finger to my head. "Two contradictory ideas."

Warren's face gets softer. "Do you know what F. Scotch Fitzgerald says?"

"What does *Scotch* say?"

"If you hold two conflicting ideas together long enough, you'll crack up." He looks as if he's going to walk over to me, and take me in his arms. Instead, he steps to the table and takes something square, navy blue and worn out of the bag.

"You brought me my purse. You must be a mind reader."

"Jumping in Fain's car must have been some big impulse. Your aunt says you even left the hose running." He frowns. "I brought you your books and clothes. I even got you your assignments for summer school. But you've missed so much you can probably kiss that goodbye."

I want to hug him, but it might make him feel worse. "You've given me my identity back."

He touches my cheek. "How could you forget who you are when you're so special?" He bends down, and tries to kiss me. I back away.

"I don't get it. How could you be in love with someone else?"

"I told you. It just happened."

"Can't you make it unhappen?"

"No."

Warren looks at the curling linoleum. He pushes a wobbly chair. "Maybe if you stay here a little while you'll get him out of your system. Where is he anyway?"

I start to say "Modesto." If I tell Warren I'm going to be alone for a week, he might not want to go home. Worse, I might not want him to leave. "Charlie's at the field."

"Does he love you?" Warren asks.

"Well. . ."

"Does he want to marry you?"

"Those are two different questions."

"I want to marry you."

"I know," I say softly. "We have our five-year plan."

"No, I mean now." He stares at me. "I want to marry you now."

"What about school?"

"Screw school. I don't want it if I can't have you. Just marry me."

"I can't believe you're asking me. You were always so definite that we should wait at least until graduate school."

"That was before Charlie Fain. Please marry me."

If Warren had asked me a month ago, I would have been thrilled. I dreamed about our not having to say good night to each other. We shared everything. It seemed wrong not to share a bed. "I wanted this for so long."

Warren's eyes get wide. "Are you saying yes?"

"I can't marry you, Warren. I'm sorry."

"Do you just want Charlie?"

I nod. "I didn't expect this to happen."

"I think you just want to play house," Warren says. "You want a home. If you want to be domestic –" he picks up the glass bottle and squirts Windex on the windows – "we can do it." He blots the window with a paper towel. "Up until now you haven't shown the slightest interest in any of this." He waves the frying pan. "You always said you were afraid you'd turn into a dull-witted housewife. If you marry me, I'll give you a home and I'll be domestic enough for both of us."

He opens the refrigerator, takes out an egg and breaks the egg into the pan. "We can have chickens in every pot. Curtains up the yin-yang. We can argue about the bills. It will be great."

"I've never seen you like this before," I say.

"I never thought I was going to lose the person most important in the world to me," he says.

"We can still be friends."

"Friends. The death kiss." He looks as if I've punched him. "What about us against the Philistines? Now, you're turning into one of them. You spend your days cleaning windows. You don't have a job. You dropped out of summer school. What do you and Charlie talk about? What was the last conversation you had?"

I shut my eyes. "We talked about his hitting and about his changing his brand of chewing gum."

"Mrs. Fain is her own person. She wouldn't drop what she was doing on a whim."

I stare at him.

"The real Mrs. Fain knows who she is," Warren says. "Charlie's mother is a grown up."

"How do you know what she's like?"

"I went to her house to get Charlie's address." He glares at me. "At the time I didn't know Charlie's address and yours were the same."

"Did you tell her I ran off with Charlie? He's going to be so upset."

"I told her I played on Charlie's college team. I had reason to come up this way and I thought I'd say hello. She's doing her Master's thesis on Hopkins. So, Charlie lies to his mother?'

"He just didn't want to worry her."

"He didn't want to tell her the truth. Is he ashamed of you?"

"Of course not."

Warren's eyes fix on the white and yellow egg in the pan. "She's worried you're going to get pregnant."

"You did tell her I was here."

"No. She told me you were in Charlie's bedroom." Warren's face is red. "How could you?" He looks past me to the bedroom and stares at the two sleeping bags. "I could just take you in there and throw you on the bed right now."

Would he do that? Would he force himself on me? If I take a step backwards, I might anger him more. I stand very still and wait.

"I thought you wanted to be my lover," he says.

"I did. I love Charlie. . .too."

Sweat wets Warren's hair. Now, even his ears are red. He's clenching white fingers. I've made him crazy. What will he do? What do I want him to do? I don't want him to touch me when he's angry like this. If he reaches for me, I could pick up the frying pan and hit him with it. I picture raw egg running down his face. We've been best friends for years. Friends don't hit each other with frying pans. But friends don't force themselves on you.

"You don't love Charlie," he says. "It's something else, entirely. It was too hard for you living at The Palms. You were having such a difficult time you even considered going back and living with your father, remember?"

Warren looks calmer now. I take a step back and he doesn't even seem to notice.

"Mrs. Fain is reading a fascinating book," he tells me. "It's called *The Feminine Mystique*. Have you heard of it?"

I shake my head. He's not going to throw me on the bed. He's not going to propose again or insist I should come home with him. He's just going to use his fine brain to come up with some screwy reason for why I love Charlie and rejected him.

"*Feminine Mystique*," I whisper.

"It's about women who don't know how to live for themselves and so they live through their husbands and children."

"My Husband He's," I say.

Warren looks confused.

"One of the baseball wives calls the other wives *My Husband He*: My husband he doesn't like Swiss Cheese. My husband he had to soak his foot all night. Raquel says if you ask one of these women how she is, she'll say, 'My husband he stole two bases.'"

Warren shuts his eyes. When he opens them again, they are filled with tears. "It's awful that you don't want me. My heart is broken and I don't think I'll ever get over it. But what's worse is that this Charlie Fain thing has revealed who you really are. You stopped being yourself and you ran off with someone you hardly know. You are a My Husband He."

18

The job is between you and one other girl." Mr. Huggins sounds friendlier over the phone than he looked in person – a pinched, sad face peering over a pile of dirty clothes yesterday afternoon.

Warren Ashburn will learn just how wrong he is about me when he finds out about my new job at Huggins' Dry Cleaners. I am my own person. I may love Charlie. I may have made his house sparkle. But I also wrote a very good essay about the spirited and strong unmarried women in Jane Austen's books. I am an independent woman who takes care of herself.

Outside, a car engine guns and stops. Doors bang. A voice in the front room shouts, "I'm back."

Charlie is here.

"I'll come in later and talk to you." My words come in a joyful rush. "Thank you, Mr. Huggins. Thank you." Mr. Huggins must think I'm in love with dry cleaning.

Charlie is in the kitchen now. His sunburned face makes his grin look even bigger. "I have a surprise for you," he tells me. "My God. What happened to this place? It looks like *Better Homes and Gardens*." His words and his gear bag landing on the table drown out Mr. Huggins words.

"You'll be hearing from me, Mr. Huggins. And thank you for your wonderful job offer." I croon into the phone and hang up. "I'm so glad to see you." I throw my arms around Charlie. "I was afraid you were never coming back."

"I've come back in triumph." One hug is all he has time for and then he's digging into his gear bag, pulling out his glove and two packs of Doublemint gum. "My surprise for you is in here somewhere." He hands me a paper bag. "Wait until you see what I got for you."

This is my first present from Charlie. I want to rip the bag open, but my thrifty mother taught me to re-use all bags and gift-wrappings. I slip my hand in slowly. My fingers find something smooth and soft and sturdy. I pull it out.

"You seemed so lost without your purse," Charlie says.

The purse is white and shaped like an envelope. "It's beautiful. It's just what I need."

Charlie frowns. He's looking at my scuffed navy blue purse sitting on the counter. "Your aunt sent your things."

"White is so much better for summer." I pat my pleated skirt. "And it goes with what I'm wearing."

"You're all in white," Charlie says. "As if you already knew." He starts smiling again. "Did someone tell you? Or are you psychic?"

He must be new at giving presents. "I heard a voice in my dream. Pamela, today you will get a white purse."

Charlie laughs. "So you think my surprise is the white purse? Look inside."

Maybe the rent money he promised me is tucked inside a compartment. Do I want the rent money? Am I ready to live around the corner from Charlie? I unsnap the purse and pull out sheets of paper too thick to be money.

"My score sheets," Charlie says. "They read almost as beautiful as Shakespeare. C. Fain. 4-for-4. First game at Modesto."

He spreads the sheets with the filled in diamonds on the table. "You'll never guess what my average on the trip was – .550. I am sizzling."

"Congratulations," I tell him. "I'm glad things are going so well for you."

"Things are going so well for us. My overall average now is .330."

"That's wonderful. I'm happy for you."

"Be happy for us. They have to start me now. I could be a jerk out in the field and they still have to put me in the lineup."

"I'm pleased for you. I really am."

"For us, you mean. Things are going well for us." His grin gets bigger. "Very well. And today's, my day off." Charlie unwraps a piece of gum, tilts his head and studies me. "If you have nothing better to do, I thought we could get married."

I clutch my purse and stare at him.

"I know I put you through hell. You were in a difficult position. You didn't know what our future was going to be like. But I couldn't ask you to marry me when I only had a .196 batting average. There are just some things you don't do. Plus, I was a total nerd in the field."

My brain feels like cotton, but those Fourth of July sparklers are going off inside me. "Do you mean if you were hitting better you would have asked me before?"

"I didn't want you to be stuck with a loser. I thought as soon as I got up to .270, but that would have been stretching it. Still, if my fielding had improved, we might have been all right."

"Your batting average was what made you sneeze when the word marriage came up? You're not allergic to the word?"

Charlie looks indignant. "Of course not. Marriage. Marriage. Marriage. See, not even a little sniff. I have an overall .330, so do you want to get hitched?"

"My aunt is going to be so happy."

"She likes baseball?" he says.

"She likes marriage."

"Then, your answer is yes?"

"Of course it's yes." I grab his hand and pump it. "Do you really want to get married?"

He squeezes my fingers and grins. "I wouldn't be asking you if I didn't. I know this was hard for you," he eyes the sleeping bags on the bed. "Living here with me and not being legal, but that's all behind us now."

No more back-street girl. No more dirty underpants on the bedpost. The world will know that Charlie and I are a couple. "After I talk to Lottie, I'll call my stepmother. She likes stuff like this. Dresses. Centerpieces. Napkins."

"We don't have time for napkins. I don't get another day off for three and a half weeks. I thought we'd drive to Las Vegas. Old Chartreuse is running good, right?" Charlie is beaming.

"You mean you want to get married today?"

"This minute. In California it takes three days to get a blood test, plus I'm sure my mom won't give her consent." Charlie looks pained. "You know she thinks getting married young and having me ruined her life. I called and asked my dad if he would write his consent. He said he would. See, he's more on my side than she is. But it won't count, because she's the one with the legal custody. He said we should go to Nevada or Mexico."

"Mexico," I shout. 'My stepmother got married there when she was 15 and it was entirely legal. My aunt can help us. Her house, where you found me that wonderful day, is only an hour from the border."

"Are you sure she'll want us to get married now?"

I hug Charlie. "She wanted us to get married two weeks ago."

●

I lead him up my Aunt Lottie's path. What if Charlie is shocked by her weight and thinks she is a freak? Will I refuse to marry him? Of course not. But still, it will hurt. The two people I love most in the world should get along. "Remember what I told you," I say.

"Your aunt weighs 300 pounds. Her house is a wreck. Dust, trash everywhere, but I'm going to love her."

Before I raise my hand to knock, the door opens. It couldn't be worse. She's in her floating pink tent (robe?) with the magenta cummerbund. A magenta bow flops on her newly permed hair. "Aunt Lottie, this is Charlie."

He takes a sharp breath. "It's nice to meet you." He extends his hand for a shake.

Her brown eyes get small. She studies his Oxford shirt, plaid Bermuda shorts, and perfect legs. "What a beauty."

His mouth opens.

She crushes him against her. His sunglasses wobble and land on her shoulder. She won't stop hugging him. Finally he breaks away. I think he's going to glare at me, and maybe even tell me we should leave. This woman can't help anyone. But he's smiling. His eyes look wet. Love at first sight.

"Come on in," she wraps an arm around each of us and steers us through the dark foyer.

This could be the shortest love affair in history. I shut my eyes, and pray. "Please don't let the house be too bad," I whisper.

She tells Charlie, "Welcome to my home."

Light from the clean—clean? — window floods the living room. The coffee table whose glass top I haven't seen for years sends back a reflection of my surprised face. Someone tied the curtains and washed the windows, but they didn't stop there. There's not a pretzel box or a magazine or a ball of dust anywhere. The furniture and floor gleam. Roses sit in a vase on the blue piano.

She couldn't have done this for me. She didn't even know we were coming. "The house looks lovely," I say.

"Thank you." She's blushing. "I have a surprise for you."

More surprises. I picture elves with brooms and dustpans and a dragon that eats old newspapers and potato chips.

"Fresh lemonade sweetened with garden strawberries." She heads for the kitchen.

Charlie shakes his head at me and runs his fingers along a freshly waxed table. "You must be one of those terrible, lint-picking fanatics." He turns, studies the picture in the familiar oak frame above the mantle. "Nice painting."

"That's a. . ." I stop. The portrait of Rose in the tub is gone.

"A barn?" Charlie says. "You think I'm so stupid I wouldn't recognize a barn?"

He thinks I made the dust up. He thinks I think he's stupid. "There used to be a different picture there," I say.

He looks at me with suspicious eyes.

"And the house was. . ."

Lottie's back with drinks in tall glasses and coasters that look like red, yellow and blue straw wheels. She didn't need coasters when she had mounds of newspapers stacked on every table. She puts the drinks down and points to Jacob's chair. "Sit." She slides the ottoman under Charlie's feet. "I've got one more surprise," she says and leaves the room again.

Charlie sips. "Strawberries and lemonade make a great double play," he says loudly. He wants to make sure that wherever Lottie is in the dark house she will hear him.

I lick strawberries off my lip and smile at my future husband who sits in my uncle's chair. If only every day could be this perfect.

The flip flop of her rubber sandals makes a happy sound on the hall floor and then she's back in the room again. "This is Boris," she whispers. She's cradling something small and fuzzy. "He's only 8 weeks old. He just left his mother." She strokes his head. "His markings make him look Russian, don't you think? He has a snowy white face framed by a black cap."

"Boris is a perfect name for him," Charlie says.

Boris wriggles and leans toward Charlie's chair.

"I was sure he was a man's dog." Lottie settles the puppy in Charlie's lap. Her arm brushes the chair. "I wish Jacob were here. My husband would have liked you."

Charlie's eyes get wide. "Most grownups think I'm a hot dog."

."A hot dog?" She looks puzzled.

"It's a sports term," I say. "It means. . ."

"A show off," Charlie says.

Lottie nods. "Usually people think I'm quote, eccentric. What they mean is I'm cracked. I live alone with my dogs and avocados. I weigh too much."

"Everyone should be as cracked as you are," Charlie says.

Lottie smiles and watches Boris lick Charlie's knee. Then, the dog lowers its head and snores. Charlie, drinking his double play lemonade looks as if he belongs in my uncle's chair.

Jacob would love him. Jacob loved anyone who loved Lottie.

"Aunt Lottie," I say. "Charlie asked me to marry him."

She hugs us both and whispers, "I just knew this would happen."

•

Everything is wonderful. So many hours I sat in my aunt's kitchen mooning over Charlie. And now, my husband-to-be is sitting in the kitchen with me. I hold his hand in mine. With my free hand I drink Postum. I am half little girl and half grown up. I'm going to be Charlie's bride.

Lottie sighs and hangs up the phone. "Even in Mexico, boys have to be 21. I'm sorry kids."

"I won't be 21 for three years," Charlie says.

So much for Plan A: Drive across the border, walk into the first office that has a *Marriage/Divorce* sign. Mickey always told me that in Tijuana they'd marry anyone, even a frog to a chicken, for a small fee. I rub eyes that suddenly feel tired. "It's not fair. Girls can marry at 18."

"Girls supposedly know themselves better." Lottie splashes hot water into a mug, spoons in Postum, and hands the cup to Charlie. "Would your mother write a letter of consent?"

"Not even if the Pope told her to." He pats my knee. "It serves you right for taking up with a baby."

Lottie raises eyebrows that today she penciled orange.

"I'm five months older than Charlie," I say. "I'm a cradle robber."

Charlie pushes his Postum away. "Well, that's that."

Lottie stares at him. "You're not going to give up so easily?" She sits and the plastic cushion sighs. "Pam fell off her bike three times, but she kept getting back on and she finally made it down the block. That's the stuff your future wife is made of."

I sink down in my chair. What if Charlie doesn't want to marry me as much as I wanted to ride a bicycle?

Charlie jerks his head and winks at Lottie. "How would you like to be my mother?"

Lottie slams her hand on the table. "Now, you're talking."

Now, they're talking, all right. Now, they're talking fraud. But everything is all right again. Charlie wants to marry me.

Lottie is grinning. She looks as though she's planning to throw eggs down someone's chimney. "I'm the right age. Why couldn't I be your mother?"

Charlie opens his arms wide. "Mom."

"What if they ask for your identification?" I say.

"We're talking Mexico. There's places down there where I can buy myself a whole bunch of new names." Her smile dies. "But it's expensive and it takes a few days."

"We don't have a few days," Charlie says.

"Maybe I could just write a letter of consent for you. Do you have something in your mother's handwriting?"

Charlie digs through his pockets. "I have a recent letter."

Lottie reads, "God will help you with your batting average." She gets paper and pen. "This is going to be easy to copy."

"Forgery and fraud. Aunt Lottie, you could get in legal trouble for this."

"Who's going to prosecute me?" Lottie says. "This is Mexico, remember? They have drug smugglers to worry about."

"It's a piece of cake," Charlie says.

Is this just a game to them? The marriage caper?

"I want our marriage to be legal and to hold up in court. I want it to be real."

"It will be real," Charlie says.

Lottie looks up from her work. "Once we present Charlie's mother with a fact accompli and give her a couple of months, she'll be planning a second wedding in the Church."

Fact accompli? No wonder Lottie flunked French. If she had taken Law, she would have flunked that, too. Still, she might have a point. If we show Charlie's mom that we're so desperate to marry, we'd even lie, she'll believe in us all right. She'll believe we're cheats.

Charlie pops his knuckles. "Our marriage will kill her."

"Mothers have to learn to let go," Lottie says.

"We're going to have a marriage based on a lie," I say.

"We wouldn't have to lie if she weren't so against people under 30 getting married. Besides, it's a stupid law. I'm old enough to make my own decision."

Lottie folds notepaper into an envelope and licks the sealer. She frowns. She sips her drink. Her face clears. Across the front of the envelope she writes, *To Whom It May Concern.* "How's my brother taking all of this?"

"He doesn't know about our marriage yet." I say.

She nods. "We should leave now." She looks out the window and studies the sun still high above the coastal hills. She takes keys for the Studebaker from the hook.

My stomach jumps. "We forge a letter and then we're off?"

"Is it what you want?" Lottie asks.

I look at Charlie's beautiful face. "Of course."

"Then, let's go." She frowns again. "I forgot something." The mistress of propriety looks worried. "You'll need a ring."

"I didn't even think about a ring," Charlie says.

Lottie takes Jacob's band off her finger, and holds the ring for a minute and then gives it to Charlie.

The circle of gold shines in Charlie's palm. Then, I know this marriage is as real as my aunt and uncle's love and as real as the pot of Gypsy stew simmering on the stove.

Charlie lifts me high in the air. He sings, "Going to the chapel and we're going to get married, and we'll never be lonely anymore."

I smile and find Charlie's face in the stream of sunlight flooding the room. I kiss my groom on the lips. This is the wedding I dreamed of.

19

As if he couldn't wait one extra second to get married, Charlie takes long strides. I skip after him. "Wait for your bride," I say.

Charlie grins. "You're right. I can't get married without you." He tugs the hem of his school sweater. "I'm sorry I don't own a sports jacket. You deserve a decent looking groom."

"Your sweater's nicer." I run my hand over patches that say CIF 1963. "You earned all your sports letters. I wish I looked more like a bride."

He smiles at the blouse with the Peter Pan collar and the skirt I've had since ninth grade. "You look perfect."

"My blouse has a scorch mark."

"It doesn't show. You're all in white. A real bride."

My white badge of courage. I am still technically a virgin. It wasn't easy, but I held out until my wedding day.

Charlie steps off the path. Crossing the freshly raked yard, his loafers disturb the even tracks of dust. He stops by a sign swinging from two posts. The sign says, *Señor Muñoz/Lawyer/ Marriage/Divorce.* In the adobe building in front of us, Venetian blinds move. Someone is watching us. Before I can stop him, Charlie picks a pink hibiscus from a bush with shiny leaves.

He tucks the stem behind my ear. The petal's ruffled edge rests against my cheek. He leans and kisses me.

Lottie locks the car, and pants past us up the path. "Come on. What are you two waiting for?"

"If everything goes the way we hope," I say, "the next time we walk on this path, we'll be husband and wife."

"If he doesn't believe our story," Lottie says, "we'll offer him a bribe."

"How do you know he'll take it?" I say.

They both stop on the path and look at me.

"Honey," Lottie says.

"This is Mexico," Charlie says.

"We'll be able to tell right away if he's that kind of man," Lottie says.

"Does he wear a sign that says, *Hi, I take bribes*?"

"You're such a baby, even if you are a bride." Lottie pats my hand. She squints at traffic. Cars, one with a door missing, and another, minus a hood, and a truck with a load of squawking chickens, crowd the street. "I locked the car, right?"

Next to the curb, a bright, new, boxy Studebaker Lark sits waiting for its lucky owner. Behind the Lark, Lottie's Studebaker looks like a sagging cocoon. Sun has faded the gray and white tweed seat covers. Dust has settled in the ridges of the upholstery's weave. Inside and out, the car is tired. "Aunt Lottie, what do we have to offer as a bribe?"

"Hap says a customer's been eyeing my painting of the threshing machine." She fiddles with the handle of her straw purse. "I can pay Mr., that is, Señor Muñoz from the profits."

I want to tell her don't count your paintings before they are sold, but she's smiling. Her round face looks so happy. She can already see her painting hanging on a wall in a fancy living room.

Lottie puts an arm around each of us. "Let's go get married."

•

Lottie steers us toward the desk. "Señor Muñoz, this is the bride and groom."

The man behind the desk, the man who controls our fate, studies us, dressed in our best and full of hope. His eyes get more tired. "Are you the bride's mother?" he asks Lottie.

She doesn't answer. She looks confused. She's trying to decide which set of lies she should tell. For just a second, I wish my aunt wasn't a basically honest person.

The fan on Señor Muñoz's desk squeaks, and sends back waves of hot air.

"My mother's dead." My voice bounces off law books and fills the crowded office. "But I'm 18." I give him my driver's license.

A turquoise ring glinting on a thick middle finger catches light from a space in the blinds. The man who watched us steal a flower from his courtyard wears an opal on his pinky.

Lottie pulls me close. "See his jewels?" she whispers. "He likes nice things. He's vain. He's ripe to be bribed." She steps closer to his desk and takes a letter from her purse. "This is from the groom's mother, Mrs. Fain."

Señor Muñoz looks even wearier. "You're not the groom's mother either?"

"No?" She makes it a question. "I'm a family friend."

He slices the envelope with a knife that has an onyx handle. He reads. He frowns. He doesn't believe the words in the letter. He doesn't believe us.

I squeeze my eyes shut and stop myself from crying.

I hear his words. "Next week I buy an air cooler. A big expense but worth it." He's smiling at Lottie, who fans her face with her hand. He turns to Charlie. "So your mother couldn't come in person?"

Charlie's neck gets red. He stares down at the dust on his loafers. "She's very busy right now."

He's a terrible liar. He's even worse than Lottie. I lean over and kiss him.

"She's just graduated from college," Lottie is saying. "Isn't that wonderful? But Eileen always was the ambitious one. I was the fun one."

"So you and Mrs. Fain are old friends?"

"We were school girls together. She sent me here today as her ambassador."

Señor Muñoz holds the letter in front of him and then drops it in the wastebasket. Charlie sucks in his breath. He stares at the paper in the trash and the envelope with the hopeful words *To Whom It May Concern* still sitting on the desk.

The lawyer blinks at Lottie. "Who are you really?"

Her face gets pink. She glances at me. Her voice comes out of the gloom. "Pam's aunt." The straw on her purse handle is starting to unravel. "Her father is my brother." Grown up Lottie looks like a shame-faced little girl. "Her mother was my best friend."

Señor Muñoz sits in a swivel chair too small for his bulk. He shuts his eyes.

So much for the marriage caper. My eyes water. So much for the marriage.

Unless I offer him a bribe. I open my mouth and wait for words to come. "Señor Muñoz, Charlie and I love each other. I'm not pregnant. We're getting married because we can't stand to be away from each other. We want to be together day. . .and night. If you won't marry us today, we'll find someone who will." Señor Muñoz's clock says 5:30. An evening sun is turning the courtyard orange. All over town, officials are closing their doors and going home. "If we can't get married today, we'll do it tomorrow or the next day."

"If they're 15 or 50, people in love act like they are children," Señor Muñoz says. He is looking at the hibiscus in my hair. Maybe he was against us from the start. If only Charlie hadn't stolen the flower. If only Mrs. Fain wasn't so against marriage.

Señor Muñoz's eyes don't look so tired now. "In cases like this I don't file the certificate. I wait until we receive consent. Parents have a way of coming around. Ninety-nine times out of a hundred, I get a letter within a month."

Coming around? I nudge Lottie. "You're Fact Accompli." I can hear the laugh, the joy in my voice.

"You're going to marry us?" Charlie twirls me around. "He's going to marry us." He pumps Señor Muñoz's hand.

"Maybe this is blackmail, but I like to think I'm just helping love along."

"You are. You are," Charlie tells the older man.

Aunt Lottie hugs us both. Her whisper warms my neck. "I just knew it would work out."

Charlie straightens his shoulders, and clears his throat. "If you. . . if you you'd like we could give you something extra."

"You're paying me my fee, no?" Señor Muñoz looks puzzled. His voice turns cold. "Then that is all I require."
Charlie's blush spreads to his ears.

"Ripe," I tell Lottie.

She purses her lips and bows her head. Her magenta bow flops. She's properly ashamed. That should be enough for me. But she patted my hand and called me a baby. I lean toward Señor Muñoz. "Your rings are lovely."

Señor Muñoz's eyes sparkle. "My wife does the settings. She's a jeweler and an artist."

"My aunt's an artist, too," I say, forgiving her. "And except for Charlie, she's the person I love most in the world. She's kind and generous."

"We can continue to discuss the virtues of your aunt or –?" Señor Muñoz opens a gold and white book that has the words *Wedding Ceremony* on the cover.

"Pamela was bald when she was a baby," Lottie says.

We all stare at her.

She's pulling handfuls of tissues from her bag. "And puny. Now, look at my niece. She's a bride with a flower in her hair."

Charlie takes the gum from his mouth and squeezes my hand.

"We are gathered together," Señor Muñoz begins.

I hold my breath and stand very still. Charlie looks so beautiful I can't believe he's mine. His face is shining. His eyes sparkle. He looks as if he just hit a home run. He says, "I do."

I throw my arms around him. "I do, too."

•

I want to remember every detail of this moment forever. I tell the bull in the velvet wall hanging, "I'll never forget you." I wink at the bull's rhinestone eyes.

Lottie grins and slips her drink to Charlie. "We did it."

Charlie sips. His eyes get wide. "We did it." He passes the white-rimmed glass to me.

"We. . ." Lime juice makes my mouth pucker. Salt tickles my gums. "We. . ." I lose my voice. Tequila is a river of fire rushing down my throat.

"God. There's nothing like a margarita." Lottie tilts the glass. Sea-colored liquid disappears. "Holy Tamale, as Jacob used to say."

Charlie kisses my ear lobe, and then his tongue wanders inside my ear for just a wonderful second. "We've been married exactly 27 minutes," he says.

My throat burns. My ears burn. If someone opens the restaurant door and lets in the slightest breeze, I might just lift off and fly across the room. Is this how everyone feels 27 minutes after they've been married?

"Jacob and I used to come here a lot that year he was selling imported items. Do you remember, Pam?"

I tell Charlie, "He took the back seat out of the Studebaker and filled the car with straw purses, sandals, and serapes."

Lottie's face is red. She licks salt from her lips. "The poor man was never meant to be a salesman."

"Then, why did he do it?" Charlie asks.

Her eyes fill with love. "He couldn't do anything else."

A waiter with smooth cheeks and fuzz on his chin brings us our food. Lottie pokes a fork through flute-shaped dough. "I've been cooking fake Mexican food for so long, I doubt if I'll recognize the real thing." She chews a chunk of beef. Beads of sweat pop out on her forehead. "Real, all right. As hot as my living room."

Chili peppers from my innocent appearing chicken enchilada explode in my mouth. "Holy Tamale." I gulp water.

Charlie drops his fork and reaches for his water glass.

"We're all gringos," Lottie says. She lifts her glass. "How about a toast?" She shakes her head. "My brain is too fuzzy."

"I'll try a toast," I say. I hold my water glass in the air and smile at the painted bull. I look at Charlie's watch. "May we always be as happy as we've been in the last 33 minutes."

We clink glasses.

"We will always be this happy," Charlie says.

"To the most beautiful velvet bull in the entire world," I say.

Lottie pours tequila into Charlie's and my water glasses. "To my husband Jacob and the best chicken enchiladas ever."

We drink tequila. "To the game of baseball and to my bride," Charlie says.

"I've got it," Aunt Lottie says. "I've got the perfect toast. Are you ready?"

Charlie kisses my ear lobe again.

Now, the velvet bull is winking at me. Aunt Lottie lifts her glass. "Whenever the two of you are together, may you always be at home."

20

This is going to be the best night of my life. This is the night when I find out what love is really about. This is the night when I lose the big V. After tonight, I will no longer be a virgin.

My aunt flicks on the light and fishes kibbles from her pocket. "I hope you don't mind sharing the room with Boris. After all, this is your honeymoon."

Just hearing the word *honeymoon* makes me shiver, makes me feel as small as the puppy squatting on his square of newspaper.

My gorgeous husband is kneeling and stroking Boris's head.

"Thank you so much Aunt Lottie. We had a lovely wedding." I kiss her round cheek and start to close the door.

"Not so fast, young lady." She wedges her foot in the doorway.

First she rushes to get us married and now when I finally am legally (well almost) married to Charlie she wants to stand and have a chat. "Thank you so much, Aunt Lottie." Now, Charlie tries to close the door.

"Not so fast, you two." Lottie's raglan sleeves, with fields of poppies embroidered in the fabric, make a swishing sound. She shoos us out to the hall. "First we go to the pantry."

"We're not hungry," I tell her.

Humming *The Girl That I Marry* she pushes us along the hall.

She stops in front of shelves of green tomatoes and cucumbers swimming in brine and dill. Slices of preserved peaches and apricots look like tiny fists. "From the cellar, well the pantry of Lottie Carey Klein." She holds a bottle in the light. "Not Bordeaux or Napa Valley quality, but this is my own Chablis."

It sounds fancy and it looks like Elmer's Glue. She pours the liquid into goblets, puts the goblets and bottle on a straw tray that matches her new coasters. She leads us back to the hall.

"Charlie," she says. "Pick up your bride and carry her over the threshold."

I can hear his heart thumping under his thin shirt. The hall light swings above me. He navigates around Boris and puts me on the bed.

Lottie sets the wine on the table, and leans over and kisses us both. "Happy Honeymoon." At the door she stops. She looks as if she's going to say something more, perhaps a hint of what to do, but instead, she smiles and shuts the door.

•

"I love my aunt, but I thought she'd never leave."

Charlie presses his lips together. He's staring at his tennis shoes. This is funny behavior for a groom. "I didn't think I'd get married for years and years," he tells his shoes. "Not until I was ancient. At least 28 or 30." He looks at me with wide eyes. "Now, you're my bride."

I pat the hibiscus. It's fresh even after one Mexican dinner and an hour drive from the border. "I'm so happy," I say.

Charlie's shoe taps up and down on the floor. Is Charlie thinking of running away? He bends down and pat's Boris's head. My husband is more interested in a puppy than me.

I bend down and untie Charlie's new, white shoelace. "May I?"

The shoe drops on the linoleum. Now, Charlie is eyeing the top button of my blouse. His fingers twitch. Then his eyes twitch. Is he nervous? He says, "Would you like some wine?"

He pours. He sips. He makes a face. "This wine tastes like topping for a sundae. Grape Sundae sounds like something Howie would think of."

My glass shakes in my hand. I can't seem to perform the simple task of bringing the glass to my lips.

"I know you might be a little nervous," he says. He pours himself a second drink. "I'm a little. . ." He gulps more wine. "I've only been with three other girls."

Only three? That's practically a scout troop. Now, I need a drink. Sugar trickles down my throat. A wave of warmth rushes through me.

"And it wasn't the same," Charlie is saying. "I mean I wasn't married to any of them."

"Three girls. That's practically an army," I say.

Charlie looks hurt.

"Does being married make you more nervous?" I ask.

"Marriage is the real thing," he says. "It's for better or worse for life. You're my bride."

I am his bride. "There's nothing to be afraid of." I kneel on the floor and pull off his other shoe.

•

For the first time ever, Charlie takes off his undershorts. Is his penis supposed to look so small and helpless? Is something wrong? Should I kiss it make it well?

Charlie is grinning. He looks proud of his poor little thing. "Meet Mr. Noodle," he says. "He's all yours."

"But he's attached to you."

"He's on loan. Like a famous painting." Charlie studies the titles of Lottie's art books. "A Van Gogh."

Charlie's penis is my Van Gogh. I kiss him to show him how proud I am of his treasure. Charlie tastes of sugared grapes. Waves of warmth rush over me. A voice in my head sings, "This is love – the real thing." I arch my back and then Charlie is climbing on top of me.

"Ready?" he says. Before I can answer or even understand what he means, he slips his penis inside. He feels soft like a paintbrush. "Pam, Pam," Charlie moans and moves Mr. Noodle deeper.

Mr. Noodle doesn't feel like a paintbrush anymore. He's hard and big and he hurts. Something is wrong. Inside me, my skin feels tight and sore, as if it is tearing. "Please go slowly," I cry. I hold Charlie and try to keep him from moving deeper inside. "Stop."

Charlie is still calling my name, but he isn't listening to me. Could he have forgotten I'm right here, under him? Tears wet my face. Pins, hot pins, hundreds of them, prick me. "Stop," I put my hands on his belly, and try to push him away. Why won't he get off me? My fists curl. My eyes snap shut. I shove him hard, but he won't budge. My tears and words get lost in his flesh.

Something warm and wet gushes down my thighs. My skin stops throbbing. I lay still and open my eyes and blink at a shimmering tube of fluorescent light. Why didn't anyone ever tell me how much it would hurt?

Charlie shudders, and grabs my shoulders. He isn't moving anymore. He rests his head against me.

I free myself and sit up.

Charlie, starting to lose his balance, props himself on an elbow. Mr. Noodle is curled like a snake. "What are you doing?"

I stare at blood on my legs.

Blood and something else, something clear and thick – semen? – stains Lottie's white sheet. I lean down and sniff. It smells nice. Like yeast in uncooked bread dough. How could something that smells so friendly be part of something so awful? "What should we do with the puddle?"

He gives me a strange look, then puts on his shirt and pants. He comes back from the bathroom with towels. He knows what to do. He knows all about blood and semen. He's been with three other girls. Did he hurt them as much as he hurt me?

Like a good housewife, he scrubs and cleans. The stain gets lighter in color, but spreads. He puts the second towel over the wet spot. He winks. "We're ready to go again."

Again? I don't want any more pain. Ever. I cover myself with an afghan. I never want to make love again.

He kisses my forehead. "You were wonderful."

"Why didn't you stop when I told you to?"

"I was so excited that I just couldn't." He looks away from me. "I'm sorry. I wouldn't hurt you for anything."

"But you did hurt me."

"I'm sorry. Charlie moves away from me and studies Boris asleep on the newspaper.

"No one ever told me how awful sex was," I say.

Charlie blinks. "You think sex is awful?" His head droops. He scowls. "I thought you'd be thrilled."

"Thrilled to be sawed in two? I thought you knew something about this."

He cracks his knuckles. "I've only been with – "

"Three other girls." I hiss the words.

"And they liked it," he says. "They thought I was wonderful."

"Why? What was wonderful about it? I've never hurt so much in my entire life. You wouldn't stop."

Charlie's face is red. "They didn't act like they were suffering. They seemed to like me fine."

"Maybe you should have married them," I say. "You should have married all three of them." I find a dry spot on the towel. He watches me blot the blood on my legs.

Charlie cracks his knuckles again. That popping sound is driving me nuts. ""Well, there was one thing different about them."

I fold the towel in a prim little square and wait.

"They weren't virgins," he says.

"Neither am I," I say. "Not anymore."

"It's supposed to get better after you're not a virgin anymore."

Could it get better? It couldn't get worse. I never thought I'd go all the way. I thought being a virgin was the same as having boring, hay-colored hair. I'd be stuck with it for life. Now, my virginity is gone. When I was younger, I never thought I'd learn to ride a bike or swim. Bike riding and swimming didn't feel very good at first either. But they didn't feel as bad as this. "This was the worst experience I've ever had," I tell Charlie.

"You said that already. How awful do you want me to feel?"

"As awful as I felt, but that's not possible."

"I'm sorry I hurt you," Charlie says. "I wanted you to feel as wonderful as I felt."

I hug myself. When I was learning to swim there was nothing I hated more than learning to put my head under water. One afternoon, Lottie threw me in a pool. I paddled and grabbed the side and then yelled at her, "Why did you do that?" She said, "Sometimes the only way to learn is to just jump in." I hated her that day. Yet, swimming was fun once I got the hang of it. Could sex be fun once I get the hang of it?

Aunt Lottie loves me. This evening she closed the door and shut me in the room. She wouldn't be winking and smiling if she thought I was in for a long night of torture. I must be missing something. "Should I have taken an aspirin or maybe even a stronger pain killer?" I ask Charlie.

Hunched on the foot of the bed, and rubbing his foot over the puppy's back, he isn't answering anymore questions.

I touch his shoulder. "I'm sorry," I say. "But my skin felt as if it were tearing."

His lower lips pout in a little boy put. "Maybe we should have used Vaseline," he says.

"What do you mean?"

"Maybe we should have used a lubricant."

"Do you think that would have helped?"

"How should I know," he says. "I'm not a girl."

He's grumpy. "But you just said. . ." I stop myself from asking about his conquests. Suddenly I don't want to know what any of the merry trio used or didn't use. This has to be the worst wedding night that anyone ever had. Charlie bows his head. He looks ready to cry. I've hurt his feelings, but sex hurt me.

If only I could do something about the pain. I picture myself tiptoeing down the hall, walking into the bathroom, opening the mirrored door of the medicine chest and searching for aspirin and Vaseline. In the next room, Lottie, wide-awake, will be listening to the sigh of the door, the rattle of the bottles. She'll know I'm having a problem. She'll know I'm flunking sex.

I eye the milky Chablis. Alcohol is a good, medicinal pain-killer Mickey always says. I shut my eyes and hold my nose and drink. It's awful. I fill the glass again and tilt my head and pour the syrup down my throat.

Charlie is watching me.

"Those chicken enchiladas made me so thirsty," I say.

Mr. Noodle grows in Charlie's lap. It must be terrible to have a penis. Charlie is angry and wants nothing to do with me, but Mr. Noodle has a will of his own. I can feel my smile. I have power over Mr. Noodle. I start on my third drink. The walls tilt – a good sign. I drink and pour and drink. The ceiling spins. Something, a bee or a fly perhaps, buzzes in my head. My spine tingles. I stick my fingers in the glass and moisten them. I slip my hand under the afghan. Charlie is watching me. I put the fingers inside me. "Lubricant," I say.

Charlie is curled up in a corner of the bed, hugging himself. I take off the afghan and move next to him. I kiss him on the forehead.

"What are you doing?" he says.

"I'm kissing my husband."

"I thought you didn't want to have anything more to do with me."

"You thought wrong." I push Charlie down on the bed and climb on top of him. I take a deep breath and put Mr. Noodle inside of me.

"Pam, are you sure I'm not torturing you or anything?" His face softens. "I don't want to hurt you."

I move slowly down on Mr. Noodle. "So far, so good." I wink at Charlie and slide down deeper.

21

I 'll just jog up that hill behind your aunt's house and I'll be right back." Charlie kisses me goodbye.

"Be careful of the ruts in the road," I tell him. He nods and shuts the bedroom door.

Thank God he's gone. It's seemed so unromantic, so unbridelike to tell my groom I had to go to the bathroom. Now, I step over the puppy on the newspaper and hurry down the hall.

I smile at the stains on the sheet. I'm no longer a girl. I'm a woman. Maybe it was all that wine, maybe it was the lubricant, but the second time with Charlie was so much better. I still feel warm and glowing inside.

I strip the bed and load my arms with linen. I tiptoe through the house. I hope the stains will wash out.

I stop at the laundry room door. A stranger with gold hair that could use a good shampoo and conditioner bends over the machine. Sprinkling soap on clothes, she must be the miracle worker who has swept away years of Lottie's dust.

My face burns. I don't want her to see our stains. I turn, start to go.

She jerks her head. "There's plenty of room left."

She's about my age, but taller than I am. She has a thin face and wary blue yes. Something about those eyes is so familiar.

She starts to take the sheets from me. "I'll do it," I say. I drape the bundle over my arm, so she can't see the stains. I dump some Tide detergent in the folds of the sheets somewhere near where I think the stains are.

"We can put a little ammonia in the wash," she says. The miracle worker has a dry voice. She tucks our towels and sheets into the machine. She adds a foul smelling liquid. "Good thing Miss Carey didn't have much wash this time."

Why does she call Lottie Miss Carey instead of Mrs. Klein?

She twists the faucets. Water gushes. "You must be Pam," she says. "Your aunt has told me all about you. You're a brain, right?"

I want to tell her I can't clean house the way she can, but for some reason the words won't come. Why do I feel as if we've met before?

"She's a wonderful woman," the girl says. "Imagine, I'm just a stranger and she sends food home with me." A small, quick smile brightens her face. "I was so lucky. As soon as I put my ad up at the high school employment office, she answered."

The girl is gangly and flat-chested, but her arms and legs are strong. She could be a tennis player or a swimmer. Those arms could churn like paddles. My knees start to buckle. I swallow and blink back tears. I would bet anything that once when she was very small and those arms were just like sticks, she tried to swim back to the person she loved most.

I inch closer. "You're – "

Her lips move. The sound of her name gets lost in the swishing of clothes and the chug of the machine.

"Rose?" I shout.

She nods.

I grab her hand. "I'm so happy to see. . .to meet you."

Her sharp chin juts. She looks surprised. She's wondering why the niece of her employer is holding her hand as if she never wanted to let go.

I can't stop staring at her. I used to beg to comb her hair and feed her peaches. I loved to hug her and feel her baby breath hot on my neck. When she was tired of being held and wriggled free from my grasp, I cried. Now the plumpness and color to her cheeks are gone. They're scooped out, hollow. She looks as if she really did belong to the woman in the gray coat and not to us.

She squeezes my fingers and shakes her head. "You are the nicest family." She is talking over my shoulder to Lottie, who is standing in the doorway.

Gripping her coffee mug, Lottie is taking in every detail of our reunion. There's a warning in her eyes. She's afraid I 'm going to say too much. She doesn't have to worry. I would never hurt her or Rose. I've never loved my aunt more than I do this minute.

"Rose is a find," Lottie says.

Rose's face is softer now. She's studying Lottie and there's a dreamy look in her eyes. The machine hums. The three of us seem sewn together by invisible threads.

Charlie creeps up behind Lottie. "What is this? The ladies' laundry room convention?"

Rose steps back. She holds up her hand and begins counting with her fingers, "I did the kitchen floor, counters, windows, and that shelf under the sink. Should I move the refrigerator and get to work behind there?"

"You should take a break," her employer tells her. "There's fresh strawberry lemonade and some peaches. "Rose, this is my new nephew."

"How you doing?" Charlie says.

"Miss Carey told me," Rose looks at me. "You all got married. Congratulations. You're lucky to be in this family."

Suddenly, I'm hugging her, cupping my hands around her sharp shoulder blades. "Don't you know anything?"

Behind me, Lottie sucks in her breath.

I hold Rose close, stroke her hair. "You have to hug me. I'm a bride. I'll bring you luck. If you hug me, someday you'll be as happy as I am today."

•

I breathe in the fresh sweet smell of peaches. Bees hum in the clover. High, white clouds sail overhead. The world is so alive. I touch Charlie's arm. Sparklers shoot off inside of me. Charlie has made me part of this bright world.

Lottie twists a stem off a branch. "I hate to see you leave."

"We don't want to go." Charlie looks at the house, the honeymoon bedroom, and the big woman picking peaches. "What if my mother never forgives me?" Charlie drops a peach in the bag. "What if she wants nothing more to do with me?"

Lottie turns and looks at the porch where Rose shakes a mop. Dust falls like snow over the bushes. "She won't stop loving you. She's your mother."

She hands me the bag of peaches. "These should last you for awhile." Then she squints, and gets a funny look in her eyes. She digs through her apron pocket. "He would want me to do this." She puts Jacob's ring on Charlie's finger.

Sunlight pours around oak branches and makes the ring the tired salesman wore for twenty years look new. Rose comes and stands behind Lottie. Lottie hugs Charlie and me. "Just remember, you're each other's family now."

I rest my head on Lottie's soft shoulder. I want to stay here with her and Charlie and Rose forever. "I'm so happy," I whisper.

Charlie hugs Lottie a final time, and shakes hands with Rose.

He slides behind the steering wheel.

"Don't worry about your mother," Lottie tells him. "She'll get used to everything."

I hug Rose.

Lottie opens Charlie's car door, sets the shoe box with the puppy on the floor. Old Chartreuse shakes and starts. Charlie rolls down the car window. "Keep right behind me."

I sit in my Plymouth and turn the key. I wave at the house, the yellow roses, the two women standing there, and then I follow Charlie down the road.

•

I tell Aunt Lottie's ring, my wedding ring, "When my father sees how happy I am, he'll be happy, too. He will love Charlie."

I spot my father's cab. Mickey keeps asking for a different taxi stand, but his boss, the owner of the Bayside Cab, says people expect the ex-boxer turned cabbie at the corner of Fourth and Wilshire. Like the statue of Saint Monica or the Totem Pole at the park, my father has become a local landmark.

I rap on the window. The local landmark looks up from a sports page and frowns. He doesn't like me hanging around his cab. I scare away the real customers. He eyes a man carrying a barbecue grill, spatula and tongs. The little man in the business suit may need a cab. "Whatever it is, make it snappy," my father says.

"Charlie and I got married." I breathe in stale cigarette smoke. "In Tijuana yesterday."

Mickey bows his head. "Jesus, Mary and Joseph." Is he praying? "Why the hell did you do a damn thing like that?"

Two cars away, a car trunk pops open. The man with the barbecue grill owns an Edsel.

Mickey waves the newspaper with a photo of Sandy Koufax in my face. "How's the punk going to take care of you? We're not talking about a Sandy Koufax or a Maury Wills here."

"I'm going to take care of me."

"Your living in a boarding house wasn't bad enough? Now, you'll be moving to the sidewalk at Thrifty's. You'll be that cowboy's neighbor." He points to a transient in dirty boots and a torn flannel shirt hunched against the sun-warmed tile wall. "I want you to have a home, a real home. You don't know how hard the world is."

Because I'm Mrs. Charlie Fain, my father thinks I'm going to live on a sidewalk.

"You could be someone with an education," he tells me.

"I am someone with an education. I'm still going to go to school."

"You'll be too busy wiping snot from your husband's nose."

"Daddy, I wanted you to be happy for me. For us."

There's a long silence. "I wanted more for you," my father says.

"I'm just fine," I tell him. "I have what I want."

Static bleats on the care radio. A voice says a customer at the landing dock on the pier wants Little Red Carey to pick him up."

"Do you want me to ride with you?" I ask.

"We're not supposed to have non-paying passengers."

"We're leaving for Cotton Valley in two hours," I say.

My father wipes his tears on the sleeve of his cabbie jacket. He opens the passenger door for me. "Does that infield up there still have pot holes?" he says.

I nod.

"Shin Splint City," he says.

•

Maybe miracles can happen. Mrs. Fain is smiling at us as if she's happy to see us. "The graduation pictures came out beautifully," she tells Charlie. "Come and see for yourself." Her smile doesn't stop at Charlie but goes right on to me. "You come see, too. After all, someday it will be your turn."

Someday in the future, she will be at my graduation. And Charlie will be beaming. But Mrs. Fain doesn't know I'm part of her family. Charlie slipped Jacob's ring in his pocket. I sneaked Lottie's ring into my purse. "We should ease mom into this sort of gradually," Charlie had told me.

Now, she ushers us through her living room into her tiny bedroom with all those bookshelves. She's studying Charlie. "You've come a long way. Are you sure the team can spare you?"

Charlie looks embarrassed. "We had yesterday off. We have a night game tonight."

"Was your friend Warren able to find you?" she asks.

"Ashburn?" Charlie says. "He was looking for me?"

"I told him you were in Cotton Valley. He said he was going up right away. I assumed he got in touch with you."

Charlie glances at me. I should have told him about Warren. It just seemed easier not to. If I tell him now, Mrs. Fain will know for sure that I was up in Cotton Valley with her son.

"The team was on a long road trip," Charlie says. "Maybe Warren came by then."

"It's a shame he missed you," Mrs. Fain turns to me. "I understood that he was a friend of yours as well."

I nod and listen to the rattle of my wedding ring bumping against my car keys in my purse. Mrs. Fain is no dummy. She probably recognized my voice on the phone. She probably has guessed that this isn't a social call. We should tell her the truth right now.

"Here are the pictures," she says with determination. If she has her way she's going to keep this visit polite and uneventful. She picks up her photograph and presses it into Charlie's hands.

The woman in the picture wears a cap and gown and waves the rolled up piece of paper in her hand as if it were a magic wand. Her certificate from the university will get her what she wants. Mrs. Fain has been her own fairy godmother.

Now she leans against a desk she must have gotten at a yard sale. She seems to draw courage from the solid piece of furniture. Layers of yellow paint don't hide the dents in the drawers or what look like tooth marks in the legs. Her smile says she loves the desk because it's hers. She earned it. And whatever we do to her, whatever ways we may hurt her this afternoon, we can't take this desk away from her.

"Here's one of you and me," she tells Charlie. Her skin glows. For the first time since I've known her, she's wearing lipstick and mascara. She's a pretty woman. Tonight, she seems to know it.

In the picture she holds up, Charlie has his arm around her. Now, he pats her shoulder and says, "My graduate."

Her worry lines are back. "I hope it hasn't been too much for you. Dinners alone. Games I didn't see. All that money spent on books, tuition, and gas. I hope that's not why. . ."

Her eyes slide away, they stare at her desk. Now they can see the chipped paint and the dents. Now, she can see me as the girl who was in her son's bedroom.

She studies the picture of herself in the cap and gown. "Education isn't a death. It isn't something you finish, like raising a son."

"I'll always need a mother," Charlie says.

She shakes her head. She doesn't believe him. "My neighbor, Mrs. Marco, keeps asking, 'When are you going to stop school?' 'My education,' I tell her, 'will continue for as long as I'm alive.'"

I can't help smiling for her. She sounds like Alice. But Alice didn't have her courage. After my mother left Kelso, she didn't step into a classroom again.

Mrs. Fain's stare leaves me quickly. "You know it's not too early to think about a particular person or period you want to study."

I turn from her and look at the yellow shelves. She really is generous. She doesn't hate me or see me as a seductress out to steal her son. "I like the Brontës," I tell her. "And Austen. And Woolf."

"Of course," she smiles. "We all do, all women do, I mean. But it's best for you to find someone who's been less written about." She rubs her eyes. Mascara smudges her lids. "It has to be someone you like. Someone you can live with for a long time." She sighs. "It's like a marriage."

"We have something to tell you," Charlie says.

She hunches her shoulders, sits in her desk chair. "What is it?" her voice sounds weary.

"Pam and I got married," Charlie says. "We wanted to tell you right away but we weren't sure how you would take the news."

She wriggles in her chair. "When did this happen?"

"Yesterday," Charlie says. "Pam's aunt took us to Tijuana."

She sniffs, but says nothing.

"I called Dad. He's real happy for us. I hope you will be, too."

"Maybe if your father had stayed with us, none of this would have happened." She looks at me, and then looks away. "He had a knack for making you happy. It's a knack I don't seem to have."

"Mom, this has nothing to do with you. I found the girl I love and I want to be with her."

"You're both way too young," she says. "You're just children playing house. It's not even real. Probably not even legal." Her eyes get bright. She looks at Charlie. "Aren't you under age?"

"Pamela and I are married." Charlie juts his jaw. "We had a ceremony. Señor Muñoz is a lawyer. We have all the paper work done. We just need one small favor. In order for Señor Muñoz to complete the filing," his voice begins to trail off, "we need a letter of consent from you."

Her face gets red. "I don't understand. You had a ceremony without my consent? Now, you want me to give you your consent?"

"We're married," Charlie says. "We did everything we have to do. But before Señor Muñoz can file all our paperwork we need a note from you. As soon as he gets your letter, Señor Muñoz will put the marriage on record."

"Dear God." Kicking the floor with her feet, she swivels in her chair. "It's all pretend. Children playing house. This is a sham and entirely illegal."

She's right. We're only half-married. It's not fair. Charlie is old enough to go to war, but not old enough to get married. "We love each other. We want to be together."

She looks at me with angry eyes. "This is emotional blackmail."

"Mom, we just need you to write a letter," Charlie says. "Don't you want us to be happy?"

"What I want is to start all over." Her smile is rueful. "So I could raise you right." She studies him. "But you'd still leave." She pushes her elbows against her desk and rests her face in her hands. Just touching her desk, seems to make her stronger. "When you were little, you'd invite friends over for dinner before asking my permission. You'd fix it so I couldn't say no. You haven't changed much."

"It should be up to me," Charlie says. "I'm a man. I'm a professional ballplayer. I should be able to choose whether I get married or not."

"Obviously the state doesn't agree with you." She sighs. "Marriage. Baseball. They're both about a hundred times harder than you think they are."

"Will you write that letter for me, for us?" Charlie asks.

"I won't do it," Mrs. Fain says.

I shiver in this sunny, book-filled room and look at Mrs. Fain. "My Aunt Lottie was so sure you would come around. We will never hurt each other the way that you have hurt us."

I tug Charlie's hand and lead him out of his mother's house.

22

If only one person besides Aunt Lottie and Rose were happy for us, maybe I'd feel more like a bride and less like a criminal. But Mrs. Soames, my ex-landlady, didn't want to hear the details of my real life romance and wedding. As soon as she saw my band, she knew I was no longer in need of a room for the unattached. Her interest in me flickered and went out. Knitting pink booties for a granddaughter she's never seen, she silenced me and turned back to her movie on television. Deborah Kerr isn't dancing with a king in this one. She and Cary Grant are having an affair to remember.

I pack the books Warren and I bought together for our future home. I fold my clothes and linens and take the picture of Alice from the dresser. I walk down the empty hall of The Palms and knock on Luna Livingston's door. Maybe she will be happy for Charlie and me. But Luna isn't home. Then, I remember it's band day at the Ocean Park Pavilion. Luna isn't here to wish me luck or tell me that Charlie and I did the right thing. I shut the door of The Palms Hotel behind me. Ocean fog blows in my face.

If only Charlie had come to The Palms with me. But he wanted to go back and say goodbye to his mother. Over the noise of crickets and traffic, I listen to the movie. Deborah's had an accident and lost the use of her legs. She's confined to a wheelchair. But she's very brave. She doesn't want Cary Grant to know of her plight. He'd only pity her. She's sure she'll ruin his life. I feel a lump in my throat. Why does love have to be so hard?

I open the Plymouth trunk, stare into what looks like a dark, empty cave. Why is Mickey worried? Why is Mrs. Fain so cold?

"Haven't you forgotten something?" a voice whispers in the dark. At first, I think it's Cary Grant telling Deborah just how foolish she's been. But the voice is too close to be coming from Mrs. Soames' television.

"Miss Carey, I mean, Mrs. Fain, are you leaving town without even saying goodbye?"

Warren's hot breath blows on my neck. He makes my new name sound like a curse. He steps out of the shadows. From the light of a street lamp, and the glare of the TV, I can see him clearly now. His mouth looks funny, twisted. His eyes are swollen. "You didn't even bother to tell me." His voice is shaking. "That's how damn important I am to you."

"I was going to tell you."

"Right." He slams down the trunk. "After all the important stuff like packing."

"How did you know about the marriage?" I ask.

"Mrs. Fain, the real Mrs. Fain called me. She wanted me to talk to you and Charlie and give up the idea of this marriage." Warren looks as if he'd like to rip the trunk from its hinges. "What about our plans?"

"We can still be. . ."

"Friends? When you married, or almost married the enemy? Charlie Fain is a dumb jock."

"He's sweet and sensitive and kind."

Warren steps close to me. "In a year you'll come crying to me that your husband doesn't understand you."

He hugs me hard, as if he'd like to crush me. His breath smells of cherry lifesavers. The smell brings back so many memories of stolen kisses. The boy, who kissed me, the boy who said he loved my pilgrim soul, now pounds my back and cries, "Damn you, Mrs. Fain."

•

The hot, dry Cotton Valley wind blows in through the bedroom window. Charlie doesn't have a dresser. I settle Alice's picture on a cardboard box. I line Charlie's trophies on the floor. I place the lion I won at the pier on the sleeping bags.

I stack Warren's and my books in the corner of Charlie's bedroom. Gently, I put the Yeats on top. Maybe, someday Warren and I can go through our books together. Maybe, someday Warren will forgive me for marrying Charlie.

I hang my white skirt and blouse with the Peter Pan collar next to Charlie's high school sweater.

Charlie's bedroom is now my bedroom, too.

•

When they see my ring they will know it's official. I'm a baseball wife. I shut the Plymouth door and step out into the bright Cotton Valley sun. I hurry toward the field. I feel so light, as if my feet were rushing me forward.

"Congratulations on your wedding." Bonnie runs to catch up with me. She touches my elbow. She's all in pink. Her hair is freshly curled. She looks like a bridesmaid. Her word *wedding* sings in my head. "Charlie told Steve all about his plans," she says. "I didn't say anything to the other wives. They thought you were already married."

"Well, I am married now." I stop walking so fast. "That's what's important."

"Of course it is," Bonnie says. "Your husband was so excited he couldn't keep the news to himself. He passed out sticks of Doublemint gum to the team, wives, and fans. He told everyone, 'The most wonderful girl in the world married me.' Then, he did a somersault right on the pitcher's mound."

I look toward the field where Charlie is taking batting practice. "I'm so lucky," I tell Bonnie.

In the bleachers, Norma cups her hand around her mouth and shouts, "What you did was so romantic."

Heads turn. Walt, and his friend with a gooey eye, and the library assistant, and Mr. Nordstrom stare. "I wish Rusty and I had done it," Norma yells. Why doesn't she just borrow a bullhorn? If I'm closer to her maybe she'll stop screaming. I walk faster.

"Congratulations." Beth slides over and makes a place for me.

"You two eloped." Norma is still shouting. Everyone is the world is looking at me. I've never had so much attention. "You're just like Romeo and Juliet," Norma says.

"Rome and Juliet died." Raquel flaps her lashes at me. "But best wishes anyway."

"Let's see the ring," Norma says.

I hold up my hand.

"It's so old," Norma says. "But it's pretty."

"Simple and elegant," Bonnie says.

Beth digs through her diaper bag and pulls out a white box with a pink bow. Little Tank reaches for it. "It's for the bride," Beth tells me.

"I can't believe it's for me," I say.

"You're the only bride here." Raquel actually smiles at me.

All the wives are smiling now. The box smells of animal crackers. I slip off the bow and lift up the lid. Inside the box sits a beautiful lace top with puffed sleeves and panty bottoms. "Baby doll pajamas," I say.

"We thought the white baby doll was the naughtiest," Norma says.

"The most like something we'd like for ourselves," Raquel says.

"We talked about it, and then I dashed out and got it," Beth says.

"It's lovely, Beth. No one has ever done anything like this for me before," I say.

"You probably never got married before," Raquel says.

"It's even more than that," I tell them. "I've never had a circle of girl friends before." I shrug. "I don't know why. Since my mother died, I've stayed away from girls my age. Or they stayed away from me."

Bonnie hugs me. "You don't have to be alone again."

•

"This is my first package from home." Charlie's smile is sad. His fingers drum a little tune on a package wrapped in brown paper. "I hurt Mom so much." "Maybe she's forgiven us," I say.

I can still see her angry eyes. We tricked her. Maybe it's her turn to trick us. Maybe she sent us a diamondback rattlesnake made of rubber. "Why don't you open it?"

Charlie's long fingers keep drumming.

I get a knife from the drawer and slice the tape. "If she's forgiven us, she'll write a letter of consent and our troubles will be over."

"She loves me," Charlie says. "She'll want us to be happy."

He searches through paper and then holds up something cotton that has pink roses on a white background.

"Are those sheets?" I ask.

He nods.

"She sent us sheets?" I say.

He grins. "She knows what we'll do in them."

Does she think about her son and me in bed together? She must accept our love. She sent us sheets. Our waiting is over.

"See, I told you. She's happy for us." Charlie is shaking his head and grinning. "There should be a letter giving her consent." His fingers search through paper. "Maybe just a note. All we need is a sentence and a signature."

He frowns, and pulls out books. He rifles through a cookbook, turns it upside down and shakes it. No letter. The second book has a dark blue cover and a long title: *The Feminine Mystique*. He holds it up and a letter falls out. "Thank God." He tears open the envelope addressed to *Pam and Charlie*. "I knew she wasn't that stubborn." He beams. "We're home free now. You'll see." He holds the note in shaking hands.

I hug him hard. "Are we legal?"

"Dear ones," he reads. "Ones. That means both of us."

I step closer and lean against him. "Well?"

His face sags. He shuts his eyes. I squint at the small, neat handwriting. "There was a sale at Penney's and I thought the sheets would go nicely in your new home. Love, Mom."

I turn the note over. I shake the cookbook, and the sheets. No more messages.

She is a strange woman. She sent sheets but no consent. I was right. She did want to trick us. She found something even better than a rubber rattlesnake.

"Damn it," Charlie says. "Why is she doing this to us?"

"She's mean or crazy."

Charlie scowls. He doesn't like me calling his mother names.

"Maybe we should call her and try to reason things out."

"I can't believe she'd hurt me like this," he says.

"Does she like to tease people?"

My question makes him draw back. "I've never seen her do a mean thing." He cradles the sheets in his arms.

I want to touch his face and tell him everything will be all right. I step toward him. He turns and walks away.

•

Wearing my baby doll pajamas, I giggle and slip between the sheets with pink roses.

Charlie opens the bedroom door. "You look wonderful," he says.

If only I could think of something sophisticated and wicked to say. "Let's try out our new sheets."

23

Mozart's *A Little Night Music* drifts in from the bedroom next door. In the moonlight I hum along and count the knots in our pine ceiling. An even number says Mrs. Fain is a fair and rational person and her consent letter is in the mail. An odd number says she's vengeful and vindictive and we're still illegal. Any day now, Mrs. Gooth will be knocking on our door and telling us she needs to see our marriage certificate or she will have to ask us to leave. Mrs. Gooth will tell the baseball club we're not legally married. The wives will demand that I return the baby doll pajamas.

Charlie stirs. I touch his warm neck. We love each other. We're not committing any crimes. Whether we're totally legally married or not should be no one's business but our own.

Charlie sits up in bed.

"Did the music wake you?" I whisper. "At least she's not talking to Anton Chekhov tonight."

Charlie blinks, looks at me. "All right, you Norwegian Nerd."

Norwegian? He can't mean me.

"So you think I can't make the team?" Charlie steps out of bed. "So you want a pivot?"

"Charlie, are you all right?"

"You got a pivot," he says. His hands reach out, and catch the air. One bare foot taps the floor. He wheels. His pajama shirt flaps. His arm arcs. "Perfect pivot," he says. He punches the air. "Up yours, Nordstrom ."

"Charlie, are you awake?"

His stare at me is glassy. I'm not in his dream. He climbs back in bed, and slips under the covers. He pulls the sheet with pink roses to his chin.

"Charlie, are you OK?" I shake him. He rests his head on the pillow. His mouth opens. He smacks his lips and smiles in his sleep.

I hug myself, and gather the sheets around my shoulder. It can't be normal, playing baseball in your sleep. What is the matter with him? Is there a cure for sleepwalking or is it something you have to live through, like chicken pox? If this pivot thing is bothering Charlie why didn't he tell me about it? Does he really think he isn't good enough to make the team? What has Mr. Nordstrom been saying about him? What kind of a wife am I to not even read my husband's press clippings?

Next door, the Mozart has stopped. A curtain moves. The woman with bouffant hair was watching our floor show. Now, her shade snaps down.

In the sudden stillness, I can hear my uneven breathing. I touch Charlie's shoulder. He's asleep. He looks at peace. Maybe punching people out in your dreams is good for you. Maybe I should take a few jabs at Mrs. Fain.

I roll over and shut my eyes. But I know sleep won't come. The woman next door will start talking to Chekhov. Or Charlie will get up to field a ball. Or the San Joaquin Bullet will roar past our living room.

The whole world is crazy.

•

I step out onto the patio. The bright morning sun turns the palm fronds to gold. The dark fears of the night are behind us. Charlie, doing push-ups, glows with health. I bend down and kiss the back of his head. "I didn't know I married a sleepwalker," I say.

"I should have warned you about my escapades." Charlie smiles the all too familiar smile of a drunk who has blacked out and wants to know all the cute and curious things he has done the night before. He pours orange juice for me. He dusts off a patio chair, and stretches his long legs. "Once, when I was 7, I got up and made myself a peanut butter and jelly sandwich. So, what did I do last night?"

"What's a pivot?"

His smile dies. "It's what's keeping me from the major leagues. Did I talk about it last night?"

"You did it."

"No? Show me."

"You want me to pivot?"

His smile comes back, turns cocky. "If you can."

The concrete feels warm under my bare feet. I pretend to catch a ball. I tag a rock. I turn and curl my arm.

"A perfect pivot." His look turns sour. He downs his juice. "If you can do it, I can do it."

- 177 -

"But my whole career doesn't depend on it. If it did, maybe I'd be so worried that I'd forget everything I knew. If you could distract yourself out there, and think of something else. Put less pressure on yourself. Then, when a pivot was needed, you'd do it without thinking."

He springs to his feet, stretches, and touches my cheek. "Maybe you could read to me while I work out."

"What would you like to hear?"

"I like the poem about the bird – something about drinking and leaving the world unseen."

He wants something cheerful to begin the day. "Do you mean *Ode to a Nightingale* by John Keats?"

He shrugs. "I don't know. You're the scholar."

I open the *Oxford Book of English Verse.* I read, "My heart aches and a drowsy numbness pains my sense. . ."

His elbows touch his toes. He nods. "That's the one." His arms clap over his head. He jumps and his feet click together. He does a perfect jumping jack. "Next comes the hemlock."

•

Someone knocks on the door. I don't want to answer. I want to sit and sip my morning coffee. The knock comes again. What if a postman with a special letter for us from Mrs. Fain is at the door?

A stranger, a woman, stands on my doorstep. She's too old to be selling Girl Scout cookies and too sexy to be a Jehovah's Witness. She wears an orange halter-top, and white shorts. She has bouffant hair, glasses and knobby knees.

"May I help you?" I ask.

"I came to see if I could help you."

I know the husky voice. I know her. She's the lady who talks to dead Russian writers. I check to make sure the screen door between us is locked.

"I'm Laura Davis, your next door neighbor. I thought if you needed anything. . ." She studies the yard, and looks at devil grass choking the roses, the dead palm branches. "Maybe you could use some garden tools. I have a hose and saw."

I don't do well with neighbors. Sooner or later my father's drinking would upset people we lived near. This lady already knows Charlie's and my night secrets.

"We don't need anything." The sharpness in my voice makes her back away. Her full lips form a little girl pout. She looks at me sadly. There is a warmth in her hazel eyes that makes me regret my words.

A Siamese cat tiptoes up my steps, and sidles up to Laura Davis, and rubs its back against her bare legs. She kneels down and pats its cream and black colored head. She cradles the cat in her arms. "This is Chekhov," she says.

Her Chekhov is a cat? I sigh my relief, and tilt my face toward sunlight filtering in through the screen. My next door neighbor may be whimsical, but she's not crazy. I unlock the door. "Won't you come in?" I eye the empty Jim Beam bottle sitting on top of her trash by the road. "For coffee?"

•

I peel my nails and squint at the field. I picture Charlie doing a perfect pivot. "You can do it," I whisper.

Steve Willis at first and Tank at center field call, "Hey, batter. Hey, batter."

Charlie, at second, cups his glove around his mouth and yells at the Marysville hitter, "When palsy shakes a few sad, last gray hairs."

The batter cocks his head and strains to hear.

Charlie shouts, "Where youth grows pale, and spectre-thin and dies."

The batter watches a pitch go by.

"Where but to think is to be full of sorrow," Charlie says.

Norma looks up from her magazine. "What's he jabbering about out there?"

"John Keats." Raquel winks at me. "Very funny."

"Charlie is working on his pivot," I tell her.

Raquel cracks her gum.

"Already with thee," Charlie yells. "Tender is the night."

The batter's swing is a split second too late.

Charlie does and a jumping jack, yells "Hemlock" and runs toward the dugout.

•

"Your Keats was wonderful," I tell him.

He grins. "I was ready. Too bad there was no opportunity for the double play." He slowly slides into the passenger side. "Every part of me hurts. I can't wait to soak in the tub."

I start the engine. "I loved your double and two singles. You're getting hot."

"You know you sound like a real fan?" He pats his chest. "And I could be an English major."

"I invited Steve and Bonnie over to dinner. I hope it's OK."

"Willis's wife is the blond who looks like Sandra Dee, right?"

Of course he'd notice Bonnie in the bleachers. He's probably wishing right now that I look like her. He rubs his neck and smiles at me. "I'm sure you'll make the best dinner that ever was."

•

Why would Charlie believe I'm a good cook when he's never tasted anything I've ever made? Whatever prompted me to invite Bonnie to dinner? Maybe I should suggest we all go out. My treat. But I don't have any extra money.

I open the cookbook I got out of the library. The pages crackle. They smell new. The lady who wrote the book says she hates to cook. She makes jokes about what the big cookbooks would tell you to do. Alice used those big cookbooks and she would have blanched, pan seared, chopped and grated. Maybe this won't be so hard after all. I smile as I get the can opener, then stir cream of mushroom soup with whipped cream and pour the whole mess onto a cut up chicken. I shove the casserole into the oven. Alice wouldn't call this dinner.

Outside the summer evening is still hot. Through the window I can watch the sprinkler. Blue jays fight over the bread crumbs I left for them. I tear lettuce at the sink. The kitchen still smells of fresh paint. On the way home from the game, I stopped at a paint store. Now, I have one window trimmed. Soon, this will be the Pennsylvania Dutch blue and white kitchen I've always wanted. Charlie said I was silly. We'd be leaving before the paint was dry.

"Something smells good. And it's not the paint." Charlie is wearing only his pajama top. It shows off his beautiful legs and perfect knees. Nureyev is in my kitchen. He kisses my neck. "Sorry I was so grumpy before."

"You had a hard game. You had very little sleep. You're under a lot of pressure."

"Let's go to bed and do something about it."

"The Willises are coming soon."

His sleepy breath warms the back of my neck, "When?"

"Seven."

He wraps his arms around me. "Then, we still have lots of time."

We don't. I still have to make the salad dressing and set the table. But he feels so good leaning against me. I close my eyes, shut out the mixing bowl and bottles of vinegar and oil waiting for me on the counter.

·

The paprika makes the chicken look like a picture of a meal in a magazine.

Bonnie cuts the chicken into small pieces and takes a bite. Her face is hard to read in the soft candlelight. At least she isn't spitting the food out. At least it's edible. I take a deep breath and wait.

"This is delicious," she says. "You'll have to give me the recipe."

"I'm just a beginner, but it's easy," I tell her.

"You could probably do anything you set your mind to," Bonnie says. Her lovely face, softened by candlelight, loses its tenseness.

"I bet you do everything well," I tell her.

"She has a beautiful singing voice," Steve says.

"Do you practice?" I ask.

"Right now," she tells me, "we're concentrating on Steve."

"She really has a fine singing voice," Steve says. "She even sang a solo for our high school assembly. What was that song?"

"I didn't think you'd remember," she says.

Steve snaps his fingers. "*Smoke Gets In Your Eyes.*"

Her hands begin to shake. She puts down her fork. "Mrs. Powers. I haven't thought of her in years. She had a beautiful voice, and she wanted to be a great singer. She had been beautiful once."

"Long before we knew her," Steve says.

"She had such gorgeous red hair," Bonnie tells the candle. "And a real sense of style."

"Yeah," her husband says, "and she ended up leading a bunch of kids through *O Tannenbaum.*"

Bonnie picks up her fork and starts eating. Why doesn't she sing anymore? What made her stop doing what she loved? Steve gets to do what he loves. Why can't Bonnie? Just because you fall in love and get married doesn't mean you stop being who you are.

•

"That was a wonderful dinner, hon." Charlie says it as if I've served him a million meals and we've been married for decades. He kisses me. "Hey, Willis, want to see my baseball stuff?"

They disappear into the bedroom. "The museum," I smile. I can still feel Charlie's kiss on my forehead. "Charlie earned so many trophies. Steve must have a lot, too."

Bonnie doesn't say anything for what feels like a long time. "I keep wondering what will happen to us if Steve doesn't make it."

She worries too. Maybe all of us wives do. "Charlie tells me not to think about that," I say. "He says he never does." I take the casserole from the table. The oven mitt feels sticky. I remember pulling the baseball glove from the trash can while Mr. Nordstrom watched. "But just last night, Charlie pivoted and made a double play in his sleep."

Bonnie opens her purse, takes out a mirror and applies her lipstick. "They're under so much pressure," she says.

"Does Steve talk to you about what's bothering him?"

"Of course. Doesn't Charlie?"

"I just don't know what I can do for him." I tear half a dinner roll and open the window and toss out the crumbs for the birds.

•

"I love your living room," Bonnie says. "It's so unusual."

Is unusual good or bad? It's probably bad. We have pillows for chairs, wallpapered lampshades, and an elephant rug by the hearth. Whatever made me think wild dried buckwheat plunked in a wine bottle could pass as a centerpiece?

"It's lovely," she says.

Unusual is good. I fluff a pillow and smile at the home I'm creating. Maybe Bonnie's right. I am the kind of person who can do what she sets her mind to. I've made a comfortable place for Charlie and me.

She settles on a pillow and stretches her legs. She looks at home here. Moonlight softens the hard corners of the living room. One of my favorite songs – *This Is Dedicated to the One I Love* – comes on the radio. Suddenly I feel so happy. Bonnie and Steve think of Charlie and me as a couple.

Charlie and Steve step into the living room. Tall, blond, even-featured, they look like brothers. They sit next to us on the rug. "What about something to drink?" Steve says. "Maybe a little wine?"

He should be drinking milk. "We don't have the right glasses," I tell him.

"It tastes the same in any glass," Bonnie says. She has never had wine in a metallic tumbler – a Blue Chip Stamp purchase. She follows me into the kitchen, to the wine jug – a Regal Foods special. She looks down at her long fingernails. "That's one of the wonderful things about being in California. Even supermarkets sell good wine."

This is not good wine. Next time it will be. If we have a next time, I will buy glass glasses.

In the living room, Charlie is leaning against the knotty pine wall. "But then I start thinking, this is it – the Major Leagues. I have to do everything right." He rubs his neck. "Pam knows. I pivot in my sleep."

I grip the tumbler. "He did a beautiful pivot last night. If he can do one when he's asleep, he can do one when he's awake."

"Just trust yourself," Steve tells him.

"That's easy for you to say," Charlie says. "Your position is safe."

"There's no such position."

"But you have something to fall back on," Charlie says and turns to me. "You've heard of Willis Polo Shirts? Steve's dad."

Alice and I used to see their ads for polo shirts in the fashion magazines. No wonder Charlie is jealous. Steve Willis Senior must have everything.

Steve Willis Junior leans against Gooth's chair. "What I want to do is play ball. If they'll let me."

"They're letting you," Charlie says.

Steve Willis Junior is not drinking his wine. "If I had your talent, it would be a different story. 'Course you don't have my discipline."

"I work hard," Charlie says.

"You don't know what hard work is."

Bonnie clinks her tumbler against her husband's. "That was a lovely dinner, wasn't it?"

"He won't take my advice," Steve tells her. "He doesn't know how good he is. It came too easy to him."

"Then, why am I only in Class A?"

"A-ball is a perfectly good place to start. They'll be moving you up soon. Unless you keep blowing it."

Charlie cracks his knuckles. "You read what Nordstrom said – I got handcuffs on my ankles."

"What does he know?" I say. "For some reason you irritate him. He likes to pick on you."

"I thought everybody would be rooting for me," Charlie folds his hands in his lap. His face gets still. "They all want to cut my throat."

"Well, your attitude is a little hard to take," Steve says. "The boasting and bowing to the fans. But nobody wants you to fail."

Charlie picks a loop of yarn from the rug. "Pam's dictionary says it means *missing or insufficient*." His cruel smile finds me. "Guess what word comes after *failure* – in your dictionary."

The dark blue spine of my Oxford Dictionary stands out on the shelf. "I don't know."

"Fain," he says.

Bonnie smoothes her skirt. Steve sips wine. "Don't make it worse than it is. It's already hard enough. Right now, you're not failing. Nobody's kicked you off the team." He smiles. "You're just not succeeding."

"Then I'm failing."

"That's not how my dad taught me to look at it."

"Maybe he can afford it," Charlie says.

"Maybe he can't afford not to." Steve finishes his wine. "He got to be president of a company because he refused to call himself a failure or give up." He hands me the tumbler and stands. "Charlie, you got it all inside out."

•

I wait for him to smile and thank me for being a wonderful hostess. But he can't seem to stop watching the car. The new Porsche hums down the street past the tumbleweed and railroad tracks.

"It must be nice to be rich," Charlie says.

"He'd rather have your talent."

He walks back inside. "Let's do the dishes."

He is bringing the tumblers to the sink. He doesn't want to look at me.

"I'm sorry you're having such a hard time," I say.

Silently, he feeds scraps to Boris and then dumps chicken bones in a garbage bag and fills the sink with suds.

"Steve may be onto something," I say. "Maybe you could work harder."

"I work plenty." He rinses a plate. "See, that's why I'm not sure I should tell you things. You analyze every little piece of information. When you're not analyzing, you're correcting."

If I had remembered to buy dish towels, I could be doing something now. I watch him put dishes in the plastic drainer. "I could just listen. I don't have to analyze anything."

He studies me.

I sink into a folding chair, and rest my hands in my lap. For some reason, I think of my mother. Would she have been proud of my dinner party? Or would she be worried that I was turning into a baseball wife? Bonnie gave up singing so that they could "concentrate on Steve." I've been too busy worrying about how to cook a chicken to read a book or call the local college about classes. The single blue trimmed window I painted gleams. It makes the room look odd.

Charlie sits in a chair next to me. Our knees touch. "I just don't know if I'm going to make it," he says. "Baseball is the only thing I can do. I'm not good for anything else."

24

Come get me."

I thought it might be Bonnie calling. Or someone selling something no one wanted, like I did once: encyclopedias that weighed more than sacks of potatoes. I never guessed it would be Mickey on the other end of the line.

"I'm at the Greyhound depot," he says.

I wasn't very good selling by phone. I kept thinking of the other person, sitting in a shabby room somewhere, listening to my pitch. I feel like the listener now. "Where are you?" I ask.

"I told you. At the Greyhound."

"I mean what city are you in?"

There is a long silence. Maybe he doesn't know. Maybe he is looking at his bus ticket to find out or hoping someone will pass by, someone he can ask. "Your city, for chrissake. I came up to see my son play ball."

I start to say, "He's your son-in law," but I stop. No more correcting or analyzing from me.

"Well? Will you come get me?"

He sounds sober. He sounds tired. He traveled a long way just to see his only daughter and his new son-in-law. "I'll be there in 10 minutes," I say.

As usual, he hangs up first.

•

My father stands in front of the depot. He grips his worn sports bag as if it were his only possession. He wears his cab uniform pants and an emerald green sports shirt. Freckles the muddy brown of river stones cover his tired face. I throw my arms around him and kiss his scratchy face. "It's wonderful to see you."

He says, "You took long enough." He ducks into the Plymouth and puts the bag on his lap. "Is the car running good?"

"Wonderful," I tell him. "It made the trip from L.A. with no problem."

He nods. "McAtee's a good mechanic. I'm glad we put that rebuilt engine in two years ago."

Today, he's the good father, reminding himself he takes care of his daughter's car. Today, I'm the good daughter, proud of my competent father. But he can't mention his friend Rick McAtee without both of us remembering the night Mickey drove this same Plymouth through Rick's new picture window – all because Rick said Mickey needed to spend more time with me.

"The engine sounds funny," he says. "Did you remember to put in oil?"

"Of course."

"Of course, nothing. You burned up that first engine."

He never told me to check the oil. He just told me he was loaning me his car. He could get along on his motorcycle. That was two years ago and he still hasn't asked to have his car back. He is a caring father. "I'll treat you to a cheeseburger," I say.

"That engine was sweeter than this one. Original equipment, you see. Built to last."

"I found a place nearly as good as Waldo's," I say.

He rubs his jaw. "I can try out my new tooth." He shows me it with his mischievous little boy smile. "I had a spill on my Suzuki."

He had another accident. I should give him his sturdy Plymouth back. He doesn't have a chance on that rickety motorcycle.

"You have to stop drinking and driving," I say.

He rubs a frayed seam on the canvas bag. "Nearly as good as Waldo's, huh?"

"I mean it," I tell him. "While you still have some of your – original equipment."

My father smiles at me. He touches the back of my hand on the steering wheel. A moment later, he is laughing.

•

"Wind in your face, roar of the crowd, crack of the bat." Mickey marches ahead of me to the bleachers with a Jimmy Cagney swagger. "There's nothing like a ball game, is there?"

I have a headache. His good cheer wears me out. Any minute now he'll be telling me a story from the days he was 12 and traveled with the Tacoma Otters in the old Pacific Coast League. He'll be happy remembering his days as a batboy. Then, he'll look at his shoes in need of polish, his baggy cabbie trousers. Then, he'll want a drink. Our wonderful visit will turn into a nightmare.

He rubs his hands together and looks at the field. "The same damn pot holes," he says happily. "You could break a leg out here. Ah, well, this is the minor leagues. What do you expect?"

One beer is all I'll let him have.

"Good turn out," he says.

"There are the wives," I tell him, then scold myself for not steering him to the visitors' side. I don't want him drinking in front of anyone I know.

Whistling, he steps up the first rung. He sits next to Bonnie. "Which one's your hubby?" he asks.

She smiles at me, at Boris at the end of the leash in my hand. She smiles at my cab driver father, who cannot be anything like her millionaire father in law. She points and says, "First base."

Mickey squints toward first, then finds Charlie in the infield. "He's as handsome as my son-in-law out there. Why, they look like twins. Tweedledum and Tweedledee."

He leans back, content with his insight. He is back on familiar turf now. He is the hero of an Irish-American movie – the rough who has been a boxer and is now a successful manager or the priest with a heart of gold. He will borrow (imitate?) the charm of actors like Cagney, O'Brien, Crosby, hoping to camouflage his real character: the rebellious and sometimes rude person he has become. But he's not rude now. He's friendly and happy to be out in an afternoon of sun, instead of driving a cab in smoggy L.A. Why am I so hard on him?

"Tweedledum and Tweedledee – *Alice In Wonderland*," he tells Bonnie in his best conspiratorial whisper. "Fine book."

For a moment, Bonnie is speechless. She is fighting a grin. She knows.

I take *Moll Flanders* from my shopping bag. I'm not going to be like Bonnie and stop doing what I do best. Even though I'm missing the summer school course on the history of the English novel, I can still read the books that are required for the class.

"I hope Steve wasn't too hard on Charlie last night," Bonnie tells me.

I look up from my book.

"I don't know what gets into him sometimes," she says.

I balance the puppy with *Moll Flanders* in my lap and say nothing.

"Charlie's been so quiet out there today," Bonnie says. "Not himself at all." I smell her apple perfume. "I'm sorry if Steve got him down."

"It isn't Steve," I say. "Charlie doesn't like my suggestions." I sigh and wonder how Charlie is going to feel about my father sitting in the stands and watching every move he makes? I try to read but the bright sun makes the words blur on the page. I put on my sunglasses. The words get lost in darkness.

"How much of the game did we miss?" Mickey asks.

Bonnie leans forward, taps Beth's shoulder. "What inning is this?"

Beth consults with Norma, then turns and smiles. "We think it's the third."

"Think?" Mickey squints at the blank scoreboard, then looks at my book. "Don't any of you watch?"

"We watch," Beth says.

"We talk," Bonnie says.

Norma is looking at my book. "Usually Pam knows the score."

"Of course," Mickey closes my book. "My daughter is a fan."

I re-open the book and shade my eyes with my hand.

Beth's baby dribbles crumbs on his mother's shoulder and on my father's shoes.

"Cute little fellah," Mickey says. "Is he a fan, too?"

Beth's eyes lose their wary look. "His daddy, Tank, is the center fielder. This is Little Tank."

Mickey pulls out his key ring and hands it to the baby. Little Tank shakes the ring and smiles a five-tooth smile. Mickey's house and motorcycle keys jingle.

"I hope you have an extra set," I whisper.

"You worry too much," my father says.

I wipe my sunglasses on the edge of my skirt and watch a batter foul off a ball. On the next pitch, he bangs a hard grounder up the middle. The shortstop gets a late jump. Charlie dashes over, scoops the ball into his glove. A man from first heads closes in on second, where the shortstop now moves to take the throw. But Charlie runs the ball to the base himself, steps on it, and throws to first for the double play.

"Way to go!" Mickey shouts.

Charlie, trotting off the field, stares out at the bleachers.

"Shouldn't he have thrown to second?" Bonnie asks Beth.

"Nah," Mickey tells them. "The shortstop already blew it. Charlie, he knows the guy's rattled, couldn't trust him. He sees he has time. Gutsy play."

I draw a deep breath, puff my cheeks, and then release the air slowly. Charlie did do the right thing. I think. He did get the double play.

I shade my eyes and begin to read.

"The kid sure looks good in the field," Mickey says. "How's his stick?"

Beth turns. Her eyes are wide.

I put my finger on the page to mark my place.

"He hits in streaks," I say as quickly as possible. "I'm not really sure just how he's doing."

"How would you know?" Mickey says. "You got your nose in a book."

"You're the one who wanted me to stay in school."

"But you're here now, aren't you? At least you could pay attention."

Beth turns back again.

"Charlie hasn't mastered the pivot," I say in a lower voice. "The second baseman has to catch the ball with his back to the runner and –"

"– turn and throw for the double play. I wasn't born yesterday, for Chri. . ." The former bat boy for the Tacoma Otters clears his throat. "It's all foot work, you see. A ballplayer's got to be quick on his feet. It's the same for a boxer. Got a jump rope?"

Both Beth and Norma turn now. Bonnie covers her smile.

I remember Mickey taking me and my friends and our jump ropes to the gym to show us the right way to skip rope. He showed us the way he had trained grown men to jump rope. I can see him telling little girls in pigtails to trust their feet.

Mickey shrugs. "Still the same scoreboard here," he tells no one in particular. "I'm sure of it."

•

"Good stance," Mickey says.

"He's been swinging too early," I tell him.

Charlie hits the next pitch hard. The ball bounces off the pitcher's glove and before the pitcher can pick it up and throw, Charlie is at first.

"Perfect," Mickey says. "You think he swings too early? He hit it right on the button."

I pet Boris. "He doesn't steal much now. He says his feet feel like bricks."

Mickey nods. "If you can't trust your feet, you can't do anything." From his shirt pocket he takes out a plastic case. He puts on reading glasses that perch on bumps of his prizefighter's nose. The ebullient motion picture Irishman is gone, replaced by Red, the athlete, cab driver, inventor, manager of athletic talent. Shrewd blue eyes flecked with yellow stare at the runner. "He can take a bigger lead off this pitcher. The guy rattles easy. No move to first, either" He presses his lips together. "First base coach is asleep out there."

Bonnie is covering her smile again.

Mickey stands and cups a hand to his mouth. "Get off the base!"

I dig my fingers into my palms. Charlie is going to hate me for sure. He looks at my father and me. Mickey waves toward second. With a nod, Charlie widens his lead from first. The pitcher turns, and throws to the base. Charlie gets back in plenty of time.

"Not even close!" Mickey yells, and his arms wave harder. "Get off of there. Get off. Get off."

Now, Mr. Nordstrom is staring at Mickey. Maybe Mr. Nordstrom will write a column about the crazy fan who thought he was a coach. On the next pitch, Charlie steals second.

A little lady with lavender curls and a score card on her lap yells, "Charge!" Mickey shakes his head and mutters. "He should see these things himself."

"Mr. Reisner said Charlie takes too many chances," I say. "Now Charlie is afraid."

"If the kid doesn't want to take chances, he's in the wrong game."

"Mr. Reisner's a big fan of yours," I tell him. "He used to see you fight in Sacramento."

Mickey nods. "The pitcher's shook now."

He isn't listening. This man, my father, who is always so hungry for praise, for proof that once he really was a champion, now just waves his arms and whispers, as though the runner at second could hear, "He might have third, too."

Out there, Charlie is grinning.

He steals third.

Picker fans clap. Walt puts two fingers in his mouth and whistles so loud, Boris's puppy, ears twitch. I close *Moll Flanders*. Bonnie squeezes my arm. "Aren't you proud?"

Mickey nods at the runner at third base. Tall, sure, ready, Charlie takes a lead.

I swallow hard. "He's not going to try to steal home?"

Beth and Norma turn in their seats. Mickey gives them a soft smile and sits. "Relax, ladies. Nobody's going anywhere now." He squints at me, and shakes his head. "I thought I taught you about taking dumb chances. Steal home. Ridiculous."

I watch the dog.

"Well," Bonnie says after the next pitch, "Charlie certainly has got his confidence back."

Charlie has, yes.

•

I use my new tongs to pull out the corn. I look at the boiling water and picture Mickey and Charlie yelling at each other over the table. Maybe Mickey is slamming his hand down, or Charlie is waving his fist in Mickey's face. I put the corn on the platter.

I carry the corn to the picnic table outside. Mickey and Charlie are sitting together in peace. Maybe we can get through this meal. Maybe we can be a real family.

"A single, a double, and a home run. You're hot, kid." Mickey bites into his cheeseburger. "Not bad," he tells me.

"I put in garlic and a dash of Worcestershire sauce, just the way you do."

Mickey takes another bite. "Not bad at all. I wish I didn't have to leave." He turns to Charlie. "I'd like to see what you're going to do tomorrow."

"We'll clean the Lodi Crushers' clocks." Charlie pours catsup on his meat. He's going to drown out the burger's subtle flavor. "Can't you stay?" he asks Mickey.

I smile at the new salt and pepper shakers. We are a real family. Charlie is glad my father is here.

"I told Kathleen I'd take the 8-o'clock bus home. I got to work. Plus, she's the jealous type. I'm away from her half an hour, she thinks I'm in someone else's pants."

"She knows you came to see us," I say.

"Yep. She's crazy."

Charlie laughs. "Well, you brought me luck today."

"Luck nothing," Mickey says. "You just stopped acting self-conscious. You're back to your old self now. I can't figure out what got into you, kid. I'm glad it's gone."

"Did Steve upset you?" I ask.

With a nod, Charlie chews the hamburger. "He started me thinking last night, who is Charlie Fain without the flash?"

"Worst thing a ballplayer can do," Mickey spreads margarine on the corn, "is think."

"Charlie's thinking all the time out there," I tell him.

"Concentrating," Mickey says. "Not the same as thinking. Good concentration keeps your mind on the game."

Charlie is nodding. "I was always so busy figuring out how I was doing, what I looked like out there, I lost track of myself and the game."

"You weren't concentrating." Mickey has a mouthful of corn. "It's a terrible thing."

"I was all flash."

"Terrible."

"But," Charlie tells him, "if you stop all the flash and just play it straight, how do you know if you're any good?"

"That's the hell of it, kid. You don't."

Charlie shivers. "Sometimes when I'm out there, I think I'm going to pee in my pants."

"But you always looked so confident," I say.

"An act," Charlie tells me. "I thought if I faked it long enough, maybe I'd believe it myself."

My father puts down the ear of corn. "You get scared in the ring, too. I got so scared I shook worse than when I had the DTs."

Like two children who've just admitted they're afraid of the dark, they smile at each other.

The gate clicks open. In lavender pedal pushers and a smear of lipstick that changes the shape of her mouth, Mrs. Davis tiptoes on the stone walk. "Oh, I didn't know you had company. I just came for the saw." She studies the brown palm branches. "That is, if you're done."

Mickey stands, offers his hand. "I'm Michael Carey, Pamela's father."

She glances at his wide wedding ring, the widest band Kathleen could find. "Laura Davis," she says.

"Laura. Very pretty name."

Trouble.

Charlie starts to clear the dishes. Reluctantly, I step into the dark garage and search for the saw. It hangs where I left it. I remember the empty Jim Beam bottle in Laura Davis's trash. I don't want them to get to know each other well enough to discover that they drink the same brand of whiskey. Heads bent, they are sitting together at my table.

"Laura's a librarian," Mickey tells me. "My daughter's going to be an English professor, did she tell you?"

I feel like an angry kindergarten teacher now. "It's 7:15."

Mickey eyes the sunset. "What about dessert? Charlie said he was making strawberry shortcake. Do you like strawberries, Laura?"

"Mickey," I say. "We have to go to the depot."

He seems to shrink in the chair. He sighs. Suddenly, he gets to his feet. "You're right. Those Greyhound people don't run on Carey time." He takes the saw from my hand. "The least I can do is carry this home for Laura."

Before I can speak, the good neighbor gives me a jovial Bing Crosby wave and leads the way to the gate.

"He'd better be back in three minutes," I say.

Charlie comes out with a sponge. "Why are you treating him like a child?"

"Guess."

"He hasn't done anything wrong."

"Not yet."

Charlie frowns at me. Maybe I am being too hard on Mickey. I always think the worst.

"Didn't you see him in the stands?" Charlie follows me into the house. "He was rooting for me." He stops at the sink, runs a finger over the edge of a plate. "He made me feel like I could do anything I wanted out there."

Inside of my 6-foot husband, a small boy touches his Davy Crockett cap for luck and waits for a daddy who is never coming home. Mickey remembers what it's like to be small and scared, and Mickey remembers what it's like to feel as though you could do anything you wanted to do.

I put my arms around Charlie and stand on tiptoes. "You're right. He came to see you play, not to cause trouble. He can tell time, read bus schedules."

He knows he has a wife waiting.

25

Ⅰf we don't leave in five minutes, Mickey will miss his bus. Purse and Plymouth keys in hand, I wait by the front door, listen to Charlie washing the dishes, think about the other window I promised I would trim in blue today, think about how another day has gone by and I haven't called the local college. I think about what is taking so long next door.

I have to step over the hose and avoid the new sprinkler head watering the rose bush. Every morning I've dumped coffee grounds around the scraggly rose bush, a trick I learned from Alice and Aunt Lottie. Now, my rose bush is sporting new red leaves. I open the gate and march next door.

•

They are on the floor. A coffee table stands between them. The table has been turned upside down. There is what looks like a twirler's baton stuck under that table.

I put my face closer to the window. There are no liquor bottles on the carpet. Maybe everything is going to be all right. "It's such a wonderful idea," Mrs. Davis is saying. "I don't know why someone didn't think of it before. It's so handy, especially for women." She winks at my father. "We just don't have your muscles."

The smell of garlic and tomatoes blows from her kitchen. A small nautical clock on the mantle ticks. At the Greyhound depot two miles away, the bus is waiting. I step back from the window and turn toward the door.

Mickey has already spotted me. "What are you doing here?"

"You're going to miss your bus."

"You're standing in the shrubs," he says.

"You'll be late," I tell him. "I came to get you."

The look he gives me tells me he knows I came to spy on him. He marches to the door and invites me in as if he lived here. "She understands," he says.

Laura Davis is smiling.

"She thinks it's going to make me a fortune, too," he says.

Laura Davis is nodding.

He steps back to the overturned table, and raps a leg with his knuckles. "This is my latest invention. It's a motorcycle jack."

"He should call it the Carey Jack," Mrs. Davis says. "The jack you can carry."

Somehow or other, that upside down table and the baton represent the jack. I stare at it for a moment, unable to grasp the meaning. "Yes, I see," I tell them.

"Laura used to ride a Honda."

I am unable to picture that either.

She steps on the end of the baton. Miraculously, and with one hand, she rights the table. "His version folds," she says, picking up the baton. "It fits in a purse. Isn't that amazing?"

That is the word I would choose for it, too. "Daddy, we have to go."

"Not yet," he says. "First, we have to go to Sears."

"Your father is so impulsive." Mrs. Davis giggles. One of her front teeth is chipped. Maybe she fell off her Honda. "He knows just how to encourage people."

"It's a gift," I say. "His real problem is telling time."

He grins at me. "I called the depot. Another bus leaves at 10." He puts an arm on Mrs. Davis's shoulder. "Laura will take me."

"I promise," she says.

"Right after we hit Sears," he tells me. "You have a Sears, don't you?"

I nod.

He nods back. "Of course you do. Everybody's got a Sears." He gives the plump shoulder a squeeze. "That's the beauty of the Carey Jack. It goes everywhere, too." Her eyes have a cheerleader's shine. She believes in him. Alice used to believe in him when he was in the ring. Kathleen believes in him now, when she's checked and made sure he's paid the bills. How much trouble can they get into at Sears?

"Have a good time," I tell them. "Call me tomorrow."

My father's words follow me out into the night. "You're a good daughter."

The good daughter walks home.

•

Charlie is waiting for me in bed. He looks wonderful. For once, Laura Davis won't be peering at us through her window. My father will be keeping her busy. I have two choices. I can either brood about Mickey or I can dive in bed and make mad, passionate love to my husband. I kick off my shoes and jump in.

Charlie grabs me. "I kept thinking about you on the diamond today."

"I never stop thinking about you," I tell him. "Charlie, could you call your mother tomorrow? Ask if she's going to write that letter for us?"

"Yes." Charlie slides a big hand down my back.

"Maybe she's already written it, and sent it to Señor Muñoz herself."

"I'm sure she has." Charlie's hand slides under my panties.

•

I dream that my mother is in the bleachers. She takes a tube of lipstick, a comb, and a compact from her purse. They fly from her hand, through the stands, toward me.

The compact hits me first. The lipstick and comb pelt me a moment later. "You weren't supposed to get married," Alice yells. "You're still a baby. You're supposed to grow up and take care of yourself. You're supposed to have a career."

I wake up. I had another bad dream about Alice? Why do I keep having them?

I slide closer to Charlie, and hold him while he sleeps. With luck this will work, I tell myself.

With luck, I won't be afraid to close my eyes.

•

Like a happy little elf, he whistles while he works. Dust covers his good shirt and uniform trousers. At the end of a furrow, he turns the tiller, sets the tines back into sandy soil and starts a new row.

Laura Davis follows him past our bedroom window.

It is 3 a.m. and they are out there gardening by moonlight. They are kicking up stones and dirt. Above the roar of the tiller, I hear my father laughing.

I hear the phone ringing.

It will all go away, I tell myself. The tiller, the phone, the laughing will go away.

I pick up the phone.

"Where is he?" Kathleen is shouting, as if she knew her husband would be outside making noise with some motor from some machine. "I waited at the depot for two hours."

Mickey is letting Mrs. Davis have a turn at the tiller now. Mickey is watching her rump. "He's here," I say into the phone. "He's right here."

"Let me talk to him."

I think of lies for him. He tried to call but the line was busy. There was a problem with our phone, with the Plymouth. He's out there right now working on my car's carburetor. He's been out there for hours. He's so tired. He's so sweet. He is a saint.

"Who is she?" Kathleen says.

"Really, he's right here sleeping. He'll be on the first bus in the morning. I promise. We had car trouble. The carburetor."

"Why didn't he take a cab to the depot?"

"He'll be on the first bus in the morning Kathleen. He'll call you."

She breathes the way some people cry. "Well, he better. And he better say he loves me first thing."

He is dancing down the row Mrs. Davis is tilling.

"He loves you," I say.

"Tell him I miss him and I love him, too."

I hold the phone to my ear, listen to the dial tone, and watch my father pick a flower and hand it to the woman steering the rototiller. What I see with my eyes open scares me, too.

•

I want my father to be a normal human being. Is that too much to ask? Harriet Nelson never had to ask where Ozzie was at 3 a.m. I tie the bathrobe cord around my middle and, for the second time tonight, I march to my neighbor's house.

"He makes dreams come true," Mrs. Davis tells me as she opens her living room door. She doesn't smell of Jim Beam. She smells of newly turned earth. She pours cocoa for me at her table. "I always wanted a big garden, but the only way to get rid of all that grass was to invest in a big machine."

On the other side of her kitchen window, dirt swirls in the breeze. There's not a blade of grass anywhere out there now. "Did you have to garden at 3 in the morning?" I ask.

"Well, your father has a bus to catch. He's very responsible, you know. I was afraid I wouldn't know how to run the tiller. But your father said if I could understand the Carey Jack, I could understand a tiller."

He comes in through the back door. He rubs dust from his face with the Irish linen handkerchief Kathleen gave him. "We ought to put some water on it. You got more wind up here than I figured."

I take a deep sniff. No Jim Beam on him either.

She puts her hand on mine. "Can you imagine – he started the machine right on the AstroTurf at Sears."

This I can imagine.

"Then, he steered it right out of the store and down the street. It was too big to fit in my car."

"Those curbs," he says, pocketing his handkerchief, "they were kind of tough at first. But I got the hang of it."

"You'd be surprised how many cars stopped to let him through the intersections, even though they had a green light."

I drink cocoa. "I'm surprised the police didn't stop you."

"What for? I was just doing a neighbor a favor."

"A neighbor?"

"Your neighbor. I know what it is to want to grow things. Remember when I dug all those irrigation ditches around the yard on Hibiscus Street?" He leans close to Mrs. Davis. "I plumbed gray water from the tub and sink out there, you see. We had the best garden in the neighborhood."

We did. Alice did. He did help, turning the compost, mending the hoses. He pokes at packets of seeds on the table. "You want to get these in the ground today. That's all decomposed granite you got out there, so you'll have fine drainage. You'll want to compost it though. Then you'll have something."

Mrs. Davis is smiling at him with love in her eyes. "Thank you, Michael. And for such a lovely evening."

He shakes her hand as if they were saying goodbye at Sunday school. He stands and rubs the back of his neck. "Well, come on," he tells me. "Finish that coca and get me to the depot."

•

My Charlie is wonderful. He recited *Ode to a Nightingale* out in the field and made two perfect pivots for two perfect double plays. He's hot at the plate, a single in the first inning, a double in the third, a triple in the seventh, and a home run in the ninth. I'm wonderful, too. I read three chapters of *Moll Flanders* while I watched Charlie.

Mr. Nordstrom is waiting by my Plymouth. I want to tell him how wrong he was about Charlie. When he sees us coming, he starts toward us. His gait is odd. He leans his weight on one leg, then swivels the other in front of him. The leg in front is straight and stiff. He hops forward on his good leg.

"What's the matter with him?" I ask.

"Shhh," Charlie whispers. He jumps in front of me. "What did you think of those two double plays?" he calls to the writer.

"How do you feel about having a chance to become the team's MVP?" Mr. Nordstrom grins.

Charlie blinks at him, then at me.

"I don't see anyone else in the running," Mr. Nordstrom says. "Do you?"

"Steve Willis. And Kahlil Gibran."

The reporter scribbles on a pad. "You were having trouble with the pivot. What turned you around?"

I wait for Charlie to say, "My wife helped me," but he shrugs and gets in the car. I slide behind the wheel, and put the key into the ignition.

"Was that your father in the stands yesterday?" Mr. Nordstrom is bending to the window, his pad at the ready. "The one who kept shouting?"

Charlie shuts his eyes. "He's my father-in-law," he says, his voice a half whisper. A moment later, he is bright-eyed and grinning. "We're a game and a half back. If we keep playing like this, we'll be Number One. Write that down."

•

"Most Valuable Player." Charlie steers a cart down an aisle. "Safeway never looked more beautiful."

The store feels cold and dark after the glare of the field. "Why didn't you tell Mr. Nordstrom I helped you with the pivot? I told you to find a way to distract yourself and then the pivot would come automatically."

Charlie looks at me for a moment, and then nods and says, "You did help me. Load up. You can have anything you want."

"But our budget."

"Our budget just got pregnant and had eight kittens." He drops sirloin steaks into the cart and then eyes the fruit.

Charlie just put steak in our grocery cart.

"Did you say once you like coconuts?" he asks.

"I've never had them."

"And you call yourself an experienced woman." He sets three coconuts on top of the steaks. I try to put them back, but he stops me. "We could move up from here. I told you I'd have to tear up this league to get there. Well, I'm tearing up this league."

"What if you go into another slump?"

He glares at me, and then turns away. "I'm the Pickers' MVP. I'm the star." He turns back, smiling. "I'm going to call my father up and tell him he definitely has to come. This may be his last chance to see me in California."

I want to tell Charlie not to get his hopes up. His father may never come. But he looks as if he doesn't want to hear my doubts, my analysis.

"We've got it made now," he says. "No more poor, get it? No more poor."

I whisper it.

He nods. "No more Palms Hotel. Or old sick cars and curling linoleum."

I picture a closet with a door and a kitchen with new curtains. "No more poor." Saying it makes me smile. I follow him down the aisle.

•

I think of the watered roses, the pruned palm, of staying. He thinks of buying suitcases and of leaving.

He pours a glass of wine and one of carrot juice. "You got to be flexible, babe. In two weeks we could be in another state."

Babe. One of those terms of endearment ballplayers reserve almost exclusively for each other. Maybe men in a team sport or in combat are really closer to each other than they are to their wives. "I don't want to go anywhere," I say. "I started the curtains for the bedroom."

"I didn't marry Heidi Homemaker," Charlie says. "I married a scholar."

The wine tastes of metal. "I talked to the admissions people at the college here. They have a second summer session class on the English Novel. That's the class I've been reading *Moll Flanders* for.

He sits, and scratches the stubble of hair along his jaw, and stares at me. "You shouldn't have to wait until the second session. You should be in school now."

I look at him, then find I can't look at him. If I were in school now, maybe I'd stop having dreams about my mother throwing her lipstick at me. "We got married," I say. "We moved. My father visited."

"Excuses," Charlie says.

"It's fun to watch you play ball."

"I am magnificent," he says, grinning. "The MVP. But even I'd get tired of watching me after awhile. Did you ask if you could get into a class now?"

"They said it was too late to register."

"Steve's dad is a big shot around here. Maybe he can help bend the rules." Charlie points to the stack of books at my elbow. "You're doing all that reading."

"But if you get moved up?"

"They have colleges in Sacagawea," he says.

I shrug. I don't even know where Sacagawea is. If I went to school now, wouldn't I be deserting Charlie?

He clinks his glass to mine. "Think about it. I want you to be happy. Sometimes when I'm in the field, I look at you in the bleachers, and your face has no expression. You look like one of the living dead."

It doesn't sound like a compliment. "The living dead?"

"You know like people you see riding on busses, going to the same job they've had for 20 years. You know how sad those birdlike little secretaries who hate their bosses look."

He thinks I'm a cross between a secretary and a canary. "My mother was like yours, only worse," I say. "She thought women shouldn't get married until they had careers. I feel guilty because I fell in love at 18." Then, I tell Charlie about my dream and how Alice pelted me with her make-up items.

He listens, scratches his crew cut. "I'm glad I don't have terrible dreams like that."

"No, you just walk in your sleep, do pivots, and punch people out."

"I mean you must really be unhappy to have a dream like that. Maybe your mother isn't the only person who's disappointed in you. Maybe you are, too." He pours himself more juice.

"I'll talk to Steve and ask him if his dad can help," I say. "And if we leave, maybe being in a class here will make it easier to get in a class in the next school."

Charlie is staring at me. He is noticing the curtains, the unfinished windowsills. "A lot of work, huh?"

I shrug again. His hand warms my shoulder. "I always thought being a ballplayer was hard," he says. "Maybe being a ballplayer's wife is even harder."

26

The woman behind the sign – *College Admissions* – tells me it's too late to sign up for the first session of summer school. "Why dear, the classes are almost over."

"What about the second session?" I ask.

"Filled up," she says. "Sometimes, we slip people in under special circumstances."

"What kind of circumstances?"

"Oh, if they need just one more class to graduate."

"I'm a long way from graduating. But I may be the winner of the June Wells Scholarship."

"The what, dear?"

"It's a scholarship for students transferring from a two-year college."

"You can check in a week or so," she tells me. She waves the next student to the counter.

"Do you know Steve Willis?" I ask. "I mean Steve Willis, senior."

She nods and waits.

"His son and my husband are good friends. Mr. Willis. . ." I try to think of a lie that will impress her. I shove papers at her. "This is my transcript," and hear myself saying, "I feel that every day I'm out of school, my brain dies a little. Before she died, my mother told me not to waste my life. I think I'm turning into a vegetable. A happily married vegetable, but still a vegetable. I would really love to take *The History of the English Novel* in your second session."

I pull my transcript back, turn away before the woman can see my tears.

•

I put on my best smile for Charlie. Just because I made an idiot of myself in front of the College Admissions lady, I don't want Charlie to think I'm sorry I'm in the stands and watching him.

The lady in a big hat points at one of the Pickers warming up on the infield. "That's my Alton, the new shortstop."

"We already have a shortstop," I say.

Her gray eyes glint, then she shrugs. "Maybe they want him for another spot. He can play any position in the infield."

I want to tell her that we have an infield, that every position is set. I keep silent and watch Coach Mackie hit hard grounders at the new player, a small boy with skin the color of porcelain who scoops up every ball, throws strong and straight to first, makes everything look easy. He's good. He's very good. The new lady glances at my wedding band. "What position does your husband play?"

"My husband is the second baseman."

"That's my son's best position." Her words scare me. Still, Charlie's position is set. "But Alton likes shortstop better," the lady says. "There's so much more for him to do."

Coach yells, "Shoot two" and drives a ball up the middle. Alton dives in back of the bag, makes the catch, somersaults and tosses to Charlie, who seems so surprised to see the ball coming out of the cloud of dust that he hesitates before throwing to first. I pop a lifesaver in my mouth. In the silence down on the field, the players watch Alton get up, dust himself off. All the Pickers are nodding to themselves. Everyone but Charlie. He looks worried. Coach Mackie is shaking his head, but grinning. "Not bad, Eibur. Not half damn bad."

Two rows in front of me, Mr. Reisner is smiling, and nodding his head. Next to him, Mr. Nordstrom is nodding too.

Mrs. Eibur lays a white hand on mine. "Your husband made a very nice throw to first." She leans back, smiles at the sky. "It's a beautiful day, isn't it?"

"Beautiful?" Raquel turns so fast her orange ponytail swishes. "You call 103 hideous degrees beautiful?"

Alton's mother bites her lip then draws a long breath, and opens a picnic hamper. The smell of dill pickles and potato salad drifts out. "Anyone want something to eat? I brought plenty." She unwraps a ham sandwich. My dog, Boris inches closer, his nose wriggling. He knocks my book, *Joseph Andrews*, off my lap.

Little Tank burps and throws up orange juice. Raquel makes a face at Beth. "How can you feed him so much on such a hot day?" Slowly, Mrs. Eibur puts the sandwich back, and shuts the hamper.

Little Tank throws up more juice. My own stomach is turning. But it isn't food or the heat that is making me sick. I tell myself Alton's somersault was just a fluke. It's something he does once a decade.

Beth puts her hand on her son's forehead. "I think he has a fever."

"Maybe you should take him home," Raquel says.

"Raquel, you're a fake," I tell her. "You do everything you can to pretend Little Tank doesn't exist, but when he has a problem, you fuss over him more than the rest of us."

Raquel shrugs. Beth smiles, then shades her eyes, and studies center field. "Big Tank expects us to be here. He says we bring him good luck. We have never missed a game."

Mrs. Eibur clears her throat and pats Beth's shoulder. "If the baby's sick, I'm sure your husband would understand."

Relief fills Beth's eyes. She puts the diaper bag in the rack on the stroller.

Norma watches. "Tank's going to be upset."

Beth glances at Mrs. Eibur. "The baby comes first." She settles Little Tank on her hip. "See you all tomorrow."

The stroller creaks. Tired wheels kick up dust. Out by the fence, past center field, Tank is calling for a ball.

Bonnie takes out her long blue thing, and starts to knit. The Pickers trot to the dugout and the Oilers take the field. The stadium announcer, still fighting his summer cold, wheezes his way through the starting lineups. The shortstop for the Pickers today is Wayne Olivares. Alton's mother sucks in her disappointment, and folds her plump hands in her lap. She ignores Raquel's hard smile and stares out into the heat, as if waiting for something worth watching to take shape out there.

•

Ducky waves Steve out, puts Alton in. Bonnie stops knitting, starts picking at her nails.

"What did the Skipper do that for?" Norma asks. "We're winning aren't we?"

"Six to zip. We're so far ahead, it doesn't matter who plays first." Raquel glances at Alton's mother. "Ducky just wants to see what, if anything, the new kid can do."

Next to me, Alton's mother is patting Boris's head and smiling. The new kid, her son, looks too small to block the base against a determined runner. And Black Bart, the Oiler's burly catcher is at the plate.

"Don't you worry Alton could get hurt?" I whisper my question. For a reason I don't understand, I want to protect his plump, wide-eyed woman from Raquel's stare.

Watching the action on the field, Mrs. Eibur shakes her head. Bart drills a ball to the pitcher. Alton catches the toss, tags the base, and then makes a Gene Kelly leap out of Bart's way.

The somersault he did in practice was not a fluke. Walt whistles. Norma looks up from her magazine. "Did he just do what I think he did?"

"Did your son ever consider dancing?" I ask.

"Baseball is his life," she says.

I try to read Charlie's face, but his head is turned away from me. He follows little Alton to the dugout. Maybe Charlie's thinking what I'm thinking: Alton may be a good fielder, but a kid that size can't have much power. It's mean of me, but I hope my suspicions are true.

"How's his hitting?" I ask his mother.

"Dependable," she says.

I take a long, deep breath. He's dependable. He isn't spectacular. The Oilers, with less enthusiasm than they usually have, take the field.

Hunched over his bat, he looks even smaller. It will be hard for the pitcher to find the strike zone.

The pitcher finds the strike zone.

Alton slugs the ball out of the park.

Picker fans are on their feet. Everyone but Bonnie. She covers her eyes with her blue thing. She has seen enough. She has seen what I've seen. Every position in the infield is at risk. Still, I can't stop my smile or the shiver that runs down my back. Alton's mother is right. At least once a game, Alton can be depended upon to smash the ball out of the park.

•

Poor Bonnie. She looks at her husband sitting on the bench, then turns away. Thank God, Charlie is still at second base. But what is he feeling out there? At least he doesn't know that second is Alton's best position. I hope he never finds out.

"I don't see the harm in just handing him a sandwich." Mrs. Eibur is fretting. "Alton must be so hungry. I brought the food for him so he would have something to eat while we drove back to the motel."

"We just don't go out there," I tell her. Today, I'm the veteran, the experienced wife. "It's an unwritten code. Players think baseball is war. They're soldiers. They can't be bothered by their women."

"But the game is over."

"They're planning the next battle."

She shuts the hamper and sighs.

Bonnie folds up her knitting. Without even turning her head and saying goodbye, she starts for the parking lot. I should follow her. We could help and console each other. I pick up Boris and stand.

"You would never guess my son nearly died when he was 6 years old," Mrs. Eibur says.

I sit back down. You can't leave someone who is telling you they almost lost their only child. "I would guess," I tell her. But I don't add the rest of my thought. He looks sickly even now.

Bonnie starts her car engine, then shuts it down.

"Alton had polio. Thank God we got it in time. He used to listen to the games in the hospital. I got him every baseball card I could find in the city. We never dreamed he could actually play. You should have seen him. That little bit of a thing." Mrs. Eibur stares out at the field. As she talks, I can see him, too — a little boy in a uniform three sizes too big for him. He is a little boy who just won't quit. She says, "I'm so proud of him."

"He must be proud of you, too. You spent months of waiting in hospitals, and years cheering in the bleachers. You nursed him and encouraged him. You never thought of yourself."

Her eyes look surprised.

I study Raquel bent over her crossword puzzle book, Norma reading her movie magazine, and Bonnie standing next to her car and tapping high heels on the asphalt. I think of me reading a book during a ball game. "Didn't you mind all the waiting?" I ask.

"Why," she says. "What else would I do?"

•

Raquel looks up from her puzzle book. "The conference at Geneva is over."

The team meeting is over. I hold onto the puppy as if he were an anchor. I don't know what to say to Charlie. Is Charlie as worried about Alton as I am?

Tank breaks away from the team and looks up in the bleachers for his wife and child. Norma shouts the bad news. "Little Tank threw up. You can ride home with us."

Raquel looks at her watch. "Seven minutes to shower and change and we can split."

I tuck the puppy under my arm and head toward Charlie. On the field, Charlie is pumping Mr. Reisner's hand. "Glad you could come, sir."

Mr. Reisner looks past Charlie and nods at Alton.

"So how do you think I'm doing?" Charlie asks the scout.

"Fine, fine," Mr. Reisner lets go of Charlie's hand, and smiles at the lady with the picnic hamper. "What do you think of your son?"

Charlie scowls, and pivots and runs toward the locker room.

•

The dugout is lost in shade. Then, a shadow moves. Charlie is sitting alone on the team bench. He is probably feeling so lost. I tiptoe closer. I long to hug him, but maybe he'd rather be left alone.

The fading sun burns my back. I try to find the right words, the words that will take some of the sting and some of the magic out of that wonderful catch and the Gene Kelly leap. I could tell Charlie, "Alton's good. But you're good, too." But Charlie won't be soothed by my words. He knows Alton is better.

Maybe there are no right words.

I grip Charlie's shoulder. "Are you all right?"

No answer. Wind hisses, and then stops. "Alton Eibur is great," Charlie says.

"He's good. But you are, too."

Charlie stands and picks up his gear. "It's a gift. It makes you believe in," he shades his eyes and stares at the swaying Eucalyptus branches, "trees, birds, God, everything."

I knit my fingers together. The puppy wriggles in my arms. Alton makes Charlie believe in God. Well, that's good, isn't it? Alton's gifts are so large they make Charlie take the better view. Charlie's always been generous. And in the grand scheme of things, it isn't really that important that Alton has more talent than Charlie. "I'm so proud of you,' I say. "You're taking this well."

He grins. "You see the way he caught my long throw near third? Me and Alton are going to go all the way together."

●

I sit at the wobbly table and sip coffee. Sunday morning church bells peal. I nibble the last of the coconut. Will Charlie still be the MVP now that Alton is on the team? The one blue trimmed window looks like a Cyclops. Today, I will paint the second window.

The phone rings. I answer and listen. Kathleen is looking for Mickey again. I twist the cord and tell her the words I need to believe. "He's probably sleeping it off somewhere."

"He's been too happy ever since he's come back from seeing you," she says.

I stare at coffee getting cold on the table. Kathleen has always been jealous of me. She forgets I exist when things are going well with her and Mickey. She only calls when there's trouble. The first time I ever heard her voice was in the predawn morning right after Alice died. Kathleen said, "Come get your father." I didn't know where Mickey had disappeared. I didn't know Kathleen existed.

Now, she says, "Make sure he's not with you. Go look."

I put down the receiver and study the almost empty living room. I start to giggle as I peer under Gooth's chair. "He's not here," I say into the phone.

There's a long silence.

What if Mickey had another accident or got in a fight in a bar or drove Kathleen's Rambler off the Santa Monica pier? Maybe he's lying dead somewhere. When I think of what my father could do to himself while under the influence, I wish I could lock him in a big rubber room somewhere where he would be safe.

"He's not dead. He's with someone," Kathleen is saying. "Someone he met in Cotton Valley." Why does Kathleen sound happiest when she's close to proving her worst suspicions are true? "He met someone up there. I just know it."

I look out the window. Laura Davis bought new blue jeans just so she could crawl through the dirt. Peering through a magnifying glass, she hunts for seedlings. If Mickey were in town, would he be on his knees, searching right along with her? She told me she had trouble "distinguishing cultivated plants from unwanted natives." If Mickey were here, would he be showing her what to pull and what to keep?

"He's not in Cotton Valley," I tell Kathleen. "Have you checked jails, hospitals, the morgue?" I swallow the last word.

"No," her voice gets small. "I was too scared."

She's always too scared. She always makes me do the difficult tasks. And if this time he's really dead, I'm the one who will have to call the funeral home. Church bells sound tinny now. Through the open window comes the smell of smoke and burning oil. A well has caught fire. This beautiful morning has turned ugly. "He's always been all right in the past," I say. "I'm sure he's fine now. But I'll call the morgue, if you call the hospitals. I'll only call you back it there's bad news, OK?"

I know the morgue number by heart. I dial and wait for the long distance operator to come on line. I watch Laura Davis get to her feet. She smiles down at her earth and stretches in the sun. The little librarian has pink cheeks. She looks happy. Is it her garden that's making her happy or is it Mickey?

He's not in the morgue.

He's on a Greyhound, humming a little tune, smiling at the scenery, counting the miles, the minutes, 'til he sees Laura Davis again.

•

I can't ask her. It's not a question you can ask and then forget. It will be part of our memories. It will cling to the garden patch and the summer sky. If I ask, we will still be neighbors, but nothing between us will be the same again. Still, still I have to make sure.

I step around the hedge that divides the yards. Kneeling, Mrs. Davis turns on new sprinklers and smiles at rainbows in the water.

Afraid to tramp on her soil, I stand at the edge of her garden. "Mrs. Davis, have you communicated with my father? Did he call or write to you?"

Her head swivels. "Why would he call me?"

"Kathleen just thought. . ." I tell the packet of seeds at my feet. "He didn't come home last night."

Laura Davis pokes at dirt on the tip of her nose. "I'm just a regular old home-wrecker." He shoulders get lost in the stiff, flannel shirt. Then, she smiles. "I'm famous for it." She stands, and lights a cigarette and puffs. "I've seen pictures of your stepmother. She's so beautiful. I should be flattered you'd even think a mouse like me would have a chance."

"I'm sorry," I step nearer. I know how she feels – pretty, but ordinary. When people pass me, or Laura Davis, on the street, they've forgotten they have seen us by the time they've turned the corner. Laura Davis or I will never be home-wreckers. We will never be like Kathleen, who kept my father busy at nights while Alice stayed up waiting for him.

27

Adusty truck rattles down the road and stops halfway between her house and ours. The truck has the words *Halligan's Fine Furniture* written across its side. Is Laura expecting a delivery?

A door squeaks. Charlie jumps out of the cab. What's he doing in a furniture truck? The driver, a man with liver spots on his balding head, a man who's getting too old for this kind of work, opens the back. He and Charlie waltz a table down a ramp. The maple table has a drop leaf and spindle legs. It looks like Alice's kitchen table. Charlie bought me a table to match the one we had on Hibiscus Street.

I run and put my arms around Charlie. "I love the table," I say. "I love you."

Charlie grins.

Laura Davis marches toward us. Her little back is straight. Her steps are quick. She looks like a toy soldier. She says, "I'll give you a hand."

She's a good soldier and a good neighbor. She'll pretend she has forgotten my question.

Charlie carries a maple chair to me. "Your seat, madam."

I sit. "It's wonderfully comfortable," I tell him. "It's perfect." My feet brush against stiff grass, grass that could scratch my new dinette set. "Shouldn't we bring the table and chairs into the house?"

But Charlie doesn't answer. He's going back to the truck. Hands on hips, the man from Halligan's is sizing up a couch. Charlie picks up a brass floor lamp and walks toward me.

"That beautiful lamp is ours?"

As if it was a Maypole, Charlie skips around the brass stand. He takes my hand and we skip around the lamp together. "I'll put the lamp in the living room corner, next to Gooth's chair," I tell him.

But Charlie isn't listening. He's back at the truck. He waltzes an end table down the ramp, and then helps the older man carry a couch.

Just how much furniture did Charlie buy? Not the whole truck load? I should help. But I can't move. My arms and legs won't work right. If I pick up anything, even a pillow, I'll have to believe all the furniture belongs to us.

"Ginger jar. I've always loved them." Cradling a yellow lamp as if it were a newborn baby, Laura Davis tiptoes down the ramp. Beaming, she tells me, "It took Herbert and me years to set up our house. You're so lucky."

Laura hands me the ginger jar lamp. The china base, heated by the sun, warms my arms. Why didn't Charlie tell me what he was planning? Maybe he was afraid I would talk him out of it. I would ask questions, analyze our financial situation. I would steal his joy. I carry the lamp into the house.

Laura Davis, interior decorator, stretches the tape across the wall. "Your couch will just fit."

Charlie lets go of the tape at his end. "I thought so." His smile is smug.

The couch has tiny flowers that match the yellow in the lamp.

"Everything is so beautiful," I say.

"I figured you needed a lift," Charlie says.

"To give someone a lift, you buy them a cup of coffee, not two rooms worth of furniture." I'm never going to learn to keep my mouth shut. "What I mean is, before you were worried about buying just one chair. You said it would be a problem to move."

"That's what trucks and delivery men are for."

"I was just thinking of the expense. But the furniture is lovely."

He grins. "I'm the MVP, remember?"

I also remember a skinny boy with pale skin who caught everything in sight.

Charlie sits in the rocker. "I bought the furniture on time." He glances at Laura Davis. "Mickey told me how. You put some money down and then make small monthly payments."

Morning coffee, cold and sour, settles in my stomach. "Kathleen called. Mickey didn't come home last night."

"No sweat," Charlie says. "Your dad's got nine lives. He's probably just sleeping somewhere in his cab."

Charlie's probably right. My father is fine. He has years ahead of him. And we have years to pay for the furniture. Behind me, Laura Davis sighs, and lights a fresh cigarette from old embers. She does like to help, to be good neighbor.

But maybe, she also wants to be around to hear news about Mickey.

"He's a survivor. He'll be fine." I want to convince myself. I want to convince Laura. I sit in the new easy chair and draw comfort from the thick corduroy. "I've always paid in cash," I say.

"And just what have you bought?" Charlie asks. "A pair of shoes and a skirt? Hey, were in the big leagues now."

"I've been buying things on time for years," Laura Davis says. "I still sleep nights."

She doesn't sleep nights. She stays up and talks to Chekhov. Still, the corduroy chair, the rocker, the couch, the ginger jar lamp are all so lovely. This house with its knotty pine paneling feels like a real home.

•

"He doesn't understand what it's like." Kathleen is crying. "I had to call the hospitals and ask if my husband was there."

I grip the cold receiver, stare at its tiny holes. "Is he –?"

"Home," she says.

"Thank God. Is he all right?"

Her sniff sounds resentful. "Nothing ever happens to him."

"He's fine," I tell the two worried faces behind me. I smile at the new kitchen table. "He is just fine."

My words make little Laura smile.

"Is he hurt at all?" I ask Kathleen.

"The bastard doesn't even have a hangover," his wife tells me. "He wasn't with another woman. There's nothing to worry about."

"I'm so glad he's all right," I say.

"He made me throw it at him," she says.

I must have missed something. *Don't ask*, I tell myself. "What are you talking about? What did you throw?"

"I threw my favorite lamp."

I cover the receiver. "She threw her lamp at him."

Charlie and Laura look puzzled.

"Pam, speak to him. Tell him he's killing me. He's wrecking our home." Kathleen's sobs get fainter and disappear.

There's a moment of silence, and then a meek, little voice says, "Hello."

"Daddy, I was so worried."

"Put Charlie on," the little voice whispers.

"But Daddy, don't you want to talk to me? I'm so relieved."

"I want to talk to Charlie," he says.

Suddenly I wish Mickey had a hangover, a headache, a sick stomach, something to remind him not to get drunk again.

"Charlie." He makes the name sound like a prayer.

Why won't Mickey talk to his daughter? He's tired of my lectures and my tears. Maybe he'll listen to his son-in-law. I wave Charlie to the phone. "Tell him to stop drinking."

"I'll tell him no more drinking." Charlie takes the phone and settles into the new kitchen chair. His face is calm. He nods twice. He clears his throat once. He isn't telling Mickey anything.

"Tell him he's killing himself," I say.

Charlie waves me away. His expression hasn't changed.

"Please tell him. He'll listen to you."

Laura Davis comes back from the living room. "Your father's really all right?"

"Charlie's talking to him now." So why isn't Charlie saying anything?

"Tell him Laura is worried too," I say.

"Oh, don't tell him that," she says. "He might get the wrong idea."

"She's worried as a friend," I say. "Tell him."

Charlie shakes his head.

"Then, I'll tell him." I start for the phone.

But Charlie hangs up. "Why did you do that?" I ask. "I wanted to talk to him too."

Charlie rubs tired eyes and then stares at me. "Please promise me we'll never fight like that."

•

Behind my sunglasses, I shut my eyes and see Charlie leap up and catch every ball that comes his way. Alton is good, but Charlie is better. At the end of the game, Rusty and Steve hoist Charlie on their shoulders. Charlie is still the MVP.

I open my eyes. My fantasy gives me courage to see the game that is actually on the field. Charlie scoops up a Manteca's hard grounder and tags second. He throws a perfect strike to Alton at first. Walt's friend, the man with the murky eye, is on his feet and cheering with the rest of the crowd. I wait for Charlie's clown bow. It doesn't come. He pulls his cap down and studies the next batter. Maybe he really believes the applause and shouts are for him.

Beth swings Little Tank. He claps his hands for Charlie. Little Tank is wearing a small brown and orange Picker cap.

Walt thumps my back. "We got it in the bag now."

He has believed in the 1963 Pickers all along. Now, the rest of the town has caught up with him. The town has Picker Fever. The disease isn't listed yet in my *Oxford Dictionary*, but it is real. It began even before Charlie came to town. But Charlie and Alton Eibur are causing the disease to spread. Retired folks, baseball wives, teenage boys, and shop owners along Main Street seem to be the most susceptible to the illness. But shy literary types sometimes get the worst cases. Coleen, Laura Davis's meek assistant, comes to every night game, and when the Pickers play in the day she spends her lunch hours in the stands. She's here now, clapping for Charlie. It must be nice to be a fan and not a worried wife.

Bonnie, her sharp shoulder blades pushing against her thin blue and white sundress, edges past two 12-year-old boys. Her legs brush against their knees, her skirt hikes up. Their faces turn bright red. She bumps their radio and knocks it down.

Raquel cups her hand and whispers, "If I were her, I'd think about staying home."

Raquel would. Maybe I would, too. But even though Steve is on the bench, even though Bonnie's face gets thinner every day, even though she's chewed her nails down past her fingertips, she still comes to the games. "She's more concerned about Steve's feelings than her own," I say.

Raquel lights one of her brown Sherman's. It looks like a skinny cigar. She says, "How much good is she doing Steve when she sits there looking as if she's attending her husband's funeral?"

I sigh and watch the Butcher batter dribble a ball to third. Norma's Rusty makes the long throw to first but the ball is way short of the bag. Alton leans out, catches it, and tags the base with his glove. The runner is out.

Norma sits up straighter. She tells Mrs. Eibur, "I've never seen a first baseman make that play before."

Raquel whispers, "She never watched the damn game before."

Norma taps Bonnie on the back. Bonnie squeezes next to Beth. "That was no put down of Steve," Norma says. "I don't think Pepitone or Skowron or Hodges could have done it."

Raquel snorts. Smoke from her cigarette blows toward the field. "Skowron."

Norma pouts. "What's the matter with being enthusiastic? We do have a shot at the division title, you know."

Raquel frowns. "I think I liked you better before you were an expert like Vin Scully. 'Course, you got a point about Eibur. He is marvelous." She glances at Bonnie. "I'm just glad he's so slight. There aren't too many skinny catchers."

"There have been a few," Mrs. Eibur says. "I looked it up once."

"You're spooky," Raquel tells her. "Your son is so talented. But most of the time you act as if all you're thinking about is what's in your picnic hamper. But you probably know more baseball than any of us."

"She does," Norma says. "She reads to me from *The Sporting News*."

"I try to keep up," Mrs. Eibur says.

"Mrs. Eibur, have there been very many small center fielders?" Beth asks.

"They're the exception," Mrs. Eibur says. "It's usually a power position. And so most of the time, they're built like your Tank."

Beth looks relieved. She bends down and kisses her son's head.

Norma studies her Rusty at third. "Just last night he was talking about when he retired he wanted to go back and work his father's farm. But Alton's not interested in playing third base, is he?"

Alton leaps up, catches a line drive, and makes the third out. A Cub Scout bangs his bongo drum. The crowd is cheering. The Butchers take the field.

"Alton likes the middle – second base and shortstop," Mrs. Eibur says.

There have been many small second baseman. Pepper pots. Alton likes second base the best. Maybe Charlie isn't waving and bowing to the crowd because he knows his position is most at risk.

"I don't think this conversation is doing us any good," I say. "We all know Alton is wonderful. We all know what could happen."

Raquel shakes her ponytail. "One Vin Scully. One shrink."

Bonnie smiles.

At the plate, Charlie hits a ball that drops in front of the second baseman's glove. Charlie beats the throw to first. Behind me, Walt shouts, "Way to go, Fain."

Alton drills a ball in the hole between second and short. Both Charlie and Alton are safe.

"Alton seemed to know just where to put that ball," Norma tells Mrs. Eibur. "We really are so lucky to have him."

Mrs. Eibur puts her fingers on her lips and nods toward Bonnie. It must have happened dozens of times. Alton joined a team and a solid, reliable player got bumped.

A red ant is crawling across Bonnie's big toe. I bend over and swat it. She flinches and stares at me. "Those things bite," I tell her.

"They're worse than bee stings," Norma says. "Last year Sally got bit. Her leg swelled so bad we had to take her to the Emergency Room. Remember, Beth?"

Beth says, "Some lady in Alabama died just from one red ant bite."

Raquel curses and puts her hands over her ears.

"Let's get out of this heat." I wrap my arm around Bonnie's shoulder and steer her past the young boys and their radio.

Norma's voice chases us. "Where are you two going? Charlie's on second. He could score."

"You should stay and watch your husband," Bonnie tells me.

"He's having a good time out there. He doesn't need me."

In the bathroom, I wet a paper towel. She looks down at the wound, but does nothing. I kneel and pat the dirt off her toe. Her skin is already angry and puffing. Her toenails are neatly clipped and painted pink. "We can get some iodine from Coach," I tell her.

She shrugs. "Maybe some ice."

There are things I should be saying to make Bonnie feel better. But what are they? Should I lie, and tell her she has nothing to worry about? If Charlie were out of the lineup, what would I want to hear?"

"You should take better care of yourself," I say. "Steve's going to need your strength."

She shuts her eyes as a "yes," and turns from me. I've made her feel guilty. She turns on the tap and splashes water on her face. "He's not sleeping anymore," she says.

There are dark circles under her eyes. He's not the only one who isn't sleeping. "When we first got here, Charlie was up all the time. I know he's worried about Alton. He's sleepwalking again. But he won't talk about Alton. We just pretend everything's the way it used to be."

Bonnie nods. There's a spark of interest in her green eyes.

"Charlie thinks Alton should play third or short and Steve should go back to first. Charlie says it will be better for the Pickers. We need Steve's bat."

"It doesn't matter what Charlie thinks." Her eyes look dead again. "He's not the manager."

"Charlie will fix things," I say.

She shakes her head, and opens her purse and stares at tubes of lipstick. She slumps against the sink.

"I don't know if Charlie can fix things," I say. "I don't know what's going to happen to any of us. I never dreamed it would be so hard just to sit in the bleachers and watch."

She edges closer to me, and suddenly she's gripping my shoulders. "Everything Steve ever hoped for is gone," she says. "And there's nothing I can do."

28

I can never decide which are worse, the red ants at day games or the mosquitoes at night games. Tonight, I slap a mosquito with Warren's and my copy of *Jude the Obscure*. I still keep trying to read at games, but my mind keeps drifting to Alton. Some days, I only use my books as weapons against insects.

"Everything's all set." Bonnie smiles at me. She looks rested tonight. Maybe she and Steve got some sleep. Maybe our talk yesterday did some good.

"Did Charlie fix things for you?" I ask. "Did he talk to Ducky and get Steve back in the lineup?"

Bonnie sighs and watches the boys from Kettle City warm up. "We haven't heard anything."

"Then, what is all set?"

"All you have to do is go to the Registrar's Office."

"I have no idea what you're talking about."

"Mrs. Ryan was very impressed with you."

"Mrs. who?"

Bonnie is still smiling. "She was Steve's father's first-grade teacher, you know."

"No, I don't know."

"She works at the college now. She told Steve's father how determined you were. And it's a good thing, too." Bonnie rests her hand on my arm. "Charlie told Steve you were having some bad dreams, something about your mother sitting here in the bleachers."

Beth stops humming to Little Tank. Norma looks up from Jim Murray's sports column. She cracks her gum.

Why did Charlie tell Steve about me? Aren't husbands and wives supposed to keep secrets for each other?

"But your mother's dead, isn't she?" Beth asks me. "It must be hard for you to have lost your mother so young."

I use the Hardy to slap another mosquito. "It is."

"See, what did I tell you about ghosts?" Norma nods at each of us. "First Marilyn Monroe and now Pam's mother. Ghosts like baseball, and we have a winning team." Norma studies me. "Now, where exactly was she sitting and was it a day game or a night game?"

"She's not here," I tell Norma. "It was just a bad dream."

"Isn't there a song?" Raquel says. "It goes something like, 'Oh, Doctor Freud, How I wish you were otherwise employed.'"

Norma frowns. "What does this Doctor person have to do with anything? Is he a ghost?"

"In a way," Raquel laughs. "If he were here, he'd say Pam's unconscious is cooking up her nightmares. She feels guilty about something." Raquel stares at me. "What exactly do you feel guilty about?"

"I don't know," I tell her.

"Well, it can't be anything major," Raquel says. "What exactly is the worst thing you ever did? Forget to wrap a used sanitary napkin with toilet paper before putting it in the trash."

Beth makes a face. "Gross."

Bonnie says, "Steve's dad asked Steve about Pam. Steve told his dad about her dream. Steve's dad is on the Board of Regents."

"The Board of Regents knows I'm having nightmares? Is there anyone in Cotton Valley who doesn't know about my dream? If we missed someone, I could get on the loudspeaker and make an announcement to the crowd. "

Raquel smiles and flips her ponytail.

"I don't think Mr. Willis told the Board about your dream. He told them you were a good student and you were in line for some scholarship you told Mrs. Ryan about."

I hug Bonnie. "You mean they are going to let me into school?"

"It's the first good news we've had for a long time," she says.

Norma taps my shoulder. "Is there some message your mother has for you or for us? For instance, Marilyn told Joe –"

Field lights hiss and go out. The rest of Norma's sentence gets lost in the sudden darkness.

"Not again," Beth whispers.

Little Tank starts to cry.

"Another damn delay," Raquel says. "We won't be home 'til midnight."

A circle of light dances across our knees. Bonnie is waving the flashlight. "Does anyone need this?"

"Is anyone hungry?" Mrs. Eibur asks. The hamper lid squeaks. The smell of dill, mayonnaise, and macaroons fills the air. "There's plenty."

If the world were coming to an end, Mrs. Eibur would be passing out food, and Bonnie would be shining her light.

"Twice in one week," Norma says. "It must be some sort of sign."

"It's a sign that we're a minor league field and that what happens to us doesn't matter," Raquel says.

"It's a sign that Fred, the maintenance man, is on another binge," Beth says.

"Beth," Norma says.

I move closer to the other women. I can't see past the circle of yellow light. "If I do go back to school," I say, "I'll miss you all. I never fit into Brownies or Girl Scouts. This is the first group where I belonged."

•

Something clicks, then there's a whirring noise and the lights blink on. I take a deep breath. Charlie is still standing at second. There are no ghosts in the bleachers.

"All you have to do is pick your class," Bonnie says. "And sign some forms."

I fix my stare on the lamp, a yellow rectangle that casts white light on the field. School. The word washes over me. A soft warm breeze lifts the tips of my hair and the hem of my skirt.

"Each class is three units of credit," Bonnie says. "You'll do twelve weeks of work in four. Tremendous pressure. You'll love it." Bonnie rummages through her purse. She takes out makeup, a screwdriver, Camembert cheese, a flashlight, and finally a catalog. "You're an English Major right? Mrs. Ryan said something about the English novel."

I look at the catalog. "Twenty novels in four weeks? I'll have to study every second. What about Charlie? He could go into another slump." I glance at Bonnie's chewed nails. "Or something worse. Plus, there's housework and cooking."

Raquel turns around and looks at me. "I thought you wanted to go to school?"

"Yes, but I'll miss all of you. And I feel as if I'm deserting Charlie."

"So, all you want in life is to be a My Husband He?"

I stare at the picture of tortured Jude Fawley on the book cover. I pick up the Hardy and thumb through the pages. Would Jude Fawley turn down the second summer session at Cal State Cotton Valley? Blind Chance stacked everything against him, but he never wanted to give up his dream of reaching those university towers. Do I want to be Pamela the Obscure?

Mr. Nordstrom is standing in front of us. He looks at Bonnie. "Are you and Steve holding up OK?"

"Fine," she lies.

"Good." He glances at the book in my hands and shakes his head. "Mrs. Fain, beautiful as he is, put your Hardy away. We make our own fate."

I meet his stare and then turn. Maybe Mr. Nordstrom is part ghost. He can read my mind. Maybe he can even tell me why I'm having nightmares. He pivots on his good leg and limps to his seat.

What an odd man. Why does he want me to put my Hardy away? Alice loved Thomas Hardy. Is there something about him that she didn't know? I pick up the catalog and read the section on British novels.

"So, what do you think?" Bonnie says. "Are you excited about the class?"

I look out toward second. Charlie is watching the batter at the plate. "Charlie must have been worried if he talked to Steve about me. I don't know what I did to deserve a husband like Charlie, or a friend like you."

"I'm the lucky one," she whispers. "You're the first girl who hasn't hated me just because I'm pretty."

"Gorgeous," I tell her.

"Gorgeous," she smiles. "And rich."

•

Just walking past the college bookstore makes my feet take bigger steps. There are so many books for me to read. I smile at students resting their backs against thick tree trunks. The students have shiny new faces. They look younger than the ballplayers I've been watching. They look as if nothing bad has happened to them yet. Does being here make them as happy as it makes me?

At the Admissions Office, I fill out the papers for my *History of the English Novel* class and hand Mrs. Ryan fresh green paper bills. The money is the same new green as the grass outside.

"Thank you, dear." Mrs. Ryan winks at me.

Bonnie told me Mrs. Ryan is a widow and working at the college is what gives purpose to her life.

I reach for the older woman's freckled hand. "Thank you, Mrs. Ryan."

"We're all in this together," she says.

I stop walking halfway down the hall and tell myself, "I should have asked Mrs. Ryan what *it* is and who *we* are."

•

The new shortstop, Alton Eibur, leaps up, catches the ball and tosses it to Charlie for the double play.

"The kid's great," Mr. Zimmer says.

"He's so excited you're here," I tell him. "After all, you were Charlie's first coach."

Mr. Zimmer squints, pushes up his Derby hat. "I mean that Eibur kid. I've never seen anything like him. He's terrific."

Norma's head swivels. She flashes a fresh lipstick smile at Mr. Zimmer, then blinks at gold pineapples and red starfish in his Hawaiian shirt. Wait till you see Alton bat. His average is a sweet .420."

"It's .423, dear," Mrs. Eibur says.

Behind me, Raquel rattles the newspaper, and looks up from the *Times* crossword puzzle.

"He doesn't need a hot bat. Not with that defense," Mr. Zimmer says. "I've never seen anybody get rid of the ball so fast. He always throws strikes. He leads the league in fewest errors."

I pat my puppy's head, and put my finger on the page in *Persuasion*. I will have to keep interrupting my reading today to look out at the field. Charlie's needs to know I'm rooting for him. He will be hurt when he learns how much Mr. Zimmer admires Alton. Charlie thinks Mr. Zimmer came all this way just to see him.

"How do you know about Alton way down in L.A.?" I ask Mr. Zimmer.

"I'm alive, ain't I? The Pickers are doing good. So is Charlie. But this Alton! It's not every day a future Hall of Famer pops up practically in your own backyard."

Charlie and the future Hall of Famer watch the Oiler batter foul one off.

"How come he's so quiet out there?" Mr. Zimmer asks. "The kid got lockjaw?"

"Alton?"

"Charlie. I don't recognize him with his mouth shut."

He's quiet because wherever he goes someone is raving about Alton.

"He's just concentrating," I tell Mr. Zimmer. Charlie charges a grounder, and throws the ball to first. "He's picked up running speed," I say.

"Alton?" Mr. Zimmer says.

"Charlie," I say.

Punching each other, the Pickers new Three Musketeers, Alton, Charlie and Steve run off the field. Knitting needles click. Bonnie is smiling again. The blue thing grows. Charlie says the new guy was moved down to Class C.

"Where's Steve hitting?" Bonnie asks Norma.

"Eighth." Norma turns to Mr. Zimmer. Her hair spray shimmers like snail slime in the sun. Now that she likes baseball, now that the Pickers are winning, she combs her hair before she comes to the park. "We need Alton's bat," she explains to the ex-Little League coach. "In fact, that's where he's most valuable. Ducky didn't know whether to have Alton lead off or bat clean up. He's got power. But he's also so fast. He's a rabbit."

The rabbit who likes to go first, get on, then take second on a wild pitch to Charlie.

With a big lead off second. Alton wants to steal third. But Charlie swings at a pitch over his head.

Mr. Zimmer clucks his tongue. "What's he doing? Playing tether ball?"

"Maybe he's a little over anxious because you're here," I tell Mr. Zimmer. I close my eyes and hope for a hit. There's a sweet smacking noise. Charlie's ball sails over the center fielder's head.

Mr. Zimmer jumps to his feet, cups worn hands around his mouth. "Good going, son."

I stand and clap for Charlie, then sit and look down at my book. I take a pen from my purse. On my notepad I write:

Even though Anne Elliot was heartbroken at the loss of Captain Wentworth, she found pleasure in the small things in life. She cared for her nephews, enjoyed Nature, people's foibles amused her. She had a rich inner life.

For some reason, this makes me think of Mrs. Ryan in the Admission's Office. Then, I picture Laura Davis bent over her seedlings, Mrs. Fain smiling at her desk. Was Mrs. Ryan telling me that we are an army of women who are in some kind of war? Does she think what Alice thought? Women, happily married, unhappily married, or single, can find joy in the small things and take pride in paying their bills.

•

I never knew a restaurant could be so beautiful. My heels sink in the thick carpet. I take Charlie's hand and point my free hand to the chandelier. "Let's walk slowly," I tell Charlie. "I don't want to miss anything."

"They're not going to make me take my hat off," Mr. Zimmer says. "I don't do that for no one."

"No sweat," Charlie tells him.

Bonnie sucks in her breath. "It is considered bad manners to wear your hat while you're eating."

Mr. Zimmer takes off his hat. Bonnie loops her arm in her husband's. "This is our special restaurant," she tells us. "We come here whenever we have something to celebrate."

Charlie squeezes my hand. Mr. Zimmer, lost in a sports coat and tie that the headwaiter insisted on loaning him, sighs.

Bonnie halts suddenly. It takes a moment for me to see a candle on a table and a waiter moving something, a chair, toward me. What should I do? If I sit where he has positioned the chair, the place setting will be out of reach. I take a step, then two. As if by magic, the thick chair slides under me. I'm safe.

A voice comes out of the gloom. "I'm going to need a derrick to get me out of this thing."

Is a derrick something like a forklift? I lean forward and search for Mr. Zimmer. He's patting the chair's velvet arm and blinking in the candlelight. His bald head gleams. "Can't they pay their electricity bill?" he says.

"Howie, dark is fancier," Charlie whispers. "And nicer."

The fry cook asks, "Are you sure it's not so people can't see what they're eating?"

First my father, and now Mr. Zimmer. Both act as if they grew up in a zoo. Bonnie will think I don't know anyone who has manners. She is probably wishing she hadn't insisted Charlie's Little League coach be the Willis's dinner guest.

Paper rattles. "I can't see the damn menu," Mr. Zimmer says. "Is it English or what?"

"'Course it's English," Charlie says. "Steak Robert. Steak Diane. Chicken catch a something. If you don't want to try something new, just ask for a plain steak and maybe some catsup." He turns to Steve. "Howie can do that, right? I mean, the point of a fancy restaurant is, you're supposed to be comfortable."

Charlie does look comfortable. He smiles at the linen napkin folded like a child's paper birthday hat.

"The point of a fancy restaurant is it's supposed to be fancy," I say. "It's fun to be fancy."

Charlie pats my knee and points to the yellow squares on a plate. "That's real butter. Isn't it beautiful?"

Steve orders a carafe of the house wine.

"I've never had wine in a restaurant," I whisper.

"Well, you're going to tonight," Charlie says.

"You're not old enough," Mr. Zimmer tells me. "In California you can't drink until you're 21." He squints at Steve. "You could be hauled off. I can see the headlines: Picker's first and second basemen spend night in jail."

Steve leans over across the table. His chin nearly touches the tip of the candle flames. "We've had liquor here before and no one's said anything."

Mr. Zimmer purses his lips.

When the wine comes, Bonnie raises her glass. "A toast to Charlie for getting Steve back in the lineup."

"Steve earned his position," Charlie says. "He's the one to toast."

We toast Charlie, and Steve. The house wine must be really good because it tastes like tree bark.

Mr. Zimmer smacks his lips. "Real thirst quencher, you know like lemon juice when it's so sour it makes your eyes squeeze. Nothing like it on a hot day."

Candlelight flickers and threatens to go out.

"So, you were Charlie's first coach?" Steve says. "Was your son also on the team?"

Mr. Zimmer doesn't answer. He rolls his breadstick in a square of butter.

"I'm kind of like Howie's son," Charlie says. "I mean I have a father and everything but. . ."

Mr. Zimmer looks up and smiles at Charlie. "The kid's dad split," Mr. Zimmer says. "Eileen, Mrs. Fain, worked for me. The kid was having a rough time. So was she. So I thought, what the hell. I volunteered to be his coach. I was surprised as anybody when he turned out to be so good. Eileen, his mother, well you never seen anybody so happy."

The memory of her, of Eileen, so happy, makes Howard Zimmer's yellow eyes sparkle. He's grinning now. He's forgotten he's in a fancy restaurant with Charlie's fancy friends. He's remembering how it was. Does Mrs. Fain know how much he loved her?

"By the way," he tells Charlie, "your mom's fine. She wanted to come up with me, but she's loaded with work."

"Howie used to be a first baseman," Charlie says.

"Professionally?" Steve asks.

"Semi-pro. Like every kid, I wanted to be a major leaguer. But I knew I didn't have it. So, I changed my dream a little." His fingers shape something – a trapezoid? – in the air. "Now, I have a restaurant. It's right on the beach. Well, across the highway. Charlie does the playing for me."

Steve looks at Mr. Zimmer for a long time. "I keep telling Charlie he doesn't know how lucky he is. Some guys I know would give up their right arm to have a dad like you."

"Aw, he. . .well." Mr. Zimmer's face turns pink. He shoves half a bread stick in his mouth.

"Howie, you never told me what you thought about Alton," Charlie says.

I gulp the fancy tree bark wine for courage. "Let's take a vacation from Alton tonight."

"Mr. Zimmer," Bonnie says. "You should try the house salad dressing. It's a vinaigrette seasoned with tarragon."

"I couldn't believe it when I read about Eibur," Mr. Zimmer says.

Bonnie whispers to me, "I tried."

"You mean the Nordstrom's clippings I sent?" Charlie asks.

"He's in all the papers," Steve says. "Everyone's writing about him."

"*The Los Angeles Times*?" Charlie sinks back in his chair.

"*Times, Examiner, The Sporting News*," Mr. Zimmer says. "Is he as good as everybody says?"

Charlie takes a deep breath. "What do you think?"

"He's the best thing that ever happened to you."

"Me? How do you figure that?" Charlie asks.

"He's just what you needed – someone with equal talent to play beside. He shows off how good you are. You'll go up together I'm sure." Mr. Zimmer points his fork at Steve. "You're good for Charlie, too."

Steve smiles and pours Mr. Zimmer more wine. "That's very kind. But I know I'm not in Alton's class."

"Don't put yourself down, son. You're a good team player, reliable. A kid like Alton's going to make you look better. He advantages everyone."

I lean back and take in the smell of fine wood, cut flowers. Everything's going to be all right. Mr. Zimmer missed his calling. He should have been a diplomat.

A waiter steps to the table and asks for our order.

"Sometimes the sauces are a little too rich," Bonnie tells Mr. Zimmer. "You could have a simple Filet Mignon."

"When in Rome," Mr. Zimmer says. "A Number 7. Steak tartar." He smiles the smile of a comfortable man in comfortable surroundings. "Steak with fish sauce."

29

I tiptoe toward the green and silver Bel Air Chevrolet. I'm going to ask Mr. Zimmer to explain to Mrs. Fain that we really need that letter of consent. Mr. Zimmer knows about love. He should be on our side.

Before I even get to his car, Mr. Zimmer pokes his head through the car's open window. Even in the moonlight, the chrome gleams. The 7- year-old car looks new. "I didn't want to be the one to tell the kid," Mr. Zimmer says.

Tell the kid what? What's Mr. Zimmer talking about? Maybe he heard a rumor that Alton is moving up to Sacagawea, Washington or maybe even Triple A. Across the parking lot, Charlie leans against the Willis's Porsche. They're talking baseball. They could be there a long time.

"Alton's very good," I tell the night air. "But Charlie's good too. I wanted to ask you. . ."

"Forget Alton. Eileen, Mrs. Fain, is seeing someone."

"Mrs. Fain is involved with a man? That's wonderful. Then she'll be more understanding of Charlie and me. She's seeing you, isn't she."

Mr. Zimmer looks up at the moon. "If I was seeing her, wouldn't she be up here with me? She could have had some of that great Trout Almandine she's always talking about. I'm glad Steve warned me off that raw steak."

Poor Mr. Zimmer. Lucky Eileen. She got her degree, put on lipstick and found herself a man. Since she's being so liberal with herself, maybe she can be nice to us and give her consent.

"Charlie's a little sensitive on the subject of his mother's dating. That's why I had backed off."

Little Charlie had wanted his mother for himself and Mr. Zimmer had respected his wishes. "Maybe she would have been more accepting of Charlie and me if she had let herself get involved with you."

Mr. Zimmer nods. He rolls the window all the way down. "It was a mistake to keep herself all bottled up. Maybe, that's why she's gone so crazy now. The truth is the guy she's seeing is a friend of yours. That no-hit kid, Warren Ashburn."

Mr. Zimmer's the one who's gone crazy. "Warren wouldn't be interested in Charlie's mother. She's old. She's over 40."

"He wanted someone to talk to about you. Eileen's always been a good listener."

"So, they talk to each other. That doesn't mean they're – together."

"Warren is an awful name," Mr. Zimmer says. "I never met a Warren I didn't hate. The kid's got terrible manners. Have you ever seen him slurp soup? I had dinner with them before I came up. He's got dirt in his fingernails. Where does a kid like that get dirt? He doesn't do any work. And she's sleeping with him."

Mr. Zimmer's got it all wrong. Warren still loves me. He just got done telling me so. "But Mrs. Fain's a Catholic."

Mr. Zimmer shakes his head and looks at me the way my father does. "She's a woman, and she sure as hell proved it to me when we were together. Then, she'd go and confess. The Church is handy that way."

I clear my throat. "Charlie and I are in an awkward situation. We're not quite legal and we feel. . ."

"At least you and Charlie aren't beating your chests and crying what terrible sinners you are. The Catholics have it made. All they have to do is say they're committing a sin, and then they confess, and they can weasel out of anything. Look at the President."

"President? The President of what?"

"President Kennedy," Mr. Zimmer says. "He does the same thing."

I smile up at the sky and let relief fill me. Mr. Zimmer is loony and consumed with jealousy. Mrs. Fain and Warren go out for coffee and talk about Charlie and me. Poor Mr. Zimmer thinks they've having a torrid affair.

"John Kennedy is a piece of work," Mr. Zimmer says.

"That's disrespectful," I say. "President Kennedy has done so much for us. He's made us believe in ourselves again. Even if he weren't the fine leader he is, he'd still be our President."

"He's got a screw loose," Mr. Zimmer says. "That's the only explanation. He's just like her."

"I feel sorry for you, Mr. Zimmer. I don't know where you get such ideas. Maybe in some sleazy magazine somewhere."

"My brother is the one that tells me," Mr. Zimmer says. "I don't think it's hit the magazines yet. The news people want to protect Kennedy. Like you said, he's the President."

Mr. Zimmer's brother is an expert on political affairs? The fry cook's brother knows the inner secrets of the White House? Mr. Zimmer is a lunatic.

"This has all been very interesting," I tell him. "Informative really. But you have a long drive ahead of you and Charlie's got a game tomorrow. I think we should call it a night."

"My brother's a caterer."

"Oh, Charlie," I call across the parking lot.

"My brother caters fancy beach parties for movie stars like Peter Lawford."

"But Peter Lawford is the President's –"

"Brother-in-law," Mr. Zimmer says.

"Some of us from the young Democrats used to park in front of his beach house, hoping that we could see President Kennedy."

"Well, you would have had an eye full. Stewardesses. Starlets. John Fitzgerald Kennedy loves them all."

Tree-bark wine bubbles in my throat. "You mean the President. . ?"

"Fools around. Just like her."

I look up. The stars, the moon, everything is spinning.

"Catholics." Mr. Zimmer spits the word.

My stomach turns. I bend down over a low fence. The full blooming dahlias turn into the leering faces of President Kennedy, Mrs. Fain, and Warren.

But Warren loves me. I can still see him smiling down at me. I can still feel the silver buttons on his wool jacket pressing against me and leaving their round imprints in my clothes. He can't be making love to someone else.

"You'll have to break it to him gently," Mr. Zimmer is saying. "Charlie's going to take it real bad."

Béarnaise sauce fills my throat. Orange and red dahlias float in front of me. I must be as selfish as President Kennedy and as wild as Mrs. Fain. Even though I'm married to Charlie, I still want Warren to love only me.

•

I'm finally here, back where I belong in a classroom where an erudite professor and intelligent students discuss great literature. I curl into the hard-backed chair and smile at the man who writes his name, *Professor Edelsen*, in chalk on the blackboard.

I open the notebook Charlie gave me. On the first page he wrote: *Best wishes to one of my two favorite students.* I shut my eyes and think of his other favorite student, his seductress mama. I shut my notebook and look up at the podium.

The professor with big ears tells us there are only a few great stories: Boy Meets Girl *(Romeo and Juliet)*, Deception *(King Lear)*, Quest *(Don Quixote)*, Jealousy *(Othello)*, and the *Cinderella* story. The excitement of boiling all literature down to a few simple formulas gets Professor Edelsen pacing again. The tail of his pin-striped Oxford shirt flaps against his rear. One shoe has a loose sole. How could a professor of English at an accredited university turn literature into a joke? If I leave right now, I still have time to catch about four innings of Charlie's game.

The professor points his chalk at me. "What great story did I steal for *Lonesome Sam?*"

Lonesome Sam, the squirrel in a cowboy hat, was my favorite cartoon. He had a skinny tail, sad eyes, and two older bushy-tailed brothers who schemed to own their father's ranch.

"You had something to do with *Lonesome Sam?*" I say.

The professor grins. "I'm Sam's creator."

This floppy man is the person who dreamed up the quick-witted squirrel I loved. But lovable squirrels are for grade-school kids, and this is a college classroom. Maybe I shouldn't answer him, but my voice comes anyway. "*King Lear?*"

"You get an. . ." The chalk flies out of Professor Edelsen's hand, and lands next to a radiator. He bends down and holds up the chalk. "A."

I squint at the man who turned one of the greatest stories of all time into a Saturday morning cartoon. He has a chalk smudge on his rather generous nose. I try to stop, but can't: I'm smiling.

The professor charges to the blackboard, and writes the words, "*Jane Eyre* — boy meets girl." He wheezes. "A love story," he sneezes. He is allergic to chalk. "Plain Jane Eyre and haughty Mr. Rochester. It's a wonderful love story of two lost souls who discover each other."

I picture Mrs. Fain and Warren naked on her couch. Then, I see them naked in Warren's car, and naked on Peter Lawford's front lawn. I want to throw my new notebook against the blackboard.

A clean, neat young man with a piece of tissue still dangling from a small, bloody cut on his chin, raises his hand. "What about their age difference?"

For a second I think this boy who doesn't even know how to shave yet can see the pictures in my mind.

"Age-smage," the professor says. "If Cordelia can be squirrel named Sam, Mr. Rochester can be Romeo."

The boy nods appreciatively. The tissue flutters to the floor and lands by the desk's front leg. Are Warren and Mrs. Fain the new Romeo and Juliet? The new Romeo and Juliet make me sick.

"What about the differences in their social classes?" a girl with makeup half way down her neck asks.

The professor sits on a desk and looks at us with doleful eyes. "In those days poor young women with no family, and no dowry rarely married. In real life, a plain, penniless governess would have remained a plain, penniless governess. But Charlotte Brontë wrote fiction. Two people who need each other find each other. Their ages could have been reversed. Jane, rich, middle-aged, hurt, bitter, but willing to test another person, and Rochester, young, just trying to make his way in the world, could have fallen in love."

Mrs. Fain and Warren need each other. They both have lost someone they love. They've both been hurt. Still, that's no excuse.

"Anyway you do it, Jane, young, and Mr. Rochester older, or the other way around, it's still *Romeo and Juliet*," the professor says.

"Or *Oedipus*," I say.

"*Oedipus*?" The talkative TV writer, opens his mouth, but no more words come out. For maybe the first time in his life, he's speechless. He tosses chalk in the air and catches it. "*Oedipus*. Boy meets girl."

The class laughs.

"You mean boy meets mommy," I say.

The class laughs again. Professor Edelsen tugs his big ear. "Well, Miss Fain, you're certainly an interesting addition to our class."

•

Norma blots lipstick on a tissue. Her eyes look worried. "He's here to move someone up."

"Or down," Beth hugs Little Tank hard.

Mr. Reisner wears Bermuda shorts and a straw hat. In his hometown, the scout looks like a tourist. Next to him is a round, pink-faced stranger who has trouble stepping up the bleachers.

Maybe Mr. Reisner's here to see Charlie, who has been tearing it up. Two days ago, his batting average was actually higher than Alton's. When Charlie came home he said, "Start packing. We're going to Sacagawea." Maybe Charlie was right. I told him I was glad I hadn't cut the fabric for the curtains yet. But what I was really thinking was that I had just bought the textbooks for my class.

Raquel pats Beth's shoulder. "You don't need to worry about Tank. He's doing great. Mr. Reisner wouldn't come all this way just to suggest that someone should be let go."

"Mr. Reisner lives here," I say. "He could just be home for a rest."

"Right. And his friend's here for the scenery." Raquel puffs smoke toward a meadow that is half pasture and half oil field. "Which do you think he wants to see most? The cows or the oil wells?"

"The Dodgers have a shot at the pennant this year," Norma says.

"Thank you, Vin Scully," Raquel tells her.

Norma scans *The Sporting News*. "Triple A's not producing the standouts the Dodgers hope for. The scouts might be here, looking for help. Maybe pitching. Maybe something else." She rubs eyes tired from so much reading. "Did Charlie hear anything?"

"No." I wave at Mr. Reisner. He waves back. He *is* here to see Charlie. Every day Charlie thinks it's going to happen today. I hide my smile behind *Jane Eyre*. Today he's right.

"What about Alton? Has he heard anything?" Norma asks Mrs. Eibur.

Alton. Why do I always forget Alton? Because I want to. Charlie and I don't talk about him anymore. There's just a phantom shortstop out there, a ghost who gets the job done but who is no threat.

The ghost's mother tucks newly waved hair under her picture hat. Overnight, gray roots have turned auburn. "Alton's happy just to be here."

She's telling the truth. Anyone can see he loves to play.

"That's what Steve says," Bonnie tells us. "But I don't believe him. Maybe they'll all get moved." She waves her slender arm. "Whoosh. The whole team up to Sacagawea, Washington."

"Wouldn't that be wonderful?" Beth tucks a blanket around Little Tank. "No one gets fired or left behind."

"That's not baseball," Norma says.

"Or life." Raquel smoothes her full skirt, and admires her new leather sandals. "It doesn't matter how good you are. It's what they need. Still, a little arsenic in the beer for the whole Dodger team would help."

Norma stares at the black armband. "I thought you hated baseball."

"If my husband plays, he might as well be the best."

"Sometimes I can't stand the waiting," Beth says. "Tank's due, but –"

"His bat's hot now," Norma tells her. "He's always had one of the best arms in the organization."

"I'm pregnant again," Beth says.

We all get very still.

Beth sighs, and smiles down at Little Tank asleep in the stroller. "We can barely afford this one."

Beth never finished high school. All Big Tank knows how to do is play ball. What will happen if he doesn't make it?

Raquel lights a Sherman. I brace myself for her angry speech about the virtues of the pill. The speech doesn't come.

We are so quiet we can hear the baseballs landing in the fielders' gloves.

Beth's eyes look dull. "They made so many promises when Tank signed."

"They'll keep those promises." Norma smiles at her and then studies Rusty warming up at third. "They'll keep all those promises."

"Something's going to happen," Beth, without a baby to hug, hugs herself. "I just know it."

"Something good," Bonnie says.

"Did you ever see that movie with Jean Simmons, Dorothy McGuire, and Maggie something? *Three Coins in the Fountain.* Three women make a wish but only one wish can come true." Norma points her scorekeeper's pencil "Mrs. Eibur. Raquel. Beth. Bonnie. Pam. Which one will the fountain bless?"

"We're six women," Raquel says. "This isn't a damn movie. One of our husbands or," she clears her throat, "our son, is going to get moved up, and the rest of us are going to get hurt."

We look at each other. Goose bumps pop out on Bonnie's arm. Beth's right. Something's going to happen and after it does, nothing will be the same. One of us won't be in the bleachers anymore. Could it be me?

I finally got myself back in school. I don't want to go. I don't want to leave my house, my friends. By some miracle, I've built a life here. But Charlie will be thrilled to be moved up. Somehow we will make it work in the next town.

"We could take bets," Raquel says. "Losers take the winner out to dinner."

Norma frowns. "Who's the winner? The person who guesses right or the person who moves to Sacagawea?"

"The person who guesses right. The real winner will be on her way to the airport. I thought the rest of us could console each other. Maybe it was a dumb idea."

"I don't like gambling." Mrs. Eibur unwraps a sandwich she plans to sneak to Alton.

I look at the plump woman in the cotton dress. She is a wonder. Since Alton got sick, she's been gambling. And winning. She'd do great in Las Vegas.

Norma checks the batting order on her scorecard. "Whoever it is, I hope he does good."

"Well," Raquel says. "The word you want is *well.*"

If Kahlil Gibran, alias Barry Silver, gets moved, Raquel will be gone. I'll miss her armband, her brown cigarettes. I'll miss her correcting Norma's grammar.

30

I look at the Lodi team, festive in red and white. They go down in order and Charlie is at the plate. I close my eyes and picture the bat hitting the ball.

The bat cracks. I open my eyes. Charlie has hit a solid single. I look at Mr. Reisner and wave. Charlie can do the job.

On the first pitch to Tank, Charlie steals second. Mr. Reisner is smiling and nudging the pink-faced man. They both are nodding.

Hello, Sacagawea.

Tank swings at a second strike. "Ducky really changed the lineup, but this is an important game. We have to go with the power," Norma says.

"We? I didn't know you were on the team, Norma?" Raquel says.

"Are you saying just because Charlie's batting lead-off he doesn't have any power?" I ask. "He can do it all."

"Just relax," Bonnie tells me. "Norma didn't mean anything."

"Of course she means something," Raquel says. "Everything that is said or done means something."

Norma sniffs. "I wasn't picking on Charlie."

"Please." Beth, staring at the plate, pats her crying baby's back. "I don't know how much more of this I can take."

The baby's father hits a rocket that bounces off the fence into the center fielder's glove. Charlie scores easily. Tank thinks better of trying for a double and trots back to first base.

"That was so close to going over," Norma says.

"Close doesn't count," Beth says. "Long single."

Norma makes a sour face. "I'm just trying to make you feel better." She glances at each of us. "Why am I always the bad guy?"

"I thought I was the bad guy," Raquel says.

We exchange smiles. Bonnie takes out a thermos, passes lemonade around. "We're going to need our strength."

Beth hands out Little Tank's animal crackers.

Kahlil Gibran is up. "A catcher who rarely tires and is always a powerful hitter," Norma says. "Ducky believes in him, and has him batting fourth. Your husband could be another Roy Campanella."

"If he were another Campy, we'd already know it," Raquel says.

"You're so hard," Norma says.

"Just honest."

"I brought lemonade, too." Mrs. Eibur is handing a metallic tumbler to Beth.

"If I had your attitude I wouldn't get up in the morning," Norma tells Raquel.

"At least I have an attitude. I'm not a movie fan one day and Vin Scully the next." Raquel chews the end of her cigarette and watches her husband swing. "Roy just struck out. Damn." She hunches down. "He hates to go out swinging. He'll be mad at himself. And mad at me. No sex tonight." She glances at the scouts. "He'll be mad at them for seeing him strike out. No sex for a week."

Mrs. Eibur's usually steady hand shakes. The drink she's handing to me, swishes, and spills. Her cheeks redden. "So sorry dear," she whispers and swipes at drops of lemonade on my knee.

Where is Mr. Eibur now? Did they have a good time together? Were they in love? Or just in sex?

"Alton's up," I say. "The lemonade's delicious. You and Bonnie could go into business."

Fans boo. "What happened?" Mrs. Eibur shades her eyes and stares at her son.

"He took a strike," Norma says.

Mrs. Eibur puts the jug next to her feet. Like a little girl in school, she sits up straight, and clasps white hands in her lap. She is like the rest of us after all. She is as nervous for Alton as we are for our players.

The pitch is a strike. Alton swings. The ball is gone. From somewhere over the fence comes the sound of shattering glass. Raquel is shaking her head. "Too bad Alton's not married. Some girl is really missing out."

Mrs. Eibur lets air escape from her mouth. She is on her feet and clapping. Spilled lemonade, Raquel's words, nothing can hurt her now.

The Lodi team watches Alton gallop around the bases, careful not to overtake Tank, who chugs home. "He's so polite," Norma says. "He's just hit a home run." She glances at me. "He's not going to show off by taking his time around the bases."

"He always was thoughtful," Mrs. Eibur says. "I never had to remind him about his manners."

Was it easy or hard for Alton to always be the good little boy? Sometimes, I catch him staring at Bonnie. His mother told me once he doesn't have much time for dating. Maybe he's afraid to hurt his mother. He won't let her know that he needs another woman in his life.

Charlie may not be the one they pick to move up, but at least he has me.

At the plate, Steve hits a pop-up. Bonnie's shoulders hunch. Norma chews her lip. Raquel nudges her. "Even you can't find much good to say to Bonnie about a dying quail hit right to the shortstop."

Mrs. Eibur glances up at Mr. Reisner, then pats Bonnie on the shoulder. "It's always so difficult on the players when they're being watched."

"Are you worried?" Raquel bats her new lashes. They're longer than the old ones. They look like little push brooms. "You know Alton will make it sooner or later."

"Alton is very good," Mrs. Eibur says. "But life is full of surprises."

If Mrs. Eibur believes that something could get in the way of Alton's success, then there are no guarantees for any of us. My mouth feels dry. My eyes hurt. Maybe I've been doing too much reading, too much watching, too much hoping. I edge past Mrs. Eibur and Bonnie who are too busy watching the game to even notice that I'm leaving.

In the bathroom I splash water on my face. Which one will the fountain bless? In the movie, was it Jean Simmons' wish that came true? This wanting is awful. It's an ache that won't go away. Charlie needs so badly to win. He has to be the one.

When I walk back to the stands, it's only the third inning and a Lodi runner is on first. This game and the waiting could go on forever. The catcher hits a grounder up the middle. Charlie tags second, pivots, and makes a perfect throw to first. Someone yells, "Whoopee!" Behind the chain link fence at home plate, Walt, stamping new cowboy boots on the pale, orange ground, makes dust fly.

In the bleachers, Mr. Reisner is smiling and nodding. He sees me and winks. I wave and call hello. I want to shout to the world that Mr. Reisner was wonderfully right to sign Charlie.

The next batter hits a hard grounder through the infield. Charlie rushes but the ball is out of his reach. Alton hits the ground, and lying on his belly he catches the ball. Popping up to his knees, he throws to first in time for the out.

At first the bleachers are quiet. No one can believe they've seen what they've seen. Walt shouts, "Al-ton." In a moment the lady with lavender curls and the shy library assistant have taken up the chant.

Now, the pink-faced man next to Mr. Reisner is grinning. Maybe he's the lucky man who scouted Alton. Raquel shakes her head and nudges Mrs. Eibur. "He's magnificent. Nothing gets past him. Nothing."

Mrs. Eibur's white hands lift up from her lap. "Why thank you dear." She looks pleased and surprised.

At second base, Charlie is still looking at the spot where Alton caught the ball. Fans are standing now. They clap and cheer and whistle. None of the cheers are for Charlie.

•

Eighth inning. Except for the steady mournful click of Bonnie's knitting needles (Steve hasn't gotten out of the batter's box yet), there is silence in our part of the bleachers. Raquel sits forward. Her crossword puzzle book is unopened in her lap. Kahlil Gibran is 3-for-4.

Sitting next to Bonnie, I have to stop myself from humming a little tune. Charlie is 2-for-4, with a pair of stolen bases. He's made three stand-out pivots. Whatever happens today, he has the satisfaction of knowing that this is the best he's ever looked.

Alton steps to the plate. The pitch is high and outside. But Alton hits it over the fence.

"Perfect day at the plate," Raquel says. "I hope he has his suitcase packed."

"Do you think he's the one who is going?" I ask in a whisper that all the women, silent and attentive, hear.

"Who else do you see out there who's that good?" Raquel says.

Mrs. Eibur, wide-eyed, and calm, watches her son cross home plate.

"But you said it's not how good you are, it's what they need," I tell Raquel.

"Don't be a baby," Raquel says. "Any team anywhere could use an Alton."

As if they heard her words and agreed, Mr. Reisner and the pink-faced man step down from the bleachers. Something heavy and awful settles in my chest, and then sinks down to my stomach.

Mr. Reisner pauses at the end of our row. "Charlie's looking good," he calls over the heads of wives.

"I'll tell him you said so."

Everyone in our row is watching Mr. Reisner. He smiles up at the white and orange sky. "Little warmer than your Santa Monica," he says. He steps down to the next rung, and calls over his shoulder, "Lemonade weather."

Mr. Reisner and his companion climb into the sedan I could recognize in any parking lot anywhere. How many times is it now that with my heart beating too fast I've watched that car turn onto a boulevard and take all my dreams away? How can Mr. Reisner talk to me about lemonade? Doesn't he know how much Charlie wants to be the one who is moved up? Doesn't he know how much I want it for Charlie?

•

Mrs. Eibur, pigeon-toed, walks to the driver's side of her car. She is just one in a series of mothers I've adopted for myself. There is no way that I am as important to her as she is to me. But maybe she will tell me that she's sorry she won't be seeing me anymore.

I stand on tiptoes and throw my arms around her large frame. "I'm going to miss you," I whisper in the puff of cotton at her shoulder.

She pats my back. "There, dear." She looks surprised. Maybe no one has made a fuss about her leaving before. "It's been lovely meeting you." She includes Raquel in her glance. "All of you."

Raquel sways and swats a fly.

"Mrs. Eibur, what about your cookie tin?" I ask. The tin has a picture of the Renoir girl with the watering can on it. "You'll want that back. I'll send it to you in Sacagawea."

She nods. She has probably left bits of herself, cookie tins, recipe cards, afghans, with mothers and wives at other fields. And with them, as with us, she has been friendly, but distant, as if she knew her talented son would keep her on the move. She hands her son a thermos of warm milk and tells him to lean back and relax. She will get him to the airport in plenty of time.

She settles her bulky frame into the seat of the older model car that she has kept spotless. The plastic seat-cover crackles.

Through the car window, Alton smiles shyly at us – Beth, Norma, Raquel, Bonnie. He rolls down the window. "Mrs. Willis?"

Bonnie steps closer. Alton's porcelain colored skin is turning red. "I was just going to say, if you and Steve are ever in Sacagawea –"

Bonnie nods. Her voice is sad. "If for any reason," she tries a smile, "we're in Sacagawea, we'll come and say hello."

"Thank you." Alton leaves the window open a crack.

Mrs. Eibur turns the key. The Packard's engine hums. She waves goodbye to Mr. Nordstrom standing next to a palm. "I'll miss you all," she says. "Take care, Pamela."

Catching the late afternoon sun, the car glides onto the boulevard. The Eiburs are gone.

•

The Pickers watch the big car carrying their shortstop get smaller and smaller in the summer haze. I squint. Maybe Charlie and I will be the next family to leave town.

Ducky Daspitt has tears in his eyes. "Our star is gone. If he can hit Double-A pitching half as well as he hits down here, he's going to go all the way." Ducky raises his pudgy hand. "He'll be up there with Wills and Koufax and Drysdale."

"For once, the skipper's right," Raquel says.

"When did you become such an Alton Eibur fan?" Norma asks. Her nose is red. She's been crying in the bathroom. She doesn't try to hide her tears. She is more honest than the rest of us. We've been standing here dry-eyed and stoic, waiting for Ducky to finish his speech.

"I always admire talent," Raquel says.

"Except when it belongs to your husband," Norma says.

Raquel looks at her for a long time. "Why do you think I fell in love with him?" Raquel says. Then, she snorts. "I certainly didn't like his taste in books – Rod McKuen and sappy Kahlil Gibran."

"Do you know how rare it is to make the leap from Class A right to the Bigs?" Ducky asks the Pickers. The Pickers shuffle their feet and look up at the sky that is losing its lights. "Only pitchers can make that leap."

Wind whistles past our cars. Ducky takes it as a cue to keep talking:

"We – all of us, players and wives – want to go home and hide, and maybe drink too much beer or soak for what's left of the day in a hot tub. Our Alton can do it. We have to carry on without him. We have to do it for us – and for him."

Little Tank starts to cry. Beth whispers to Norma, "I'm going to get the baby out of the wind. Tell Tank I'm in the car."

"See you tomorrow," Bonnie calls to her.

Beth nods. She wraps a blanket a little more tightly around her son. "I guess we'll all be here."

"We're still in first place," Ducky is saying now. "Even without Alton, we can win this division. Manteca's three back. By Labor Day they'll be in the dust. With Silver behind the plate and Tank in center, Willis at first and Fain at second– we can do it." Ducky's voice gets stronger. "We'll win it all."

•

If only I could make my husband's shoulders stop sagging and take the tired look away from his eyes.

"You were spectacular today. Mr. Reisner told me to tell you." I pull the sheet with pink roses, (his mother's pink roses) to my knees. "You'll be next. Raquel, Bonnie, even Norma, all say you'll be next."

"Experts," he says. He's been sitting at the edge of the bed staring at his slippers for half an hour.

"It's just a matter of time," I say.

He fiddles with the buttons on the new pajamas his mother sent him. Did she buy new pajamas for Warren, too? That angry feeling bubbles up in me again. I'd feel so much better if I could smash something or someone. But I have to control myself. I can't let Charlie know about Warren and his mother.

He has too much else to worry about. "Everyone says how good you are."

"Three perfect pivots," he tells the slippers. "Three damn pivots."

"They were beautiful," I say.

"Not beautiful enough." He wraps the plaid bathrobe more tightly around him. "When I saw Mr. Reisner and the other guy in the stands, I was sure they were there to see me. I can't believe it. I did the best I could, the absolute best. And it wasn't enough."

"All any of us can do is our best," I say.

"Then, I tried to tell myself there was some other reason. Maybe the Double-A shortstop got injured. But Yours Truly is a shortstop, too. Then, I thought maybe the Double-A coach's daughter had a crush on Alton. But I just couldn't see Alton as a lady-killer. The guy looks like a slice of Wonder Bread."

I sigh. How do you compete with a boy who hits four home runs in a single game? I squeeze Charlie's hand. "Alton deserves it though, doesn't he?"

Charlie yanks his hand away and blows on his fingers as if my touch had burned him. He stares at me with angry eyes.

I look away and slide deeper under the sheets. "I'm sorry. Even you said he was good."

He nods and lets slippers drop from his feet. He climbs in bed, pulls the covers to him, turns off the light.

Silence. The puppy scratches. A radio hums in Laura Davis's bedroom. An owl hoots in the cotton field. I picture Charlie and me on a plane, holding hands and flying to Sacagawea.

In the dark comes a sleepy whisper: "Alton deserves it."

31

The black-framed clock on the cork board wall says 12. In the big clock on the university tower outside, chimes begin to ring. High noon. The Pickers will be taking the field. If only I could be in two places at once. If only I could be in the stands cheering Charlie and here in the classroom with my notebook and freshly sharpened pencil.

The door bursts open, and lets in the hot valley wind. Professor Edelsen charges to the blackboard and writes, *Persuasion*.

"Marriage is a serious business," he wheezes. "In Jane Austen's time, it was about the only business a woman could enter. She had to choose right the first time. She didn't get a second chance." He turns and points a piece of broken chalk at me. "Did your mother object?"

"What?"

He points. "You're wearing a wedding ring. You are married aren't you? You're not wearing that for show?"

I shake my head.

"And you're what, 18? And you're a serious girl."

I want to crawl under my desk, or better yet, run away.

He winks at the class. "I can tell by her essays that she's serious. They're thoughtful, and there's not a hint of fancy or the usual romantic notions."

Is he saying I'm abnormal?

"So your mother must have been surprised you wanted to marry so young."

"She didn't know," I say. "She's dead."

His eyes get surprised, then sad. "I'm sorry. You're so young." His voice begins to trail off. "It never occurred to me."

Everyone is staring at me. The room grows quiet. Professor Edelsen slinks behind the podium. Why do I feel like a freak just because I lost my mother? Why do I still miss her so much? Shouldn't I be over it by now?

"I am married," I whisper, looking at all the fresh, virginal faces, feeling as if I'm confessing a crime.

"Your mother would be very proud of you," the professor says.

"Would she?" I stare at my wedding ring.

His voice keeps coming. "You're bright, thoughtful."

I blow out air. "Aren't we supposed to be talking about *Persuasion*?"

He nods. "Another failed experiment in bringing life to literature." He tugs his ear. "Actually there are some more parallels than I realized. Did you have a guardian, an older woman, your mother's friend to advise you?"

The boy with tissue paper on his chin is staring at me as if I were some specimen in a bottle.

"Aunt Lottie," I say.

"And she was more cautious because she loved you and because she was taking over for your mother," Professor Edelsen says. "She didn't want you to make a mistake. She tried to persuade you to wait."

"She drove us to Mexico so we could get married," I say.

Students laugh. A boy next to me in cut offs and a surfer shirt (a surfer shirt 100 miles from the ocean?) bangs his book on the desk. The creator of *Lonesome Sam* opens his mouth, but no words come out. He taps chalk against his forehead.

I hear my own voice say, "Actually I did identify with Anne Elliot. My mother would object. Maybe she would even talk me out of it. She wouldn't like Charlie. So you see, there is a connection."

What's the matter with me? I'm confessing to a room full of strangers, a room full of virgins.

Professor Edelsen's eyes brighten. "Thank you, Mrs. Fain." His knees bang the podium. "I'm sorry if I mentioned things that caused you pain." He clears his throat. "Getting back to *Persuasion*, it would be an easy matter for a Lady Russell to persuade even a girl as much in love as Anne Elliot not to marry before her husband's future was set. Too much could go wrong."

I press my palms against my eyes. Would I have married if Alice were alive? Even dead, her persuasive powers are strong. I am here in a classroom where she wanted me to be. Why did she have to die? Why is there still this dark, empty hole inside of me? It seems whatever I do – fall in love with a wonderful boy like Charlie, go to school – I still can't fill up that empty hole inside me. My head bangs. Tears build behind my eyes. I open my purse, take out my Plymouth keys. I stand and start for the door.

"Mrs. Fain," the professor's voice stops me. "I've upset you. I'm so sorry." Professor Edelsen's heavy eyelids sag. He looks ready to cry. "You reminded me of our heroine, quiet and humble. I couldn't resist the comparison. I didn't know about your mother. I thought, because of your experience, you would bring something unique to us. Most girls your age aren't married, you know."

"I know. I'm a freak – half-woman, half-girl," I whisper. "I don't belong with the other students."

"You bring your life experience to the classroom," he says. "You have something important to contribute," he says. "You're one of the best students I've ever had. You're well read. You love literature. And you have a rich life experience that makes your understanding of literature very special. You are going to be a wonderful teacher."

"How did you know that that's what I want to do?"

"Because you have a gift for it," he says.

I let Professor Edelsen grip my elbow and steer me back to my seat.

•

"I wanted this clock to remind us to make the most of every moment we have." I hold up a wrought iron rooster with a clock in its tail.

Charlie blows on his coffee. "It's ugly."

"It didn't cost us anything," I say. "I bought it with Blue Chip Stamps."

"They should have paid us for keeping it here out of view. We're performing a public service."

I find the stud and hammer the nail into the wall. I hang the clock on the nail and step down the ladder. "It looks even better on the wall."

Charlie squints. "It's worse."

I take the clock down and wrap it in paper.

"What are you doing?" he asks.

"I'm bringing it back to Blue Chip. This is your home. You're supposed to like what's here."

He gets up from his chair, slips the clock from its paper and hangs the clock on the wall. "You like it, and maybe it will grow on me."

•

"I got an A on my essay," I tell him.

"Umm." Charlie sets a plate of scrambled eggs in front of me.

"Professor Edelsen says I'm one of the best students he's ever had."

Charlie sits and opens the sports page.

"You were right to encourage me," I say.

No answer.

"The eggs are very good," I tell him. "You should eat before yours get cold."

"Eibur," Charlie says. "Damn, he did it. He's in Los Angeles. Absolutely no one makes that jump."

"Maybe it's a misprint or another Eibur."

Charlie glares at me. "Another A. Eibur? Baseball must be full of them – Andrew Eibur, Allen Eibur, Arthur Eibur."

I can just see old-fashioned Mrs. Eibur in her picture hat, with her hamper on her lap, sitting in that huge, brightly lit new stadium. "Ducky said he would do it."

"That was just a lucky guess. Daspitt's a minor league coach. If he knew anything, he'd be in Los Angeles, too."

Charlie is so touchy. I jump up and get bread from the fridge. "More toast?"

"Toast? Eibur's in L.A. with Drysdale and Koufax, and you want to know if I want toast?"

He's touchy and hurt. He believes he should have been the one to be moved up.

"One damn summer is all it took Eibur," Charlie says.

"The L.A. Dodgers. I thought you'd be happy for him. He de. . ."

"Deserves it," Charlie says. "Yes, he does. But don't I deserve something, too?"

"You have a start. Class A ball is a good beginning." My voice sounds tired. The one-girl pep squad is running out of pep. I rinse my plate at the sink.

Charlie looks out the window. "Whatever team I played on, I was always the best. I was the one who was so gifted."

I smile at the sun shining on the new roses. "It does feel wonderful to be best at something, even if it is only for a second. Of course you would want to hold onto that for as long as you can. But no one can be the best all the time."

"Why not?"

"I don't know. There are so many talented people out there."

"But don't you see, baseball is all I have. I'm not like Willis with his father and a million-dollar company. Or Alton, who is smart and has his mommy to take care of him. My father was a no show, and even my mother didn't always show up at my games."

"But no one has taken baseball from you." I look at the clock. It's 10 after 11. "I have to get on the road for class." I bend down and kiss Charlie's neck. "I'm sorry."

He blinks. "You're going now with Alton in LA?" He closes the newspaper and folds himself into the chair.

"Your turn will come," I kiss him. "I promise."

He bows his head.

How can I leave now when he needs me most? What kind of a wife am I? I leave when my husband's hurting. I walk to the bedroom and find my keys and purse. I should stay. But right now, at this moment in time, I'm the best student in Professor Edelsen's class. I can't help it. I like being the best, too.

Back in the kitchen, on the radio, Matt Monroe sings a song about leaving. He's going to leave softly.

"I'm not going forever," I tell Charlie. "As soon as class is over, I'll be back. I'll have plenty of time to drive you to the game if you need me too." I whisper. "You're still the best to me."

Charlie shakes his head. He doesn't need me later. He needs me now.

Feeling like the rat I am, a rat in a skirt and stockings, I pick up books and close the door softly.

•

Charlie looks confident out on second base. I rushed home from school early and cooked him fried chicken and corn. Now he's shouting, "Put a bunch of bulls together and what do you get?"

Charlie has his spirit back.

The Dairyland batter checks his swing at a high pitch.

"This guy's not going to do anything," Charlie puts his glove on his shoulder, pats it as if it were a pillow and pretends to sleep.

Raquel turns to me. "Is he all right?"

"Of course," I say. "He's just trying to rattle the batter."

The batter, tall, lean, but still strong, scratches his scrawny neck, wiggles his body, and then grips the bat. He looks angry and mean. He swings at a ball that's high and outside. Charlie stretches and yawns and sleeps again. The batter hits a high fly into the infield. The second baseman reaches, and catches the ball. One out. Charlie tosses the ball in the air and plays a private game of catch.

"Is that legal?" Norma asks. "I mean that's the official ball."

"Fain." Ducky jumps out of the dugout, and trots toward the field.

Charlie throws the ball to the pitcher. Ducky, looking more tired than I've ever seen him, shuffles back to the bench.

A new batter steps to the plate. He eyes Charlie and spits out tobacco. Charlie waves and says, "Bye bye."

The batter hits a grounder up the middle. Charlie dodges in front of Wayne Olivares, our shortstop, and scoops up the ball, but his throw to Steve at first is too late. Charlie shouts, "Hey, Olivares. Go back to D ball or Little League. Maybe then you can play your position."

Wayne Olivares is studying his shoe. Steve yells, "Shut up, Fain." Charlie shrugs.

Norma stares at me, and then looks at Bonnie. "I thought those two were buddies, Tweedledum and Tweedledee."

Bonnie keeps silent. Her knitting needles click.

I tell Norma, "Steve knows it's not like Charlie to be cruel. Steve's just trying to help."

The Bull's hottest hitter, their center fielder, Evan Clay, nicknamed Cassius, stomps on home plate, and cocks the bat over his large shoulder. Charlie holds up two fingers and says, "Double play."

Cassius smacks a hard grounder. Charlie tags second and pivots. He throws a perfect strike to first. Steve stretches. The ball thuds into his mitt. The Dairyland team is gone. The Pickers trot off the field. Charlie is still standing at second. He shouts, "Put a bunch of bulls together and what do you get? A pile of manure."

•

The Dairyland Bulls lead 4 to 3, and the tying run's on first. The winning run, Charlie Fain is at the plate. The winning run thinks he's Fred Astaire. He tips his cap and dances around the bat.

Charlie's clowning isn't hurting anyone, but for some reason it's irritating Ducky. Ducky is marching toward the plate.

"He's going to throw him out," Norma says. "The umpire should have done it innings ago."

"Charlie will feel terrible if he gets pulled," I say.

Fred Astaire sees Ducky stop just short of the on deck circle. Fred's suave smile disappears. Charlie Fain, the Picker's determined second baseman, picks up the bat and hoists it above his shoulder. Ducky steps back, waits, watches. The pitcher goes into his stretch to hold the runner close, then hurls a fastball. Charlie Fain knocks it out of the park.

rs. Fain? This is Halligan's." The voice on the phone is young and crisp and female.

She is the voice of Halligan's. If the Dodgers can have a voice, I guess a furniture store can too. "What can I do for you, Halligan's?"

"Your time payment is overdue."

"My husband pays the bills," I say.

"Your husband is two weeks late."

"That can't be. Charlie is always so responsible."

"We're almost into another payment time period."

"I'm sure there is a mistake in your accounting," I say.

She sounds angry. "There is no mistake."

I tell the voice of Halligan's, "Charlie prides himself on paying his bills on time. But I'll double check." I hang up.

•

I nibble a potato chip and tell myself that Kahlil Gibran's moving up to Sacagawea is not as bad for Charlie as Alton's jump to Los Angeles. Kahlil has played in Cotton Valley for two seasons. Charlie might even be inspired by the catcher's determination.

Barry and Raquel Silver live in a garage. The Silvers don't believe in owning furniture. Ducky sighs and sinks his round frame into a paisley floor cushion. With his short legs tucked under his plump bottom, he does look like a mama duck waiting for her eggs to hatch. But all of Ducky's eggs are rolling away. "They're ruining me," he says. "Stealing all my talent, piece by piece."

Barry Silver, alias Kahlil Gibran, the host and man of the hour, grins and pours Ducky more beer.

Ducky glares at a balloon that swings above him from a raw beam. His eyes say he'd like to smash the balloon and then get really serious and roll a few heads around in the punch bowl. He wags his finger in Barry's face. "You can hit. You can pick guys off." He glances at Barry's wife, Raquel. Slumped against the wall of the room that the Silver's call home, she guzzles wine from a Dixie cup. Her short skirt doesn't quite cover the hole in the thigh of her black leotards. The manager tells Barry, "You can take punishment like nobody else."

Barry stirs Hawaiian punch with a swizzle stick. "You're going to be OK, Skipper."

"Not without you," Ducky bows his head. "You play hurt. You play with pneumonia, with bruises and welts. For God's sakes, you're a catcher and you're allergic to dust and grass."

Freckled, broad-faced, big shoulders, Barry looks as strong as a new barn. "He has allergies?" I ask.

Ducky turns and blinks. He's forgotten I was sitting on the floor next to him. "Asthma," he tells me. "When he wheezes, he sounds like a damn Church choir." He soft-punches Barry. "Remember the time you played on crutches?" He slumps deeper into the pillow. "Now, they're taking you away."

"I'm going to miss you, Skipper." Barry's voice gets lost in his throat. "But you'll be OK."

"Ah, hell," Ducky says.

I look up at Barry. "You played behind the plate on crutches?"

"Nah. I just pinch hit."

"But that's amazing. How could you hold onto your crutches and a bat at the same time?"

Under the roots of his rust colored hair, Barry's scalp turns pink. He smiles at me. "Sometimes you got to do what you got to do. I hobbled up to the plate and just sort of tapped the ball. Didn't bother to run it out, but we got the run home."

I can see why Raquel fell in love with this big teddy bear of a man. I glance at her. She is bent over her drink and paying no attention to Barry or me.

"Wife stealing again, Silver?" Charlie slaps Barry on the back. Barry, still leaning on his imaginary crutch, wobbles. "Congratulations," Charlie tells him. "You got what you deserved."

I sip sweet punch. Charlie is happy for his teammate. "You're next," Barry tells Charlie.

"That's what everyone said when Alton got moved."

"The only reason I'm going first is the Double A guy got injured. Raquel said she put a voodoo spell on him. Maybe it worked."

"Right, voodoo." Charlie opens a fresh beer. "That's the only reason. It can't be that you're that good." He winks. "You're that good, Gibran. And don't let anyone tell you different."

Charlie's eyes are red, white and blue. "Barry played on crutches," I tell my husband, the patriot.

"Gibran knows how to win," Charlie says. "He's probably just like me. He was a winner all through Little League and Pony League and high school and college. He knows how to do that. The problem is we come up here and we have to learn how to be good losers."

"We're not losing," Ducky says. "Even if they are taking all the good ones away."

Charlie looks out the window and tells the small, run down houses and oil wells with towers fragile as Tinker toys, "I'm still here."

"Yeah, but for how long?" his manager says. "You're the next one out of here."

Charlie smiles, relieved. He bends down and pats the plump shoulders. "You worry too much."

"If a pennant's going to happen here in my life time, it's going to happen now. We got the horses and the chemistry. We're the ones getting all the luck, the come from behind wins, the clutch hits. We got it all. I pray every night." Ducky makes the sign of the cross. "Don't take Silver. Don't take Tank. Don't take Fain."

Norma steps to the serving table. She clinks glasses with Barry, and nods at me. "Didn't I always say he was another Roy Campanella?"

"She always did," I tell the catcher. "He has so much courage," I tell Norma. My voice is loud. My tongue is thick. Just how much beer have I had? "He played on crutches. He has asthma. You were right, Norma. He is another Campy."

Barry's cheeks are red. "I better check on that dip." He hurries to the farthest corner of the room.

He wanted to get away from me. "What did I say?" I ask.

"What didn't you say? Barry doesn't like to be the center of attention," Charlie tells me.

Ducky glances at Raquel, who puffs on her brown cigarette. "Maybe that's why he picked our hostess with the mostest. Who'd notice him with her around?" He rubs the fuzz on the side of his head. "What are we going to do without Silver?"

"We'll still get that pennant," Charlie says. "No sweat."

Ducky's eyes widen. "You got a crystal ball?"

"We're four and a half up. You still got me, Steve, Tank, and Rusty. You're in Fat City. I could probably do it for you all by myself."

"It looks like that's what you're trying to do," Ducky says. "You're not helping out there."

"I was 3-for-4 yesterday."

"Your mouth was 10-for-10."

Charlie taps his head. "I'm using psychology and getting them rattled."

"All you're doing is making the other teams mad," Ducky says.

"Listen to him," Norma tells Charlie.

"We're going to have a riot out there someday because of you, Fain." Ducky squints, and gazes past brick and wood bookshelves at something only he can see. "Benches cleared and guys punching each other out and winding up in the hospital. It won't be a pretty sight, and it will all be because of you and your mouth."

Charlie bites a potato chip, and then gets quiet. His eyes look worried. Then, he points a chip at Ducky's nose. "'Cause of me, Daspitt, you're going to win it all."

•

Raquel has been in the bathroom crying for half an hour. If only someone would help her. But how do you offer comfort to someone as strong-minded as Raquel? Wouldn't it be like giving chicken soup to a grizzly bear? Barry taps on the particleboard. His big, freckled hand trembles. He whispers, "Honey, are you OK?"

Over the sound of running water, sobs get louder.

"For God's sake, what a racket," Ducky says.

Barry's knocks make the thin boards shake. Norma stares at the quaking walls. "What if the whole flimsy thing falls down and Raquel's just sitting there on the toilet for everyone to see?"

"Not a pretty picture," Ducky says.

"If only they had rented a regular, apartment, instead of this dump, then at least there'd be some place for the rest of us to go," Norma says.

Ducky says, "There is a place for us to go – home."

Barry is looking at me. "Maybe you could talk to her."

"Me?"

"She says you're her friend."

"I am, but I don't know if she likes me that much."

"She talks about you all the time."

I stand taller, and square my shoulders. The Pickers who have been standing in a group break up and form a path. Everyone looks at me, and then their eyes shift. They stare longingly at potato chips and dip. The Pickers can go back to their good time. Pamela is going to slay the dragon.

"Raquel," I rap. "It's me, Pam."

"Go away," she sobs.

Maybe we weren't such great friends after all. I turn away, and then I see Barry's worried eyes. "I have to use the bathroom," I say.

The lie works. She opens the door and I slip inside.

She's a mess. Her eyes are puffy and one set of lashes dangles on her cheek. She points to the toilet. "So go."

Thank goodness I'm wearing a skirt. I pull down my underpants, and sit on the seat. On the other side of the door, the party-talk sounds loud and artificial.

She splashes water on her face and turns off the tap. From a cupboard under a sink, she takes out a fresh sanitary napkin. "Is anyone saying anything about me?"

"Why would they be saying anything about you? You've only been in here half an hour sobbing. They think you might have something against Sacagawea, Washington."

"I hate Sacagawea, Washington," she says. "It rains all the time. It has two pulp mills and they both stink."

"That's what we've all been saying. Raquel hates Sacagawea."

She blots tears with the sanitary napkin. I stare.

"Haven't you seen anyone dry their face before?" she says.

"Don't you have towels?"

She blows and wipes her nose. "I've got to get some use out of these things."

"Don't you need them for your period?" Then, I know. "This isn't about Sacagawea," I whisper. "You're pregnant."

"Smart as whips, these college girls."

Are the party sounds on the other side of the door suddenly quieter? "You were so proud of your pills. How could it happen?"

"Barry went on the road. I thought why bother when my husband's in Lodi? When he came back I started them again. I didn't know you were supposed to take them even when you weren't screwing."

Screwing is an awful word. Why can't she say, "making love?" Maybe to her it isn't making love. Maybe it is just screwing. And now, she's pregnant.

"I'm so sorry," I tell her.

She drops cigarette ashes in the Dixie Cup. "Me, too."

"Maybe you could get. . .an abortion."

"They're too dangerous. My cousin died from one. She bled to death. Besides, Barry wants LB."

"LB?"

"Little Bastard."

"Why would you call your baby such an awful name?"

"The doctor says the kid's the size of a lima bean. I told Barry that's what LB stands for."

Imagine a baby the size of a lima bean. Wouldn't it be amazing if Charlie and I had our own lima bean growing inside of me?

Raquel sighs. "Stay in school. Don't let your husband touch you. Don't get trapped. You'll have to live your life for both of us."

She wants me to stay in school for her. She's another Alice – yelling instructions from the sidelines. I tear off toilet paper and pretend to wipe myself. I flush the toilet. Raquel's not watching my pantomime.

She pulls down her lip and stares in the mirror. "I'll probably lose all my teeth."

"They say one baby, one tooth," I tell her.

"Naturally, you'd have the gory, up-to-the-minute facts."

"Norma's the one with the gory facts. I'm the one who's going to school for you. You can always get another arm band."

Raquel's mouth opens wide.

"One band for baseball, one for LB. And you'll have to buy an account book. My friend Warren's mother kept a running account in her head of everything he owed from the second he was born." Just saying Warren's name makes me feel close to tears. "But you can do better. Write it all down. Start now.

One hour of mental anguish at Barry's celebration party. What would that be worth?"

"Hypocrite," she says. "What about going to school while your husband's acting like crazy Jimmy Piersall?"

"What are you talking about?"

"Charlie's so wild. You saw him dancing with the bat."

"He's just trying extra hard. It's because of Alton."

Raquel looks at me for a long time. "He needs to learn how to roll with the punches."

"He has a lot of punches to roll with. Warren is. . .screwing Charlie's mother."

Raquel's eyes get big.

"Charlie doesn't know. I figure he had enough problems." I lean against the particleboard and listen to the party noise. "You are going to have a child and if you call him Little Bastard and make him pay for your unhappiness, you're just putting one more unloved person like Warren into the world."

"OK. I won't call him Little Bastard." Raquel hands me the Dixie cup. "Have some Ripple."

The wine is sweet and has a punch. "Charlie's mom is a bookkeeper," I say. "How Freudian. You don't think Warren's just trying to give her something back. She's a mommy and he wants to balance the books?"

"That's too complicated. They're both just lonely. What did Warren's mother have against him?"

I pour more Ripple into my cup. "The list starts with her labor pains and the hospital bill, and ends with paying for electricity when he studies."

"In 18 years," Raquel says, "Lima Bean could screw one of my friends just to make up for all the crap I caused him."

I lift my cup. "I'm going to get gloriously drunk. Do you want to join me?"

"Pregnant in Sacagawea. Talk about *No Exit*." Raquel takes the cup from me. "You just don't look right with that in your hand. And it might not be good for the bean. Besides, it won't solve anything. In the morning, you'll still have an unhappy husband and I'll still be going to that rainy hellhole."

"I'll miss you," I say.

She pours the Ripple down the sink. "I'll miss you, too."

•

"You'll be next." I kiss the top of Charlie's head. "Would you like some coffee?"

"I have a game tomorrow." Charlie glances at the rooster clock. "Today. It's 2 a.m. Alton is in L.A., Silver is going to Sacagawea, and all's wrong with the world."

I put water on the stove for my coffee. "I know you're disappointed. I'm so sorry, honey."

His eyes squeeze. He stands, and pours himself a glass of milk.

"They called from Halligan's. They must have made a mistake. They're under the impression that we're late on our payment."

"They'll have to learn to wait just like the rest of us."

"So, we do owe them?"

He drinks and makes a face. "I forgot about all that beer. It wrecks the taste of milk."

He starts to dump milk down the sink. My voice stops him. "Don't waste it."

"Don't waste it," he mimics. But, he puts the milk back.

"We have to pay. You signed a contract. You agreed."

He shrugs. "I'll take care of it first thing in the morning."

"Do you promise?"

He gives me a beer-milk kiss. "I promise."

•

I tell myself that Warren might be happy to hear from me. He might even say he misses our friendship. Or he might tell me he hates the sound of my voice and he never wants to hear from me again.

I pull the new maple chair next to the phone. The line that goes all those miles from my kitchen to Warren's mother's house crackles.

"I need your help," I say.

"Already?" Warren says.

"I know you and Mrs. Fain are. . .close."

Silence. Even the line stops humming.

"And you probably still care about me," I say. "Two contradictory ideas."

"You got that right," he says.

- 262 -

"She won't consent to our marriage. We need a letter. Could you talk to her? Charlie is having a hard time and it would be one less thing for him to worry about."

There is another long silence. "I'll do it for you," Warren says.

33

Rusty and Tank trot to their positions. Charlie stops in front of the visitor's dugout and tells the Lodestone Crushers, "You guys might as well get back on your bus and go home."

"Drop it, Fain," the visitor's coach says.

I hug myself. Charlie was so mellow at the Silver's party. Why does he have to start up again?

"Suckers," Charlie is saying. "You drive 90 miles in the heat just to get embarrassed."

A Crusher with a wide face and stick-up blond hair gets to his feet. He waves a fist at Charlie. "You're garbage, Fain."

Another Crusher pushes the man back down on the bench. "Save it for the game, Moose."

"See Moose?" Charlie says. "You're only embarrassing yourself."

Steve Willis wraps his arm around Charlie and leads him toward second.

"That's why we need you here," a voice behind me says. "You can tone your husband down. That's a wife's job."

"He's always clowned around," I tell the faded blue shirt. For some reason, I'm afraid to look at Walt's eyes.

Walt holds a popcorn box out to me. A peace offering? "Did you see Alton with the Dodgers? The kid's an inspiration. He shows us just how good we can be."

Alton is the reason my husband needs toning down. "Charlie just likes to get the other team rattled," I say. "He thinks that's his job."

"He needs to stay cool."

Carrying a hot dog and a basket of fries, Walt's buddy, the man in the check shirt, comes padding up to us. He wears a patch over one eye. He looks like a chubby little pirate. He smiles at me. "What do you think of your husband?"

"Charlie's just fine," I say.

"Better than fine. He hit for the cycle yesterday. Didn't he tell you?"

"No." Why didn't he tell me? Doesn't he see hitting for the cycle as a victory?

"Even the Crusher's lead-off man is a giant," Walt is saying.

The Crusher at the plate stands over 6-feet tall. He has three chins. They look like stairs. A little tap of the ball and the ball he hits could be half way to the Pacific. Fans on the visitor's side are chanting, "Seve, kill. Seve, kill."

Seve? Must be short for *sever*.

"They're all giants," the man whispers and bites into his hot dog.

Seve whacks the first pitch into the hole between third and short. Norma's Rusty watches the ball bounce off his glove, then scoops it up.

"An error and the lead off is on," Walt mutters.

"I got a lot going on this season," Walt's friend tells me. "I promised the wife if we win we'll go to the Grand Canyon and take one of those burro rides to the bottom."

"Eibur would have gotten that," Walt says.

"Eibur." The man takes a handkerchief from his pocket and blots his good eye. "He looked like Caspar the friendly ghost, but could he play. Right, Walt? 'Course these guys can play, too. Your hubby helps a lot."

Hubby is one of those women's magazine terms. There are lots of articles about the care and treatment of hubbies. Scowling at second, my hubby looks as if he's eaten splinters for breakfast.

A tall, thin man with wire from a transistor radio plugged in his ear, calls from the stands, "Hey Walt. How long is Tank's streak now?"

"Fifteen games," Walt says.

The man pulls the plug out of his ear. "You should be calling the game. That Bozo said it was only 13."

Walt stirs his Slurpee. "Last year Tank had a 30-game hitting streak and no one was here to watch."

On the base path, Seve takes a big lead. Charlie yawns and puts his glove on his shoulder and pretends to sleep. "Fain, cut it out," Ducky yells from the dugout.

Seve is halfway to second. "Relax, Duck." Charlie bare-hands the ball our new catcher tosses to him.

Seve trots back to first.

"Charlie's just keeping the Crushers off balance," I tell Walt.

Walt is watching Seve run again. Our catcher's throw is late. Seve knocks Charlie down and slides under his leg.

Charlie falls head first into the base path. He's lost in the dust. I stand on tiptoes and try to see past Pickers running on the field.

"Don't worry," Walt's friend says. "Your hubby's tough."

Charlie stands and brushes off dirt.

"See?" Walt's friend rubs his good eye. "What did I tell you?"

"Seve's safe." Walt tells the air. "Kahlil Gibran would have made that play."

Charlie shouts at the batter, "Hey, Pee Wee. Go home."

Pee Wee, the Crusher catcher, a shrimp of 6-feet with forearms that look like ham bones, slams a ball over Charlie's head. The ball bounces into center field in front of Tank's glove. Seve's slide to the plate beats Tank's throw.

Walt says, "These are routine plays and we can't make them."

Seve gets to his feet, and jabs his thumb at the Picker crowd. The score is 1-0.

Pee Wee takes a lead off second. Charlie calls to our pitcher: "Step off!" The runner goes. The pitcher steps off the rubber, but his throw to third is just a heartbeat late. Ducky yells, "Are you guys asleep out there?"

"Charlie's not asleep," I tell Walt and the man in the check shirt. "He's the one who saw the play." Charlie rubs his shoulder. "And he's playing hurt," I say.

•

The score is 3-0. The Pickers went out one-two-three in the first. Now, Moose, the Crusher's first baseman, the one who called Charlie "garbage" is at first, and another power hitter, their right fielder, is at the plate. A trumpet blares on the Visitor side. Fans yell, "Charge."

The hitter cracks a ball up the middle, past the pitcher. Charlie grabs the ball and heads toward second base. Over the blast of the trumpet, Walt shouts, "Double play."

Charlie's foot tags the base. He pivots and fires the ball toward first. Moose looks like a little truck as he charges down the base path. "Why doesn't he stop?" I ask Walt. "The play's over. He's out."

Moose lowers a shoulder and knocks Charlie off his feet, and takes him halfway to center field.

"That's why he didn't stop," Walt says. "Those Crushers want blood."

Charlie's lost in the dust again. "He's hurt," I say.

The man in the check shirt sucks in his breath and whistles.

Seve, Pee Wee, Moose, and all those other monsters in gold have something against Charlie. Charlie gets up slowly. He's all right.

Walt crushes his Slurpee cup. "And they say football is a tough game."

"What is this?" I ask him. "Some kind of holiday – get Charlie Fain day?"

The man with the eye patch taps Walt on the shoulder. "I'm going. Call me later and tell me who won." He shakes his head at me. "I came to see baseball. Not war."

"Maybe Charlie shouldn't try to rattle those guys. They all think they're John Wayne, or worse. See what I mean?" Walt points to home plate. The new batter has hair in his ears, two teeth missing, and a tattoo. They must have found him in a cave. He pounds the ball deep into left field. It's a triple. Walt eyes Ducky who is showering the dugout with sunflower seeds. "Maybe you could talk to the manager and get Charlie out for his own good."

Someone is tapping me on the shoulder. Bonnie is smiling. "Why didn't you let me know you were coming to the game? We missed you." She tells Walt, "Pam's been such a stranger."

"You're her friend," Walt says. "Tell her she should talk to the manager and get Charlie out of the game."

Bonnie's eyes widen. "Is he hurt?"

"He will be," Walt says.

"Usually we don't interfere," Bonnie says. "The guys don't like it. Besides, they all fight. It's part of the fun for them."

"I've watched a lot of baseball," Walt says. "This looks particularly vicious."

I tell Walt, "If one more bad thing happens, I promise I'll talk to Ducky."

•

I bend down and smile at Little Tank. "He looks as if he's grown an inch since I saw him last."

"He's teething. It's murder," Beth says.

"For him and for her," Norma says.

"You were right that I love the challenge of school," I tell Bonnie.

She opens her knitting bag. Her blue thing covers her lap.

"I had to write three essays in one day. I've never felt so alive," I say. "Now, we're going to be reading Thomas Hardy – *The Mayor of Castorbridge.*" I find Mr. Nordstrom's striped beach chair in the crowd. Mr. Nordstrom is bending over his notepad. "We already read *Jude the Obscure.*"

"Awful," Norma says.

"Thomas Hardy is awful?" I ask.

"Every time you look, one of those Crushers is on base," Norma says.

Seve takes a lead off first. "But they don't stay long," I tell her. "They knock Charlie down, run the bases and tag home."

"It's not that bad," Norma says.

It's that bad. But Bonnie, Norma and Beth don't seem surprised. Maybe all of Charlie's little insults have added up. Maybe the Crushers are carrying one large grudge.

The batter hits a pop fly right to Charlie's glove. Charlie tags the bag for the second out. Seve charges him, and rolls him on what has become a path into center field. "Stop them." I'm on my feet and screaming.

Ducky jumps out of the dugout, and yells at the plate umpire and the Crusher manager, "What are you guys trying to do? Get my second baseman killed?"

"That's exactly what they're doing," I shout.

The umpire doesn't say anything. He's watching Charlie roll. Charlie stops. The dust settles. Steve and our shortstop help Charlie to his feet. Bonnie says, "He's all right."

Charlie stumbles to the bag. Seve at second grins.

"Hey, Bozo," Charlie holds up the ball and shouts, "You're out."

Walt has his back to the field. He shades his eyes with his hand and looks at me.

"I've got to get Charlie out of the game before something really awful happens," I say.

"You'll only embarrass him," Bonnie says.

"I'd rather have him embarrassed than dead."

"He'll never forgive you," Norma tells me. "You know how they are. He'll think you're acting like his mother."

"The other guys will make fun of him," Beth says. "Once I wanted Tank to leave a game because he twisted his ankle. You should have heard the guys ride him. Tank didn't talk to me for three whole days."

"So, I'm just supposed to wait until the game's over or they take him out on a stretcher. Whichever comes first."

"You worry too much," Bonnie says. "The umpire will stop it."

Maybe Bonnie's right. I don't want to hurt Charlie's pride. I turn from Walt's stare and sink in my seat.

•

Charlie fences with the bat and points its tip at the pitcher. "Ready or not, here I come."

The pitcher doesn't wait for Charlie to take the proper batting stance. The ball whizzes past Charlie's ear. He ducks just in time. The umpire calls the ear-grazer a ball.

A second pitch, a strike, rips past Charlie's shoulder. He stoops and backs away from the plate. "I should have talked to Ducky and gotten Charlie out of the game," I say. "That pitcher's trying to hit him."

"He's been asking for it," Norma says. "But I don't think anyone would really hit him."

"Of course not," Bonnie pats my knee.

Norma looks up from her scorecard. "They wouldn't hit him, because if he's hit by a pitch they have to put him on base."

"You do care," I say.

She shrugs and watches the pitcher wind up. The ball flies toward Charlie's knee. He jumps back in time to miss the ball.

"My God," Norma says. "They do want him dead." She turns to me. "He may be loud and obnoxious, but he's a good player. He doesn't deserve this."

"We should do something," Bonnie stands. "I'll talk to Mr. Daspitt."

She's too late. The pitch heads like a homing pigeon for Charlie's face. Charlie curls up and rolls on the ground.

""Did the ball hit him? He could be unconscious," I say.

"Or blind," Norma says. "That ball could have smacked him in the eye."

I stare and try to see Charlie through the dust and crowd of players surrounding him. Bonnie's arm is around me. Her watch ticks. Beth is crying.

The crowd breaks up. Charlie stumbles to his feet and slaps dirt from his sleeves, and his pant legs. He searches through a dust cloud for his bat.

He can see. He's conscious. He's all right for now. Coleen, the library assistant, gets to her feet and claps for Charlie. Charlie grins.

But the pitcher is grinning too. "Ready or not, here it comes."

Charlie's ready. The pitch starts off fast. Charlie swings. The ball sinks low, and falls just to the right of the plate.

"Strike," Norma says.

Charlie curses, and flips his bat in front of home plate.

Norma sighs and watches Charlie stagger to the dugout. "Maybe he should have let the ball hit him." She winks at me and rubs her red nose. "Not hard, but we need a man on or we'll never catch up."

34

I'm so sorry," I tell Charlie. He's a mess of cuts, scratches, and bruises. There's a gash across his forehead. One eye puffs and threatens to close. He looked better before I washed off the dirt and dried blood. "I'll make you better." I pour Campho-Phenique on a cotton ball. Where do I start? I dab his knee. "Why didn't the umpire stop the game? Didn't he see they were after you?"

"'Course he saw." Charlie grabs the cotton ball and slaps a welt on his thigh. "You're too timid. By the time you're done, gangrene would set in and we'd have to amputate." He frowns at his legs. "It looks like a damn topographical map. Mountains of swelling and valleys of bruises." He hoists himself to the edge of the tub and lifts one leg and stares at the jagged cut on his calf. "There's the San Andreas Fault."

"How did you get that?"

"Seve thought my leg was a skating pond." He hands me the cotton ball. "I can't reach."

I squeeze the cotton and let the medicine run down the cut. "Maybe you shouldn't be the one to rattle the other team. Maybe you should just play baseball."

"That is baseball." He winces and grips the edge of the tub. "Do you have to be so rough?"

"First I was too timid. Now, I'm too rough? Does it sting?"

He glares at me through his good eye.

"Those Crushers are bullies," I tell him. I look down at the San Andreas Fault on Charlie's leg. The fault is turning red. I rub his neck and whisper, "They shouldn't be allowed to treat you that way."

Suddenly his good eye gets bright. For some reason, he's grinning. I don't like his smile. He has a new horrible plan. It's something so awful it makes him grin.

"You will take my advice won't you?" I ask. "Don't bait them and they won't treat you that way."

He squeezes my hand. "You're right, babe. They shouldn't be allowed to treat me that way."

•

At the plate, Seve shouts, "Hey Fain. Watch me." Seve points the tip of the bat on the ground and tap dances.

At second base, Charlie watches and says nothing. Good. Charlie listened to me. He'll concentrate on being a fine ballplayer. He'll do nothing to aggravate the Crushers.

Norma runs her finger through freshly cut and waved hair. She eyes the new scoreboard. It's painted a dark, shiny green. The numbers are black against a white backing. "The Crushers got three runs in the first inning," Norma says.

If Raquel were here, she'd tell Norma that we all know how to read a scoreboard.

Norma sighs. "It's only the second inning."

"I feel sick," Beth says.

"We could still pull it out from here," Norma tells her. "They're a tough team, but it's not impossible."

Beth stands and lifts Little Tank from the stroller and hands him to me. "I'm going to throw up." She runs to the bathroom.

Little Tank smells of powder and apple sauce. He's so plump, I feel as if I'm holding a dumpling. What do I do with him? He studies me. He knows I don't know what to do. I should give him to Bonnie or Norma. But Beth trusted me.

"I'm glad Raquel's not here." Bonnie pats Little Tank's chin. "Imagine the hard time she'd give Beth about a second pregnancy so soon."

"Maybe her reaction would surprise you," I say.

Norma tilts her head.

"Raquel's always so sure about everything," Bonnie says.

"People change," I say.

"Not Raquel," Norma says.

Little Tank wriggles. He wants to get away from me. If Raquel were here, she'd be in the bathroom throwing up right alongside Beth.

Now, the baby's gurgling and pressing wet lips to my neck. I can't believe how much he likes me. I hug him and feel his warmth. So, this is what holding a baby is like. I look out at Charlie at second. He stands calm and still. Maybe someday we will have a child together.

A bat smacks a ball. Pee Wee, the Crusher catcher, is running to first. The ball zips past Rusty at third. "Damn." Norma spits out sunflower shells. It won't be long before she's chewing tobacco.

Seve steps up to the plate. Even his head seems oversized. He bends at the waist in imitation of a Charlie Fain clown bow. Stone-faced, Charlie turns and watches the pitcher wind up. Seve lets a strike blow by. He hits the next pitch hard, and up the middle. Charlie scoops it up, pivots and tags second.

"Turn two," Norma screams.

Pee Wee starts a late slide. His hand starts down the bag. No. It's not the bag he's after. He's reaching for Charlie's legs.

The batter puffs slowly toward first.

Charlie drops his arm and throws sidearm, hitting the sliding Crusher runner in the face.

It can't be. Charlie couldn't have hit him on purpose. He had plenty of time to make the throw to Steve Willis at first. Pee Wee skids in the base path. He looks stiff. He's out cold.

And Charlie is grinning.

He hit him on purpose. This was his plan. I hug Little Tank hard, and feel my tears. How could Charlie do it?

Steve and the team mangers kneel by Pee Wee. Pee Wee is unconscious. "We need an ambulance," Bonnie says.

"Coach Mackie already called," I say.

White-faced, Coach Mackie runs from the office to the field.

"He could die," Norma says. "Or it could be even worse. Just this spring some high school kid was hit like that. Now, he's paralyzed from the waist down."

I squeeze Little Tank and try to get courage from his warmth and softness. "It had to be an accident," I say. "Charlie wouldn't hurt anyone on purpose. He's a very gentle person."

"I don't think that Crusher Seve agrees with you." Norma points to the field.

Seve slugs Charlie in the face, in the chest and in the stomach. Charlie doubles over and kicks Seve in the groin. Wayne Olivares squeezes between the two of them. Now the three of them are waltzing. They dip their knees, curl their elbows and kick their feet. The waltz turns to a polka. It's horrible. I stand and clutch Little Tank. "Charlie stop."

"We better call two ambulances," Norma says.

The restroom door bangs open. Beth, hair flying, skirt flapping, looks at me, and at Little Tank, and then starts to run to her husband on the field. Mr. Nordstrom blocks her.

He says something to her, and links his arm in hers, and escorts her to the bleachers.

Mr. Nordstrom glances at me holding the baby. He must blame Charlie for the shouts and yells coming from the field. "Don't do this, Charlie," I call.

Even though I'm shouting, Little Tank takes slow, even breaths, and stays asleep. Beth is starting to cry. I offer her her child, but she shakes her head. I hold Little Tank as if he were an anchor.

Whoops ring from the Crusher's dugout. Four or is it five Crushers run to the field. Mr. Nordstrom says, "War."

He grips his pen. He's not writing anything. He looks as if he'd like to be out there, stopping what he's watching. But what can Mr. Nordstrom , with his bad leg, do?

Bonnie rushes toward the fence and cups her hands and shouts, "Steve, stay out of it."

Steve isn't listening. He's running into a gold and blue Crusher chest.

"They've got my Rusty," Norma cries.

Her Rusty has joined Charlie, Seve, and Wayne in the polka. Her Rusty is pushing his glove in Seve's face.

The benches clear. The only two men not fighting are Mr. Nordstrom and Pee Wee. Even Ducky, and the round, little umpire have joined the dance.

Norma glares at me. "This is all your husband's fault. You heard Ducky. He warned him."

I nod and close my eyes. Behind my lids I see the graceful shortstop I fell in love with. My Nureyev was not a brawler. My Nureyev was not a murderer.

I feel someone squeeze my shoulder. I look up and see my face reflected in Mr. Nordstrom 's glasses. "You can't blame a wife for a husband's behavior," he says.

•

The little umpire is standing on the pitcher's mound. He shouts through a bullhorn. "Everyone off the field, or there's no game."

Heads lift. Fists stop in mid-air. Shoulders hunch. Angry scowls turn to sheepish grins. Tank looks at his pregnant wife in the bleachers. He shrugs his shoulders, and slaps dust off his sleeves and shuffles to the Pickers dugout.

Ducky, the Crusher manager, and an attendant carry Pee Wee on a stretcher to an ambulance. Fans cheer Pee Wee. Pee Wee is a hero. But he can't hear their cheers.

If the catcher's a hero, then my husband must be the villain.

A siren rings out. The siren's wail stops the fans' cheers. In the sudden quiet I wonder what will happen if Pee Wee dies?

Charlie will get the fame he's been wanting. People will talk about him the way my father said they talked about the boxer Emile Griffith who killed Benny Kid Paret in the ring. They'll talk about him in whispers.

Umpires and managers huddle around the mound. The sportswriter glances at me and walks unevenly to his canvass chair. Subdued, all business, the professional ballplayers take their positions.

The game resumes.

•

Any minute now we'll hear the news that Pee Wee is all right. Ducky will step to the bleachers and tell us, "All the guy had was a mild concussion."

Norma smacks her bubble gum. She won't turn to look at me. She talks to Beth. "Those Crushers are copycats."

Beth rocks Little Tank. The baby's eyes flutter and blink at me. Little Tank doesn't hold it against me that I'm married to a potential murderer.

"Guess what their first baseman's name is?" Norma asks Beth. "Moose. First they have Pee Wee. Now, they have Moose. Moose Steinman. Can you believe that?"

Beth believes that. She sings a lullaby.

"Just because he's big and plays first base, he's got to be called Moose. I mean Tank is original. Bruiser is original. But Moose?"

Bent over her blue thing, Bonnie smiles at me. Her smile says though my husband is a potential murderer, she's still my friend.

Charlie steps to the plate. Crusher fans boo. Norma stops talking. Beth hums, *Rock-a-Bye Baby*. Bonnie's needles click. Pamela, the sort-of Catholic, prays, "Please let Pee Wee be all right. Please, let Charlie get through this game without any more problems."

The pitcher aims at Charlie's middle. Charlie doesn't budge. Why won't he just take one step back? Isn't one player in the hospital enough for Charlie? Does he want to get hit so he'll have an excuse to start another fight?

Bonnie puts her knitting on her lap and watches.

The second pitch is high, tight and fast. Charlie ducks but stands his ground.

Charlie hits the next pitch, a high fastball up past the pitcher. Charlie is off the plate and running toward first. The shortstop's throw is late. I take a deep breath. Charlie is going to be safe.

I shut my eyes. When I open them again, Steve Willis is at the plate and Charlie is taking a modest leave off first. But the pitcher isn't taking any chances. He throws the ball. The ball zooms over Moose Steinman's head. The first baseman leaps up and makes the catch. Charlie's foot is on the bag, but Moose tags Charlie hard, smack in the center of his chest. The tap takes Charlie's breath away. It drives him off the base and into the dirt.

Crusher fans cheer. Their Moose is doing what they want him to do – kill my Charlie.

Charlie stands and shoves the first baseman. Moose rocks, but keeps his ground. Suddenly the little umpire is there, jumping up and down, yelling, and breaking them apart. "You'll be out of the game and into the showers."

"Take them out now." Walt steps on to the field. "Take them out before there's more trouble."

Now, the Crusher fans are booing Walt.

"Who is that guy – is he someone's relative?" Norma asks.

"He's my friend," I say.

"Yeah, well he shouldn't be on the field."

If Raquel were here, she'd ask Norma who appointed her the Commissioner of Baseball. "Walt means well."

Norma crushes her bubble with her thumb. "He's not supposed to be out there."

"And you're not the Commissioner of Baseball," I say.

Surprised, Norma opens her mouth and lets pink gum dribble on her chin.

Bonnie looks at the plate where Steve is watching a strike go by. She touches my shoulder. "Your Walt is right. We should get Charlie out."

I stand up. Bonnie is right behind me. We squeeze past Beth and Little Tank.

Charlie shouts, "Mother May I?" He takes three steps off the base.

"Mother May I. The things he comes up with." Norma tries to stop her smile, but can't. She blushes and chomps on gum. "He's got balls."

Beth stares at her. "Norma."

"Well, he does."

"Hey, Mother." Charlie takes four steps.

I walk down one stair and then another.

The pitcher tosses the ball to Moose. Charlie jumps back to the base. Moose tags him in the chest, and shoves him in the dirt.

"Not again," Bonnie says behind me. We jump down to level ground and push our way through the crowd toward the fence.

"That's my husband out there." I push past a tall man in a Dodger cap, and a girl with cotton candy.

Through the holes in the chain link fence I see Charlie. He wobbles, falls, and then gets up again. There's a new angry bruise on his cheek. His eyelid is puffy. But he still throws a punch right to Moose's jaw. Moose totters, and stumbles, but he's standing. He blinks. He rocks. He throws down his glove. He's going to kill Charlie for sure.

The little umpire is there – squeezing himself between them. He grabs Charlie's shirt. "Fain, get out." He jerks his thumb. "Moose."

"It's over." I hug Bonnie.

"Everything's going to be all right now." Walt watches Charlie walk off the field.

Charlie is nursing his right hand.

•

The X-ray shows two broken fingers.

35

Maybe the hot tea and tomato soup, both so warm and soothing, will perk him up.

Propped by pillows, and wearing a plaid bathrobe, Charlie sits in bed and watches a cooking show.

"Soup and tea?" I ask.

He blinks and holds two broken fingers, supported by a slender splint, to his lips. "Never over-cook roast beef," he repeats what the man on television is saying. "You pay top money for the prime cut. You don't want to ruin it."

My stomach rumbles. Roast beef sounds so wonderful. We're running low on money and on food. I ask Charlie. "Do you want to share a bologna sandwich?"

Charlie shakes his head, and watches the chef whip something and pour something. "Yorkshire pudding is complicated," Charlie says. "It's all in the whipping. But it's worth the effort."

With his broken fingers on one hand and his sore wrist on the other, he won't be able to use an eggbeater for months. I step to the kitchen and return with a straw.

The Galloping Gourmet pours wine and toasts the viewers at home. Charlie tilts his head and winks at me. "I'll have Yorkshire pudding. Prime rib, very rare." He bends down and sips soup through the straw.

"I'm so sorry this has happened to you," I say.

"And plum pudding for dessert."

•

"How are your fingers?" I ask.

No answer. Charlie picks up the scissors with his better hand and tries to clip a recipe out of a newspaper. He puts the scissors down and sighs at the screen.

Johnny Carson raises thick eyebrows at his late night audience. "You're saying husbands and wives should talk about. . . "

"Everything," the lady psychologist, with a nice smile and nice waves in her hair, says.

"Even, you know. . .?" Johnny says.

"Whatever is bothering a couple, that's what they should talk about."

"When did the doctor say your cast could come off?" I ask Charlie.

Charlie turns pages of *Woman's Day* magazine.

"There should be no secrets between husbands and wives," the lady psychologist says.

Johnny tugs on the V-neck of his sweater. He looks nervous. Is he married? Are their things he's not telling his wife?

"How did you feel when you punched Moose?" I ask.

Charlie gets up, and punches the TV button. The room turns dark.

•

I dial the phone again. When Mrs. Fain hears my news, she'll come and fix Charlie tomato soup. She'll help him get better and she'll help him find his hope again. She's always been a good mother. She'll be a good mother now.

The good mother still doesn't answer her phone.

•

Mr. Zimmer shouts over the whir of the stove fan, "Eileen's in the mountains."

"Do you have the number there?"

He doesn't answer my question.

I listen to the rattle of dishes. A car honks in the far away parking lot. "She said she wanted her privacy," he says.

She's on a Catholic retreat. She's praying for forgiveness for being with Warren. She told me she loves to go once a year. The skinny pines make her feel closer to God. God will forgive her. I'm not so sure her sort-of daughter-in-law will. But she's the only one who can help Charlie. "Can I leave a message for her through the Church?"

"What Church? She's up at Lake Arrowhead screwing your friend."

She's not praying. She's screwing. I blink and stare at dark tea. They're there together at his aunt's cabin where we were going to go someday when I felt "ready to be a woman." I never felt ready. I wrap the string and tag of the tea bag around the cup handle. Now, he has a real woman.

"The jerk had engine trouble on the way up. They called, and asked me what they should do. He has a Fiat. Who the hell ever heard of a Fiat?"

"It's his parent's car. It overheats easily."

- 279 -

"She overheats easily," he says.

There's a pause on the other end. I can imagine Mr. Zimmer standing there, aiming a moody stare at the steam rising from the grill. "Is there something I can help you with?" he says.

This is going to hurt Mr. Zimmer almost as much as it hurts Charlie. "Charlie's had an injury. He broke two fingers."

Mr. Zimmer whistles. "Tough break."

"He wanted you and his mom to know."

"How did it happen?"

"There was a problem at first base. He's taken it very badly. He's just sitting around and watching TV as if his life were over."

"Very tough. You want me to come and cheer him up? He takes everything too much to heart. For him, it's always all or nothing."

This probably isn't the first time Mr. Zimmer's been willing to leave his restaurant to help Charlie. "If he doesn't get better, I'll call you again."

"Tell the kid I love him," Mr. Zimmer hangs up.

•

This may be the very thing to get Charlie going again. I glance at him. His eyes have red rims. He reeks of Vicks. He sits on the edge of the bed and rubs fingers over his red-gold stubble, the start of his Viking beard. He stares at the screen. His eyes brighten. One of his favorite shows, *Girl Talk,* is on.

"Did you know there are stages in child development? Today, we're doing Terrible Twos." He smiles at the panel of girls – all women over 21.

I turn the knob to Channel 10, local news.

"What did you do. . .?" Charlie doesn't finish his sentence. He studies the TV screen.

Hands on knees, nervous smiles, Steve Willis and Ducky Daspitt look like prisoners of war. "Though we lost Eibur, Fain, and Silver, we still have got a great chance," Ducky tells the camera. "Fain could come back soon. By the way, Pee Wee, that Crusher player is OK."

Charlie jumps out of bed and turns the television back to his program.

"Mr. Daspitt's talking about you," I say.

"Not anymore," Charlie says.

I reach for the knob. Charlie blocks me.

"Bonnie thought you'd want to see Steve," I say. "Maybe it would cheer you up."

"*Girl Talk* cheers me up."

"Don't you want to hear about the team?"

His shoulders sag. "There's no way they can take the division now." He pauses, and flicks the channel back to Ducky and Steve. He tells the screen, "I thought I was the greatest thing since sliced bread. Now I can't even play A-Ball."

"You were playing brilliantly. Your fingers will heal."

"The universe didn't want me to play. Eibur and Silver getting sent up, two broken fingers, they're signs. This is not Charlie Fain's season." He switches the channel and climbs back into bed. He pats the covers and makes a place for Boris.

On the television, a moon-faced woman with puffy blond hair smiles into the camera. "If you're patient and willing to give up a little sleep, and a neat house, there's no reason the Twos can't be terrific."

Maybe Charlie is going through a negative stage. Maybe he is just two. He certainly is terrible. I study the moderator and her experts. They don't stay home and chase 2-year-olds in those skirts and heels.

"Steve wants you to come to the games," I say. "You're still a Picker. It will be good for the team. Your friends can help you. I don't know how to make you feel better."

Charlie pats the dog's head. "Boris needs me here."

"You need to talk about what's bothering you. It can't be healthy keeping everything inside. Isn't that what they say on all those shows you watch? Spouses need to be honest."

So, why am I pretending that what he's doing is all right with me?

Charlie hums the *Girl Talk* theme music, and watches the plump woman fade to a commercial.

"At least let me drive you to the office. If you get your insurance form and half pay, that will remind you of how much you contribute. Plus, we could use the money."

He sighs, and shuts off the TV. "Tomorrow they're doing meals that freeze and please. Maybe you could watch with me?"

"Maybe if you're not going to be with the team right now, we should think about one or both of us getting a job."

"I have two broken fingers, remember?"

"I know, but maybe there's something you can do."

Charlie turns a cigarette pack inside out and rolls it into a ball. "I could be a one-armed paper hanger or a one-handed fish cleaner." He tucks the puppy under his good arm. "We'll have Boris, the partially trained pimp, sell pencils and Charlie."

He slips off his robe, and puts on jeans and a sweatshirt. He clips the leash onto Boris's collar.

"You're going for another walk?" I ask. "You'll be gone for hours. And when you come back, I'll ask what you saw and you'll say nothing." I slide my arms around his waist. "Please don't go. We should talk. I want to help you. You must hurt so much."

He squints. "I just can't talk." He yanks the leash and pulls the dog out of the room. A second later, the front door thuds shut. The gate clicks.

I hurry to the living room. Out the window I see them, a boy and dog jogging alongside the railroad track. They get smaller and smaller. Soon they're lost in the dust they raise as they run.

•

Maybe if I bring home money and add it to the money he's earning on half pay, he'll see how much he's accomplished. But maybe the half pay will only make him feel worse. It will remind him that right now he isn't playing ball. I stare at large color photographs of tractors decorating two walls. The tractors look as if they're heading right toward me.

I turn and stare at pictures of baseball teams. Mr. Miller, the Picker's owner, has two loves in his life − his tractor business and his baseball team.

"May I help you, Mrs. Fain?" Grace Everett, Mr. Miller's secretary, looks at home behind the honey colored desk. At day games, she wears glasses, hats, and long sleeves to protect her smooth skin and perfect hair. Maybe the rumors are true. Maybe Mr. Miller has three loves: tractors, baseball and Miss Everett.

"I came about Charlie's half pay," I say. "You know, I told you on the phone." I stand straight, the way Alice taught me. I'm not sure why I feel like a beggar.

The team secretary rifles through insurance forms. Grace Everett's hair is the color of champagne. Her stylish glasses her heart-shaped face give her a schoolgirl look. "You must be so excited that the Pickers are in first place," I say.

"It's wonderful for Mr. Miller. He's never had a winner before."

"But I thought. . ." Above her, a brown and yellow banner with the words "Central Valley 1953" flaps in the breeze from a fan.

"Mr. Simpson, Simpson's Paints, owned the team then." She glances at team pictures fading on the wall. She opens her checkbook and starts to write.

Just watching her pen move across the check gets me jumpy. What if Charlie gets mad at me for asking for his check without his permission? It is his money.

"Mr. Miller's being generous you know. But that's his way." Grace Everett smiles indulgently. "He doesn't have to pay anything. Charlie took himself out of the lineup."

"But Moose threw him in the dirt. He had to defend himself."

She stops dating the check and looks at me. Her eyes twinkle. "They all fight. They're just little boys. But it sure is exciting when they have a winning team." She writes Charlie's name on the check. "Mr. Miller tells me Charlie is sitting at home instead of on the bench."

I look down at my scuffed sandals.

"He's probably ashamed," Grace Everett says. "He knows he brought all this trouble on himself. That may be why he hasn't asked for his half pay himself. He feels he doesn't deserve it."

I turn away from her and look at all those proud faces in the picture of the last winning team. I read their names and then stop. Neil Nordstrom was voted the team's most valuable player. I find his broad face and blond hair. He's changed so little. "Mr. Nordstrom played ball?" I ask.

"He was wonderful. He played second base."

Neil Nordstrom was once the Picker's MVP, and second baseman. No wonder he gave Charlie a hard time. No wonder he rooted for him.

"Everyone says he would have made it to the Bigs for sure," Grace Everett says.

"What happened?"

"He got cancer. The doctors had to amputate."

I can feel my eyes get wet. "Mr. Nordstrom told me, 'We make our own fate.' How could he say that when cancer made his fate?"

She lays her pen on the desk and looks at his picture. "He stays close to the game and he's a friend to Mr. Miller and the team."

I feel disloyal, but I can't help asking, "What would Mr. Nordstrom have done if his only illness was two broken fingers?"

She pushes the form and check in my hands and leads me to the door. "Take care of yourself, Mrs. Fain. Maybe we'll see you next year."

"If Charlie has half the grit of Mr. Nordstrom, we'll be back."

In the Plymouth I look at the check. It will just cover the rent. There will be nothing left over for food.

•

I look at the blackboard with the words *The Return of The Native* written across it. Some of the happiest moments of my life have been right here in this classroom. If only I knew for sure that I could keep coming here. I shut the empty classroom door. I've never been a quitter before. But since I've met Charlie, I've dropped out of summer school once and now I'm going to do it again. All that work and now the three units of credit could just blow away. My footsteps hardly make a sound as I march down the corridor to Professor Edelsen's office.

•

"I gave you an A plus on your *Great Expectations* paper."

"But you said you never gave A plusses."

"I never did until now." Professor Edelsen studies me. "You're the best student I ever had and now you're telling me you may have to drop my class. I know it's because of me."

For once, he's not asking a question, he's making a statement.

- 284 -

"I hurt you by comparing you to Anne Elliot. I shouldn't have made your private life public."

"I was surprised," I tell him. "I didn't see the connection then."

He sneezes and rubs his nose with a big plaid handkerchief worn thin from washings. "My jokes are a way to connect and to make you kids see that literature reflects life. I didn't mean to hurt you."

I look at his books and at his surprisingly neat desk. "You're a good teacher. I want to be a teacher, too." I glance out the window at a ball field in the distance. "I'm not dropping your class because of you. My husband and I are out of money. I have to work."

"You shouldn't quit on yourself now."

"It's just temporary."

"That's what everyone in your situation says. But they don't come back. They wind up saying school isn't the real world. It's not relevant." His pale eyes blink. "But Jane Austen and Thomas Hardy have so much to teach us about living. What about student loans or scholarships?"

"I am up for a scholarship from Santa Monica College. But we need the money now. My husband's an out of work ballplayer."

"Charlie Fain is gifted," he says. "Two broken fingers won't get in his way for long. But you have gifts, too. I could give some money to you, a loan so you can finish this course. You can pay me back when Charlie's playing again. You deserve the help."

Maybe I do deserve the help, but it would be unusual, maybe even improper for him to help me. Charlie might worry that the professor was interested in me. "The loan might hurt Charlie's pride," I say. "I'm sorry. But you were right about *Persuasion*. My mother wanted more for me than just marriage. I think she felt trapped. I feel guilty when I go against her beliefs. In fact, I was wondering if I could bend the rules just a little." I take a deep breath. "I hate to miss your lectures. But maybe I could have someone tape them. And I could come and take the final."

For some reason, this makes his eyes water. Something creaks. He's opening his desk drawer. He hands me a weathered hardback book. The lettering says it's called *Awakening* by a woman named Kate Chopin.

"My mother liked this book," he tells me. "Maybe your mother knew it, too?"

I shake my head.

He writes down the date and time for the class final. "Thank you for not giving up on yourself."

36

Ⅰf only I knew the right thing to do. I stare at the pretty
woman in the gray suit. She looks as if she always does
the right thing.

If I do this, Charlie won't have to worry about money
anymore. Maybe he'll be so relieved he'll put on his uniform
and go back to the park. Or maybe he'll be so angry that I've
taken over his responsibilities, he'll go back to bed and never
get up again. But is earning money only Charlie's
responsibility? Don't I eat our food, and sleep in our rented
house? Most of the heroines I love – Jane Eyre, Moll Flanders,
even Pamela the servant girl – had to make their own way in
the world. But when they got married, their stories and,
presumably, their troubles ended. Still, why shouldn't
married women pay the bills?

I look at the pretty woman in the gray suit. She wears a
thick gold wedding band. And she doesn't look the least bit
guilty that she works and is in charge of other women.

"I'm Sue Lynn Brown, you're trainer," she says. "You've
all been accepted into the Wise Owl Department Store
training program. We do have a dress code. Wise Owl
workers wear only black, beige, gray or brown suits and
dresses. We do permit white blouses." She frowns. "We don't
allow tweeds."

I glance around the room. I'm in my blue dress. One older
woman wears a plaid shirtwaist. The girl in front of me is in
pink. Our smiles at each other are guilty. We look like a flock
of parrots.

"You will learn the principles of selling and how to wait on
customers." Sue Lynn smiles. "You will learn how to operate
our Wise Owl cash registers and how to process the Wise Owl
charge card. You will learn how to work with cash.

I sit up straighter. *Cash* is a wonderful, soothing,
reassuring, word. It will be a pleasure just to touch the
money. If I have cash, I will be able to buy food for the table.
If I have even more cash, I may be able to pay for the table.

•

"I hope you'll be happy. I got a job. I did it for us."

"Umm." The ghost in the plaid bathrobe buries his face in
a halo of Vick's Vapor Rub steam.

"I'll be making $1.65 an hour."

"Um."

"It's at the Wise Owl. I learned to work the register."

"You didn't have to get a job," Charlie says. "I'm handling things."

"It's just temporary. I'm what they call a floater. If you want, I'll quit when you go back to playing ball."

Charlie tells the TV, "People are going to say Charlie Fain is a jerk making his wife go out and work. I think you should quit. Something will come up. My fingers will heal or. . ." The front door bell rings. Charlie cocks his head. "Or someone will come to our door with a pile of money."

"I'm coming," I call over Boris's bark. I hurry through the kitchen. At least I got the worst part over with. I told Charlie about the job.

At the door, I smooth my dress, then wobble in my high heels. Mr. Nordstrom is standing on our porch. He says, "I came to interview your husband. Is he in?"

"I'll get him." I walk as far as the kitchen and then remember my manners. I step back to the living room and open the screen door. Maybe Mr. Nordstrom's talking to him will remind Charlie how important he is to the team. Still the little girl playing dress up, playing house, I say, "Please come in."

Mr. Nordstrom smells of shaving cream and too much cologne. Maybe he has no one in his life to tell him he is wearing too much cologne. I point to the new chair. "If you'd like to sit."

I wish I could take my words back. In order to sit, he has to walk across the room. And to be polite, I should stay and watch. Something inside his pants' squeaks. Is the artificial leg attached at the hip or at the knee? How much did they have to amputate? He reaches the chair, and then takes a moment to settle in.

"Your place is homey," he says.

The living room is neat and clean. Fresh roses sit in a vase. In the kitchen, the tea kettle's whistle turns to a roar. "Get that will you?"

Charlie stands in the narrow archway that separates the kitchen and living room. He's closer to the kettle than I am.

Boris yips, and dashes into the room and jumps on Mr. Nordstrom's white, chino pants. The hem of the pants rides up over a white sock. I turn my head so I won't see anymore. I scoop the dog in my arms. "Isn't it wonderful?" I call over my shoulder to Charlie. "Mr. Nordstrom is here to see you."

"What do you want?" Charlie asks him.

Mr. Nordstrom looks at the floppy robe, the red-rimmed eyes and beard. "I came to check on the franchise."

"Franchise." Charlie almost smiles, then shakes his head and turns to me. "Can't you do something about that racket on the stove?"

I brush past Charlie and turn off the gas flame. It's too quiet in the living room. I stand in the archway. Mr. Nordstrom is staring at his polished shoes. "Would you like tea with milk and sugar?" I ask.

"Just milk, thank you," he says.

Charlie's face is neutral.

Mr. Nordstrom opens his notebook and asks, "How are your fingers?"

"Broken," Charlie says.

"But they're mending, right?"

Charlie rolls an empty cigarette pack into a neat, small ball.

"When will you be back in the lineup?"

With his left hand, Charlie lobs the ball into a wastebasket. Every day when I come home from school, there are paper airplanes and silver balls waiting for me on the floor.

"Doctor Houston and the others must have some idea of how you're doing," Mr. Nordstrom says.

Charlie sinks into Gooth's chair. "What do they know?"

"Plenty," Mr. Nordstrom says. "They saved my life."

Charlie studies Mr. Nordstrom. For a moment, he looks like the old Charlie, the Charlie who understands and cares. He squints. His eyes lose their softness. He lights a cigarette and blows smoke across the room.

"What do you think about your Pickers?" Mr. Nordstrom asks.

"I haven't been following."

"They're three games up on everybody. They are going to do it. You can see it even in the way they walk. They know they're winners. This is the first time in 10 years we win a pennant – and you're part of it. That's got to be great medicine."

Charlie yawns.

"What do you think of Alton?" the reporter asks.

"Alton who?"

"Mr. Reisner found him four years ago in South Carolina. He tore up Triple A last year until he injured his shoulder. The management wanted to start him easy, so they brought him here before they sent him up. I don't think Eibur will be in L.A. much longer. Marichal made short work of him yesterday. The kid's not quite ready yet. In a couple of years you and he will be fighting it out for the same spot." Mr. Nordstrom bats the smoke. "Are you interested in any of this?"

"You hear that? Alton didn't just jump from A-Ball to the big leagues. No one does that. Mr. Nordstrom's saying you're going to be every bit as good as Alton," I tell Charlie. "Isn't that wonderful?"

"Wonderful, my ass." He looks at Mr. Nordstrom . "I have nothing to say."

"But you're news," the reporter says.

"Old news," Charlie says. "I don't mean to be rude, but, why don't you leave?"

They stare at each other. I can feel my palms sweating. The rooster clock ticks. In the bedroom, Boris's nails click. He's pawing the door.

Mr. Nordstrom bends over his clipboard. Is he going to tell all of Cotton Valley how bitter Charlie is? "I hate to see you making the same mistake I made," the reporter says. "I thought Class A was nothing. I was sure I was going all the way. We won the pennant here and I didn't even go to the team party. I didn't understand that that was my last team party ever."

Charlie's face softens. He looks close to tears. "That must have been very hard for you." Then, his face turns weary. "But that's you and this is me. I have nothing more to say, so why don't you just leave?"

I think of the pennant waving in Grace Everett's office. I can see the 1953 team picture and the determination in the MVP's eyes. "He wants you to win," I tell Charlie.

"If you don't go on your own, I'll throw you out," Charlie says. "Artificial leg and all."

"He doesn't mean it," I say.

Mr. Nordstrom puts his hands on the arms of the chair, braces himself and gets to his feet. He studies Charlie. "Did you ever consider that maybe you wanted this injury, Fain? It's a custom-made excuse for not moving up."

Charlie's hands make fists. He looks foolish standing there in his bathrobe. He looks like a punch-drunk fighter.

I tug on his sleeve. "Don't do this."

"Before you break your other hand," Mr. Nordstrom tells him, "think about this. Life's always easier when you have excuses. You can tell your friends and grandchildren you had the talent to go all the way, but you had a bad break. That's easier than doing the best you can and maybe finding out it's still not enough. You can take that punch now."

Charlie sags, and sucks in air. He studies Mr. Nordstrom, and turns. He doesn't look at me. Maybe he's even forgotten I'm here. He shuffles into the kitchen and after a long moment, the bedroom door thuds shut.

•

I've opened every box in the glove department for the plump, stylish lady in the sundress. She picks up a pair of pale yellow gloves. "I have a yellow suit that I adore. I'll buy these."

She frowns. Is she going to change her mind again? I wait.

"I'm not sure about my new son-in-law to be," she says. "Men act nice at first and then they get crazy on you. It's their hormones."

"Hormones?"

"Whatever that male hormone is. They needed it when we were back in the caves. So they'd be the ones to spear the animals. But now they live in houses and drive cars, but they still have those hormones. What can you do? Try not to worry and buy nice things."

Maybe Charlie's only trouble is his hormones. His male hormones made him order a sportswriter out of the house. I sigh and put the gloves in a box.

•

The house is dark. There's no barking dog, no TV glare. If only Charlie were home and in his bathrobe. At least I would know that he's safe.

I turn on lights and open windows. In the bedroom something catches my heels. I trip, then pick up Charlie's bathrobe where he dropped it (threw it?) on the floor. Where is he?

Maybe he's apologizing to Mr. Nordstrom, or visiting the Pickers.

I set the table for two and warm the tuna noodle casserole I made before going to work. The tuna is salty. The noodles taste like paste. Tuna and noodles were never meant to meet in the same casserole.

I sweep the kitchen and wash my dishes. I leave Charlie's place set. I call Mrs. Fain again and listen to the phone ring in the empty kitchen. She and her baby boyfriend are never coming down from that cabin at Lake Arrowhead. She's forgotten she has a son.

Her son has forgotten he has a wife.

Burned and dry and still warming in the oven, the tuna in mushroom cream gravy looks as appetizing as dirty snow. I slam the oven door shut, put Charlie's clean silverware back in the drawer. Charlie's never missed dinner before. Something terrible must have happened. I sink into Gooth's chair, the only chair in the house that is paid for. I wait.

Keys rattle in the lock. The door squeaks open. In the dark I call, "Are you all right?"

He snaps on the ginger jar lamp. He's holding a bouquet of long stem roses. "Hi, there, sports fan. I'm sorry about dinner." He doesn't look sorry. He's grinning and smiling down at a bag of groceries. "Have you eaten yet?"

My feet hurt. I rub swollen ankles, and sore toes. I have salesgirls' feet. Soggy tuna settles in my stomach. My eyes are tired from reading English novels and staring at the clock. I lean back in the chair. He wants to eat. All I want to do is sleep. "Why didn't you call?"

"I bought steak and champagne," he says.

Something wonderful must have happened. He saw Doctor Houston. His fingers are healing. He'll be back in plenty of time to help the Pickers take the division title. I sit up. "When do you start playing again?"

His grin fades. He taps a finger to his head. "I'm using my brains now. I figured out a way to take care of my family."

He steps into the kitchen and sets groceries on the table. I follow him. "You didn't see a doctor? Then what have you been doing all this time?"

"Studying. I found out I'm not so dumb as everybody thought. I have a head for detail." He pulls a racing form from his pocket. "There's a fortune in racing," he says. "If you're smart and know how to play."

He's late because of horses? I glance at the form. The name *Yankee Doodle Dandy* is circled in red.

He kisses me and opens the bottle with his good hand. "We're going to drink a toast to *Crimson Streak*. The horse was off at 12-to-1 and won by two lengths." He hasn't looked so happy in weeks.

The cork pops and hits the wall. Champagne bubbles over. We didn't have champagne when we got married or when Charlie won MVP. But we're going to have it now. He pours the drink into Blue Chip Stamp tumblers. Bubbles make my nose itch. "I'm not sure I'll like it," I say.

"Everyone likes champagne," he says.

I should be happy that he's happy. The champagne is sweet and bubbly, but it goes down the wrong way.

Charlie opens the oven door, and takes out the casserole. He makes a face. "What is that?"

"It was your dinner."

He dumps it in the garbage. "How do you like your steak?"

•

For the first time in days Charlie kissed me as if he meant it. I smile down at my sleeping husband. He was in such a hurry to make love. I had almost come to believe his excuses about breaking his cast or re-injuring his finger. But after the champagne, he wasn't worried about anything. Now, that he's had this triumph with horses, he'll feel like a winner again. He'll be able to rejoin his team.

I have to go to the bathroom. I wrap my robe around me, step out of bed and onto a pile of Charlie's clothes. I hang up his shirt and then reach for his pants. A slip of paper falls from his pocket. There's something written on the paper. Maybe it's something we need to keep. I squint in the moonlight. I can't make out the words.

In the bathroom, I close the door and turn on the light. The scribbled message reads, *Silver Slipper 4-to-1*. Is 4-to-1 good or bad? I pull a piece of paper from his pocket. Paper spills like confetti. I read, *Rooney's Girl in the 5th. Henry's Hope, 3-to-1 in the 8th.*

His front pockets bulge. I dig my fingers in and touch a wad of bills. I pull them out. I weigh the bills in my palm and count $800.

I would have to work three months at the Wise Owl to earn what I hold in my hand. I open the door a crack. Charlie is asleep. Maybe I should wake him and tell him how wonderful he is. He won the money to pay back all our bills. I can cut down my time at work and not miss one more class. I kiss the bills. I can be a full time student again.

Charlie had more champagne than I did. He might not appreciate being awakened. He might not even remember how much money he has. I'll wait until morning to talk to him about the money. But what if he's still asleep when it's time for me to go to work? If I leave the money with him, he might spend it on something frivolous – a treat for us that we can't afford.

I shut the bathroom door again, but quietly. Where can I hide $800?

can't believe you sold that Modern Library book." Blue-haired Mrs. Wheeler's lips press together. They form a *U*. She can't be smiling. Everyone says she's a battle ax and battle axes don't smile. "We move two of those books a month, and that's if we're lucky. You sold one the first day!"

Mrs. Wheeler really is smiling. I stand taller. "The lady said she wanted to read something different. So I told her Kafka wrote about a man who discovered he was a cockroach."

"Cockroach?" Mrs. Wheeler shudders. "Kafka. We'll have to reorder." Mrs. Wheeler picks up her purse. "I could use a cigarette." Her left eyelid flutters.

Do battle axes wink?

"Usually when we have a floater, I stay in the department all day. But I'm confident you'll handle everything just fine. The Literary Guild reserves are under the register. If a member picks up a book, make a note in her file. The files are in – "

"The top right-hand drawer," I say.

She nods and walks to the elevator in back of the department. "I've been at the Wise Owl since it first opened. I'm old and demanding." She licks a flake of lipstick off her mouth. "I like people who work hard. People like you. They think here that I don't know they call me a battle ax."

"I think you're very nice."

She nods and punches a button and steps inside the elevator. Doors close.

I'm alone in the Book Department. I pick up a feather duster and brush shiny book spines. Why is it that older women who are smart and work hard and pay attention to details are always called battle axes? If I work hard enough, maybe someday I'll be a battle ax, too.

•

I hand the stout woman her two new hard covers *The Joy of Cooking* and *How I Lost a Hundred Pounds on a Liquid Diet*. She moves slowly to the elevator.

"Which book do you think she'll read first?" I ask.

"Liquid Diet," Mrs. Wheeler whispers at my elbow. "What some women won't do to lose weight." One skinny bookseller to another, we smile.

The elevator doors open. Puffy eyes, hollow cheeks, hung over, my husband Charlie steps out.

I'm ruined.

He's wearing his green and gold high school letterman's sweater. "So this is where you're hiding," he says.

Mrs. Wheeler looks up from her Guild records.

"I'm not hiding," I whisper. "I'm working." I step away from the register and slip my hand under his elbow. I lead him to the shelves farthest away from Mrs. Wheeler. "Would you like something from the children's department?"

He blinks. "Where's my money?"

I whisper, "I'm so proud of you. You got enough to pay our bills and maybe even have some left over."

"Where's my $800?" he says.

"It's our money, isn't it? I mean we're a team. I just wanted the money to be safe until you were feeling well enough to handle it."

"I can handle it right now."

At the register, Mrs. Wheeler cocks her head.

"Where is it? I searched the damn house."

I close my eyes. What does Mrs. Wheeler think of her new floater now?

"I earned that money," Charlie says. "I used my brains and I solved our problems. We have nothing more to worry about."

"You mean you're going to pay Halligan's today? The girl in the credit department will be so happy."

"We can buy our own furniture store. Just give me the money."

"Will you pay Halligan's?"

"I told you, I have everything taken care of." He waves his arms and knocks down books.

I kneel and pick up the new *Mary Poppins*. His elbow bumps *Alice in Wonderland*. It tumbles to the floor. "Just tell me where the money is." His voice is getting louder.

"Shush, Charlie. I don't want to lose my job."

"Mrs. Fain, may I speak to you?" Mrs. Wheeler looms over the best seller rack. She crooks her finger. I slink to the register. "What's going on here? Who is that person?"

"A relative," I tell her. I swallow hard and taste stale champagne. Aunt Lottie would be so ashamed of me for not admitting that Charlie is my husband. Aunt Lottie said that Charlie and I were supposed to be a family now. I'm supposed to trust him. Now that he's had his thrill, he won't need to play the horses again, will he? I hurry back to a scowling Charlie. "The money's in the tail of the rooster-clock."

He grins and kisses my cheek. "You did the right thing, babe. You'll see. We're going to be in Fat City."

"I just want you well and our bills paid."

"That's what I want, too." Head bobbing, arms swinging, ready to take on the world, he saunters past the register. He salutes Mrs. Wheeler. "Hi, boss."

The doors can't close soon enough. What if Mrs. Wheeler fires me for making a scene is her sedate book department? The elevator taking Charlie away hums. My heart is beating faster. I've never been fired before.

"I'm 70," Mrs. Wheeler says. "But I tell them I 'm 60. They're going to make me retire someday. I want someone special to take over the department. Maybe it will be you." She sighs. "I shouldn't make a judgment about your family after seeing only one relative, but it looks as if you're going to need a good job."

•

Old Chartreuse's engine sputters and fades. Charlie is home. He clicks the gate shut. "I'm so glad to see you," I call. "Were they surprised at Halligan's when you came in with all that money?"

He's weaving up the path. At the door, he bends down and kisses me. He tastes of beer. "I'm sorry I'm late."

"You're not so late. I made grilled cheese sandwiches. So tell me about your day."

"There's nothing to tell."

"But you went to Halligan's?"

Charlie shakes his head. I march to the kitchen. "But you promised."

"I promised I would solve our problems and I will."

I slice each sandwich into two triangles and a narrow center strip. "You shouldn't have saluted Mrs. Wheeler," I say. "She's a nice lady."

"She's a battle ax."

"She's gainfully employed."

He sits at the table. I slide a bowl of tomato soup in front of him.

"I don't think I can manage soup now." He stares at his sandwich. "Triangles?"

"My mother always cut sandwiches this way. She called it Ladies' Luncheon Style. It was her attempt at gentility."

It was her attempt to forget her husband drank a little too much. So, why am I cutting sandwiches into triangles? This is my attempt to forget my husband doesn't keep his promises. This phony gentility must be something in my genes. Or maybe it's my adaptation to the environment. If I cut toast into triangles, I won't pour hot tomato soup on my husband's head. A laugh rattles and then explodes in my throat. If Charlie keeps not paying our bills, I'll be very busy trying to cover up and make things seem better than they are. Soon, I'll be converting milk cartons to vases and tacking chintz onto the toilet seat.

Charlie studies me. "What's the joke?"

"History repeats."

He shakes his head and pushes food away. "I'm just too tired." He gets up from the table and staggers across the kitchen and shuts the bedroom door behind him.

•

Maybe he still has the money. Maybe he just had a beer or two and everything else just slipped his mind. Charlie is snoring. I slip out of bed, and tiptoe across the room. The closet door squeaks. I hold my breath. My fingers slide into his pants pocket. He stirs. I pull my hand out, and grab my robe. If he asks what I'm doing, I'll say I felt chilly. He goes back to sleep. In his pockets, those little slips of paper have multiplied. There's no comforting wad of money. He spent all his money on what – more horses? This was his plan, his way to take care of his family. I should never have told him where the money was. I should have paid Halligan's myself.

Next door, Laura Davis is playing something sad and scary. It's a funeral march. Our money is dead.

•

In the mailbox there's a powder blue envelope addressed to Charlie and me from Mrs. Eileen Fain. I tear open the seal and scan the neat handwriting. Mrs. Fain has let Señor Muñoz know she consents to our marriage. A stay in the mountains changed her mind. We will be getting our certificate soon. She is praying that Charlie's fingers are healing. She is making plans to come up and help us. Charlie and I are husband and wife. I slip the letter in my pocket and burst into tears. I can't wait to tell my legal husband the news.

But I don't know where he is.

•

"I'm so happy to see you," I tell my father. "I hope you can help me solve this."

"You should have called me sooner." Mickey squares his shoulders and steps off the Greyhound bus. "I'll straighten him out."

"Aren't you going to say you're happy to see me, too?"

"I'm here, aren't I?"

I sigh. He's right. He is here and maybe he can help get Charlie's mind back on baseball. He grips his canvas bag, and blinks in the morning light. "Where did you park, Sacramento?"

I lead him up the quiet block and open the door for him. It squeaks.

"A little maintenance," he says. "One lousy can of 3-in-1 oil, that's all this beauty needs. But no, you're going to drive her until she falls apart, *blam*, on the highway, and you have to pick her up piece by piece." He throws his bag on the beauty's frayed back seat. "Where's Charlie?"

I sink into the driver's side. "I don't know. He just disappears, then he comes back with little pieces of paper and no money."

"Drive through town," he says. "We'll find him."

•

"This is fun," I say. "We rarely have any father-daughter time anymore. Cotton Valley is a pretty little place." I point out the window. "This is the city hall, and the courthouse. Everything has been rebuilt since the last earthquake. I think they did a wonderful job."

"Don't you have any brains?" Mickey says. "I didn't ask for the scenic tour."

"You said drive through town. This is the civic center."

"Civic center, right. The local bookie has his shop right next to the mayor's office. On the fancy door there's a big brass sign." Mickey holds his hands up and shapes the sign in the air. "*Bookie.*" He shakes his head and looks at me with disgust. "Don't you have a pawn shop and a pool hall?"

"How am I supposed to know where the criminal element hangs out?"

"You're my daughter aren't you?" He sighs. "Go back toward the depot."

I drive a few blocks and then slow the car to a crawl past a row of storefronts that start with a dry cleaners with dirty windows. "Is this better?"

"Stop." Mickey points to a space in front of Rolly Wynn's Liquors. "Park." He shoves the car door open. "Wait."

Chin held high, all business, he marches into Rolly Wynn's as if stalking a wounded boxer across the ring.

I lean back and stare at the cleaner's awning, whitened with bird droppings and flapping in the breeze. Why is my father so hard on me? Am I really as dense as he thinks I am? Do you have to be some kind of he-man like my father to understand car maintenance and horse racing?

A bell rings. Rolly Wynn's door shuts. Mickey grins his *I told you so* smile and dances a jig on the sidewalk, tugging his son-in-law to the Plymouth.

•

Mickey drops his canvas bag on the porch and leads Charlie to the yard where my roses bloom. It's a good, private place for a talk. Mickey will tell Charlie he can't keep gambling. Maybe, Charlie, who misses his own father, will listen to mine.

I unlock the door, and pick up Mickey's bag. I set it down again. Mickey brought barbells or bricks.

The house is cold and dark. In the kitchen, breakfast dishes wait. I fill the sink with suds and open the window and let in morning sun. A mockingbird sings. A towhee whistles. Then a human voice says, "Jab with your left, lead with your right."

Jab?

I press my face against the window screen.

"That's it," Mickey shouts.

Charlie, his right hand lifted high, looks happier than he has in weeks. He aims a punch at Mickey's chest.

I toss the wet sponge in the sink, and hurry out to the yard. Bright light makes me blink. Boris yips. He thinks I want to join in the play. He nips at my ankles. The two gladiators, sparring in the sun, are too busy to notice me.

"Watch out for your splint," I say.

Charlie keeps punching and missing. Mickey laughs, ducks, dances away, then moves closer to his opponent.

"Daddy, stop it. This isn't why I asked you to come."

Still dancing, Mickey looks up surprised. "If he's going to fight, he's got to learn how to make his punches count." He jumps away and grins. "I dropped bigger than me, a lot bigger, with just one punch. It's all in turning from the heels, like this." He whirls and punches.

He's so fast he takes my breath away.

Charlie nods and watches.

"You try," Mickey says.

Wooden, slower, Charlie makes the same move.

"Good," Mickey says. "Again."

"Daddy, stop it."

"Let me handle this sweetheart," Mickey winks. "Don't get in the way of my plan."

Plan? Mickey's plan is to teach Charlie to box. Next time, Charlie will be able to kill someone for sure. What kind of a plan is that? Maybe calling Mickey was a terrible idea. It is the delinquent leading the delinquent.

I walk toward the house. New grass spears my feet. Though anger makes my fists clench, though I'm ready to land a few well-placed punches of my own, I'm still the good wife and the good daughter. I call over my shoulder, "Dinner's in the refrigerator. I'm working the late shift."

•

The hushed voices coming from the living room tell me the pugilists are up early. But the windowpanes aren't rattling, and the walls aren't shaking. Has all the sparring, punching, and jabbing stopped because someone is lying unconscious in there? Before Charlie had a chance to defend himself, did Little Red Carey knock him out, blind him, and maim him?

Mickey's plan was to keep his son-in-law bandaged and in traction. Then, he'll stay out of trouble.

Maybe they're just talking about me. Maybe one of them remembered my birthday. Today, I'm 19. Maybe they're making plans for a cake and a party, and a present. To let them know I'm up, I hum, and open a squeaky cupboard. I slurp coffee.

I'm 19. I'm almost all grown up. If Alice were here, we'd be women together. We'd be friends. I take a deep breath. My beautiful sphinx of a mother answered questions with riddles. Why do I miss her more, not less, as years go by? I carry my cup into the sun-brightened living room. I'm ready for hugs and kisses, a chorus of the song that belongs to me today.

They are sitting on the carpet in front of the unpaid-for coffee table. A pile of books – Marx, Dickens, Steinbeck – lies between them. Mickey's traveling library, a staple of his cab, used to impress his customers, and routinely to bowl them over with facts – facts they don't expect or want.

"Forget all those queens and kings," Mickey is saying. "History's simpler than that." With a wave of his arm, he dismisses royalty, the pomp in Trevelyan's *History of England* that Charlie is holding. "History's just the Haves versus the Have-Nots. The Haves murder, pillage and rape. The Have-Nots are on the receiving end."

Happy Birthday to me.

Mickey grins at me. "Welcome to my little seminar. I'm teaching your hubby the real way of the world."

In the real way of the world, can a cab driver's confused Catholic, sloppy Socialist view of history change his son-in-law's mind about gambling? There is a plan in here somewhere. Mickey is telling Charlie that material things – possessions – aren't that important. Charlie won't feel so badly on half pay. His confidence will be restored and Charlie won't need to play the horses anymore. Maybe my father isn't demented. Maybe he's a genius.

"You'll be late for work," Mickey says, turning back to his books.

"It's company policy," I tell him, "that employees don't work on – "

"Church." Mickey punches the thick history book, knocking it out of Charlie's hands. "Damn Church tells the

Have-Nots to be grateful for crumbs. They're sinners, see? So they have to love their suffering, because that's what brings them closer to God."

"On their birthday," I say.

"Right." Mickey nods at Charlie. "So, did you ever think about how the Church keeps people from dreaming?"

Charlie shakes his head. His eyes are wide. He's playing dumb, playing the role the Brothers assigned him in grammar school, the role that is bad for him. Charlie makes it easy for Mickey to feel superior to him. Watching Charlie play that role makes me feel sad, and it makes me want to slug him.

"The happiest people," Mickey is saying, "are supposed to be the ones who suffer the most. Take old Stanley with the newsstand in front of Thrifty's. He's got arthritis so bad he can't even fold the papers, but he thanks God every day he has those winos to keep him company. See, poor people, sick people, blind people, they're more noble."

Charlie nods. Maybe that's why he's so anxious to blow our money: so we'll be better. We'll be noble.

"This is ridiculous," I say.

"Ridiculous?" Mickey pats the dust-colored cover of *The Grapes of Wrath*. "John Steinbeck is ridiculous? He understands how a decent man just can't get a break."

"What about me? I'm a decent woman." I sink into the unpaid-for chair. Any day, the old man from Halligan's will come to take our furniture away. "I bought you a bus ticket so you'd help me with my husband. All you do is give punching lessons and lectures." I wait for tears and wonder why they don't come. "This is my birthday, damn it."

"Of course it is." Mickey pats my head, winks at Charlie. "These things mean so much more to a woman." A $5 bill appears in his hand, as if by magic. "Here you go. Buy yourself a cake on me."

Just touching the money makes me weep.

"There now," Mickey says. "This is supposed to make you happy."

"Happy birthday, darling." Charlie kisses the top of my head. "And many more."

Many more like this? I want to slug both of them. Yet, as if it were a crumb from the last piece of bread on earth, I crumple the $5 bill in my fist. I'm not going to hit anyone. I don't have it in me. What I'm going to do is stop crying and then go out and buy my cake. I'll probably wind up singing *Happy Birthday* to myself. And I'll tell myself tomorrow that it was a happy birthday. I hate this part of me. It makes me feel as if I were dying. Maybe Mickey is right about suffering and nobility. You can't be any nobler than dead.

"What kind of cake should I get?" I ask my father. "Chocolate?"

38

I look at the groceries in my cart – freshly baked bread, Ritz crackers and my favorite soup, Minestrone. I feel better already.

"I'm sorry, Mrs. Fain." The checker doesn't look sorry. She looks tired. Her skinny finger points at a slip of paper with my last name and others on it, taped to her register. "You're on the list for bad checks."

I clutch my preferred customer card. "I don't understand."

"Your last check must have bounced."

"But we have $50 in our account. The balance in my checkbook proves it. It's a mistake."

The checker taps her finger on my name, then shakes her head. "Do you wish to pay for your items in cash?"

This can't be happening. I would never write a check for funds I didn't have. I feel like a cheat when I get to the library after closing and have to slide a book in the overnight slot. "Can I talk to the manager."

The checker frowns, then waves to a young man across the store. Behind me, a man nudges his basket into my back. The manager is an apple-cheeked boy with a badge and a mustache. He looks at the list on the cash register and then at my check cashing card. He clears his throat. His breath smells of pink bubble-gum. "This is a joint account. Your husband may have written a check and forgot to tell you."

It can't be true. Charlie wouldn't do this to us, would he? He knows how tight our budget is – how we have to make every penny count. He wouldn't go out and write checks on money we don't have. From my wallet, I take the $5 Mickey gave me, and look over my groceries. I try to pick what we need most and what we can afford. Milk, bread, beans, and a few other staples will add up to less than $5

The checker is holding a bottle of Scotch and a long kitchen knife the man behind me is buying. If I ask Charlie about the bounced check will he tell me the truth or will he say, "Those Bozos at Regal don't know how to count."

"Mrs. Fain," the assistant manager is saying, "your check, the one that came back, was for twelve dollars and thirty cents. Maybe you could pay your bill now."

Now, he's telling me we owe them money for food we've already eaten. How can Charlie expect me to live like this?

What is the matter with him? What is the matter with me for trusting him? I hand the manager my $5. "Put this on our account."

No money in my wallet, no groceries in my arms, I square my shoulders and walk out of the store.

•

I have 12 blocks to go. The traffic light is turning red. I press the gas pedal to the floor. My Plymouth speeds through the intersection. Please don't let them have started my cake.

•

The cake sitting on the counter has white frosting and two layers. I'm not too late. This is not my cake. The cake I ordered was to have only one layer. Karl, the baker, will understand about canceling my order. This is a minor league baseball town – people come up short all the time.

The cake is decorated with green leaves framing yellow roses so perfect they look alive. Red candy script spells out "Happy Birthday, Pamela."

I didn't ask for a fancy cake. I wanted something plain, something that suited me. How did he know I love yellow roses? Was it just another lucky guess, like the guess he made with Little Tank?

I stand on tiptoes and smell the sugary cake and look down the short hall that connects the waiting room to a kitchen. With his back to me, his shoulders straining the seams of his white shirt, Karl works at a big table, rolling out sheets of dough. For Little Tank's 9-month birthday, Karl made a clown cake with whipped cream hair, chocolate eyes and a cherry nose. How did he know Little Tank loved clowns? But he did know. He cared and he didn't charge more for the special ingredients or for his extra time. Now, Karl is whistling, fluting doughy edges for a pie. He loves his work. He's good at what he does. His gifts make him generous, make him want to give people more than they ask for.

But maybe this cake wasn't Karl's idea. Maybe it was Charlie's. What if Charlie used some of our checking account money for this lovely cake? I could forgive Charlie then.

If Charlie didn't pay for this cake, I'll have to tell Karl, the Honorary Picker, I can't pay him what I owe. I will be a welcher, at least until I get my paycheck.

"Do you like your cake?" A girl steps out of a small, side room. Stitched in red across her uniform is her name: *Ella*. She's Karl's daughter.

"The cake is beautiful," I say.

She brushes flour from her arms. She must have been watching her father, maybe helping, then he sent her to the counter to help the customer. Now she is waiting for my money.

I open my purse. Can I write a check? Mickey says he's broke, but he must have some spare change. Then, I'll ask Mrs. Davis and then maybe Mrs. Wheeler. I look away from Ella's wide face and glance at the roses on the cake. "About my bill."

"There is no bill," Ella says.

My head feels lighter. Charlie did order the cake for me.

Ella's eyes meet mine. She is smiling. "All paid for."

"When did my husband come in?"

"Not your husband. Mrs. Bonnie Willis ordered it for you two days ago. There's a card." She hands it to me. "Happy Birthday from Bonnie, Norma, Beth, Raquel, and Frances Eibur."

A lump sits at the back of my throat. This beautiful cake is a gift for me on my birthday from my friends. But what could I have done to deserve so much generosity? A line from a Rossetti poem builds tears I know I won't be able to stop: *It is the birthday of my life.*

"We weren't sure what to do when you came in and asked for a cake," Ella is saying. Her fingers fly, fitting my cake in a box and tying it with a string. "But father said to play along and don't spoil your surprise." She slides the box to me. "Happy birthday, Miss."

The box feels solid and good in my hands. On the birthday of my life, I don't cry. I make a wish, a promise. I'll never let Charlie or anyone else put me in this position again.

•

The doorknob flies out of my hand and bangs against a wall. The speech I've practiced all the way home is ready to explode past my lips: No more lies, Charlie, and no more gambling. From now on, I write all the checks, because I'm in charge of our family finances.

Nothing comes out. No one is here. Books litter the floor. Charlie's robe sits on a chair. His pajamas, the ones his cradle-robbing mama sent, lie on the couch. Those horrid little bicycle wheels are staring back at me, taunting me. I would give anything to tear those pajamas to shreds, but I'd only have to buy him a new pair. I can't afford new pajamas. Thanks to my irresponsible husband, we can't afford food.

The phone starts ringing. I step past the mess on the floor, and stop next to the refrigerator in the kitchen. I listen to the motor of the big white machine hum along with the phone. The receiver feels cold in my hand. I can't speak.

"Mrs. Fain?" The man's voice is soft and reassuring. "Hello?"

"Yes."

"Mrs. Fain, Dan Lowell Junior, here at California Gold Savings and Loan." His voice has changed. It sounds dry now, dusty, as if he's been out panning for nuggets all day and has come back empty.

Bonnie introduced me to Dan Lowell in the bleachers. "He's just graduated from Stanford," she said. "Now, he's vice president."

He said, "Vice president of my father's bank."

Now, I tell him, "I meant to stop in today."

"You did?"

"Yes, I want to cover the check my husband wrote."

"I see. That would be appreciated."

"Could you please transfer the money from our savings account? I can come in later to sign a form if you need me to."

Over the phone line, down at the bank 20 blocks away, typewriter keys click, a fan whirs. Dan Lowell clears his throat. "We would have transferred the money for you automatically. Unfortunately the balance in your savings account stands at $20 − the minimum to keep your account open. Your checking account is overdrawn, by $110."

We are overdrawn $110 and our savings are gone, too? This can't be true. Charlie had $800. How could he possibly have needed more?

"Are you sure?" I ask the Stanford graduate. "There couldn't be a mistake somewhere?"

"I'm certain there is no mistake," Dan Lowell says. Then, the dry voice vanishes. Someone at the bank put the radio on.

Bobby Darin is singing *Mack The Knife*. The knife is out of sight.

"Mrs. Fain?" Dan Lowell is back.

How could Charlie take our savings without my knowing? We have a joint account. Could Charlie just withdraw our funds without my signature?

"Mr. Lowell, are the withdrawal slips in order?"

"Of course." The dry voice is prim.

Tears prick my eyes.

"Mrs. Fain. We would appreciate it if you cover the over draft by tomorrow."

"Of course." I make my voice as dry and prim as his.

What if I can't come up with the money? How could Charlie have gone through so much money so fast? Why is he so desperate? Why didn't I see what was happening? I should have tried to get him to see how crazy he was acting. Then, we wouldn't be deadbeats.

What can a banker like Dan Lowell do to us? He could tell Mrs. Wheeler at work how unreliable we are. He could talk to the Pickers. I grip the receiver. He could garnish Charlie's salary. Mr. Reisner, Mr. Nordstrom, Steve, Bonnie, everyone will know what Charlie and I have done. This is the birthday of my life, the day I see my life for the awful mess it is.

He clears his throat. "Mrs. Fain, I probably shouldn't say this. Who am I to be judging you? But forgive me. You've had more advantages than the other baseball wives have had. You're bright and you go to college." Typewriter keys click on his end of the line, the refrigerator hums on mine. I wait. "You're too smart to be in this situation," he says.

I want to argue with him and tell him I'm not the one who bounced checks all over town. But a second ago, I was telling myself that this was Charlie's and my problem. Because Dan Lowell shook my hand one sunny morning in the bleachers, and because he saw some spark in me, I've made a hard job harder. "I'm sorry for the trouble I caused you. I'll bring the money in as soon as I can."

I hang up.

•

I stare at the phone. Dan Lowell said I was too smart to be in this situation. So, why am I in this situation? Some of this has to be my fault.

I open the third drawer in the kitchen cupboard and search through old gas, electric and telephone bills. The passbook for our savings is gone. I slam the drawer shut. How could I not know what Charlie was doing? Why do I always believe what I tell myself? *Mickey's not going to drink. Charlie is taking care of the money.* I've read English novels and sold books, and sewed curtains while my husband forged my signature and stole our money.

I don't get to be this stupid.

In the living room, I sink into the easy chair and make myself as small as possible. If only I could disappear completely. It's not as if I hadn't been warned. I've grown up on prophecies from *The Book of Alice.* "Be smart," she told me. "Never live hand-to-mouth. Keep some money tucked away that your husband doesn't know about."

"I'm supposed to hide money from the man of my dreams?" I was 12 and in love with love.

She said, "We marry our fathers, that's what you have to know."

She pointed her burning cigarette at a picture of her dad in a photograph album. Albert McMullen, a narrow-faced man in overalls as treasurer for the Kelso Logger's Aid Society. He used his friends' and neighbors' money to buy himself a new truck. He was sent to jail. Schoolmates threw rocks at little Alice. Only plump Charlotte Carey took her side. The McMullen's lost their home and had to move in with cousins.

"Why do we marry our fathers?" I asked.

Alice hugged me hard. "Keep asking questions, honey."

I kick the pile in front of me. Mickey's books and Charlie's clothes are all clumped together and form a single mess. I squeeze my eyes shut, and rest my head on the arm of the chair. "Alice, I didn't want to believe you then. I don't want to believe you now." Thick corduroy feels wet. I can't cry on the chair. It has to go back to the furniture store.

I stand and straighten the shade of the brass lamp. I rub my eyelids and try to make the image of Charlie dancing around the May pole-lamp go away. My stomach rumbles. At least I still have my birthday cake.

•

In the kitchen, I sing *Happy Birthday* to myself. I get a plate and fork, and untie the baker's daughter's knot. I plant a candle in the frosting next to a single rose. I find one of Charlie's matches, and watch my birthday flame get bigger.

I don't make a wish. I make a promise. "Alice, 19 years ago you gave me life. I'm smart. Money doesn't go and come by magic. I'm going to pay attention to what's going on and I'm never going to get in a situation like this again."

I blow out the candle, dig my fork in, and take the first bite.

•

I turn my head quickly away from the rack of pinup magazines. I glanced at a picture of a brunette in pasties and black bikini panties. My face burns. Why do store owners display those magazines? I guess they know the pictures capture men's attention.

Maybe I should be wearing pasties and a little black bikini when I sit down to talk with Charlie about our financial situation. Maybe if bouncing checks and blown savings accounts don't get his attention, lacy bikini pants will.

Overhead, a long tube of light sputters and burns out. Rolly Wynn's liquor store is falling apart. I hurry past a shelf of Jim Beam, and walk deeper into the store. "I'm looking for Charlie Fain," I tell the man behind the counter.

"I never heard of him."

The man is a moron, blind or a liar. Behind him in a plastic frame is a picture of the 1963 Pickers. I jab my thumb. "Number 7."

The clerk squints at the photograph. He's at least 30 and he still has acne. It must be all that good clean living that keeps him in such good shape. "I can't see so good in this light," he tells me.

"Charlie's tall and blond with a crew cut. He's adorable when he isn't gambling. Today, he's with an older, stocky, red-haired man."

"Nope." The clerk pulls a cowboy hat down low on his forehead, and shuts his eyes. He wants to make me disappear.

But I'm not going anywhere. "Charlie was just in here yesterday."

A door leading to a room at the back of the store opens. A man with stringy gray hair steps out. He stuffs bills into the pockets of new jeans. He walks past me. His boots creak and his breath whistles through spaces where there used to be teeth.

I stare past the clerk's big shoulders at the door to the back room. Is that where Charlie is making his bets? The clerk is watching me now. What they're doing back there is illegal. The cowboy of Rolly Wynn Liquors isn't going to let me anywhere near the back room.

"Do you have *Woman's Day*?" I ask.

"What?"

"It's a monthly magazine."

The clerk frowns.

"Maybe you could look?"

He shrugs and walks toward the front, past the magazine rack. I start to follow, then turn, run past the counter, toward the back room.

The clerk's voice, then his footsteps chase me. "Hey, you can't go in there."

"Watch me," I open the door.

Through the smoke, past the glare of the TV screen, I see the two of them. They are two rotten peas in a rotten pod. They sit together and confer over a racing form. They glance at a blackboard that is leaning against the wall. Their faces are so damn scholarly, as if they were searching for a cure to cancer. I throw the checkbook on the table. "Just what the hell are you doing?"

Startled, Charlie looks up.

"Shhh," Mickey says, "this is a place of business."

"Business? You call a bunch of unwashed, unshaven, hung-over men playing horses a business?"

Charlie tells horses running a track on the TV screen, "You don't understand."

I grab a racing form and wave it in my husband's face. "You're ruining us."

Something raps on my shoulder. I turn, and look up at a big chest. The clerk is standing behind me. "You don't belong in here," he says, and then calls to a corner. "Boss?"

Rolly Wynn is sitting alone in the dark. He's drinking the best Scotch money can buy – Glenlivet. Rolly Wynn is not worried about paying his bills. He's not half as worried about me as his cowboy employee is. He sighs and gets woozily to his feet.

Mickey jumps up. "I'll handle this." Hooking his hand on my elbow, the traitor tries to steer me away from Charlie.

"What are you doing here?" I ask Mickey. "Were you worried Charlie couldn't get into enough trouble on his own?"

"This is part of my plan," Mickey whispers. His breath smells of cigarettes and coffee. At least he's sober. "I got to find out how he works, so I can show him he's wrong." His eyes plead with me. "Go home."

Sandwiched between my father and the clerk, I grip the edge of the table. I had come here to reason with Charlie, so what was I doing yelling and throwing my checkbook around? A dog yips. Boris, tail thumping against a table leg, leaps and licks my stockings. As if he were really happy to see me, a smile breaks out on Charlie's face.

"Why didn't you tell me about the checks?" I ask softly now. "I couldn't buy groceries. I felt so ashamed."

Charlie leans across the table and kisses me. "I'm sorry you had a hard time, but everything's under control now." He pushes the checkbook toward me. "You can write all the checks you want. You never have to be embarrassed again."

I take the checkbook. "You wiped out our savings," I say. Why am I telling him what he already knows? Why don't I have the courage to tell him what he doesn't know? I think he's out of control. "We have to cover the overdraft by tomorrow. You used up all our money."

"It was his money too," Mickey says.

"You shouldn't be encouraging him," I say.

"Shhh." Charlie puts his fingers to my lips. "Your father's just trying to help. We're going to be fine. I got a present for you." He drops a role of lifesavers on the table.

He must be crazy. "Don't you get it? Even lifesavers are out of our budget."

"Your father understands me," Charlie says. "Why can't you? He's helping to build me up here. Why can't you get on the team?"

"We can be a team," I say. "But for right now, maybe I should organize the family finances. I'm going to work overtime." The speech I practiced sounds tired and weak now. It's a sandbag trying to block a tidal wave. "Maybe we can find something for you to do now. Before you know it, you'll be back on the team."

I glance around the room at the unwashed locals. Charlie is smiling at me now. He looks as if he's been waiting all his life for me to say these words to him. He feels about as guilty at being caught in the backroom of Rolly Wynn's as Boris does. He pushes the chair away from the table. Still wearing that demented grin, he walks toward me. Wrapping his arm around my waist, he says, "I don't need another job. His whiskers nick my ears. "We're going to get everything we want."

He steers me past the yawning clerk, tables, chairs, and silent men. In the corner, Rolly Wynn is watching me. I'm a threat as menacing as a kite on a string. He is waiting for me to blow away.

"You have to stop gambling right now," I tell Charlie. "Or we'll be ruined."

Suddenly I'm flooded in sunlight and standing in an alley.

Sweat drips down my face and seeps under the tight fitting collar around my neck. Something slippery, wet gravel, crunches under my heels. "You don't get to spend all our money and not tell me," I say. "That's not what grown-up married people do."

Tugging my hand, Charlie is leading me down the alley. "One day soon, maybe tomorrow, you'll go to the bank," he says. "You'll be nervous. The teller with chopsticks in her hair will look grim, but her eyes will twinkle. She'll check the balance sheet, then say, 'Mrs. Fain, you have $3000.' Her wrinkled face will break into a smile. 'Your husband fixed everything. You can quit your job and concentrate on your schoolwork.'"

Shading my eyes, I try to find Charlie in the bright light. He stops walking and puts his arms around me. Like the lady in his tale, his eyes are twinkling. He must believe his own lies. He's conned himself.

Overhead, puffy white storybook clouds sail by. My high heels find sandy holes between the stones and dig in. He's not a grown up. He's an 18-year-old who still belongs in nursery school. He really does believe he's doing this awful thing for us. "It's a beautiful dream," I tell him. "But it's just a dream."

A voice over my shoulder has a lilt to it: "Still, wouldn't it be grand?"

I blink. Mickey-Bing, the Irish-American leprechaun, has appeared out of nowhere.

"You're making everything worse," I tell my father. "You're feeding lies. Don't you both know how much trouble we're in?" The lump that's been sitting at the edge of my throat all day is back. So are the tears. If I start to cry now, I won't stop, and they'll think I'm the weak one, the one who's deluded. "I have to go to work."

I slide over gravel. Air blowing out from the back of the dry cleaners adds even more heat to the stiff, dry wind.

At the corner, I stop. Maybe I shouldn't give up so easily. Maybe if I put it all down on paper for Charlie, he'll be able to see how wrong he is. Numbers don't lie.

I turn, and walk back toward him. A jeep kicking up clouds of dust rolls down the alley. By the time the dust cloud settles, I've made my way back to the cleaners. I look through the glare for my husband and father. They're gone. The door to the liquor store clicks shut.

The three wooden stairs sway under my footsteps. I twist the doorknob. The door is locked. Just running my hand down the door makes the paint peel and the wood splinter. My fingers ache to do more damage. I'd like to rip the door from its hinges.

What I need is Carrie Nation's band of women and their axes. One swing and the door would fall. One slash and goodbye TV screen, goodbye horse races. Carrie Nation and her crew could demolish Rolly Wynn's backroom in five minutes.

Past Rolly Wynn's trash cans, a pair of shoes and mound of cloth wait in tall weeds. Sun-bleached penny loafers, once mahogany in color, now are the same lemon-brown as the dying horseradish that hides them. The wool checked jacket still has good buttons and looks soft enough to double as a pillow. Do the shoes and jacket belong to someone who begs for coffee money in front of the Greyhound depot in a second, better pair of shoes? Past the dry cleaner's vent, wind, or maybe a man's feet pressed the weeds flat for a bed. The man in front of the depot is coming back. This patch of alley is his home.

If Charlie had to wear the vagrant's penny loafers would he be as smart as the vagrant is? If Charlie had only two pairs of shoes left, would he be gambling one pair away?

I wade through dry, crackling weeds. Cattails prick my dress. Little spears dig through my stockings, and attack my legs. I brush and brush, but there's no getting rid of those stickers. I grip my purse. Three pennies clink at the bottom. I will be getting my paycheck at the end of the week, but Charlie could spend the money in a second. If I keep doing things Charlie's way I could end up without a home. I can almost taste the sour, begged-for coffee.

•

"This may be the worst idea I've ever had," I say. "And it's not going to solve the whole problem."

Grace Everett is tapping a sharp pencil on her blotter. Six more sharp pencils sit in a cup.

"Charlie and I are in some financial difficulty," I say.

"Mr. Miller handles the players' problems," she tells me. "I hate to bother him now. He's getting ready for harvest and fall planting. It's the store's second busiest season."

"I don't want to bother Mr. Miller or you, but Charlie and I are in debt. Dan Lowell says they might have to garnish Charlie's wages. I was thinking if you gave Charlie's check," I take a breath, "directly to me I can pay off what we owe. I'll make sure he still eats well and gets to the doctor."

Grace Everett fiddles with a paperweight, a model of one of the John Deere tractors that Mr. Miller sells in the store. Beth and Norma say that Grace is in love with Mr. Miller. He loves her back. But he has a wife somewhere in LA. So he and Grace are discreet. She's stroking the tractor wheels and watching them spin.

"If the bank does have to take some of Charlie's salary," I say, "it could get to the press. It could hurt Mr. Miller."

"I understand the difficulty of your situation," she says. "But you're taking Charlie's wages from him is so drastic. You need to be gentle with him. He's in a lot of pain right now. They hate to admit their failures, especially if they're partly at fault. They're not as tough as we are. You need to give him time to work it out."

"But he's betting on the horses. He wiped out our savings."

Her face changes. "I see." She pushes the tractor next to the cup of pencils. It rolls to a stop. Her face is pink. "I'll ask Mr. Miller. I'll handle it as a request. You can pick the check up at 3 o'clock Wednesday. That's when I make them out."

Grace will point her pencil at Mr. Miller's shirt pocket and tell him what she thinks is good for him and the Pickers. A minute later, Mr. Miller will make his decision. My shoes squeak. I step to the desk. "I don't know how to thank you."

"I like your husband." Her face looks soft. She looks ten years younger. "We both do. Only the three of us have to know. The matter will be confidential."

•

In the mail I find Aunt Lottie's hand-painted birthday card of yellow roses.

•

"You've got to come get him," I tell Kathleen.

"Is he drunk?" she asks.

"Sober."

"Sometimes he's worse then."

I kick my father's books under the chair. "Could you drive up and take him home? As soon as I get my paycheck, I'll reimburse you for the travel expenses."

"If I come way out there, I'll kill him," she says. "He's missing work and losing money. But you tell him to come home right now."

He won't come. He's having too good a time teaching Charlie everything he knows. I can hear Kathleen sniffling. She must have one of her "Mickey colds." Whenever they fight, she gets sick. Maybe she doesn't want him back this time. Maybe she's tired of taking Contac, rubbing herself with Vicks Vapo Rub, sneezing in her customer's faces.

I turn from his books, and look outside where our neighbor, Laura's corn is reaching half way up to her windows. I remember her muddy knees, and her tears. What do women like Kathleen and Laura see in Mickey anyway? Do they just like trouble?

"Whenever you have a problem, off he goes," Kathleen says. "He doesn't give me a thought. You always come first with him."

Maybe I do. I stare at his windbreaker folded neatly on the couch. Last night, he used his jacket as a pillow. Maybe it wasn't so easy for him to leave Kathleen. He does want to help his only daughter. Am I ungrateful because I want him to go home?

"I can't come now," Kathleen is saying. "We have a mortgage payment. I can't miss work."

"Think of it as an investment," I tell her. "You give up one or two days of work, but then you'll get his paycheck, too."

"Maybe he won't want to come home," she says.

"Once he sees you. . ."

"It will jog his memory," she sniffs.

I tell her the truth. "He does love you."

"He shouldn't have to be reminded he's married."

She's going to bang the phone down. They're the only couple I know who include the cost of buying new phones in their annual budget. I hold the receiver away from my ear. Her voice is soft, muffled by her cold, and the distance between us. "By the way," she says, "Happy Birthday."

"Thank you," I hang up.

My growling stomach reminds me I had nothing to eat or drink except for birthday cake. My legs ache. I feel as if I've been climbing stairs for hours. I need food and rest. I open the refrigerator. It's empty except for two eggs and a stalk of celery. Kathleen said I come first with Mickey. Charlie said he's doing these crazy things for me. If the both care about me why are they ruining my life?

39

There's a tap on the back door windowpane. Bonnie's sunglasses are too large for her heart-shaped face. She presses freshly colored lips together. She looks nervous.

She's probably angry. I haven't even called to thank her for the cake. I open the door. "The cake is so beautiful," I tell her. Steam from the rice I'm cooking blows into her pale face. "It was such a lovely surprise."

Cool in her ice-white sheath, she brushes past me. Her new leather shoes make the cracked linoleum look more faded than usual. "I thought we were friends," she says.

She is my friend, but what have I ever done for her? I pull out a chair. My hands are stained with red juice. "I wanted to call, but I just got. . .busy. How about a piece of your wonderful cake and –?" The only beverage I can offer her is water.

Still standing, she frowns at diced onions, sliced chili peppers, and chopped tomatoes. I haven't been too busy to pick Laura's garden vegetables for dinner. Bonnie slips her sunglasses and car keys into her straw purse. She's going to stay. She's going to stand forever silent in my kitchen.

Gas flames lick the bottom of the stainless steel pan. The rice is burning. I dump rice into a bowl. "Time just got away from me."

She frowns at Aunt Lottie's recipe-card. It reads: *The Underpaid Artist's Special – Spanish-Rice.* Goose bumps pop out on her thin arms. She thinks I'm lying about the time. She thinks I'm some kind of superwoman who has everything under control. She couldn't guess how relieved I was to find the rice tucked away in a corner of the almost empty cupboard. She wouldn't believe I could get myself into such a mess.

"You should have told me you were in trouble," she says. "I came the moment I heard."

I sink into the chair I offered her. How did she find out? Over coffee, Dan Lowell Senior whispered to Steve Willis Senior that young Steve's loud-mouthed, second baseman friend had run through his savings.

"Don't be angry at Grace," Bonnie says. "She told me because she was worried. She knows I'm your friend."

It wasn't Dan Lowell. It was *This-will-be-between-the-three-of-us-confidential* Grace. Why should Mr. Reisner's dad waste paper and money on the *Cotton Valley Gazette* when the news gets out anyway? Everyone in town has a mouth that works overtime.

Bonnie sits in a chair opposite me and hugs herself. "If you had told me earlier, you could have kept going to classes. Professor Edelsen called to tell me he was worried about you working too hard, keeping up on all that reading and working at the Wise Owl."

"I feel terrible," I tell her. "You and Professor Edelsen and Grace Everett are all trying to help me."

"The problem isn't you," she says. "It's gambling."

She makes *gambling* sound like the curse word it is.

She's going to tell me to leave Charlie. She's going to say no man is worth this aggravation.

"You're doing this all wrong," she says. "You're going to ruin your marriage. Steve was very depressed when he was on the bench. He thought he was a failure. He thought he would lose me because I wouldn't love a failure. If I had interfered with his relationship with the Pickers he would have felt even worse."

I study the mound of rice between us. "We owe so much money." I recite the litany. "I'll get my Wise Owl paycheck in two days and Charlie's pay check the next day. Mr. Lowell might wait until then."

Bonnie isn't listening. She's rummaging through her purse. She takes out a fountain pen that is leaking red ink. She opens her checkbook. "You can't take away a man's pride," she says. "He needs to feel he's in charge. You can help him get involved in the team. Grace said he could do some pinch running."

"You expect Charlie, the world's greatest second baseman, to pinch run?"

"He'll do it," Bonnie tells me, "if you make him feel important enough."

"I'm sick of the old marriage game," I say. "Though he's lazy, drinks, gambles, the husband is a king, a peacock, while his uncomplaining and industrious Alice or Bonnie or Pamela, keeps everything going. Wives shouldn't have to pretend."

She nods. "That would be nice." She rips the check from the book. "Take the money. Pay me back when you can."

I stare at my name, Pamela Fain. The dot above the "i" looks like a drop of blood. "Bonnie, I just can't. If Charlie finds out, he'll feel worse."

"If he finds out you want to take his paycheck before he even sees, he'll kill you. He's going to stop this craziness. It's just a little period of adjustment."

Outside, Old Chartreuse sputters to a stop. Doors slams. Boris yips. Charlie starts singing *Happy Birthday*. He carries a long white box with a fancy pink bow. He bought me a present. Maybe that's where some of our money disappeared. Why didn't he give me the gift this morning? All of our money couldn't have gone into what is in that box.

Mickey, hands in pocket, chin in neutral, not singing a note, follows his son-in-law up the walk.

"Just play along," Bonnie saying. "Pretend he's doing everything right." She slips the check into my apron pocket. "The money is for you to save your marriage. Everything will work out. You'll see."

I finger the check and sigh. All the women's magazines tell wives to lie. Could all these good little women be right?

Keys rattling in the lock sound tinny. Charlie is still singing. Boris, a bow tied to his collar, runs to me and jumps. His paws leave prints on my dress. His nails scratch my nylons. I can picture Bonnie's white sheath smudged with alley dirt. Waving the slotted spoon, I shout, "Go away." Boris cringes and slinks under the table.

Charlie bows and puts the box in my lap. "For the birthday girl."

"It's a beautiful package," I tell him. The birthday girl wants to tie the fancy ribbon around Charlie's neck and pull.

"It's from the best store in the whole valley," Charlie says. "It's called Miss Rochelle's." He winks at Bonnie. "Your rich friend here told me where to go."

It's not enough he had to waste money on a present when we have no groceries. He had to find the most expensive shop in town.

"Come on, open it," he says.

Layers of tissue paper hid something pink. Paper slides to the floor. I hold up an angora sweater with gently puffed sleeves and lace around neck. I used to pretend I had a sweater just like this in my dresser on Hibiscus Street. I lay the sweater against my cheek. It is soft and luxurious.

"It's so beautiful," I tell Charlie. He does love me. He isn't purposely trying to drive me crazy. "I'm not sure we can afford it."

Bonnie sucks in her breath.

Charlie's shoulders sag. "I paid for the sweater in cash so you wouldn't worry."

What cash? Does he have some money left over? I step up to my husband and slide my arms around his waist. "It was wonderful of you to remember my birthday." I pat his back pocket. It's flat. There are no bills hiding there. I hate my smile, but I keep patting and smiling. I'm a sneak and a hypocrite.

"That color is perfect for you," Bonnie says. "It brings out the pink in your cheeks. You look like a girl in a Renoir." She tells Charlie, "You have excellent taste."

Charlie is smiling now. He holds the sweater up to me. "Pam doesn't know how pretty she is."

Pretty Pam smiles and pats one last pocket. Is the price of the sweater enough to cover what we owe the grocery store? I search through tissue paper and hunt for a receipt. It's not there.

"Aren't you going to try the sweater on?" Charlie asks.

I slip it over my head. It feels soft. "Beautiful," Bonnie and Charlie say together.

I touch the Renoir-pink angora. The painter knew about colors. He could paint a girl with hair the color of wet hay and make her look beautiful. If only I could keep the sweater.

"What is that glop?" Mickey is staring at the rice. "That's my sister's recipe, right? That's her favorite dish – boiled cardboard."

Pressing the sweater against my cheek, and feeling the wool's softness one more time, I fold the sweater and bury it in tissue paper. "It's Spanish rice," I say. "With Laura's tomatoes we won't have to spend a cent on food for days."

"My sister killed her husband," Mickey says.

Bonnie's eyes get wide.

"The poor bastard had allergies," Mickey says. "Charlotte's not happy unless the dust is waist high. Pam loves her. But she's a freak. Am I right? She weighs 300 pounds."

Bonnie rocks on her high heels and rummages through her purse. She pulls out her car keys.

"But it was the oils in her paints that did it. She gave Jacob emphysema." My father turns to me. "You want us to eat food a 300-pound killer recommends?"

"We'll go out to eat," Charlie says.

Bonnie kisses me on the cheek, whispers, "Happy birthday," and walks toward the door.

To make up for my father's outrageousness, I call, "You were right about everything."

She nods and turns the doorknob.

Mickey's voice stops her. "You can't go without having a piece of Pam's cake." He opens the refrigerator and takes out the cake. He whistles. "Isn't it a beauty? I bought it for her."

Confused, Bonnie looks at the half-eaten cake and then at me. "Bonnie bought that cake," I say. "She ordered it days ago. It's from all of the wives. It was a lovely surprise."

Mickey squints. "What about my $5?"

"I used it to pay some of our debt to the grocery store," I whisper.

Mickey opens his mouth, but no words come out. Bonnie's car keys jangle.

"What are the sad faces for?" Charlie says. "We got a home run here." His hand slides under his letterman's sweater. He takes a roll of bills from his shirt pocket. He grins at me, and then winks at Bonnie. "See my system works. This is only the beginning."

I stare at the lovely money. "All of our problems are solved," I say. "I was so worried at the grocery store when they said our check bounced and when Dan Lowell called about our savings account, I didn't know what to do. But you have the money."

Charlie is nodding and smiling. "It must have been so hard for you. I'm sorry you had to go through it."

"It was a nightmare," I say. "How much money do we have?"

"Here." He hunts for a bill inside the roll. A $5-bill flutters down. "Gas money."

The bill lands at my feet. It's another damn $5-dollar hand out. "How much do you have?" My voice bounces off of thin walls. I'm shouting.

Charlie's fists curl around paper, then he steps away from me and backs next to shelves that hold dishes: "$317."

"I'm so glad." I move closer to him. "We owe the grocery store and the bank, but we're going to be all right. I can take the money down right now to Dan Lowell." I glance at the rooster clock. It's 4:35. He's still there. I can call up Grace, tell her the deal's off. I take the check out of my apron pocket and give it back to Bonnie. "If you give me the money now," I tell him, "this really will be a happy birthday."

"The bank can wait," Charlie says. "This is just seed money for the big kill. See, we're playing with their money now. That's how the big boys do it."

"Seed money? Weren't you listening to me? We owe money all over town."

"We're going to use the money to get more," Charlie says. "We'll be rolling in money."

"We have to pay what we owe now."

Charlie is still grinning. "It's all taken care of. Pretty soon we'll have so much money Dippy Dan Lowell and his polka dot tie will be coming to us for a loan."

Charlie's lunatic smile makes my fingers tremble. I grab something from the shelf and throw it across the room. Four chunks of blue and white china splatter on the linoleum. The chunks break into bits.

There is silence except for the bitter hum of the empty refrigerator. I'm just like Kathleen. When I'm worried, I throw a plate or a lamp or a phone, as if that will solve my problem.

I stare at the broken saucer of Alice's that had lost its cup years ago. Charlie wraps his high school sweater more tightly around him. Still grasping the cash, he stares at me and sits in a chair.

"Pam didn't mean it," Mickey says.

I reach for my broom and dustpan. I kneel and sweep. Pam did mean it.

Bonnie bends down. She brushes china into the dustpan with her bare hand. She has tears in her eyes.

"You'll cut yourself," I tell her. I dump Alice's saucer in the trash.

"What did you do that for?" Charlie asks.

Everyone is watching me and waiting for an answer. All I know is I've turned into my stepmother. Give me a few more weeks and I will be waving a butcher knife and chasing Charlie around the table.

"I buy you a beautiful present," Charlie says. "I bring home money. You throw a plate. It doesn't make sense."

"I'm sorry. I just want to pay off our debts. I'm not myself." But what if this loud, saucer-throwing person who dreams of strangling her husband with fancy pink ribbon is the real me?

Mickey shakes a stubby finger in my face. "Didn't I always tell you violence was wrong? I didn't bring you up this way."

"Just how many times have you been tossed in jail because you slugged someone?" I ask.

The refrigerator hums. The rooster clock ticks. Bonnie is staring at the floor.

Mickey pokes the cake, licks frosting from his fingers. He makes a face. "Too sweet."

Charlie cracks his knuckles. "What's the deal with Grace?"

"She's going to. . . I asked for your check so I can pay the bills."

Mickey whistles. "God."

"Gabby Grace," Charlie says. "Now, everyone will know you don't trust me. You don't trust me, do you? You don't think I can take care of anything. You're treating me like a bad child."

"Pam's done the wrong thing," Mickey says. "Once it's explained to her, she'll tell you how sorry she is."

Charlie gets to his feet. "Just go to the Pickers' office right now. Tell Grace you changed your mind and I'll pick up my checks."

Bonnie wraps her arm around my shoulder. "I'll drive you right now."

"I'll go too," Mickey tells Charlie. "I'll straighten this out."

"Do you need your purse?" Bonnie asks me.

They look at me with shiny faces. They're all waiting for me to be a good little girl and do as I'm told. "I'm not going anywhere," I say. "I don't want to change the arrangement I made with Grace. If Charlie doesn't have any money he can't gamble. I don't want his paycheck to be more seed money."

"It's my paycheck," Charlie says.

"But they're our debts."

"I showed you the money we have," Charlie says. "What more proof do you need that we're going to be OK?" His elbow bumps a chair. He studies the flowered cushion and frowns at the rungs on the chair's ladder-back. His frown says the rungs are going nowhere, just like this conversation. Charlie shoves the chair. It doesn't move. He pushes again. The chair wobbles, and thumps to the floor. It lies on its side.

I should right the chair. But, I don't want to fix another thing. My fingers ache to break more dishes. I step closer to the crockery shelf, and study what I have left of Alice's dinnerware.

"Why are you doing this to me?" Charlie says.

"Why are you gambling our money away?"

"See, you don't believe in me," he says.

"You may not agree with Charlie's actions, but at least you can let him have his pay check," Bonnie says. "We should go before the office closes."

"Who made you our certified public accountant?" Charlie asks.

"Bonnie's on our side," I say. "She's trying to help."

"You don't go to outsiders. You should have called my mother if you were so worried. She could have at least lent you grocery money. She wants to come and help us out anyway."

"Right now she's helping Warren," I say. "They're in the mountains."

"Mountains?" Charlie says.

"She doesn't have time to come up here and open a can of tomato soup. She's too busy making love with Warren."

"Now honey," Mickey says. "You just don't come out in the open and say something like that."

"You do if it's the truth," I say. "And your wife wants to kill you."

"Yeah, well, that's not exactly a news flash," my father tells his shoes. "Kathleen was born with a stiletto in her hand."

"My mother and wimpy Ashburn?" Charlie says. "You've misunderstood something – or you're making it up."

"I don't have that much imagination."

"But she's old enough to be. . ."

"His mother," I say.

"She's my mother," Charlie says. "My mother doesn't do things like that."

"She must have done it at least once," Mickey says with a little smile.

Charlie looks awful. His face is a Renoir-pink. It isn't becoming. Maybe I should have kept my information about his mother's love life to myself.

"My mother's a Catholic," he says. "She doesn't believe in sex outside of marriage."

Doesn't she? I think of the bed sheets with the lusty pink roses she sent to us.

"Mr. Zimmer told me," I say softly. "He wanted me to tell you when the time was right. I guess that time isn't now."

"This can't be true," Charlie says. "Maybe Howie's drinking too much of that beer he puts in his chili."

"I shouldn't have told you," I say. "I wanted to hurt you because I was hurt."

"Once I thought she had a thing for one of her bosses at the accounting firm," Charlie says. "We would be talking about the Dodgers chances for the pennant and she'd find some way to worm this guy's name into the conversation. I told her I was sick of hearing about him, and she got real quiet. Maybe I was too hard on her." Charlie shakes his head. "But taking up with no-hit, no-field Ashburn."

"He must do something right." Mickey clears his throat. "Excuse me, Bonnie. Pam's boyfriend wasn't all that bad. He was smart, and he worked hard."

"Now that Warren's safely out of my life," I say, "you can afford to throw a few compliments around."

Charlie wraps his arms around his chest and hugs himself. All the color has left his face. "I don't believe any of this."

Bonnie whispers, "He needs you now." She nods at Charlie who is slumped over the table. Mascara has dried in lumps on Bonnie's lashes. Sweat runs down her nose. She's chewed off her lipstick. An afternoon with my family has done her in. Before another Carey-Fain skeleton can march out of our pantry, Bonnie heads for the door.

Outside, the engine of her grape-green Oldsmobile hums. I'm glad she's going. She won't have to witness any more of our awfulness. And I won't have to watch her watching us.

"Jes-u, before you went to the Pickers," Mickey says, "you should have talked it over with me."

"Jes-u? What happened to Jesus and his jockstrap?" I ask.

"You shouldn't have said anything about his mother," Mickey says. "The boy was already upset. You don't have to hit someone when they're down."

I glance over at Charlie. "What am I supposed to do?" I ask my father. "Coddle him? Your way isn't accomplishing anything. He thinks I don't trust him, just because I'm mad he blew our money."

"He's not trusting himself," Mickey says. "Don't you see that, sweetheart?"

"I'm still in the room," Charlie says.

"He's right not to trust himself," I say. "He's not trustworthy."

Charlie bangs his fist on the table, and turns to me. "Are you going to go to the Pickers and call this thing off?"

"I'm not sure."

"Damn it, do you know how this makes me look?" Charlie grabs the Plymouth keys from the hook and heads for the door. "If you won't do it, I'll tell them myself. I earn the checks. This is my money. You had no right to embarrass me in front of the team."

I run after him. "But you're going to spend the money before you even get it."

He slams the kitchen door in my face. A second later, he's gunning the Plymouth's engine. The car jerks forward, and lurches into the street.

My fingers curl around the $5-bill. What am I doing so wrong? Why is my husband leaving me?

"You got a set of keys for Charlie's junk heap?" my father asks.

"Why do you want them?"

"I've got to find him before he spends that money. This is only the eighth inning here. We still got some at bats."

I hand him Old Chartreuse's key. Mickey winks at me. "Your father will take care of everything." He shuts the screen door behind him.

40

If only Charlie were here. At least I'd know that he's safe and alive. Where could he be at 3 a.m.? And where is my father, the great protector of restless son-in-laws?

Spanish rice and six pieces of birthday cake sit like a fist in my stomach. Out the living room window, headlights swing up the road. Those lights must mean that Charlie is coming home. He's all right. Soon, he'll be jiggling the key in the lock. I'll open the door and tell him, "You're never going to do this to me again."

Headlights capture the round white head and big shoulders of an owl perched on a wire above the railroad track. A motor hums. The owl turns gray, then black, then disappears. The car, one cracked tail light glowing, moves on.

He's not coming home. I wrap my robe more tightly around my middle. Maybe Mickey found him at Rolly Wynn's. They got in a fight with some locals and now they're both lying dead in an alley.

There's nothing more to worry about. All I have to do is wait. The police will call and ask me to come and identify the bodies. I'll inform Kathleen and Mrs. Fain. The three of us can set up funeral arrangements. Should we have two separate masses? It would be cheaper to have one funeral for both of them.

Now a train whistles. A circle of fiery light cuts its way through the darkness. The circle gets bigger. The train rumbles and then roars. Brown cattails growing by the track turn red. The owl, barely moving its wings, lifts off into the safety of darkness. Orange and yellow lights swirl. The living room looks as if it's on fire. I close my eyes, and block my ears with my hands. Windowpanes rattle, walls shake and the floor rises under my feet.

I hold onto the walls, the mantle, the backs of chairs, and make my way to the kitchen. In light cast by the 323 freight train from Stockton, I see Alice sitting at my table. A paperback mystery, cracked at its spine, lies with its pages open. Alice is wearing her white nylon robe with puffy sleeves. Her cigarette glows. She's looking out the window and waiting.

On the shelf, her dinner plates clatter. I blink and she's gone. I touch the chair where she was sitting. It's finally happened. All the worry, all the adding up of numbers, have finally pushed me over the edge. I've gone bonkers.

Past the living room, the train rumbles, and then hums. The kitchen goes dark. I turn on the light, take a seat opposite Alice's, and stare at the vacant chair. How many nights did she spend waiting and entertaining herself? She hummed Gilbert and Sullivan's *Oh Wandering Maid*, changing the words to *Oh Wandering Man*.

Wacko that I am, I reach for a strand of her hair. My fingers touch air. If only she was here, I wouldn't be alone. We could wait and sing together.

●

Even with the windows closed I can still smell bacon frying. It makes my stomach grumble. Next door, Laura is fixing her favorite breakfast: eggs, orange juice and toast. I'm hungry for something besides rice and birthday cake.

Linoleum is already hot under my feet. Today is going to be a scorcher. In the bathroom, I splash water on my face, zip my navy blue skirt, button my white sailor blouse. I rub flesh-colored cream under my eyes and make the dark hollows disappear. I finger in rouge and bring color to my cheeks. I look like a schoolgirl again.

I slide the pin of the Wise Owl badge through my blouse. The pin pricks the skin on my finger. The badge transforms me from schoolgirl to businesswoman. Clothes and makeup are wonderful. No one would guess that a few short hours ago I was tossing dishes at my husband. No one would guess I was up late last night planning funerals.

Warmed-over rice fills my stomach. I wrap a hunk of birthday cake in wax paper for my lunch. I find my purse, and then remember there's $5 in my apron pocket. I'll be able to buy groceries after work. I search for my car keys. I look out the living room window. No car.

Damn. My Plymouth could be in an oil field, a cotton field, or a ball field. It could be turned over in an irrigation ditch. If Charlie has totaled it, I'll total him.

How am I going to get to work? I could ask Laura to drop me off on the way to the library. But I don't want to admit that Charlie didn't come home. I could tell her something's wrong with the car. I shut my eyes. I'm sick of lies.

Then I remember: Cotton Valley has a small, municipal bus with a short, lady driver perched on a high seat. She stops at First and Valley Drive at 8 a.m. If I hurry, I might be able to flag her down. I lock the house. Hot air, stiff as the starch in my blouse, stings my face.

A brown mound lies on the grass near a flower bed. It's a man. Mouth gaping, fingers open, head resting in the stones I use for mulch under the rose bush, Mickey is out cold.

For some reason, words to an Eddie Fisher song come to me. I can feel my mean smile. I sing. *"Oh my papa/to me he was so wonderful/Oh my papa/to me he was so good."* I step closer and tap my papa's shoe with my foot.

He closes his mouth and smiles. I tap him again. He giggles. Just where does he think he is? Who does he think I am? One of his cocktail waitresses?

The wet clover I kneel in makes me shiver. I shake Mickey's shoulder. "Where's Charlie? Is he all right? Where's the Plymouth?"

One eye opens and shuts. Both eyes open and try to focus. The right eye wanders. He sighs and closes his eyes. I'm not the girl he wants to see.

"Where did you leave Charlie's car?" I ask. "I have to go to work."

He lifts his head and stares at a thorny branch. His mouth opens. "Yuck."

"I have to go to work at the book department," I say.

He bats a rose bush. "Is this my funeral? Where's the music? I told them to play *The Rose of Tralee.*"

He's farther gone than I thought.

He ducks his chin, curls up like the bug he is, and rolls away from the bush. "Damn roses." He sits up. "Look where you made your father sleep. All those flowers and wet dirt and bird song. I thought for sure you were burying me."

"Where's Old Chartreuse?"

He rubs his beard. "I got to wash. Why the hell didn't you let me in? I knocked on your door all night."

"I didn't hear you."

"I got old Delbert up," he says. "I saw his lights on, and his curtains move."

"Delbert Rollins?"

"Of course Delbert Robbins. How many Delberts do we know?"

"Delbert Rollins, not Robbins. Delbert Rollins lived on Hibiscus Street in Santa Monica," I say. "That was 10 years ago. This is 1963. We're in Cotton Valley."

Mickey shuts his eyes and dozes.

I shake him and knock a stone out from his collar. "If you were truly where you said you were last night, I would have heard you. I was up waiting."

He opens an eye. "I got to pee."

"Where's Charlie?"

"Rolly's." Mickey grins and blows stale alcohol breath in my face. "Rolly's. Not Polly's, Solly's, or Molly's." He rubs his eyes. "Your hubby just needs some time away from you." He studies an inchworm climbing a blade of grass. He looks up at the sky. "It's a pretty day, don't you think?"

"Is the Plymouth at Rolly's? Where's Old Chartreuse?"

He gets to his knees and falls back on his haunches. "Broken. You wouldn't understand." He pokes my Wise Owl badge.

"Which car is broken? I need to get to work."

"When Charlie comes back, you tell him how sorry you are. A man's supposed to wear the pants." Cabbie trousers, the pants my father wears, are torn at both knees and soaked with dew. "You made a mistake," he says.

"I'm just trying to pay our bills," I say. Damn it. Why do I always argue with him when he's drunk? There's no way I can win. Something in me, some sickness, makes me keep talking. "I'm not going to settle for the kind of marriage Alice had."

He juts his chin. "She was too damn bossy. Too full of herself."

"Alice was bossy?"

"Just like you." He purses his lips and cocks his head. "If you were truly where you said you were, I would have heard you." He shakes his head. "Horseshit."

"You made her miserable," I say.

"You always bring this crap up. How I broke her heart. It's the same damn broken record." He takes a flask from his back pocket and drinks. "It takes two to tango. Two to wreck a marriage. But you never see that."

I reach for the bottle. He pulls it away and tucks it under his jacket. "You have no loyalty. I'm the one who braided your hair and put those damn bows in and took you to kindergarten."

"You're going to kill yourself," I tell him.

He squints at me. "What do you care? You let your father sleep in a rose bush." He turns and looks up at the house. "Let me in. A man's got to wash up."

He's still drunk. He could break the furniture, urinate on the rug, or scald himself with water he boiled for coffee. Still, he's my father and I should let him sleep it off in a real bed. My fingers dig through my purse. "I can't find the house key."

He steps toward me and whispers, "Just give me the key."

"I'm not sure where it is."

"You just don't want me in your house," he says.

"That's not true," I say. Then, I know he's right. I don't want him puking on the floor. "Maybe you could rest outside for awhile. I'll come home at lunch time and let you in."

"Just give me the damn key." He pushes me, knocks me down and grabs my purse. I slide and sit in wet grass. One knee bumps against a rose bush. My stocking tears.

This can't be happening. He's lost all control. He's always said his hands were weapons and he would never use them against his little girl. But he shoved me, made me fall, and now he's pawing through my purse. He pulls out the keys and waves them in my face. "I came all the way to help you and this is the thanks I get. You won't even let me in your house."

He throws the purse at my feet and weaves up the walk.

I brush dirt and wet grass from my face. He looked as if he wanted to kill me. I wanted to kill him. Keys rattle. He leaves them dangling in the lock and slams the door.

I reach for my purse and get to my feet. My heels punch holes in the wet grass. On the porch I take keys from the door. Inside, the house is still and bathed in sunlight. So, peaceful, as if nothing could go wrong. He knocks over the coffee table. I follow his muddy tracks across the living room carpet, through the kitchen, to the bathroom.

I stop at the bathroom door. Water's running in there, gushing into the basin, maybe spilling onto the floor. He could be passed out and sleeping in a puddle. Can a man drown in water on the bathroom floor? If a man wanted to die enough he could. Does Mickey want to die? I know the answer. He thinks his daughter doesn't love him. He thinks his daughter blames him for everything that's wrong in her life. Why should he want to live? It would be easy for him now. Standing in a stream of water, all he has to do is flick on the light or plug in his razor. It would be over in a second.

I rap on the door. "Daddy, you can't stay in there. It's not safe."

No answer.

"Daddy, turn off the water and whatever you do, don't put on the light."

He still doesn't answer.

I knock harder. The door gives. He's sitting on the toilet, his boxer shorts and trousers are draped around his knees. Passed out. I turn to the sink and away from the sight of graying red pubic hair and a small, folded penis. I twist the faucet, and yank the sink's plug. The floor isn't too bad. It's just a small trickle of water by the basin.

If I can take his liquor away and put him in bed, he'll sleep. He'll be safe for awhile.

I should take his money too. There's a store only three blocks away that he probably knows about. A liquor store is the first thing he looks for when he comes to a new neighborhood.

I kneel and inch along the floor on my knees. His head is drooped to one side. He's snoring. I pluck the flask from his back pocket. So easy. Now for the money. Deep in his frayed pocket, I find keys and his thin, black wallet. I put the flask on the floor, and take out all four singles. I slip the wallet back into his pocket. My elbow bumps his knee.

He stirs. One eye opens. He stares at the bills in my hand. "Thief."

He stands and his pants fall to his ankles, his boxers cling to his calves. "What the hell?" He looks down at himself. His face gets red. "God damn son of a bitch." He stares at me. "You're a pervert."

Something bitter bubbles in my throat I'm going to be sick. I grab his flask, slam the bathroom door and run to the kitchen.

At the sink, I try to throw up, but nothing comes. I twist off the bottle cap. It's stuck. Mickey is already yanking the bedroom door. He charges across the kitchen. His trousers are zipped, and his belt is buckled. How did he pull up his pants and get in here so fast? He's had plenty of practice.

"That's my property," he yells.

Amber colored whiskey dribbles down the sink. I should have thrown the flask out the window. He shoves me and grabs the flask. Whiskey sloshes and spills on my skirt and blouse. The strong, woody odor makes me sneeze. I smell like a still. I'll have to change my clothes before I go to work. I'll be late and the time will be docked from my paycheck. And for what? One more lost battle.

He smiles and takes a long drink. Tucking the flask under his belly, he crawls on his knees. The cap has rolled under the stove.

I could get down on the floor with him and try to get the flask back. But I won't. I've already torn one stocking. Besides, he might shove me again. Or even hit me. Who knows what he's capable of now?

I tuck his money in my skirt pocket and splash cold water on my blouse. The stain grows.

"I got it." He caps the flask and jumps to his feet. His smile is awful. "Now, where's my money?"

"You'll just buy more liquor," I say. My voice squeaks. I'm a little mouse.

He grins. "That's the whole idea."

He stretches and puts the flask on top of the refrigerator behind an empty bowl. He studies me and sees his bills sticking out of my pocket. I should have hidden the money in the tail of the rooster clock. It would have taken him half the day to find it. By then, I could have gotten help, called the police, done something.

"Just give me my money and we won't have any more problems," he says.

"No."

"Damn ingrate. It's my money." He knocks down a chair. One of the slats falls out.

"Why do you have to wreck everything?" No more mouse. I'm shouting and crying now.

He springs and misses the bills in my pocket by half an inch. I shove the table between us and use it as a shield. He steps around his corner of the table. I step around mine. He sings, *Pop Goes the Weasel*. On the word *Pop*, he pushes his side of the table against me and backs me into the sink.

"Daddy, stop it. I'll call the police."

He squints and shoves the table. It lands on its side.

He's in the living room now. I step over table legs, and follow him to the phone. I pick up the receiver. He yanks the jack from out of the wall and pulls the receiver from my hand. The telephone flies across the room. It skids over an end table, knocks down a jar of dried flowers, and then lands just inside the kitchen.

He jumps on the new easy chair. Red unfocused eyes, arms flapping, he looks like a bat, an evil, foul-smelling bat who's between me and the front door.

I have to get away. I run to the kitchen. He's after me. His warm, alcohol breath beats on my neck. I weave around the fallen table.

"Give me my money," he screams.

I stumble over the chair, then catch myself.

A white, freckled fist whizzes past my ear. It can't be true. Little Red Carey is throwing punches at me, his daughter.

"Daddy, stop it." I turn and face him. He backs me up against the crockery shelf. He hates me. I am his enemy. The fists keep coming. I duck, curl up, and make myself as small as I can. Something big and hot hits my ear. My ear throbs. My father hit me.

"Give me the money," he says.

He's crazy. He isn't going to stop. He doesn't care who I am. Not anymore. He doesn't even care if he kills me. All he wants is his money and his liquor.

My knees buckle. Something wet dribbles down my legs. I hold out the bills and wave them like a flag.

He lowers his fist and snatches the money. He smiles an awful smile and counts the bills. He puts the money in his wallet. He shakes his head at me. "You're a wimp. You're hopeless. I could eat you for lunch."

He opens the oven door and takes out a new, unopened bottle of Jim Beam. The bastard could start his own liquor store. He's the one who's hopeless. What kind of a father is happy because he can outwit and terrify his child?

41

Someone raps on the back door. "Christ," Mickey spits. Shading her eyes, Laura Davis presses her face against the screen. "Is everything all right, dear?"

Neighbors have been asking me that question ever since I can remember. I've always pretended for myself and for them that my father and I were fine. Didn't all families fight from time to time? Break a vase here? A chair there? Weren't all families violent? I cup my hurt ear with my hand and step to the door. For once in my life, I tell the truth. "Everything's terrible."

Mickey brushes hair from his forehead, and checks his fly. "Don't let her in," he says.

"Why not?" My hand grips the doorknob. "Are you afraid you're going to beat her up, too?"

"I feel sick," the coward whispers. Laura Davis is his last fan. He doesn't want the little librarian to know that gentle, good-hearted Michael Carey terrorizes his daughter. "I need rest." He weaves around the fallen furniture, then pauses in the bedroom's doorway. "Don't try anything cute while I'm asleep."

What does he mean by cute? Stealing his whiskey? Trying to stop him from electrocuting himself? Doesn't he know how close he's come to dying? He stands in my bedroom blinking at the floor and trying to remember where he is. He kicks the mattress and tries to free his foot from his shoe, a loafer. It's too complicated a task for the great Red Carey. He kicks again. The loafer clings to his sock. I should be grateful he has the decency to take off his shoes before sleeping in my bed. He bends over, swipes at his shoe and misses.

"Ah, hell." He ducks his chin and collapses on the bed. Still wearing his shoes, he pulls my covers over him. He's down for the count.

I open the back door and let Laura Davis in. A rectangle of sunlight floods the kitchen. Laura looks at the phone and cord on the floor. She kneels and picks up a slat from the chair. "Oh dear," she whispers. She fixes her stare on the stain on my blouse. "I was afraid of something like this. I wasn't sure what to do. But now I know I should have called the police. Your father pounded on my door for hours. He wouldn't go away. He kept calling me Delbert." She lifts her gaze. "Does that make any sense?"

"Delbert was a neighbor of ours a long time ago."

"He was crying, 'Tell Alice I love her.' It's frightening what alcohol does. It takes a decent, loving man and turns him into a wild person. I blocked the door with my bookcase. I kept telling him to go away."

Poor Mrs. Davis, moving bookcases in the middle of the night. She had to crouch by her front door because she was afraid my father might break in and hurt her.

"I'm so sorry," I tell her. "He really is a menace to himself and everyone else. Maybe he always was and I didn't realize it."

"I was afraid he might hurt you." She studies my face. "Did he?"

I close my eyes and see those white fists. My ear throbs. "Yes, he never has before but – he punched me and hit my ear." I stand and wait for tears to come, but they don't. I'm just numb.

"Let me fix you a cup of tea," she says.

•

The front doorbell rings. Has Mickey frightened another neighbor who has now come to complain?

"Would you like me to go to the door?" Laura asks.

The maniac in the bedroom is my responsibility. "I'll go." I weave around the overturned coffee table and open the door.

Mr. Nordstrom , in a crisp white shirt and corduroy slacks the color of Wheaties, is standing on my front porch and smiling at me. He says, "Why didn't you tell me?"

I smooth my hair over my ear, and straighten my whiskey-stained blouse. "Why didn't I tell you what?" Maybe there's good news. The Double-A club needs a second baseman and the doctors decided Charlie is well enough to play. "Is it something about Charlie?"

He steps closer toward the screen. "I know it's early. But I just couldn't wait. Aren't you going to invite me in?"

From the kitchen comes the sound of scraping. Mrs. Davis has set up the table and is pushing it across the floor. I should tell Mr. Nordstrom I'm sick. Or I need fresh air and I would like to visit on the porch. But I just promised myself no more pretending, no more lying to neighbors and acquaintances. I reach for the screen handle then remind myself Mr. Nordstrom isn't a neighbor. He's a reporter. If Mickey wakes up and starts another scene, Mr. Nordstrom might not be able to keep the news to himself that Charlie's father-in-law is a nut case.

"What is it you want?" I ask.

My rudeness doesn't stop the sportswriter's smile from getting bigger and lighting up his tan face. "Your father is Little Red Carey."

"Guilty," I say.

"Little Red was the greatest little fighter I ever saw."

"My father is," I swallow the words, "passed out in my bedroom."

"If only I knew Red Carey was here at our park," Mr. Nordstrom tells me, "watching our team."

"Terrorizing our neighborhood," I whisper.

"It's a hell of a story you cost me," he says.

I could give him a story. Little Red keeps in shape by using his daughter as a sparring partner. Little Red and the Picker's second baseman spend their days gambling and their nights carousing.

"I'd like to interview you," Mr. Nordstrom is saying. "What is it like growing up the daughter of a champ?"

If only I could tell Mr. Nordstrom, or someone, anyone the truth: I hate my father.

Horseshoes of sweat under the sportswriter's arms stain his shirt. Climbing steps in this heat must have worn him out. How does he do it? Walk across lumpy fields. Go to team parties. Root for the Altons and Charlies and Little Reds. I couldn't do it if I were in his position. I would be too bitter. But he got up early and drove here on a hot morning just to talk to me about Mickey.

He takes a notepad from his shirt pocket. "Did Little Red teach you what he knows about winning?"

I taste the cold rice from breakfast. Little Red taught me what he knows about losing.

Eyes shining, Mr. Nordstrom watches me through the screen. Maybe rooting for others keeps him alive. He did tell me, *"We make our own fate, Mrs. Fain."*

"Was my father really that good?" I ask.

"He was one of those rare guys who never let you down. He always gave you what you hoped for and more. He never stopped punching. Your father, Miss Carey, was the best."

The best.

"Did you ever see him fight?" Mr. Nordstrom asks.

"My mother told me about him." Alice watched him. Alice cheered. Would she want me to give up on him now? Would she think he was worth saving?

"I named my Cairn Terrier Little Red," the sportswriter tells me. "We play a game where I wave a towel. He grabs it in his teeth. I lift him and the towel three feet off the ground. He snarls and grunts, kicks his legs in the air. But he keeps biting and holding on. When I put him down he wants to play again. It's the damndest thing I've ever seen."

The drunk in the bedroom would be surprised there's a dog named after him. The drunk in the bedroom was once a man other men could admire. The drunk in the bedroom was the man who taught me never to give up on myself. I open the screen door and wave Mr. Nordstrom in.

With his left hand he grips the doorjamb and swings his leg up over a rise in the doorway. He rests and gazes at the overturned coffee table. "Al, Mr. Reisner, is crazy about your dad, too."

"Please sit," I tell him. I busy myself with pillows on the couch and wait for the sound of uneven steps to stop. He settles in the new easy chair. His gold hair and bright eyes light up the living room. "Are you and Mr. Reisner good friends?"

"His dad gave me my job. We spend summer nights on the Reisner porch drinking lemonade. Two bachelors and a retired editor talking about a boy's game."

"When I was a little girl, I thought Little Red was a hero. But all little girls believe their fathers are heroes."

"Yours really was."

I shut my eyes and think of Mickey and his egg sheller. Mickey and his motorcycle jack. Mickey teaching Mrs. Davis how to rototill. Mickey skipping rope with Charlie. I start to cry.

Mr. Nordstrom pats my shoulder. He crossed the room so softly I didn't even hear his footsteps. "It's Fain isn't it?"

I don't answer. I wipe my face with the sleeve of my whiskey stained blouse.

"He needs a lot, that guy," Mr. Nordstrom is saying. "Some of the really talented ones do."

Mr. Nordstrom is still an MVP. Still the one who never stops caring. I turn my head away and look out the window at the empty railroad tracks. What happened to him isn't fair. Knowing him now, I'm sure that even as a boy he did everything right. He could have made it all the way.

Watching Mr. Nordstrom, and with a finger to her lips, Mrs. Davis creeps closer and pounces on the phone. She tucks it under her arm. Its cord sags like the tail on a dead animal. She scurries away.

Mr. Nordstrom is staring at his shoe. Does he put his sock and shoe on before he attaches the leg? I wait for him to look up again.

"I don't know if I have what it takes to deal with Charlie," I say.

"There's only one way to tell. He's at Wynn's liquor store." Mr. Nordstrom studies dried mud on the carpet. "I guess he took it pretty hard about asking for his paycheck."

Damn small towns and the busybodies who inhabit them. Poking, interfering, they leave you no room to be safe and to hide. Mr. Nordstrom knows about the checks, Charlie's gambling. And Mickey's drinking? Probably. A bartender friend of his probably called and said some drunk claiming he was Little Red Carey was throwing up in his bathroom and peeing on his floor. Mr. Nordstrom knows everything.

"You probably think I'm awful," I say. "Bossy, wearing the pants. But we owe money. I thought I had to do it."

Mr. Nordstrom looks surprised. "Fain wouldn't have gotten this far without you."

"That's not how he sees it. I get in the way of his gambling. I hurt his pride."

"His pride is his worst enemy. It's good you showed him he can't get away with everything. He takes himself too seriously, and he doesn't take the game seriously enough. As soon as he gets those two things resolved, he'll be all right."

"You mean he's too self-centered?"

"I mean he takes his personal problems out onto the field."

"But he has a lot of personal problems."

"He can't ask baseball to fill up the holes in his life. He's got his worth all tied up in how he does out there. If he has a bad day, he's bad. If he does well, everyone loves him. It's a set up for failure."

"How can I help him?"

"Just keep doing what you're doing. Do it your father's way. Just keep punching. Do you need a ride to Wynn's?"

A soft snoring sound comes from the bedroom. "There's something else I have to take care of first."

He nods, and starts for the door. I watch him make his way down the steps. He says baseball can't make up for the holes in Charlie's life. But isn't that I'm always trying to do, too? I try to fill in the missing pieces for Charlie and my father. In between being furious at them for gambling or drinking, I'm puffing them up and pretending what they do is all right with me. I lie to them. I lie to everyone else. I lie to myself. Even Pamela, the innocent and pure servant girl, learned how to trick her master.

I march to the kitchen, yank open the silverware drawer and grab my big cutting knife. I tell Mrs. Davis, "I need your help."

She looks up from the table. She's setting out napkins, donuts and coffee. The hand holding the white plastic cup starts to shake.

I grip the wood handle and wave the blade. "You know I feel almost good about this," I say.

She jumps up and holds a napkin to her mouth.

"In fact, I should have done this years ago," I say.

Eyes bulging, her sand-colored moccasins making no sound, she follows me through the kitchen. I fling open the back door, let sun and bird song into the house. At the clothesline, I stand on tiptoes and aim. *Whack.* A chunk of rope falls. Three inches of rope still dangle from the pole. I lift my knife, and whack the second line.

Someone coughs. Behind me, a branch moves. Red fruit, the size of a Christmas tree ornament, waving above her head, Mrs. Davis peers around a pomegranate bush.

"Just one more minute, Laura," I sing. "The rope's a little stubborn."

Thwack. Done. Heading for the steps, looping the rope around my shoulder, I call, "Hurry. Hurry. We don't have much time."

White-faced, Mrs. Davis follows me. I stop by the kitchen table. "We're going to go in the bedroom now," I whisper. "If we can avoid it, it's better not to wake him."

Goose bumps break out on her skinny arms. "You're upset. You don't know what you're doing."

"I know it's scary," I tell her. "But this is the best way. You'll see."

"God forgive you. You haven't thought this through. Please let me have the knife," she says.

"If you want it you can have it," I say.

She takes the knife from me. "I'm glad you're calming down. Just because your father was violent doesn't mean you should be violent too. Now give me the rope."

"But we still need it," I say. "We're not done yet."

She jumps in front of me and blocks my way to the bedroom door. "Two wrongs do not make a right. Whatever he may have done to you, he's still your father – and you still love him."

"Of course I do. That's why I'm doing this."

"I see," she nods. "You want to put him out of his misery. There is a sort of strange logic to what you're doing." She points the knife at me. "But I'm not going to let you do it."

The whole world's gone crazy. I'm throwing saucers and now my timid little neighbor wants to slice me up like one of her fancy cheeses.

"Laura, I've had a rough night and a not so terrific morning. I don't need you waving that thing at me."

"Your father doesn't need you stabbing him or strangling him with your clothes line."

"I'm not going to strangle him."

Her eyes widen. "What are you going to do with the rope?'

"I'm going to tie him up and take him somewhere where he can get some help. He's a danger to himself." I rub my sore ear. "And to others. I thought I'd take him to AA."

"I'm glad you're not going to kill him. But one meeting isn't going to change his mind about his entire life," Laura says. "There are hospitals, treatment programs that offer long range solutions."

"A hospital seems so drastic," I say.

"As drastic as dying of alcoholism?" She puts the knife on top of the refrigerator and takes one end of the rope. "I grew up on a farm. I used to rope the cows." She's allows herself a slow, remembered smile. "Let's just see how ornery Michael Patrick Carey can be."

42

The fluorescent tube brightening the hall where we sit blinks and dies. I stare at peeling paint on the wall. I wish this place had fresh paint, comfortable couches, welcoming cups of coffee. I wish it didn't look like what it is – a state hospital for alcoholics.

"I don't belong in here." Sandwiched on the bench between me and Laura, Mickey is still shivering. Eyes narrowed, he watches the nurse with legs like dumplings unlock the door and let herself back in the ward. "The only people here are dunks and losers." He looks small, gray-faced, and old. "I'm freezing. I need a blanket."

"When the doctor comes back, we'll get you a blanket," I tell him.

"Do you promise?" he asks.

"I promise." The man who terrified me only a few hours ago is now weak with the shakes and as frightened as a kid on the first day of school. I'm my father's jailer now. I'm the one with power. I bestow blankets and broth.

Once I made up my mind, it was easy to get him here. He woke up in Laura's car. I was driving. He was hungry, tired and confused. I bought him breakfast to go at Denny's, then locked the food in the trunk and told him he could eat just as soon as he signed the commitment papers. Little Red Carey gave up his freedom for a scoop of scrambled eggs and two slices of dry toast.

Maybe taking my father to the hospital was too drastic. There is nothing here to give him comfort or hope.

A stocky man with mismatched socks, pale cheeks and two tufts of carrot colored hair, hurries past. "Dr. Corcoran," I call. "We're still waiting."

The head of San Joaquin State Hospital Alcohol Ward turns, nods, and ducks into a doorway. He doesn't care that my father has the shakes and might start hallucinating any minute.

Mickey's teeth chatter. "You expect that guy to help me? He can't even dress himself."

Laura holds a cup from the vending machine to Mickey's lips. "Chicken soup will warm you, Michael," she says.

Dr. Corcoran peers around a corner. "Miss Carey?" A paper slips out of his hand. He bends, picks it up and uses it to wave me over.

"I'll be right back," I tell Mickey. "Don't try any funny stuff. Remember you made a promise."

He blinks and slumps on the bench. He looks too weak to run away, too weak for any funny stuff. Something squeezes inside of me. How can this be right when it feels so wrong?

"I wanted to talk to you about payment," Dr. Corcoran says.

"Mickey might have insurance at his work. I have a job. I can take care of him."

Dr. Corcoran's smile is quick, nervous. "Some state funding is available for these cases."

I stare at carrot tufts. These cases? Does that mean there are other Mickeys out there? Drinking and crazy behavior are such common occurrences that the Great State of California anticipates them?

Dr. Corcoran fiddles with a wall switch. Fluorescent tubes hiss, dim, and then brighten again. "Our patients need the time to go through withdrawal. We give them tranquilizers and Disulfiram – Antabuse. If they take alcohol while on Antabuse, they'll vomit – it reacts with the ethanol in whiskey. Makes them wish they were dead."

Locked up. Tranquilizers. Induced illness. It sounds awful. Why does Mickey have to suffer so much? There must be an easier way for him to get well.

"What is the length of stay in these cases?"

"One or two months," Dr. Corcoran tells me. "We've discovered recently that alcohol destroys brain cells. Once they're gone, they can't regenerate."

My father's brain is dying.

"A high percentage of our patients never have another drink," Dr. Corcoran says.

If Mickey stops drinking now, he won't lose any more brain cells. He won't be falling off his motorcycle or getting into fights. He won't be blacking out, or dreaming about snakes, or forgetting decades of his life. I glance at him, white-faced and shaking. "He looks so helpless," I say.

"He is helpless," Dr. Corcoran says.

•

Mickey holds my hand and whispers: "I want to go. I don't like it here."

"They're going to help you," I say.

"I'm Shane." A tall man with thinning blond hair and a cowboy string tie pumps Mickey's hand. "I'm an alcoholic."

Mickey backs away from the alcoholic.

Shane blows coffee breath in my face. "I've been sober 27 and a half days." Shane's eyes don't work together. His right eye stares at me, the other veers off and looks out at the dayroom where men with pale faces huddle around the TV.

Mickey lets go of my fingers and ducks behind a rubber tree plant.

Shane squats. Pulling back a leaf to get a better view of Mickey he says, "You're going to be fine. Just let go and let God."

Mickey's eyelids shut.

Laura stoops, and pats Mickey's hair. "This is for your own good," she croons.

Mickey curls into a ball.

"He just needs a little time," Dr. Corcoran says.

Time and then what? In 27 and a half days he'll be in as good a shape as Shane? How can this place be good for Mickey when he's so frightened he's rolled up into a ball?

The ball uncurls. Mickey jumps up and bolts for the door. A male nurse throws his cup with Parcheesi dice on the floor and runs after my father. My father's famous freckled hands try to twist the door handle. The handle doesn't move. "It's locked." Mickey sobs and slumps to the floor.

Shane kneels on the foyer rug next to Mickey. "I know you're scared."

Yellow flecks in Mickey's eyes look like flames. He stares at me. "How could you bring me here? Don't you love me at all?"

"We're all scared at first," Shane says. "Hell, I still pee in my pants at least once a day." Shane looks over at Laura. "I'm sorry, little lady."

The blush brightening her cheeks makes her look pretty.

"You got a nice wife," Shane says. "You have someone to come home to."

Laura sucks in her breath, waits. Mickey nods. It's all right with him if Shane thinks Laura is his wife.

"Do you like baseball?" Dr. Corcoran puts an arm around Mickey's shoulder, leads him to a circle of men seated in front of a TV screen.

The men are so quiet, you'd think they were in church. Sandy Koufax is shutting out the Giants. Backing up Koufax at second base is a skinny little kid with porcelain-colored skin.

"Daddy, look that's Alton Eibur," I say.

Mickey's eyes brighten.

"Do you always try to fix things for your dad?" Dr. Corcoran asks me.

I don't answer.

Dr. Corcoran sits next to Mickey on the rug. "When was the last time you saw a game without a beer in your hand?"

"You're making him feel worse," I tell the doctor. "He's in strange surroundings and he's going through withdrawal."

"See, you're trying to fix him." Dr. Corcoran grins at me. "I bet you're a terrific enabler. You probably fix coffee and soup for him when he's hung over."

"I take him for B-12 shots."

"And lecture him about not drinking anymore."

"It's bad for him," I say. "I care about my father."

"You're doing a wonderful job of keeping your father sick. You give him soup and then you lecture him. You rescue him and then you punish him. Meanwhile what about you? Do you think about yourself? Do you care about you?"

"Of course."

"Who do you worry about more? You or your father?"

"My father's the one with the problem."

Dr. Corcoran studies me. "The best thing you can do for your father is let him solve his own problems, and put yourself first. Make yourself the center of your life, and let everyone else take care of themselves."

"I don't know how to do that."

"Then learn," he tells me.

I stare at Alton Eibur on the screen. Who am I when I'm not trying to get someone sober or stop someone from gambling? I slip in my own needs, going to school, studying, mulching a rose bush, only when a crisis isn't going on. Then, I ask people like Mrs. Wheeler or Betty in the admissions office to bend rules for me because I have "problem relatives." I'm not much different from Mrs. Eibur. Take away her picnic hamper and her son, and she's a ghost in a picture hat, a ghost in her own life. Alice warned me and warned me. Why didn't I listen? I shiver and wrap my father's blanket around me.

"Talk about delusions," Shane is bragging to Laura. "I thought I was a row boat with holes in my sides and bottom. So I covered myself with Wet Patch. The tar stuff you put on a roof when it's raining to stop a leak? Wet Patch on my arms, my belly, even my – you know."

I stare at Shane, 27 and a half days sober. He's better off than I am. He knows he's sick. Instead of living a life, I've been trying to plug up the holes with Wet Patch. I let Mickey and Charlie interrupt my schoolwork, my job at the Wise Owl. If I ever finish anything, it's only because one of them has had a good week.

Dr. Corcoran is patting Mickey's hand. "Do you think you want to stay with us for awhile? Do you think we can help you?"

Mickey has never painted himself with Wet Patch. What if this place makes him worse? Sicker? Mickey holds out his hands to me. I kneel and hug him. He feels so light in my arms. He's been wasting away. How could I let him get so thin? "Do you want to stay here at the hospital?" I ask.

He nods.

"But a few minutes ago you were trying to get out."

"I need help," he says.

"But is this where you belong? With a guy who thinks he's a rowboat? Maybe we can find a nicer hospital."

"There still will be a problem," my father tells me.

"What problem?"

"Me. Whatever place you take me to, I'll still be there."

EPILOGUE

Will Charlie love the new me? Will he love me after I tell him he has to be responsible for his life and I have to be responsible for mine? If I tell him I'm not going to be his Mrs. Eibur or his mother, will he just go out and find someone else to prop him up?

Charlie is sitting at a table in Rolly Wynn's back room. His skin is clear and dull. The skin of a funeral parlor corpse. His high school letterman's sweater falls in folds around his hunched shoulders, as if he's shrunk a size. He says, "Did you hear the news?"

For a second I turn back into the good baseball wife, the future Mrs. Eibur. I stand at attention and wait for information. It doesn't come. "Whatever it is, we can handle it," I tell him. "I won't let you fail." Then, I remember Dr. Corcoran's grin. "Well, if you fail, you fail."

Charlie stares at me, then glances at Rolly Wynn sitting in his corner, sipping a hot toddy. If only I could hold Charlie and comfort him, but his eyes tell me he wants nothing from me. His stare fixes on rain dripping from the ceiling into a roasting pan on the floor.

"It's not your fault you broke your fingers," I say. "Well, maybe in a way it was your fault. You did provoke a fight. But all of you guys fight. They still shouldn't have released you from the team."

Charlie glares at me. "No one released me from anything." He pets Boris who is sleeping under the table. "They were considering moving me up to Double A," he says.

"Double A is very very good," the old cheerleader says. "Most people don't make it for years. They must think you're exceptional." I shut my eyes and see Shane covered in Wet Patch. Was someone always rooting for him, too? "Of course, if you don't think you're exceptional," I tell Charlie, "I guess that's your problem."

"Am I in Double A?" Charlie asks. He looks out the window, and studies the rain-drenched street. "Do you see lakes and fir trees? Are we sitting in a bar in friggin'

Sacagawea?" He shrinks deeper into his sweater. "The Pickers are in the playoffs. So, they're leaving me here."

"They need you," I say. "But if the fact that your team needs you doesn't matter to you, that's how you get to see it. It's your life."

Charlie glares at me again. "They needed Alton, too. But they sure moved him in a hurry. I start next spring in this dump."

"They asked you back? That's wonderful." Then, I hear the echo of his words and snap at him: "Do you think our home is a dump?"

"Wonderful, my ass. They want me to prove myself all over again." He rolls a napkin into a ball and tosses it into a wastepaper basket three tables away.

I watch water overflow from the pan and spill onto the hardwood floor. Rolly Wynn doesn't care that his floor is getting ruined. To stop myself from solving Rolly Wynn's problems and searching for a mop, I turn and look at TV. Jack LaLanne is doing sit-ups, one after the other, all the while talking and smiling. Jack LaLanne does 30 sit-ups.

Charlie snaps a pencil in two. "Reisner says I should play winter ball." Charlie squints at the TV. LaLanne is running in place now. "What's that wimp wearing? Ballet slippers?"

"That wimp is an athlete who takes care of himself."

"You don't understand how hard this has been," Charlie says.

What I don't understand is why I even tried to be Mrs. Eibur when Charlie never worked as hard as Alton. "You may never make the major leagues, but if you don't, it won't be because of two broken fingers," I say.

"You never broke a bone. You don't know how much it hurts," Charlie says. "You don't understand about injuries. I may never be able to throw the ball the way I used to. Or hold a bat. I could be washed up at 18."

"Is that why you're acting washed up? Sitting around with a bunch of people whose careers were over decades ago? My father broke his hands, but he still went on fighting. He broke his nose, his jaw, his ribs."

"He must have been a mess," Charlie smiles.

"He still kept punching," I say. "Two little fingers and you give up? But of course, that's your choice. It's your career, not mine."

Charlie stares at water on the floor.

"I put Mickey in the hospital," I tell him while looking at Rolly Wynn, hoping he hears. "In the drunk ward."

Charlie's eyes get wide. "Is that what you're going to do to me? Toss me in some institution? Mickey didn't even have a reason to drink. He had done it all." Charlie shakes his head. "Your father believes in me."

"Drinking is a sickness," I hear myself saying. "A way of filling up the holes in your life. Maybe gambling is a sickness like that, too. And maybe so is worrying about others and giving them advice instead of concentrating on myself."

"I gambled because of Alton," Charlie says. "Maybe I broke my fingers because of Alton, too. Hell, I don't know. And my no-show father. He has a lot to answer for. He's the reason I'm here in Wynn's backroom, instead of on the field."

"Alton isn't a reason," I tell my husband. "He's your excuse. So is your father. I know about excuses. I blamed you and my father for missing work, for having to go to work in the first place, for starting summer school late, for missing a lot of class. I blamed Mickey for everything that's wrong in my life since the moment of my birth."

"You don't think your father messed you up?" Charlie asks.

"You heard what Mr. Nordstrom said. We all love our excuses. Alton has been yours. My father has been mine. You can either believe your father and agree you're not worth driving a few miles to see you play ball, or you can believe Mr. Zimmer, Mr. Nordstrom, Mr. Reisner, and Mickey and realize you have talent, and that you can make it from here. Mr. Nordstrom told you Alton played Triple A before this year. He worked his way back up again. Nobody makes it from Single A to Dodger Stadium in one year. Alton works his ass off."

Charlie mouths the word "ass" then starts to smile again.

"How many people even get as far as Single A?" I say.

Charlie points his thumb at the next table. "Slim Knudsen, the guy with his face in the French fries, holds the record for the longest hitting streak in his division."

"You still have a chance to go all the way," I tell Charlie. "Mr. Reisner's on your side."

"Reisner works for the Dodgers. He's on the Dodgers' side."

"Why shouldn't you have to prove you can play for them?"

"I thought I already did," Charlie says. He digs his fingers into the folds of worn wool. "You don't know anything about winning."

I shut my eyes and listen to rain sloshing in the pan. "Maybe you're right. I'm too busy pouring coffee down Mickey's throat or giving you a pep talk to notice what my grade point average is or why I may have gotten turned down for my scholarship. I don't know how to live my own life, never mind how to live with someone else."

Charlie looks at me and his eyes get wary. "What are you trying to say?"

"What happens to our marriage if it gets two broken fingers? Do you give up on that, too?"

"Of course not," he says. "Why would you think that?"

"You gambled all our money. You don't come home. Why wouldn't I think that?"

Charlie looks away from me and studies two regulars who have staggered over to the pool table and are now waving cue sticks and arguing about the rules. "When I make it all the way," he says, "I'll be so good, so famous, my father will come to the games."

Charlie wants his fantasies and his excuses more than he wants me.

"You better play ball because you love it," I whisper. "Don't do it for me or your father or because you think if you do it well, someone will finally love you. Do it for you, or don't do it at all."

I watch him stare at nothing. I step back from the table: "I'm not going to try and make people love me anymore. I'm not going to fix them so they will love me when they are all better. I'm still going to be a teacher. I'm still going to have a home. What I'm not going to do is invest in a marriage that you walk away from – quit on – just because you stubbed your toe."

I start for the door. I don't look back.

Charlie runs after me. He stops me outside in front of Rolly Wynn's leaky awning. His eyes look strange. Wet. Could he be crying?

"What is all this stuff you're telling me? " he says. "If I fail I fail, and it's my career, not yours, and it's my fault I broke my fingers and I love my excuses and you don't care if I play ball or not?"

"It's your life," I say.

"But it's your life, too."

"I'm not married to baseball," I say. "I'm married to you."

"It sounds like you don't even want that anymore."

"I don't want to take responsibility for your gambling debts or your bad moods. I want to do something for myself."

"Like what?" Charlie asks.

I stare at muddy puddles on the sidewalk. "I want to get an A on my exam for Professor Edelsen's class. Guess what book I was supposed to have finished reading before I started running around town trying to pay off our debt? *Pamela*, by Samuel Richardson. Alice named me after the servant girl, and I didn't even finish the book about her."

I twist my arm free of his fingers. "And I want to try for another scholarship. I want to finish hooking the rug that Alice started. I want to trim the other window in the kitchen. Right now, our dump of a house, which I happen to love, looks like it has a damn Cyclops living in it."

"You want to give up on me because you want to paint a window blue?" Charlie says.

"I'm not giving up on you," I say. "And I'm also not giving up on me."

Charlie stares at me for a long moment, and then turns and walks back into Rolly Wynn's.

I put Old Chartreuse's keys on the seat of the car, and climb into my Plymouth and drive home.

•

Our repaired phone keeps ringing. It could be the hospital or Aunt Lottie. I push the door open and run through the house. How will Aunt Lottie take the news? I put her brother in the hospital and my marriage is a mess.

In the kitchen, I reach the phone. "Mrs. Fain, is it true that Little Red is in the hospital?" Mr. Nordstrom sounds out of breath, as if he ran to make this call. "Your father has a lot of fans rooting for him. You showed true courage committing him."

"I only did it because. . . Actually, it was his decision. He knows he has a problem. He's the one with the courage."

Outside, a car engine rattles and dies. The front door is open. Cold air and a little rain blow into the house. Charlie walks into the kitchen, and drops our savings passbook on the table. Without a word, he walks out. I hear the front door slam.

I guess that's it. My marriage is no longer a mess. It's over. I could run after Charlie and what – beg him?

"Little Red is lucky to have you," Mr. Nordstrom is saying. "So is Charlie. How does he feel about possibly getting off the disabled list tomorrow?"

I stare out the window. "He didn't even tell me," I say. "You'll have to ask him how he feels."

Charlie has just walked out of my life. I glance at the savings book – the last thing with our names on it.

"What was Charlie's reaction to signing another one year contract with the Pickers?"

I can't answer. Charlie said he had to keep proving himself to everyone. He said he had another year in this dump. I touch the kitchen curtains I sewed by hand, and feel the tears come.

Something heavy falls in the living room. Is Charlie still in the house, or did a burglar come to steal our unpaid for furniture? I pull the phone cord as far as it will go and peer through the archway.

Charlie's back is to me. He put the chair back next to the table. One by one he is picking books off the floor and placing them in the bookshelves. Why is he straightening the living room? Does he want to stay and work things out, or does he just not want to leave the house in such a mess?

"Mrs. Fain, is he pleased the Pickers want him back?"

"You'll have to ask him yourself, Mr. Nordstrom," I say loud enough for Charlie to hear. "But maybe he is. I don't always understand him."

Over his shoulder, Charlie catches me looking at him. He smiles.

"Call you back in a while," he tells the telephone as he slips past me in the archway. He squeezes my shoulder. Whistling, he walks into the kitchen, opens the cupboard, takes out a brush and a can of blue paint.

ABOUT THE AUTHOR

One of the first women admitted to the American Film Institute screenwriting program, **PENNY PERRY** received a special grant through the efforts of two-time Academy Award-winning writer-director George Seaton, to produce a film based on her script, *A Berkeley Christmas*, which aired on PBS.

A seven-time Pushcart Prize nominee in both fiction and poetry, she was born and raised in Santa Monica, the setting for her first collection of poetry, *Santa Monica Disposal & Salvage* (Garden Oak Press: 2012).

She has taught poetry and creative writing at workshops in Southern California and at the Poetry Center in Paterson, NJ, and teaches preteens in workshops for the *Kids! San Diego Poetry Annual.* Her reviews of poetry collections have appeared in *Excuse Me, I'm Writing* (excusemeimwriting.com) and in *Poetry International* (San Diego State University).

Widely published as a poet, her work has appeared in *Lilith, Earth's Daughters, LIPS,* the *Paterson Literary Review* and the *San Diego Poetry Annual.* Her fiction has appeared in *Redbook* and *California Quarterly.*

Selling Pencils, and Charlie is her first novel.

ACKNOWLEDGMENTS

For their indefatigable support of and help on this book:

JOYCE SPARLING   DHR FISHMAN   CLAIRE WACHTEL
EMILIE JACOBSON   WILLIAM HARRY HARDING

CREDITS

Author photo and cover design: by **TAAX**

Made in the USA
Las Vegas, NV
31 August 2021